I SHUDDER
AT YOUR TOUCH

I SHUDDER
AT YOUR TOUCH

22 TALES OF SEX AND HORROR

EDITED BY
MICHELE SLUNG

A ROC BOOK

Acknowledgments

"The Revelations of 'Becka Paulson" by Stephen King. Copyright © 1986 Stephen King. Used by permission of the author.

"Sea Lovers" by Valerie Martin. From *The Consolation of Nature*. Copyright © 1988 Valerie Martin. Reprinted by permission of Houghton Mifflin Company.

"Psychopomp" by Haydn Middleton. Copyright © 1991 Haydn Middleton. An original story used by permission of the author.

"A Glowing Future" by Ruth Rendell. Copyright © 1987 Kingsmarkham Enterprises Ltd. Reprinted by permission of the author and the author's agent.

"The Tiger Returns to the Mountain" by T.L. Parkinson. Copyright © 1991 T.L. Parkinson. An original story published by permission of the author and the author's agent, The Pimlico Agency, Inc., 432 Park Avenue South, New York, New York 10016.

"Consanguinity" by Ronald Duncan. From *The Fourth Ghost Book*, edited by James Turner. Published by Barrie & Rockliff Ltd., London, 1965.

"Keeping House" by Michael Blumlein. Copyright © 1991 Michael Blumlein. An original story published by permission of the author.

"The Villa Désirée" by May Sinclair. Copyright © 1926 May Sinclair. Reproduced by permission of Curtis Brown Ltd., London.

"Cleave the Vampire, or, A Gothic Pastorale" by Patrick McGrath. Copyright © 1991 Patrick McGrath. An original story published by permission of the author.

"The Swords" by Robert Aickman. Copyright © 1975 Robert Aickman. Published by permission of The Pimlico Agency, Inc., agents for the estate of Robert Aickman.

"Salon Satin" by Carolyn Banks. Copyright © 1991 Carolyn Banks. An original story published by permission of the author.

"Wings" by Harriet Zinnes. Copyright © Harriet Zinnes. First published in *New Directions 52: An International Anthology of Prose and Poetry* (1988). Reprinted by permission of the author.

ROC IS A TRADEMARK OF NEW AMERICAN LIBRARY, A DIVISION OF PENGUIN BOOKS USA INC.

PRINTED IN THE UNITED STATES OF AMERICA

ISBN 0-451-45079-5

This book is dedicated
to the memory of three dear friends—
David E. Pickford, Herbert H. Denton, Jr.,
Maurice Braddell—original spirits, all

CONTENTS

In nothing is individual fancy so varied and capricious as in its perception of the horrible. To one person a story is terrible beyond all imagination: to another, it is merely grotesque.

DOROTHY L. SAYERS, The Omnibus of Crime

They had not sailed a league, a league,
  A league but barely three,
Until she spied his cloven feet,
  And she wept right bitterlie.

The Daemon Lover, traditional ballad

It was for the instant confounding and bottomless, for if he *were* innocent, what then on earth was *I*?

HENRY JAMES, The Turn of the Screw

PREFACE

As I invite you to be seduced by this collection of extremely varied *frissons*, I feel obliged once again to cite the friend whose dry comment, when I informed him of my desire to put together such a book, was "What horror story *isn't* about sex?" Of course, he was (almost) completely right, and the eroticism inherent in those things authors intend to frighten us can be as obvious as a vampire's embrace or as subtle as the imperfectly perceived corruption permeating Henry James's *The Turn of the Screw*.

From the maddening yet marvelous reticence of that sublime novella to the no-holds-barred attitude found in, say, Clive Barker's extravaganzas of the macabre is a vast distance. And between the two, those so inclined can easily find a wide range of shocks and thrills inspired by human—as well as inhuman and nonhuman—sexuality. As I have written elsewhere, the potential for vileness, depravity, brutality, and unspeakable despair stemming from matters sexual is nearly limitless, and so, too, is the vulnerability. Sensuality is energizing, and it can also be annihilating; and something so inexplicable, yet so grounded in the reality of the flesh, as desire obviously can provide a basis for fiction that is insidiously disturbing, even dangerous.

But, perhaps, since we readily accept that the presence of

sexual imagery and sexual menace are as much a part of horror literature as the very idea of fright itself, I should concentrate on the promise of my title, *I Shudder at Your Touch*. It, of course, presents a tantalizing double message, which is this: whether one shivers in pleasure or pleasurable anticipation, or whether one recoils shudderingly, in dread, the gooseflesh raised is the same. And, as I note later, in my introduction to "Cleave the Vampire, or, A Gothic Pastorale," by Patrick McGrath, the truth is that anyone who relishes the sensations aroused by the looming shadow of a caped monster does experience at least a moment's fleeting disappointment when the creature is forced to slink away, unsatiated. Or, put in another way, what *was* King Kong going to do with Fay Wray?

Now, to love what we fear is, indeed, a perverse notion, and so is its opposite. But the linkage of the sexual instinct with the will to death existed long before Freud, and my own favorite expositions of the theme can be seen in the anonymous English and Scots folk ballads, which I first heard and read as a teenager, at about the same time that I was discovering the delights of supernatural literature.

For example, in one stanza of "The Unquiet Grave," a dead lover, mourned with too-excessive fervor, warns,

> You crave one kiss of my clay-cold lips;
> But my breath smells earthy strong;
> If you have one kiss of my clay-cold lips,
> Your time will be not long.

And that second line, already doom-laden in its lure, can alternately read, in a more explicit American variant, "But the call of death is strong." Or, to take a look at another famously thrilling ballad, "Lady Isabel and the Elf-Knight," one finds a fair lady—married, actually—who, having eloped with the spellcasting Elf-Knight, a sort of fairyland Mr. Goodbar, manages to turn the tables and murder instead of being murdered.

Such recurring folk motifs as these, with their blend of arousal and mysterious doom, lingered in my young mind like unearthly caresses. And the power of the "demon lover" was to haunt me—as it did Elizabeth Bowen, Shirley Jackson, and Sylvia Townsend-Warner, to name only three writers whose treatments of the theme soon were to mark them as kindred spirits. Moreover, as a result, I found myself receptive to all manner of eerie storytelling, seized by this secret passion of mine in a world where Ned Nickerson passed for a sex object and Tony Perkins had not yet become once and forever Norman Bates.

Back then, the landmark stories for me, those tales which proved so deliciously unsettling that I had to read them again and again and again, included Arthur Machen's "The Great God Pan" and "The Novel of the Black Seal," with their not-quite described hints of obscene rituals and appalling ecstasies; Hugh Walpole's "The Silver Mask," which follows a middle-aged woman's sexual enthrallment to its hideous conclusion; Ralph Milne Farley's "The House of Ecstasy," a crude but still nightmarish pulp teaser about sexual slavery; and E. F. Benson's "The Man Who Went Too Far," yet another vision of Pan's unholy power.

Also: J. Sheridan Le Fanu's "Carmilla," an exquisite portrait of a predatory lesbian vampire, startling in its graphicness given its late Victorian origin; Helen R. Hull's "Clay-Shuttered Doors," a story of love, death, and resurrection that prefigures *Pet Sematary*; Robert Hichens' "How Love Came to Professor Guildea" (included here); May Sinclair's "Where Their Fire Is Not Quenched" (see my introductory note to her "The Villa Désirée"); and the novel *The Haunting of Hill House*, Shirley Jackson's perfect shadow-show projection of sexual repression.

Really, though, if I'm to be honest, I'd have to agree with Edith Wharton, herself a superb ghost story writer, who once explained that she often had a difficult time falling asleep if she knew a volume containing a particularly scary story was resting on a downstairs library shelf. Thus, these tales of horror *themselves*, I believe, are like demon lovers, simultaneously attracting and repelling. And I know that I myself, before I turned off the light, would always make certain that Sayers' *The Omnibus of Crime* or August Derleth's *The Night Side* was safely in a drawer where any cloven hoof it might extrude in the night would not be seen by me.

But, demon lovers aside for a second, our sexual selves are surely where we are most private and often secret. And it goes without saying that this hidden part of our nature, as disinclined to clear exposure as any vampire is to sunshine, takes on enormous force when it appears not just in weird fiction but in mainstream writing as well. Violation, victimization, betrayal through loving unwisely, and the consequences of all manner of unnatural acts are hardly fates reserved just for those in the literature of horror. It is, though, in Henry James's phrase, that other "turn of the screw," the unexpected opening of the trapdoor into the unknown, which makes all the difference.

Witness, in this collection, for example, the importance of a metal trunk or a pair of white tennis shoes—the "overtones of strangeness in ordinary things," as H. P. Lovecraft once described it, or, again to quote James, "the strange and sinister embroidered on the very type of the normal and easy." Offered here is a world of both slowly unfolding surprises and sudden shocks: take one step forward and you'll just as likely find yourself hastily taking two backward seconds later.

Willy-nilly, these authors' ambivalences—the ones they've themselves already had time to unleash and examine—will find their way into your own, taking hold. And the beasts that lurk in these pages, then, are of the sort that won't be found in any cage, nor would you want to—although, come to think of it, they might very well be crouching under your bed right this very minute. . . .

In conclusion, I want to say that I believe much recent horror fiction, as well as film, could rightly be termed misogynistic. Additionally, the ever-escalating levels of violence and gore depress me because they seem to be not about fantasy or imagination but about body count, pure and simple, and also about towel-snapping displays of machismo viciousness. Nor am I one who thinks this genre—made up of fragile elements despite its bravura air—can survive the departure of the moral quality that, historically, has been its underpinning. Although I am as intrigued as the next person by ambiguity, as should be clear by now, I am revolted—not titillated—when evil is allowed to triumph and the innocent suffer to no creative purpose.

Though I didn't exactly plan it this way, I find that many of these stories I have chosen have female protagonists. Yet, of those, quite a few are by men—writers like Stephen King, Clive Barker, Terry Parkinson, Christopher Fowler, and Tom Disch, whose work I greatly admire. And I'm fascinated to see this, as well as being immeasurably pleased by the intuitive acuteness that I feel such psyche-teasing tales as "The Tiger Returns to the Mountain" or "Jacqueline Ess: Her Will and Testament" exhibit. There isn't, to my mind, any antiwoman sentiment being expressed here, rather the contrary, I think. And *all* of these stories, really, should provoke us not only to shudders and shivers but to contemplate what other kinds of responses are triggered in us when sensations of love and betrayal, romance and carnality, sexual exploitation and vulnerability, are taken to the very edge . . . and beyond.

I SHUDDER
AT YOUR TOUCH

THE REVELATIONS OF 'BECKA PAULSON

STEPHEN KING

"Oh, she supposed she must have had *some* idea of what all his recent preoccupation had meant, must have known there was a reason he was never after her at night anymore."

No wife wishes to find herself betrayed, even if, like Rebecca Paulson, she's more than half glad her husband has ceased to demand his conjugal rights. One imagines that most women (and 'Becka certainly doesn't rank as exceptional—not at first, anyway) would prefer that any truth liable to cause extreme emotional pain remain buried, like the moth-eaten woollens and mildewed books she discovers at the back of the downstairs hall closet. Yet it is 'Becka's fate, as we shall see, to experience revelations . . . of a very special kind.

Displaying his remarkable instinct for precisely offsetting the monstrous with the mundane—and vice versa—Stephen King gives us, in this extraordinary ordinary heroine, 'Becka Paulson, a definition of the "walking wounded" that transcends psychobabble.

What happened was simple enough—at least, at the start. What happened was that Rebecca Paulson shot herself in the head with her husband Joe's .22-caliber pistol. This occurred during her annual spring cleaning, which took place this year (as it did most years) around the middle of June. 'Becka had a way of falling behind in such things.

She was standing on a short stepladder and rummaging through the accumulated junk on the high shelf in the downstairs hall closet while the Paulson cat, a big brindle tom named Ozzie Nelson, sat in the living-room doorway, watching her. From behind Ozzie came the anxious voices of *Another World*, blaring out of the Paulsons' big old Zenith TV—which would later become something much more than a TV.

'Becka pulled stuff down and examined it, hoping for something that was still good, but not really expecting to find such a thing. There were four or five knitted winter caps, all motheaten and unraveling. She tossed them behind her onto the hall floor. Here was a Reader's Digest Condensed Book from the summer of 1954, featuring *Run Silent, Run Deep* and *Here's Goggle*. Water damage had swelled it to the size of the Manhattan telephone book. She tossed it behind her. Ah! Here was an umbrella that looked salvageable . . . and a box with something in it.

It was a shoebox. Whatever was inside was heavy. When she tilted the box, it shifted. She took the lid off, also tossing this behind her (it almost hit Ozzie Nelson, who decided to split the scene). Inside the box was a gun with a long barrel and imitation wood-grip handles.

"Oh," she said. "*That.*" She took it out of the box, not noticing that it was cocked, and turned it around to look into the small beady eye of the muzzle, believing that if there was a bullet in there she would see it.

She remembered the gun. Until five years ago, Joe had been a member of the Derry Elks. Some ten years ago (or maybe it had been fifteen), Joe had bought fifteen Elks raffle tickets while drunk. 'Becka had been so mad she had refused to let him put his manthing in her for two weeks. The first prize had been a Bombardier Skidoo, second prize an Evinrude motor. This .22 target pistol had been the third prize.

He had shot it for a while in the backyard, she remembered, plinking away at cans and bottles until 'Becka complained about the noise. Then he had taken it up to the gravel pit at the dead end of their road, although she had sensed he was losing interest, even then—he'd just gone on shooting for a while to make sure she didn't think she had gotten the better of him. Then it had disappeared. She had thought he had swapped it for something—a set of snow tires, maybe, or a battery—but here it was.

She held the muzzle of the gun up to her eye, peering into the darkness, looking for the bullet. She could see nothing but darkness. Must be unloaded, then.

I'll make him get rid of it just the same, she thought, backing down the stepladder. *Tonight. When he gets back from the post office. I'll stand right up to him. "Joe," I'll say, "it's no good having a gun sitting around the house even if there's no kids around and it's unloaded. You don't even use it to shoot bottles anymore." That's what I'll say.*

This was a satisfying thing to think, but her undermind knew that she would of course say no such thing. In the Paulson house, it was Joe who mostly picked the roads and drove the horses. She supposed that it would be best to just dispose of it herself—put it in a plastic garbage bag under the other rickrack from the closet shelf. The gun would go to the dump with everything else the next time Vinnie Margolies stopped by to pick up their throw-out. Joe would not miss what he had already forgotten—the lid of the box had been thick with undisturbed dust. Would not miss it, that was, unless she was stupid enough to bring it to his attention.

'Becka reached the bottom of the ladder. Then she stepped backward onto the Reader's Digest Condensed Book with her left foot. The front board of the book slid backward as the rotted binding gave way. She tottered, holding the gun with one hand and flailing with the other. Her right foot came down on the pile of knitted caps, which also slid backward. As she fell she realized that she looked more like a woman bent on suicide than on cleaning.

Well, it ain't loaded, she had time to think, but the gun *was* loaded, and it had been cocked; cocked for years, as if waiting for her to come along. She sat down hard in the hallway and when she did the hammer of the pistol snapped forward. There was a flat, unimportant bang not much louder than a baby firecracker in a tin can, and a .22 Winchester short entered 'Becka Paulson's brain just above the left eye. It made a small black hole that was the faint blue of just-bloomed irises around the edges.

Her head thumped back against the wall, and a trickle of blood ran from the hole into her left eyebrow. The gun, with a tiny thread of white smoke rising from its muzzle, fell into her lap. Her hands drummed lightly up and down on the floor for a period of about five seconds; her right leg flexed, then shot straight out. Her loafer flew across the hall and hit the far wall. Her eyes remained open for the next thirty minutes, the pupils dilating and constricting, dilating and constricting.

Ozzie Nelson came to the living-room door, miaowed at her, and then began washing himself.

She was putting supper on the table that night before Joe noticed the Band-Aid over her eye. He had been home for an hour and a half, but just lately he didn't notice much at all around the house—he seemed preoccupied with something, far away from her a lot of the time. This didn't bother her as much as it might have once—at least he wasn't always after her to let him put his manthing into her ladyplace.

"What'd you do to your head?" he asked as she put a bowl of beans and a plate of red hot dogs on the table.

She touched the Band-Aid vaguely. Yes—what exactly *had* she done to her head? She couldn't really remember. The whole middle of the day had a funny dark place in it, like an inkstain. She remembered feeding Joe his breakfast and standing on the porch as he headed off to the post office in his Wagoneer—that much was crystal clear. She remembered doing the white load in the new Sears washer while *Wheel of Fortune* blared from the TV. That was also clear. Then the inkstain began. She remembered putting in the colors and starting the cold cycle. She had the faintest, vaguest recollection of putting a couple of Swanson's Hungry Man frozen dinners into the oven for herself— 'Becka Paulson was a hefty eater—but after that there was nothing. Not until she had awakened sitting on the living-room couch. She had changed from slacks and her flowered smock into a dress and high heels; she had put her hair in braids. There was something heavy in her lap and on her shoulders and her forehead tickled. It was Ozzie Nelson. Ozzie was standing with his hind legs in her crotch and his forepaws on her shoulders. He was busily licking blood off her forehead and out of her eyebrow. She swatted Ozzie away from her lap and then looked at the clock. Joe would be home in an hour and she hadn't even started dinner. Then she had touched her head, which throbbed vaguely.

" 'Becka?"

"What?" She sat down at her place and began to spoon beans onto her plate.

"I asked you what you did to your head?"

"Bumped it," she said . . . although, when she went down to the bathroom and looked at herself in the mirror, it hadn't *looked* like a bump; it had looked like a hole. "I just bumped it."

"Oh," he said, losing interest. He opened the new issue of *Sports Illustrated* which had come that day and immediately fell into a daydream. In it he was running his hands slowly over the body of Nancy Voss—an activity he had been indulging in (along with any and all of those activities likely to follow) for the last six weeks or so. God bless the United States Postal Authority for sending Nancy Voss from Falmouth to Haven, that was all he could say. Falmouth's loss was Joe Paulson's gain. He had whole days when he was quite sure he had died and gone to heaven, and his pecker hadn't been so frisky since he was nineteen and touring West Germany with the U.S. Army. It would have taken more than a Band-Aid on his wife's forehead to engage his full attention.

'Becka helped herself to three hot dogs, paused to debate a moment, and then added a fourth. She doused the dogs and the beans with ketchup and then stirred everything together. The result looked a bit like the aftermath of a bad motorcycle accident. She poured herself a glass of grape Kool-Aid from the pitcher on the table (Joe had a beer) and then touched the Band-Aid with the tips of her fingers—she had been doing that ever since she put it on. Nothing but a cool plastic strip. That was okay . . . but she could feel the circular indentation beneath. The *hole*. That wasn't so okay.

"Just bumped it," she murmured again, as if saying would make it so. Joe didn't look up and 'Becka began to eat.

Hasn't hurt my appetite any, whatever it was, she thought. *Not that much ever does—probably nothing ever will. When they say on the radio that all those missiles are flying and it's the end of the world, I'll probably go right on eating until one of those rockets lands on Haven.*

She cut herself a piece of bread from the homemade loaf and began mopping up bean juice with it.

Seeing that . . . that *mark* on her forehead had unnerved her at the time, unnerved her plenty. No sense kidding about that, just as there was no sense kidding that it was just a *mark*, like a bruise. And in case anyone ever wanted to know, 'Becka thought, she would tell them that looking into the mirror and seeing that you had an extra hole in your head wasn't one of life's cheeriest experiences. Your head, after all, was where your *brains* were. And as for what she had done next—

She tried to shy away from that, but it was too late.

Too late, 'Becka, a voice tolled in her mind—it sounded like her dead father's voice.

She had stared at the hole, stared at it and stared at it, and then she had pulled open the drawer to the left of the sink and had pawed through her few meager items of makeup with hands that didn't seem to belong to her. She took out her eyebrow pencil and then looked into the mirror again.

She raised the hand holding the eyebrow pencil with the blunt end toward her, and slowly began to push it into the hole in her forehead. *No,* she moaned to herself, *stop it, 'Becka, you don't want to do this—*

But apparently *part* of her did, because she went right on doing it. There was no pain and the eyebrow pencil was a perfect fit. She pushed it in an inch, then two, then three. She looked at herself in the mirror, a woman in a flowered dress who had a pencil sticking out of her head. She pushed it in a fourth inch.

Not much left, 'Becka, be careful, wouldn't want to lose it in there, it'd rattle when you turned over in the night, wake up Joe—

She tittered hysterically.

Five inches in and the blunt end of the eyebrow pencil had finally encountered resistance. It was hard, but a gentle push also communicated a feeling of sponginess. At the same moment the whole world turned a brilliant, momentary green and an interlacing of memories jigged through her mind—sledding at four in her older brother's snowsuit, washing high school blackboards, a '59 Impala her Uncle Bill had owned, the smell of cut hay.

She pulled the eyebrow pencil out of her head, shocked back to herself, terrified that blood would come gushing out of the hole. But no blood came, nor was there any blood on the shiny surface of the eyebrow pencil. Blood or . . . or . . .

But she would not think of that. She threw the pencil back into the drawer and slammed the drawer shut. Her first impulse, to cover the hole, came back, stronger than ever.

She swung the mirror away from the medicine cabinet and grabbed the tin box of Band-Aids. It fell from her trembling fingers and clattered into the basin. 'Becka had cried out at the sound and then told herself to stop it, just *stop* it. Cover it up, make it gone. That was the thing to do; that was the ticket. Never mind the eyebrow pencil, just forget that—she had none of the signs of brain injury she had seen on the afternoon stories and *Marcus Welby, M.D.*, that was the important thing. She was *all right*. As for the eyebrow pencil, she would just forget that part.

And so she had, at least until now. She looked at her half-eaten dinner and realized with a sort of dull humor that she had been wrong about her appetite—she couldn't eat another bite.

She took her plate over to the garbage and scraped what was left into the can, while Ozzie wound restlessly around her ankles. Joe didn't look up from his magazine. In his mind, Nancy Voss was asking him again if that tongue of his was as long as it looked.

She woke up in the middle of the night from some confusing dream in which all the clocks in the house had been talking in her father's voice. Joe lay beside her, flat on his back in his boxer shorts, snoring.

Her hand went to the Band-Aid. The hole didn't hurt, didn't exactly throb, but it *itched*. She rubbed at it, but gently, afraid of another of those dazzling green flashes. None came.

She rolled over on her side and thought: *You got to go to the doctor, 'Becka. You got to get that seen to. I don't know what you did, but—*

No, she answered herself. *No doctor.* She rolled to her other side, thinking she would be awake for hours now, wondering, asking herself frightened questions. Instead, she was asleep again in moments.

In the morning the hole under the Band-Aid hardly itched at all, and that made it easier not to think about. She made Joe his breakfast and saw him off to work. She finished washing the dishes and took out the garbage. They kept it in a little shed beside the house that Joe had built, a structure not much bigger than a doghouse. You had to lock it up or the coons came out of the woods and made a mess.

She stepped in, wrinkling her nose at the smell, and put the green bag down with the others. Vinnie would be by on Friday or Saturday and then she would give the shed a good airing. As she was backing out, she saw a bag that hadn't been tied up like the others. A curved handle, like the handle of a cane, protruded from the top.

Curious, she pulled it out and saw it was an umbrella. A number of moth-eaten, unraveling hats came out with the umbrella.

A dull warning sounded in her head. For a moment she could almost see through that inkstain to what was behind it, to what had happened to her

(bottom it's in the bottom something heavy something in a box what Joe don't remember won't)

yesterday. But did she want to know?

No.

She didn't.

She wanted to forget.

She backed out of the little shed and rebolted the door with hands that trembled the slightest bit.

A week later (she still changed the Band-Aid each morning, but the wound was closing up—she could see the pink new tissue filling it when she shone Joe's flashlight into it and peered into the bathroom mirror) 'Becka found out what half of Haven already either knew or surmised—that Joe was cheating on her. Jesus told her. In the last three days or so, Jesus had told her the most amazing, terrible, distressing things imaginable. They sickened her, they destroyed her sleep, they were destroy-

ing her sanity . . . but were they wonderful? Weren't they just!
And would she stop listening, simply tip Jesus over on His face,
perhaps scream at Him to shut up? Absolutely not. For one
thing, He was the Saviour. For another thing, there was a grisly
sort of compulsion in knowing the things Jesus told her.

'Becka did not connect the onset of these divine communica-
tions with the hole in her head at all.

Jesus was on top of the Paulsons' Zenith television and He
had been in that same spot for just about twenty years. Before
resting atop the Zenith, He had rested atop two RCAs (Joe
Paulson always bought American). This was a beautiful 3-D
picture of Jesus that Rebecca's sister, who lived in Portsmouth,
had sent her. Jesus was dressed in a simple white robe, and He
was holding a shepherd's staff. Because the picture had been
created ('Becka considered *made* much too mundane a word
for a likeness which seemed so real you could almost stick
your hand into it) before the Beatles and the changes they had
wreaked on male hairstyles, His hair was not too long, and
perfectly neat. The Christ on 'Becka Paulson's TV combed His
hair a little bit like Elvis Presley after Elvis got out of the army.
His eyes were brown and mild and kind. Behind Him, in perfect
perspective, sheep as white as the linens in TV soap commer-
cials trailed away into the distance. 'Becka and her sister Co-
rinne and her brother Roland had grown up on a sheep farm in
New Gloucester, and 'Becka knew from personal experience
that sheep were *never* that white and uniformly woolly, like
little fair-weather clouds that had fallen to earth. But, she
reasoned, if Jesus could turn water into wine and bring the dead
back to life, there was no reason at all why He couldn't make
the shit caked around a bunch of lambs' rumps disappear if He
wanted to.

A couple of times Joe had tried to move that picture off the
TV, and she supposed that now she knew why, oh yessirree
Bob, oh yes indeedy. Joe, of course, had his trumped-up tales.
"It doesn't seem right to have Jesus on top of the television
while we're watching *Three's Company* or *Charlie's Angels*,"
he'd say. "Why don't you put it up on your bureau, 'Becka? Or
. . . I'll tell you what! Why not put it up on your bureau until
Sunday, and then you can bring it down and put it back on the
TV while you watch Jimmy Swaggart and Rex Humbard and

Jerry Falwell? I'll bet Jesus likes Jerry Falwell one hell of a lot better than he likes *Charlie's Angels.*"

She refused.

"When it's my turn to have the Thursday-night poker game, the guys don't like it," he said another time. "No one wants to have Jesus Christ looking at them while he tries to fill a flush or draw to an inside straight."

"Maybe they feel uncomfortable because they know gambling's the Devil's work," 'Becka said.

Joe, who was a good poker player, bridled. "Then it was the Devil's work that bought you your hair drier and that garnet ring you like so well," he said. "Better take 'em back for refunds and give the money to the Salvation Army. Wait, I think I got the receipts in my den."

She allowed as how Joe could turn the 3-D picture of Jesus around to face the wall on the one Thursday night a month that he had his dirty-talking, beer-swilling friends in to play poker . . . but that was all.

And now she knew the *real* reason he wanted to get rid of that picture. He must have had an idea all along that that picture was a *magic* picture. Oh . . . she supposed *sacred* was a better word, magic was for pagans—headhunters and Catholics and people like that—but they came almost to one and the same, didn't they? All along Joe must have sensed that picture was special, that it would be the means by which his sin would be found out.

Oh, she supposed she must have had *some* idea of what all his recent preoccupation had meant, must have known there was a reason why he was never after her at night anymore. But the truth was, that had been a relief—sex was just as her mother had told her it would be, nasty and brutish, sometimes painful and always humiliating. Had she also smelled perfume on his collar from time to time? If so, she had ignored that, too, and she might have gone on ignoring it indefinitely if the picture of Jesus on top of the Sony hadn't begun to speak on July 7th. She realized now that she had ignored a third factor, as well: at about the same time the pawings had stopped and the perfume smells had begun, old Charlie Estabrooke had retired and a woman named Nancy Voss had come up from the Falmouth post office to take his place. She guessed that the

Voss woman (whom 'Becka had now come to think of simply as The Hussy) was perhaps five years older than her and Joe, which would make her around fifty, but she was a trim, well-kept, and handsome fifty. 'Becka herself had put on a little weight during her marriage, going from one hundred and twenty-six to a hundred and ninety-three, most of that since Byron, their only chick and child, had flown from the nest.

She could have gone on ignoring it, and perhaps that would even have been for the best. If The Hussy really enjoyed the animalism of sexual congress, with its gruntings and thrustings and that final squirt of sticky stuff that smelled faintly like codfish and looked like cheap dish detergent, then it only proved that The Hussy was little more than an animal herself—and of course it freed 'Becka of a tiresome, if ever more occasional, obligation. But when the picture of Jesus spoke up, telling her *exactly* what was going on, it became impossible to ignore. She knew that something would have to be done.

The picture first spoke at just past three in the afternoon on Thursday. This was eight days after shooting herself in the head and about four days after her resolution to forget it was a *hole* and not just a *mark* had finally begun to take effect. 'Becka was coming back into the living room from the kitchen with a little snack (half a coffeecake and a beer stein filled with Kool-Aid) to watch *General Hospital*. She no longer really believed that Luke would ever find Laura, but she could not quite find it in her heart to *completely* give up hope.

She was bending down to turn on the Zenith when Jesus said, " 'Becka, Joe is putting the boots to that Hussy down at the pee-oh just about every lunch hour and sometimes after punching-out time in the afternoon. Once he was so randy he drove it to her while he was supposed to be helping her sort the mail. And do you know what? She never even said 'At least wait until I get the first-class into the boxes.' "

'Becka screamed and spilled her Kool-Aid down the front of the TV. It was a wonder, she thought later, when she was able to think at all, that the picture tube didn't blow. Her coffeecake went on the rug.

"And that's not all," Jesus told her. He walked halfway across the picture, His robe fluttering around His ankles, and sat down on a rock that jutted out of the ground. He held His staff between His knees and looked at her grimly. "There's a lot going on in Haven. Why, you wouldn't believe the half of it."

'Becka screamed again and fell on her knees. One of them landed squarely on her coffeecake and squirted raspberry filling into the face of Ozzie Nelson, who had crept into the living room to see what was going on. "My Lord! My Lord!" 'Becka shrieked. Ozzie ran, hissing, for the kitchen, where he crawled under the stove with red goo dripping from his whiskers. He stayed under there the rest of the day.

"Well, none of the Paulsons was ever any good," Jesus said. A sheep wandered toward Him and He whacked it away, using his staff with an absentminded impatience that reminded 'Becka, even in her current frozen state, of her long-dead father. The sheep went, rippling slightly through the 3-D effect. It disappeared from the picture, actually seeming to *curve* as it went off the edge . . . but that was just an optical illusion, she felt sure. "No good at all," Jesus went on. "Joe's granddad was a whoremaster of the purest ray serene, as you well know, 'Becka. Spent his whole life pecker-led. And when he came up here, do you know what we said? 'No room!' that's what we said." Jesus leaned forward, still holding His staff. " 'Go see Mr. Splitfoot down below,' we said. 'You'll find your Haven-home, all right. But you may find your new landlord a hard taskmaster,' we said." Incredibly, Jesus winked at her . . . and that was when 'Becka fled, shrieking, from the house.

She stopped in the backyard, panting, her hair, a mousy blond that was really not much of any color at all, hanging in her face. Her heart was beating so fast in her chest that it frightened her. No one had heard her shriekings and carryings-on, thank the Lord; she and Joe lived far out on the Nista Road, and their nearest neighbors were the Brodskys, those Polacks that lived in that slutty trailer. The Brodskys were half a mile away. If anyone had heard her, they would have thought there was a crazywoman down at Joe and 'Becka Paulson's.

Well there IS a crazywoman at the Paulsons', isn't there? she thought. *If you really think that picture of Jesus started to talk to you, why, you must be crazy. Daddy'd beat you three shades of blue for thinking such a thing—one shade for lying, another shade for believing the lie, and a third for raising your voice. 'Becka, you ARE crazy. Pictures don't talk.*

No . . . and it didn't, another voice spoke up suddenly. *That voice came out of your own head, 'Becka. I don't know how it could be . . . how you could know such things . . . but that's what happened. Maybe it had something to do with what happened to you last week, or maybe not, but you made that picture of Jesus talk your own self. It didn't really talk no more than that little rubber Topo Gigio mouse on the Ed Sullivan Show.*

But somehow the idea that it might have something to do with that . . . that

(hole)

other thing was scarier than the idea that the picture itself had spoken, because that *was* the sort of thing they sometimes had on *Marcus Welby*, like that show about the fellow who had the brain tumor and it was making him wear his wife's nylon stockings and step-ins. She refused to allow it mental houseroom. It might be a miracle. After all, miracles happened every day. There was the Shroud of Turin, and the cures at Lourdes, and that Mexican fellow who had found a picture of the Virgin Mary burned into the surface of a taco or an enchilada or something. Not to mention those children that had made the headlines of one of the tabloids—children who cried rocks. Those were all *bona fide* miracles (the children who wept rocks was, admittedly, a rather gritty one), as uplifting as a Jimmy Swaggart sermon. Hearing voices was only crazy.

But that's what happened. And you've been hearing voices for quite a little while now, haven't you? You've been hearing HIS voice. Joe's voice. And that's where it came from, not from Jesus but from Joe, from Joe's head—

"No," 'Becka whimpered. "No, I ain't heard any *voices* in my *head*."

She stood by her clothesline in the hot backyard, looking blankly off toward the woods on the other side of the Nista Road, blue-gray-hazy in the heat. She wrung her hands in front of her and began to weep.

"I ain't no heard no *voices* in my *head*."

Crazy, her dead father's implacable voice replied. *Crazy with the heat. You come on over here, 'Becka Bouchard, I'm gonna beat you three shades of blister-blue for that crazy talk.*

"I ain't heard no *voices* in my *head*," 'Becka moaned. "That picture really did talk, I swear, I can't *do* ventriloquism!"

Better believe the picture. If it was the hole, it was a brain tumor, sure. If it was the picture, it was a miracle. Miracles came from God. Miracles came from Outside. A miracle could drive you crazy—and the dear God knew she felt like she was going crazy right now—but it didn't mean you were crazy, or that your brains were scrambled. As as for believing that you could hear other people's thoughts . . . that was just *crazy*.

'Becka looked down at her legs and saw blood gushing from her left knee. She shrieked again and ran back into the house to call the doctor, MEDIX, somebody. She was in the living room again, pawing at the dial with the phone to her ear, when Jesus said:

"That's raspberry filling from your coffeecake, 'Becka. Why don't you just relax, before you have a heart attack?"

She looked at the TV, the telephone receiver falling to the table with a clunk. Jesus was still sitting on the rock outcropping. It looked as though He had crossed His legs. It was really surprising how much He looked like her own father . . . only He didn't seem forbidding, ready to be hitting angry at a moment's notice. He was looking at her with a kind of exasperated patience.

"Try it and see if I'm not right," Jesus said.

She touched her knee gently, wincing, expecting pain. There was none. She saw the seeds in the red stuff and relaxed. She licked the raspberry filling off her fingers.

"Also," Jesus said, "you have got to get these ideas about hearing voices and going crazy out of your head. It's just Me, and I can talk to anyone I want to, any *way* I want to."

"Because you're the Saviour," 'Becka whispered.

"That's right," Jesus said, and looked down. Below Him, a couple of animated salad bowls were dancing in appreciation of the Hidden Valley Ranch Dressing which they were about to receive. "And I'd like you to please turn that crap off, if you don't mind. We don't need that thing running. Also, it makes My feet tingle."

'Becka approached the TV and turned it off.

"My Lord," she whispered.

Now it was Sunday, July 10th. Joe was lying fast asleep out in the backyard hammock with Ozzie lying limply across his ample stomach like a black and white fur stole. She stood in the living room, holding the curtain back with her left hand and looking out at Joe. Sleeping in the hammock. Dreaming of The Hussy, no doubt—dreaming of throwing her down in a great big pile of catalogues from Carroll Reed and fourth-class junk mail and then—how would Joe and his piggy poker-buddies put it?—"putting the shoes to her."

She was holding the curtain with her left hand because she had a handful of square nine-volt batteries in her right. She had bought them yesterday down at the town hardware store. Now she let the curtain drop and took the batteries into the kitchen, where she was assembling a little something on the counter. Jesus had told her how to make it. She told Jesus she couldn't build things. Jesus told her not to be a cussed fool. If she could follow a recipe, she could build this little gadget. She was delighted to find that Jesus was absolutely right. It was not only easy, it was fun. A lot more fun than cooking, certainly; she had never really had the knack for that. Her cakes almost always fell and her breads almost never rose. She had begun this little thing yesterday, working with the toaster, the motor from her old Hamilton-Beach blender, and a funny board full of electronic things which had come from the back of an old radio in the shed. She thought she would be done long before Joe woke up and came in to watch the Red Sox on TV at two o'clock.

Actually, it was funny how many ideas she'd had in the last few days. Some Jesus had told her about; others just seemed to come to her at odd moments.

Her sewing machine, for instance—she'd always wanted one of those attachments that made the zigzag stitches, but Joe had told her she would have to wait until he could afford to buy her a new machine (and that would probably be along about the 12th of Never, if she knew Joe). Just four days ago she had seen how, if she just moved the button stitcher and added a second needle where it had been at an angle of forty-five degrees to the first needle, she could make all the zigzags she wanted. All it took was a screwdriver—even a dummy like her could use one of those—and it worked just as well as you could want. She saw that the camshaft would probably warp out of true before long because of the weight differential, but there were ways to fix that, too, when it happened.

Then there was the Electrolux. Jesus had told her about that one. Getting her ready for Joe, maybe. It had been Jesus who told her how to use Joe's little butane welding torch, and that made it easier. She had gone over to Derry and bought three of those electronic Simon games at KayBee Toys. Once she was back home she broke them open and pulled out the memory boards. Following Jesus's instructions, she connected the boards and wired Eveready dry cells to the memory circuit she had created. Jesus told her how to program the Electrolux and power it (she had, in fact, already figured this out for herself, but she was much too polite to tell Him so). Now it vacuumed the kitchen, living room, and downstairs bathroom all by itself. It had a tendency to get caught under the piano bench or in the bathroom (where it just kept on butting its stupid self against the toilet until she came running to turn it around), and it scared the granola out of Ozzie, but it was still an improvement over dragging a thirty-pound vac around like a dead dog. She had much more time to catch up on the afternoon stories—and now these included the true stories Jesus told her. Her new, improved Electrolux used juice awfully fast, though, and sometimes it got tangled in its own electrical cord. She thought she might just scratch the dry cells and hook up a motorcycle battery to it one day soon. There would be time—after this problem of Joe and The Hussy had been solved.

Or . . . just last night. She had lain awake in bed long after Joe was snoring beside her, thinking about numbers. It occurred to 'Becka (who had never gotten beyond Business Math in high school) that if you gave numbers *letter* values, you could unfreeze them—you could turn them into something that was like Jell-O. When they—the numbers—were letters, you could pour them into any old mold you liked. Then you could turn the letters back into numbers, and that was like putting the Jell-O into the fridge so it would set, and keep the shape of the mold when you turned it out onto a plate later on.

That way you could always figure things out, 'Becka had thought, delighted. She was unaware that her fingers had gone to the spot above her left eye and were rubbing, rubbing, rubbing. *For instance, just look! You could make things fall into a line every time by saying* $ax + bx + c = 0$, *and that proves it. It always works. It's like Captain Marvel saying Shazam! Well, there is the zero factor; you can't let "a" be zero or that spoils it. But otherwise—*

She had lain awake a while longer, considering this, and then had fallen asleep, unaware that she had reinvented the quadratic equation, and polynomials, and the concept of factoring.

Ideas. Quite a few of them just lately.

'Becka picked up Joe's little blowtorch and lit it deftly with a kitchen match. She would have laughed last month if you'd told her she would ever be working with something like this. But it was easy. Jesus had told her exactly how to solder the wires to the electronics board from the old radio. It was just like fixing up the vacuum cleaner, only this idea was even better.

Jesus had told her a lot of other things in the last three days or so. They had murdered her sleep (and what little sleep she had gotten was nightmare-driven), they had made her afraid to show her face in the village itself (*I'll always know when you've done something wrong, 'Becka,* her father had told her, *because your face just can't keep a secret*), they had made her lose her appetite. Joe, totally bound up in his work, the Red Sox, and his Hussy, noticed none of these things . . . although he had noticed the other night as they watched television that 'Becka was gnawing her fingernails, something she had never done before—it was, in fact, one of the many things *she* nagged *him* about. But she was doing it now, all right; they were bitten right down to the quick. Joe Paulson considered this for all of twelve seconds before looking back at the Sony TV and losing himself in dreams of Nancy Voss's billowy white breasts.

Here were just a few of the afternoon stories Jesus had told her which had caused 'Becka to sleep poorly and to begin biting her fingernails at the advanced age of forty-five:

•In 1973, Moss Harlingen, one of Joe's poker buddies, had murdered his father. They had been hunting deer up in Greenville and it had supposedly been one of those tragic accidents, but the shooting of Abel Harlingen had been no accident. Moss simply lay up behind a fallen tree with his rifle and waited until his father splashed toward him across a small stream about fifty yards down the hill from where Moss was. Moss shot his father carefully and deliberately through the head. *Moss* thought he had killed his father for money. His (Moss's) business, Big Ditch Construction, had two notes falling due with two different banks, and neither bank would extend because of the other. Moss went to Abel, but Abel refused to help, although he could afford to. So Moss shot his father and inherited a lot of money as soon as the county coroner handed down his verdict of death by misadventure. The note was paid and Moss Harlingen really believed (except perhaps in his deepest dreams) that he had committed murder for gain. The *real* motive had been something else. Far in the past, when Moss was ten and his little brother Emery but seven, Abel's wife went south to Rhode Island for one whole winter. Moss's and Emery's uncle had died suddenly, and his wife needed help getting on her feet. While their mother was gone, there were several incidents of buggery in the Harlingens' Troy home. The buggery stopped when the boys' mother came back, and the incidents were never repeated. Moss had forgotten all about them. He never remembered lying awake in the dark anymore, lying awake in mortal terror and watching the doorway for the shadow of his father. He had absolutely no recollection of lying with his mouth pressed against his forearm, hot salty tears of shame and rage squeezing out of his eyes and coursing down his face to his mouth as Abel Harlingen slathered lard onto his cock and then slid it up his son's back door with a grunt and a sigh. It had all made so little impression on Moss that he could not remember biting his arm until it bled to keep from crying out, and he certainly could not remember Emery's breathless little cries from the next bed—"Please, no, daddy, please not me tonight, please, daddy, please no." Children, of course, forget very easily. But *some* subconscious memory must have lingered, because when Moss Harlingen actually pulled the trigger, as he had dreamed of doing every night for the last thirty-two years of his life, as the echoes first rolled away and then rolled back, finally disappearing into the great forested silence of the up-Maine wilderness, Moss whispered: "Not you, Em, not tonight." That Jesus had told her this not two hours after Moss had stopped in to return a fishing rod which belonged to Joe never crossed 'Becka's mind.

•Alice Kimball, who taught at the Haven Grammar School,

was a lesbian. Jesus told 'Becka this on Friday, not long after the lady herself, looking large and solid and respectable in a green pantsuit, had stopped by, collecting for the American Cancer Society.

•Darla Gaines, the pretty seventeen-year-old girl who brought the Sunday paper, had half an ounce of "bitchin' reefer" between the mattress and box spring of her bed. Jesus told 'Becka not fifteen minutes after Darla had come by on Saturday to collect for the last five weeks (three dollars plus a fifty-cent tip 'Becka now wished she had withheld) that she and her boyfriend smoked the reefer in Darla's bed after doing what they called "the horizontal bop." They did the horizontal bop and smoked reefer almost every weekday from two until three o'clock or so. Darla's parents both worked at Splended Shoe in Derry and they didn't get home until well past four.

•Hank Buck, another of Joe's poker buddies, worked at a large supermarket in Bangor and hated his boss so much that a year ago he had put half a box of Ex-Lax in the man's chocolate shake when he, the boss, sent Hank out to McDonald's to get his lunch one day. The boss had shit his pants promptly at quarter past three in the afternoon, as he was slicing luncheon meat in the deli of Paul's Down-East Grocery Mart. Hank managed to hold on until punching-out time, and then he sat in his car, laughing until he almost shit *his* pants. "He laughed," Jesus told 'Becka. "He *laughed*. Can you believe that?"

And these things were only the tip of the iceberg, so to speak. It seemed that Jesus knew something unpleasant or upsetting about everyone—everyone 'Becka herself came in contact with, anyway.

She couldn't live with such an awful outpouring.

But she didn't know if she could live without it anymore, either.

One thing was certain—she had to *do* something. *Something.*

"You *are* doing something," Jesus said. He spoke from behind her, from the picture on top of the TV—of *course* He did—and the idea that the voice was coming from inside her own head, and that it was a cold mutation of her own thoughts . . . that was nothing but a dreadful passing illusion. "In fact, you're almost done with this part, 'Becka. Just solder that red wire to that point beside the long doohickey . . . not that one, the one next to it . . . that's right. Not too much solder! It's like Brylcreem, 'Becka. A little dab'll do ya."

Strange, hearing Jesus Christ talk about Brylcreem.

Joe woke up at quarter of two, tossed Ozzie off his lap, strolled to the back of his lawn, had a comfortable whizz into the poison ivy back there, then headed into the house to watch the Yankees and the Red Sox. He opened the refrigerator in the kitchen, glancing briefly at the little snips of wire on the counter and wondering just what the hell his wife had been up to. Then he dismissed it and grabbed a quart of Bud.

He padded into the living room. 'Becka was sitting in her rocking chair, pretending to read a book. Just ten minutes before Joe came in, she had finished wiring her little gadget into the Zenith console television, following Jesus's instructions to the letter.

"You got to be careful, taking the back off a television, 'Becka," Jesus had told her. "More juice back there than there is in a Bird's Eye warehouse."

"Thought you'd have this all warmed up for me," Joe said.

"I guess you can do it," 'Becka said.

"Ayuh, guess I can," Joe said, completing the last conversational exchange the two of them would ever have.

He pushed the button that made the TV come on and better than two thousand volts of electricity slammed into him. His eyes popped wide open. When the electricity hit him, his hand clenched hard enough to break the bottle in his hand and drive brown glass into his palm and fingers. Beer foamed and ran.

"EEEEEEOOOOOOOOOAARRRRRRRRUMMMMMMMM!"Joe screamed.

His face began to turn black. Blue smoke began to pour from his hair. His finger appeared nailed to the Zenith's ON button. A picture popped up on the TV. It showed Joe and Nancy Voss screwing on the post office floor in a litter of catalogues and Congressional newsletters and sweepstakes announcements from Publishers' Clearing House.

"No!" 'Becka screamed, and the picture changed. Now she saw Moss Harlingen behind a fallen pine, sighting down the barrel of a .30-.30. The picture changed and she saw Darla Gaines and her boyfriend doing the horizontal bop in Darla's upstairs bedroom while Rick Springfield stared at them from the wall.

Joe Paulson's clothes burst into flame.

The living room was filled with the hot smell of cooking beer.

A moment later, the 3-D picture of Jesus exploded.

"*No!*" 'Becka shrieked, suddenly understanding that it had been her all along, her, her, her, she had thought everything up, she had read their thoughts, somehow read their thoughts, it had been the hole in her head and it had done something to her mind—had souped it up somehow. The picture on the TV changed again and she saw herself backing down the stepladder with the .22 pistol in her hand, pointed toward her—she looked like a woman bent on suicide rather than on cleaning.

Her husband was turning black before her very eyes.

She ran to him, seized his shredded, wet hand . . . and was herself galvanized by electricity. She was no more able to let go than Brer Rabbit had been after he slapped the tar baby for insolence.

Jesus oh Jesus, she thought as the current slammed into her, driving her up on her toes.

And a mad, cackling voice, the voice of her father, rose in her brain: *Fooled you, 'Becka! Fooled you, didn't I! Fooled you good!*

The back of the television, which she had screwed back on after she had finished with her alterations (on the off-chance that Joe might look back there), exploded backward in a mighty blue flash of light. Joe and 'Becka Paulson tumbled to the carpet. Joe was already dead. And by the time the smoldering wallpaper behind the TV had ignited the drapes, 'Becka was dead, too.

SEA LOVERS

VALERIE MARTIN

"The people on the shore will find their clothes, but they will never find the lovers."

The vast and secretive sea hides much from land-bound creatures, and the passions of its denizens, as we know from myth and fable, only deceptively resemble those of humans. Valerie Martin, whose gift is for subtle blendings of elegance and aberrance, invites us on a late-evening walk along a deserted strip of beach. What waits there, however, knows no appeasing; this unseen watcher is a presence as implacable as the ocean, and, like the lulling motion of the foamy waves, it masks its unpredictable violence with a tantalizing sensuousness.

On moonless nights the sea is black. Ships sail upon it and shine their lights through the double blackness of water and air. The darkness swallows up light like a great yawning snake. On the beach people walk, looking out to sea, but there is no sign of the ships, no sign of the drowning sailors, no sign of anything living or dead, only the continual rushing and ebbing of water sucking and sucking at the shoreline, drawing the innocent, foolish lovers out a little farther. They are unafraid, showing each other their courage. They laugh, pointing to the water. No one can see them. They slip off their clothes and wade in. The waves draw them out, tease them, lick upward slowly about her pale thighs, slap him playfully, dashing a little salt spray into his eyes. He turns to her, she to him; they can scarcely see each other, but they are strong swimmers and they link hands as they go out a little farther, a little deeper. Now the waves swell about them and they embrace. She is losing her footing, so she leans against him, allows the rising water to lift her right off her feet as she is pressed against him. He pulls her in tightly, laughing into her mouth as he kisses her.

They can't be seen; they can't be heard. The people on the shore will find their clothes, but they will never find the lovers. A solitary mermaid passing nearby hears their laughter and pauses. She watches them, but even her strange fish-pale eyes can barely see them; the night is so black, so moonless. She could sing to them, as she has sung to other drowning mortals, but she is weary tonight and her heart is heavy from too much solitude. She has not seen another of her kind for many months. She was nearly killed a few days ago, swimming near a steamship. Her head is full of the giant engine blades, of that moment when she looked up and saw that she was a hair's-breadth from death. That was when she turned toward shore. She is swimming in with the tide, even as the lovers are sucked out and down. When she drops beneath the surface of the water, the mermaid can just see the woman's long hair billowing out around her face. Her mouth is open wide in a silent scream. Oh yes, the mermaid thinks, if she could be heard it would be quite a racket. People would come running for miles. But the sea filled her mouth before the sound could get out and no one will ever hear her now. She clings to the man, and he, in his panic, pushes her away. This started out as such a lark. It was a calm, hot, black night and the white sands of the beach made all the light there was. They had wandered along, stopping to kiss and tease, laughing, so happy, so safe, and now this: she was drowning and he could not save her. Worse, worse, she would pull him under.

The mermaid rises above the crest of a wave and looks back

at them. She sees only one pale hand reaching up, the fingers splayed and tense, as if reaching for something to hold; then the water closes over that too.

The sea is full of death, now more than ever. The mermaid has, twice in her short life, found herself swimming in a sea red with blood: once from a whale struck by a steamship, once from men drowning during a war. Their ship had been torpedoed and most of them were bleeding when they hit the water. The sharks had done the rest. That time she had dived beneath the battle, for the noise was deafening and the light from the explosions dazzled her so that she could scarcely see. One of the men clutched at her as she swam away, but she shook him off. She disliked being seen by men, even when they were about to die. She could amuse herself singing to them when they couldn't see her, when they were wild-eyed and desperate, clinging to a broken spar from a boat shattered by a storm, or treading water in that ridiculous way they had, with those pathetic, useless legs; then she would hide among the waves and sing to them. Sometimes it made them more frantic, but a few times she had seen a strange calm overtake a drowning man, so that his struggles became more mechanical, less frantic, and he simply stayed afloat as long as he could and went under at last quietly, without that panicked gagging and struggling that was so disgusting to see. Once a man had died like that very near her, and she had felt so curious about him that she drifted too close to him, and in the last moment of his life he saw her. His eyes were wide open and startled already from his long, bitter struggle with death; he knew he was beaten yet could not give up. He saw her and he reached out to her, his mouth opened as if he would speak, but it was blood and not words that poured over his lips and she knew even as he did that he was gone. She had, by her nature, no sympathy for men, but this one interested her.

It was a cold, calm night and the man was so far from land that it would be days before his body was tossed up, bloated, unrecognizable, on some shore. He had been sailing alone in a small boat, far out to sea; she had, in fact, been watching his progress for days. The storm that had wrecked his little craft was intense, but quickly over, and he had survived it somehow, holding on to pieces of the wreckage. Then it was a few days of hopeless drifting for him. She watched from a distance, listened to him when he began to babble to himself. Near the end he stunned her by bursting into song, singing as loud as he could, though he had little strength left, a lively song that she couldn't understand. When he was dead she did something she had never done: she touched him. His skin was strange, he was already stiffening, and she was fascinated by the feel of it. She took him by the shoulders and brought him down with her, down where the water was still and clear, and there she looked at him carefully. His eyes fascinated her, so different from her own. She discovered the hard nails on his fingers and toes. She examined his mouth, which she thought incredibly ugly, and his genitals, which confused her. Gradually a feeling of revulsion overtook her and she swam away from him abruptly, leaving him wedged in a bed of coral and kelp, food for the bigger fish that might pass his way.

Now she remembers him as she swims toward shore, and her thin upper lip curls back at the thought of him. She is being driven toward land by a force stronger than her own will, and she hates that force even as she gives in to it, just as she hated the dead man.

It is dark and the air is still. Though the sea is never still, she has the illusion of calm. She swims effortlessly just beneath the surface of the waves. She is getting close to shore, dangerously close, but she neither slows nor alters her course.

She is acquainted with many stories that tell of the perils of the land, stories similar to the ones men tell about the sea, full of terror, wonder, magic, and romance. The moral of these tales (that she can no more live on land than men can live in the sea) has not escaped her. She has seen the land; she knows about its edges and she has seen mountains rising above the surface of the water. Sometimes there are people on these mountains, walking about or driving in their cars. This coast, which she must have chosen, is flat and long. There is white sand along it for miles and behind the sand a line of green, though in the darkness its vivid colors are only black before white before gray. The mermaid can scarcely look at it. She is caught up in the surf that moves relentlessly toward land. For a while she can drop beneath the waves, but soon the water is too shallow, and when her tail and side scrape against the hard sand at the bottom she shudders as if death had reached up suddenly and touched her. The waves smash her down and roll her over. Her tail wedges into the sand and sends a cloud over her; she feels the grit working in under her scales. She raises her webbed hands to wipe it away. It is different from the sand in the deep water; it feels sharp and somehow more irritating and it smells of land.

It's useless to fight the waves. She lets her body rise and fall with them, rolling in with the surf as heavy and unresisting as a broken ship or a dead man. Soon there is nothing but sand beneath her, and the water ebbs away, leaving her helpless, exposed to the warm and alien air. The pounding she has taken has left her barely conscious. She lies on her stomach in the sand, her arms stretched out over her head, her face turned to one side so that what little water there is can flow over it. Her long silvery body writhes in the shallows and she is aghast with pain. From the waist down she is numb and she lifts her head as best she can to look back at herself. She can hardly feel her tail, rising and falling in the sand, working her in deeper and deeper, against her will. It is horrible, and she is so helpless that she falls back down with a groan. Something is seeping out of her, spilling out into the sand. It is slippery and viscous; at first she thinks she is bleeding, then she imagines it is her life. She moans again and struggles to lift herself, pushing her hands against the sand. She opens and closes her mouth, gasping for water. Her skin is drying out; it burns along her back, her shoulders, her neck. She presses her face down as a little trickle of water rushes up near her, but it is not enough and she manages only to get more damp sand in her mouth. She lifts her head and shoulders once more against the unexpected weight of the air, and as she does, she sees the man.

He is running toward her. He has left his fishing gear to the whims of the sea and he is running toward her as fast as he can. Her heart sinks. He is in his element and she is at his mercy. But in the next heartbeat she is struck with cunning and a certainty that flashes up in her consciousness with the force of memory. In the same moment she knows that her lower body is now her own, and strength surges through her like an electric current. He must not see her face; she knows this. She spreads her hair out over her shoulders and hides her face in the sand. Her body is still, her strong tail lies flat in the shallows, as shiny and inert as a sheet of steel.

She listens to the slap of his bare feet against the hard wet sand as he comes closer. Soon she can hear his labored breathing and his mumbled exclamations, though his words are meaningless to her. This is a big catch, but it will be a while before he understands what he has caught. In the darkness he takes her for a woman, and it is not until he is bending over her that he sees the peculiar unwomanly shape of her lower body. For a moment he thinks she is a woman who has been half devoured by an enormous fish. He looks back at the shore, as if help might come from it, but there is no help for him now. His hands move over her shoulders. He is determined to pull her out of the water, not for any reason but that she has washed up on the shore and that is what men do with creatures who wash up on the shore. "My God," he says, and the pitch of his voice makes the mermaid clench her jaw, "are you still alive?"

She does not move. His hands are communicating all sorts of useless information to him: this creature is very like a woman, and though her smooth skin is extraordinarily cold, it is soft, supple, alive. His fingers dig in under her arms and lift her a little. She is careful to keep her face down, hidden in the stream of her long hair. This hair, he can see even in the darkness, is almost white, thick, unnaturally long; it falls voluptuously over her shoulders. He is losing his grip; she is heavier than he imagined, and he releases her for a moment while he changes his position. He straddles her back now. She hears the squish of his feet as he steps over her head and positions himself behind her. As he does he takes a closer look at her long back and sees the line where the pale skin turns to silver. "What are you?" he says, but he doesn't pause to find out. His hands are under her arms again; one of them strays over her breasts quickly, momentarily, as he lifts her. Her heart is beating furiously now so that she can hear nothing else. For one second she hangs limp in his arms and in the next she comes alive.

She brings her arms quickly under her and pushes up so suddenly and with such force that the man loses his balance and falls over her. She is, thanks to the sea, several times as strong as he is, and she has no difficulty now turning over beneath him. He struggles, astounded at the sudden powerful fury of the creature he had intended to save, but he struggles in vain. They are entwined together in the sand, rising and falling like lovers, but the man, at least, is aware that this is not love. Her strong arms close around him and he can feel her cold clawed hands in his hair. His face is wedged against her shoulder, and as he breathes in the peculiar odor of her skin, he is filled with terror. She takes a handful of his hair and pulls his head up so that she can look at him and he at her. What he sees paralyzes him, as surely as if he had looked at Medusa, though it is so dark he can see only the glitter of her cold, flat, lidless eyes, the thin hard line of her mouth, which opens and closes beneath his own. He can hear the desperate sucking sound fish make when they are pulled from the sea. She rolls him under her as easily as if he were a woman and she a man. With one hand she holds his throat while with the other she tears away the flimsy swimming trunks, all the protection he had against her. Her big tail is moving rapidly now, pushing her body up over his. Her hand loosens at his throat and he gasps for air, groaning, pushing against her with all his strength, trying to push her away. She raises herself on her arms, looking down at him curiously and he sees the sharp fish teeth, the dry black tongue. Her tail is powerful and sinuous; it has come up between his legs like an eel and now the sharp edge of it grazes the inside of his thighs. It cuts him; he can feel the blood gathering at the cuts, again and again, each time a little closer to the groin. He cries out, but no one hears him. The mermaid doesn't even bother to look at him as she brings her tail up hard against his testicles and slices through the unresisting flesh, once, twice, three times; that's all it takes. His fingers have torn the skin on her back and he has bitten into her breast so that she is bleeding, but she can't feel anything as pain now. She drops back over him and clasps his throat between her hands, pressing hard and for a long time until he ceases to struggle.

Then she is quiet but not still. Carefully she takes up the bleeding pocket of flesh from between his legs; carefully cradling it in her hands, she transfers it into the impression she left in the sand before this struggle began. The sea will wash it all away in a minute or two, for the tide is coming in, but that's all the time she needs. She pushes the sand up around this bloody treasure; then, exhausted and strangely peaceful, she rolls away into the shallows. The cool water revives her and she summons her strength to swim out past the breakers. Now she can feel the pain in her back and her breast, but she can't stop to attend to it. As soon as the water is deep enough she dives beneath the waves, and as she does her tail flashes silver in the dark night air; like great metal wings, the caudal fin slices first the air, then the water.

On the shore everything is still. The waves are creeping up around the man, prying him loose from the sand. Little water fingers rush in around his legs, his arms, his face. Already the water has washed his blood away. Farther down the beach his fishing gear floats in the rising water. His tackle box has spilled its insides; all his lures and hooks, all the wiles he used to harvest the sea, bob gaily on the waves.

Farther still I am walking on the shore with my lover. We have been dancing at a party. The beach house is behind us, throwing its white light and music out into the night air as if it could fill the void. Inside it was hot, bright; we couldn't hear the waves or smell the salt air, and so we are feeling lightheaded and pleased with ourselves for having had the good sense to take a walk. We are walking away from the house and away from the dead man, but not away from the sea. I've taken my shoes off so that I can let the water cool my tired feet. My lover follows my example; he sheds his shoes and stops to roll up his pants legs. As I stand looking out into the black water and the blacker sky it seems to me that I can see tiny lights, like stars, flashing in the waves. "What are those lights?" I ask him when he joins me, and he looks but says he doesn't see any lights.

"Mermaids," I say. I could almost believe it. I raise my hand and wave at them. "Be careful," I say. "Stay away from the shore." My lover is very close to me. His arms encircle me; he draws me close to him. The steady pounding of the waves and the blackness of the night excite us. We would like to make love in the sand, at the water's edge.

PSYCHOPOMP

HAYDN MIDDLETON

"His fear made no difference at all to the wanting."

Few stories whose themes locate sexuality squarely in the realm of the macabre are as basic, as primal, as this one. For one thing, Haydn Middleton, captivated like so many writers before him with the horrific potential of the classic warning, "Be careful of what you wish for . . . because you may get it," understands that one's past is a very, very dangerous place to explore. Unhappily for Red, his 45-year-old hero, Middleton also intuits (with a nod to Freud) that there can be, really, only one logical stopping place on any backward journey.

Moreover, the ennui of male mid-life crisis, a too frequently hashed-over—and, thus, too depressingly familiar—starting point for contemporary fiction, is here reinvented. The result: Middleton envisions for us one man's descent into years of yesterdays, a seemingly innocent, not quite inadvertent trip that picks up dizzying momentum with each antinostalgic shock effect.

At the age of forty-five, Red reached a strange impasse. It was as if a mirror lay across his horizon, blocking off the future, showing him only the way that he had come.

At first Red wanted to smash the mirror and break on through to the other side. But when he looked more closely at the reflected images, he found that he liked them. They touched him in ways that nothing in his present life could touch him. Instead of smashing the mirror he became seduced by it. He continued to work but lost interest in food, drink, and conversation. He spent long hours sleeping—in a different room from his wife—trying to regain in dreams a sense of his younger self.

Red didn't understand this sudden passion for his own past. His wife urged him to see a therapist, but he insisted that nothing was wrong with his mind. Losing patience, his wife then told him to take a mistress, someone half his age, to put the spring back into his step. Yet in twenty-five years of marriage Red had never been unfaithful; and this, he felt sure, was not the time for anyone—or anything—new.

Red and the marriage deteriorated. His wife booked a make-or-break holiday for them on a sunny island. They made love every night for a week, but Red found the gulf between past and present impossible to bridge. He loved his wife, but craved the girl of twenty-five years before, not this elegant and infinitely more accomplished development of that same girl at forty-five.

On the last morning of their holiday Red sat hunched on the beach, staring out to sea. His wife lay beside him, propped up on her elbows, reading a magazine. She glanced at him, then eased herself into a sitting position.

"Darling," she said, handing him the magazine. "I think I've found out what's wrong with you." She pointed to the piece that had caught her eye.

It was a wry little column headed "Death by Longing." The writer claimed that nostalgia was spreading like an epidemic through every aspect of modern life. But whereas no one today thought it harmful, seventeenth-century doctors had seen nostalgic affliction as a physical disease. There were explicit symptoms. Sufferers were believed to have died of it.

Red handed back the magazine with a shrug and a smile.

"But it's just what you've got, isn't it?" said his wife, her expression unreadable behind huge sunglasses. "You're wasting away with nostalgia."

Red shook his head. His eyes fell to the grains of sand that clung to his wife's breasts. Forty-five-year-old breasts—and still good to look at. But he was looking with forty-five-year-old eyes. He ached when he remembered how different it had been at the very beginning, when the two of them had been twenty-five years younger, in front of a roaring winter fire, in a tiny house on a hill . . . Red gazed back out to sea. His wife sighed, stretched herself on the sand, then began to read the article again.

At the end of September Red was due to attend a weekend conference in the south. He would be staying within easy driving distance of the town where he had been born and raised. On the night before he left home he went to his wife's room. She was sitting up in the bed. "Yes?" she said.

Red couldn't speak.

"There's nothing for you here," she told him. "But take a look around that godawful town of yours while you're down there. Relive the good times."

Their eyes met. She stared at him with pity rather than contempt. "You'll probably enjoy yourself so much," she said before reaching up and switching off the light, "you won't even bother to come back."

Red arrived at the conference centre late on Friday afternoon. By Saturday lunchtime he could restrain himself no longer. Facetious as his wife's suggestion may have been, it was one that he had to take up. Red made his excuses and walked out of a seminar. Heading toward the car park, he stopped on an impulse, turned, and made instead for the small rail station.

He wanted to approach the old place by train—the way he had approached it with his wife-to-be at the end of their first chaste winter term at college. Then he wanted to go from landmark to landmark on foot, reverently retreading the paths of his youth, childhood, and infancy.

But he had to wait an hour for the right train. It was a sultry afternoon. Red sweated freely as he paced the platform. His carriage on the train then smelled of urine and was thick with flies. By the time he pulled into his hometown he was feeling irritably unromantic.

He had last been back thirteen years before, for his mother's funeral. On leaving the station concourse he decided against paying a visit to her grave. It was the remoter, more resonant past that he had come to explore.

The town had never been attractive. Nothing seemed to have changed much. Perhaps there was more litter on the roads; perhaps the faces of the people had become a little more pinched. Within an hour Red had passed his school, his church, his park, the houses of various friends, relations, and teachers from his unexceptional past. He didn't look closely at any of these landmarks. Seeing them as they really were, rather than as reflections in his mid-life mirror, he'd felt curiously uninterested. As he continued on his way he walked faster, looking into the far distance, or down at his aching feet, but seldom, now, at what he was passing.

He stopped at the bottom of a steep, terraced street. From where he stood he couldn't see the house. It was a short way up on the left-hand side: the house in which, forty-five winters before, he had been born; the same house in which, twenty years later, he had first made love to the girl who would be his wife, at the start of a bitterly cold Christmas vacation.

But something made Red hesitant about entering the street. The trip so far had not been a success. He shrank from the thought of a mighty anticlimax in front of this last landmark— the house that contained his most cherished memories of all.

To fortify himself, he doubled back a short way, entered a bar that he had favored in his youth, and ordered a whiskey. The proprietor, still the same man after all the years, didn't recognize him, and he failed to respond to any of Red's attempts at conversation.

Crushed, Red stared down at his drink. He had no stomach for the whiskey. In truth he had no stomach for the whole town. His wife had been right: it *was* godawful. He marveled that his memory could have played such tricks on him. He slunk out of the bar and headed once again in the direction of his old street. This time, however, he didn't even reach the junction.

After a dozen paces he checked his step, threw back his head, and grinned. It wasn't worth it. It just wasn't worth it. At last he saw the sheer absurdity of it all: the mirror, the passion, coming back on the train—all, all, impossibly ludicrous.

He turned on his heel and strode, then broke into a trot, in the direction of the station. A train was due in fifteen minutes. He could be back for the six o'clock seminar. There was even time to phone his wife before the train arrived. He wanted to hear his wife's voice. More important, for the first time since he had seen the mirror, he wanted to feel her touch. If she sounded responsive when he phoned, he would drive straight back to her that night.

At the station he went into the bar and bought himself a large whiskey. He raised the glass and drank to his own successful exorcism of himself, there—in his drab and graceless home town—on a late afternoon in September.

Red finished his drink, opened the bar door, and returned to the platform. He noticed the man at the table outside before he saw the girl sitting next to him. Red hadn't seen the man for at least twenty years. His name was Page. They had been at school and college together, but had never been close. At college, however, Red's wife had been a friend of Page's future wife. The two women still kept in touch intermittently.

Red moved up the platform, turned, and eyed Page harder. Tanned, casually dressed, and looking startlingly youthful, he was swirling the beer in the bottom of his glass. He appeared to be paying no attention to the girl who was whispering in his ear. The girl. Not his wife. Red looked at her now.

She was young and slim. A shock of wild golden hair obscured most of her face. She wore a thin white sleeveless vest, a short black skirt, and woven sandals. Beneath the plastic table—Red saw—one of her long legs was hooked over Page's thigh. With one hand she played with the hair behind his ear. With the other she was kneading his crotch.

Red looked away. When he looked back, almost at once, the girl had both hands on Page's shoulder and was gnawing at his ear. Twice Red saw the raw length of her tongue through the paler pink lipstick. Page, however, remained impassive. It was as if he were sitting there alone.

The girl swung her leg off Page's thigh. She tapped both feet on the ground, tossed her hair from her eyes, then glanced straight at Red. He felt himself blush. She had caught him feasting his eyes on her and he couldn't look away. He smiled at her, almost in apology. She smiled back. Page, still studying the dregs of his drink, remained oblivious.

Red turned awkwardly and browsed among the racks of books. His face burned. There was a weakening at his ankles, a pulsing in his shoulders. He closed his eyes and his head teemed with the vision of her painted, overlong fingernails, openly pawing at Page's genitals. He glanced back. She seemed to be remonstrating with Page. Remonstrating or trying to convince him of something. The urgency in her face seemed all at odds with the languid arrangement of the rest of her body.

It was a wide face, beautifully formed if not exactly beautiful. Wide, high-cheekboned, and very, very open. In mid-whisper she turned her head. Again her eyes alighted on Red. She smiled, far more frankly than before. Red looked down. There was a large black shoulder bag at Page's feet. Just one bag, Red thought in a rush: Either they've packed everything into the one bag—or *else she isn't going with him.* . . . Crazily excited, he picked up a paperback and paid for it. Then he remembered, as if from a parallel life, that he had planned to phone his wife.

He stepped a little closer to Page and the girl, reading the blurb on the back of his book. The words swam in and out of focus. He sensed an intense brightness around him. The imminence of his train's arrival was announced over the loudspeakers. On hearing this, Page shifted himself in his seat until he seemed to be looking right through the girl. She cupped his face between her hands, moved her open mouth against his, and ate at him.

As she kissed him—and there was no suggestion of reciprocity about it—she slid further forward in her seat. Red watched. He watched her lodge her own crotch against Page's knee, and begin to rub herself against him.

Red looked around as if in appeal. People stood all over the platform, reading, talking, eating. Not one of them was watching the girl's performance. They seemed as heedless as Page himself. Red's train eased itself to a standstill in front of him. He watched Page rise, turn, and hoist the bag over his shoulder. The girl stood, too. Red saw her fingers splayed across Page's shoulder blades as she embraced him. A farewell embrace—Red had no doubt of that. No doubt at all. Page turned toward the train, until he stood at right angles to Red. The girl turned with him, one of her legs bent at the knee and nuzzling between his parted legs.

Passengers were leaving and joining the train. Red threw down his book and walked quickly toward the row of telephone kiosks. At the moment that he passed the embracing couple, the girl looked up and over Page's shoulder. She met Red's eye. Her timing couldn't have been better. But her face was not the face that Red might have anticipated. It wasn't soft from the single-mindedness of her embrace. Instead it broke into the sweetest smile. A little girl's smile, practiced and collusive. A smile for Red. It seemed to say: *He's going, but that doesn't have to be the end of the world. . . .*

Red walked on dizzily to the first kiosk and punched out his own number.

"Yes?" said his wife before he had time to turn and resume his observation.

Red had no idea what he wanted to say. Guards were slamming the train's doors. Red closed his eyes, aware of this moment's importance. "I love you," he said in a quaking voice.

"You don't," his wife replied at once. "How's the old place looking?"

"How did you know I was here?" he asked, turning—and suddenly panicking because he could no longer see either Page or the girl. His wife didn't answer his question. "I've seen Page," he said, craning his neck to left and right.

"So you've taken your mirror with you?"

Red frowned. "Why?"

She laughed. "You know why, you fool. Page killed himself nine years ago. He went back to that hole of a town to do it too. He must have had the same problem as you." She put down her phone.

Red gazed at his train as it pulled out of the station.

As soon as his wife had spoken of Page's death he remembered her telling him about it nine years before. It was even possible that she had come down for the funeral.

Page's body had been found on the railway line. There had been some suspicion—eventually unproven—of foul play. Red couldn't understand how he had forgotten something so hauntingly memorable. Yet he knew that he had made no mistake. The man with that girl had been Page.

For the first time Red considered that he really might be ill. Nothing physical, nothing connected with any fey seventeenth-century notions about nostalgia, and not exactly a mental derangement either. But perhaps—just perhaps—he was suffering from some peculiar sickness of the memory.

And now there was no sign of either Page or the girl. And Red would have to wait two hours for another train. And he had wrecked any chance of an immediate reconciliation with his wife. As he left the kiosk he swore aloud at the length of empty platform. He slouched along to the bar and pushed back the door.

The girl was sitting alone at the table just inside, fingering the stem of a full glass of wine. Beside the glass stood an untouched, freshly poured beer. The girl looked up at Red as he entered. She smiled a welcome.

Neither Red nor the girl spoke as they sipped their drinks. Occasionally the girl smiled. Close to, Red saw the darkness of her nipples beneath the vest. When she crossed her legs, her knee brushed his. He had never known such unqualified desire.

Then she stood. He stood too. Outside the bar she walked just one step ahead of him to the exit, then down into the station parking lot.

Red had never expected it to be like this. He had often dreamed of going with another woman. But he had always imagined that this woman would be an old friend, someone he virtually loved, whose sexual spirit he would have to exorcise if their friendship were to go on. He hadn't guessed that lust, pure and simple, would force him to change the habits of a lifetime.

The girl led the way to a small car. Red fell further behind, to watch the athletic grace of her walk. She wore the vest and skirt very lightly. He pictured her bronzed body, with those raw red flashes at tongue and fingertips. He pictured the presents for Page—or whoever—that she made of her nakedness. And Red wanted it so badly for himself. He wanted it all.

Neither of the car's doors was locked. Red got in. As the girl started the engine he placed his hand high on her thigh. She reacted only by putting the car into gear and driving away at speed. When she stopped at some traffic lights, Red moved his hand from her leg, touched the back of her neck, then drew her toward him so that they could kiss.

Her mouth opened at once but her tongue remained flaccid. Red was aware of the clashing of their teeth. He remembered how eager she had been with the lover from whom she had just parted. That man. The man who couldn't have been Page. Did she—it occurred to him—expect to be paid? Before she performed for him? Was *that* what he was getting himself into?

Suddenly it seemed so obvious. But even if she did need payment, Red still wanted her. His pride had gone. He would pay through the nose. He would give her everything he had, and get the very best she had to offer.

The lights changed. Red disengaged himself, cleared his throat, and spoke to her for the first time.

"The man you were with at the station," he said. "Was his name Page?"

The girl shrugged and shook her head with a smile. She didn't know; it didn't matter or else she wasn't going to tell him. One way or another, they weren't going to talk about it.

Red stared out at his home town. The girl was taking exactly the same route from the station that he had taken on foot. As twilight fell, prematurely for the time of year, the roads looked grimmer than ever. And inside the car it had grown chilly, far colder than it had been outside all day. Red glanced at the girl. Her skin looked less bronzed; her nipples had risen like dice against the underside of her vest. Red looked away with a shiver. They passed the bar in which he hadn't drunk his whiskey. The girl signaled a left turn.

As she swung the car, rather too quickly, into the steep street, Red gasped. Before he could speak she shifted gears and drove them to a halt. Red flushed and stared at her, wide-eyed. They were outside his old home.

"What is this?" he demanded, but his voice had no authority.

She opened her door and left the car. He watched her walk around to the front gate, open it, approach the front door, then let herself in.

Red couldn't bring himself to look at any part of the house save its open front doorway. He was afraid to be there. This was nothing to do with any sickness of the memory. This was as real as the hands that were trembling at the ends of his arms. But he wanted the girl. He wanted her. His fear made no difference at all to the wanting.

Keeping his eyes down he climbed out of the car. It was bitterly cold and nighttime dark. The streetlamp overhead painted his stunted shadow onto a pavement filmy with ice. A residue of frozen snow had banked up against the house's front-garden wall. Red breathed fast and shallow, more frightened than he had ever imagined, but famished for the girl. Too famished to ask questions.

He could see into the tiny house's main room through the doorway. All was darkness, save one small area lit by the glow of a dying fire. Stretched out on that floor, twenty-five years before, by the light of a fiercer fire, he had possessed for the first time the only woman in his life.

Red wanted to weep. Whatever was happening to him, he knew that he should go from that place, run from there. Instead he stepped closer. At the edge of the illuminated area, he distinguished the shape of the girl.

She was standing with her back to him, her head lowered. She held onto a piece of furniture, stiff-armed, as if she were bracing herself. Her legs were slightly parted. She was naked from the waist down.

I'll pay you, Red thought deliriously, feeling as if he were being dragged into the house by his groin, I'll forget about being afraid. I'll forget everything that has ever happened.

He was in the passageway, he was in the room. He pulled off his clothes, grasped the girl's shoulders, and slid into her from behind.

She was wet but she made no sound. Neither did she flinch. Red urged himself deeper, but still he could spark no response. She received him as if her own body were elsewhere.

Red kissed her neck. He gnawed at the raised vertebrae above the neckline of her vest. He slipped his hands under her arms to cup her breasts. There wasn't a trace of excitement in her. Again Red remembered how she had been at the station. He needed her to be like that with him. He couldn't do without it. He leaned against her, thrusting feverishly. His hands moved from her breasts and fastened onto her hip bones.

He felt such shame. He would have wept if he had felt capable of tears. But an unexpected lassitude took hold of him. He pushed himself higher still into the girl, wanting only to end it now and be done. But he couldn't spend himself. This had always been his way: unless the act had at least a degree of mutuality, he could not bring it to a conclusion. He closed his eyes. His penis had begun to soften.

"Why?" he whispered into the girl's still-braced back.

"It's not me," she said in reply. And when Red dropped to his knees behind her, she turned and elaborated, almost sadly, "It's not me that you want."

Red hung his head. The girl stepped away from the desk against which she had been holding herself. He heard her pull her vest over her head. There was a crackle of flames as she threw it into the fire.

When Red looked up, he saw that she was kneeling too, her back to him. He frowned at what he saw. Her back seemed less sinuously long than before. Her hair seemed shorter. It was darker for sure, and—as he looked closer—arranged in a style that had gone out of fashion before she had been born.

"Oh, Christ," he murmured as she twisted her neck to show him her profile. "Oh, Jesus Christ . . ."

"Is it me?" she asked without looking at him. "Is it me that you think you want?"

Red cried out a taut, strangled little cry. He was staring in disbelief at his own wife. She was twenty years old.

He crossed the floor to her on his hands and knees.

It was her. Flawlessly young. It really was her, just as it had been Page on the platform. Red put out a hand and touched her silken cheek. He pressed one finger to her virgin lips.

"I love you," he breathed.

She smiled. Then she laid herself out for him. Flat on her back, hands clasped over her sex, just as she had lain, on that same part of the floor, twenty-five years before. The fire beside her roared, fueled by more than one flimsy vest, lighting her breasts for Red's eyes.

Red was above her, exhausted before he began. His penis parted her hands and forged up into her. His wife—this girl who would be his wife—stayed motionless. A smile lingered on her lips, but there was a distant look in her eyes, as if she were seeing right through the ceiling and up into the bedroom where Red's mother had slept above them on that first fine night.

It was no good. She would not move with him. After several minutes Red fell down into her. Her face, neck, and breasts were cold, although he felt that the fire was singeing every hair on his own body. He stopped moving. Already he was collapsing inside her.

"It wasn't like this," he gasped, screwing up his face with the effort of speaking. "Not for me. Why are you making it like this?"

She didn't answer. Red slipped out of her loveless form, turned from the fire, and pressed his face into the floor.

He heard her get to her feet. He heard her leave the room, mount the narrow staircase, and climb into the creaking bed in the room above. His mother's bed. The bed in which Red had been born.

In spite of his despair, Red felt incensed. She had no right to that bed. It wasn't her bed to be in. The fire was now so high its flames seemed to be leaping through the room. Red stood.

He was smaller than he had been when he entered that house. Less than half the size. He made unsteadily for the door. It was no cooler in the hall, or even on the stairs. The higher he climbed, the hotter it seemed to become.

Outside the bedroom he heard her tiny cry within.

From the doorway he saw her curled inside the bedclothes. He couldn't see her face as she writhed from side to side in the great bed. She was whimpering. A sound he hadn't heard from a woman before. A small, ominous sound that, he sensed, presaged a catastrophic, all-consuming scream.

He stepped into the room. She heard him enter, and stilled herself.

"It's me that you want," she said to him—in a new but unmistakable voice from Red's remotest and most resonant past. "Now please *me*."

Red hung his head. At last he could weep. The tears coursed down. This was worse than anything he could have dreamed.

"Please me," said his mother again from beneath the blankets.

Red shook his head, vehemently. "But I'm so hot," he whined through his tears.

He spoke with the voice of an infant. *Her* infant. He felt as if the whole of him were on fire. The only cool place, he knew, would be where she wanted him to be. The only cool place. The oldest place of all.

She kicked her legs free. He saw her. He saw her hand, holding her glistening sex and offering it up to him between two fingers. She looked huge.

"Kiss me," she said, and Red knew that he wouldn't be able to refuse. This couldn't end in any other way.

He opened his mouth and tried to speak but he was too young. Far too young for speech. And he was on the bed with her, crawling on his stomach between her splayed legs, screaming his despair into the heat and the dark.

"Good," she coaxed him as his lips fastened onto her. "Good, good . . ." And she was thrashing again, holding his head hard against her crotch as she rolled from one side of the bed to the other. "Good . . ."

He bit on her with his toothless gums, but not because he wanted to please her. She arched her back in frenzy, she swung her legs wide apart. And Red saw, within her, a huge cool canopy of glass. Reflecting glass. His head was moving closer to that canopy. This would be the truest end. He was breathing in the glass. He was seeing them all, feeling them all, twisted and distorted the reflections of everything that he was leaving behind.

Then his mother screamed—the catastrophic scream that Red had sensed in her first tiny cry. And he felt her hand on his bottom, just moments before she propelled the whole of him deep inside herself, and then sealed off any possible exit.

Editor's note: A psychopomp, for those who have not previously encountered this vivid and marvelously strange word, was, in ancient Greek myth, a conductor of souls to the place of the dead.

A GLOWING FUTURE

RUTH RENDELL

"He liked her to be angry and fierce; it was her love he feared."

Jealousy may not be counted among the seven sins, but its deadliness has never been in question, and a woman scorned may only be biding in her time. Ruth Rendell, along with Patricia Highsmith (and only seemingly in a lighter vein, Fay Weldon) is one of contemporary fiction's Gypsy witches, stirring the tea leaves of sexual obsession. Almost invariably the forecast is doom, and to begin one of her stories or novels of psychological suspense is to abandon onself to a creeping awareness of that fate.

For any ordinary reader engrossed in one of Rendell's remorseless tales, a typical reaction, I think, is to pull away from the page, to resist however briefly the hypnotic force of the spell she casts, in order to examine and reassure oneself of one's own normality. What a relief it is then to remember, if only for an instant, that we—though, of course, not her characters—exist apart from the inevitable highly unpleasant conclusion.

But do we?

Rendell's genius, in this chilling portrait of love's other face,

*is that she reminds us, as she so often does, of how vulnerable
each everyday life—even yours—is to the loosening of restraint,
to an uncontrollable emotion, to an act of horror.*

"**S**ix should be enough," he said. "We'll say six tea chests,
then, and one trunk. If you'll deliver them tomorrow, I'll get
the stuff all packed and maybe your people could pick them up
Wednesday." He made a note on a bit of paper. "Fine," he said.
"Round about lunchtime tomorrow."

She hadn't moved. She was still sitting in the big oak-armed
chair at the far end of the room. He made himself look at her
and he managed a kind of grin, pretending all was well.

"No trouble," he said. "They're very efficient."

"I couldn't believe," she said, "that you'd really do it. Not
until I heard you on the phone. I wouldn't have thought it
possible. You'll really pack up all those things and have them
sent off to her."

They were going to have to go over it all again. Of course
they were. It wouldn't stop until he'd got the things out and
himself out, away from London and her for good. And he
wasn't going to argue or make long defensive speeches. He lit a
cigarette and waited for her to begin, thinking that the pubs
would be opening in an hour's time and he could go out then
and get a drink.

"I don't understand why you came here at all," she said.

He didn't answer. He was still holding the cigarette box, and
now he closed its lid, feeling the coolness of the onyx on his
fingertips.

She had gone white. "Just to get your things? Maurice, did
you come back just for that?"

"They are my things," he said evenly.

"You could have sent someone else. Even if you'd written to
me and asked me to do it—"

"I never write letters," he said.

She moved then. She made a little fluttering with her hand in
front of her mouth. "As if I didn't know!" She gasped, and
making a great effort she steadied her voice. "You were in
Australia for a year, a whole year, and you never wrote to me
once."

"I phoned."

"Yes, twice. The first time to say you loved me and missed me and were longing to come back to me and would I wait for you and there wasn't anyone else was there? And the second time, a week ago, to say you'd be here by Saturday and could I—could I put you up. My God, I'd lived with you for two years, we were practically married, and then you phone and ask if I could put you up!"

"Words," he said. "How would you have put it?"

"For one thing, I'd have mentioned Patricia. Oh, yes, I'd have mentioned her. I'd have had the decency, the common human-ity, for that. D'you know what I thought when you said you were coming? I ought to know by now how peculiar he is, I thought, how detached, not writing or phoning or anything. But that's Maurice, that's the man I love, and he's coming back to me and we'll get married and I'm so happy!"

"I did tell you about Patricia."

"Not until after you'd made love to me first."

He winced. It had been a mistake, that. Of course he hadn't meant to touch her beyond the requisite greeting kiss. But she was very attractive and he was used to her and she seemed to expect it—and oh, what the hell. Women never could under-stand about men and sex. And there was only one bed, wasn't there? A hell of a scene there'd have been that first night if he'd suggested sleeping on the sofa in here.

"You made love to me," she said. "You were so passionate, it was just like it used to be, and then the next morning you told me. You'd got a resident's permit to stay in Australia, you'd got a job all fixed up, you'd met a girl you wanted to marry. Just like that you told me, over breakfast. Have you ever been smashed in the face, Maurice? Have you ever had your dreams trodden on?"

"Would you rather I'd waited longer? As for being smashed in the face—" he rubbed his cheekbone "—that's quite a punch you pack."

She shuddered. She got up and began slowly and stiffly to pace the room. "I hardly touched you. I wish I'd killed you!" By a small table she stopped. There was a china figurine on it, a bronze paperknife, an onyx pen jar that matched the ashtray. "All those things," she said. "I looked after them for you. I treasured them. And now you're going to have them all shipped out to her. The things we lived with. I used to look at them and think: Maurice bought that when we went to—oh God, I can't believe it. Sent to her!"

He nodded, staring at her. "You can keep the big stuff," he said. "You're specially welcome to the sofa. I've tried sleeping on it for two nights and I never want to see the bloody thing again."

She picked up the china figurine and hurled it at him. It didn't hit him because he ducked and let it smash against the wall, just missing a framed drawing. "Mind the Lowry," he said laconically, "I paid a lot of money for that."

She flung herself onto the sofa and burst into sobs. She thrashed about, hammering the cushions with her fists. He wasn't going to be moved by that—he wasn't going to be moved at all. Once he'd packed those things, he'd be off to spend the next three months touring Europe. A free man, free for the sights and the fun and the girls, for a last fling of wild oats. After that, back to Patricia and a home and a job and responsibility. It was a glowing future which this hysterical woman wasn't going to mess up.

"Shut up, Betsy, for God's sake," he said. He shook her roughly by the shoulder, and then he went out because it was now eleven and he could get a drink.

Betsy made herself some coffee and washed her swollen eyes. She walked about, looking at the ornaments and the books, the glasses and vases and lamps, which he would take from her tomorrow. It wasn't that she much minded losing them, the things themselves, but the barrenness which would be left, and the knowing that they would all be Patricia's.

In the night she had got up, found his wallet, taken out the photographs of Patricia, and torn them up. But she remembered the face, pretty and hard and greedy, and she thought of those bright eyes widening as Patricia unpacked the tea chests, the predatory hands scrabbling for more treasures in the trunk. Doing it all perhaps before Maurice himself got there, arranging the lamps and the glasses and the ornaments in their home for his delight when at last he came.

He would marry her, of course. I suppose she thinks he's faithful to her, Betsy thought, the way I once thought he was faithful to me. I know better now. Poor stupid fool, she doesn't know what he did the first moment he was alone with her, or what he would do in France and Italy. That would be a nice wedding present to give her, wouldn't it, along with all the pretty bric-a-brac in the trunk?

Well, why not? Why not rock their marriage before it had even begun? A letter. A letter to be concealed in, say, that blue-and-white ginger jar. She sat down to write. Dear Patricia— what a stupid way to begin, the way you had to begin a letter even to your enemy.

Dear Patricia: I don't know what Maurice has told you about me, but we have been living here as lovers ever since he arrived. To be more explicit, I mean we have made love, have slept together. Maurice is incapable of being faithful to anyone. If you don't believe me, ask yourself why, if he didn't want me, he didn't stay in a hotel. That's all. Yours—and she signed her name and felt a little better, well enough and steady enough to take a bath and get herself some lunch.

Six tea chests and a trunk arrived on the following day. The chests smelled of tea and had drifts of tea leaves lying in the bottom of them. The trunk was made of silver-colored metal and had clasps of gold-colored metal. It was rather a beautiful object, five feet long, three feet high, two feet wide, and the lid fitted so securely it seemed a hermetic sealing.

Maurice began to pack at two o'clock. He used tissue paper and newspapers. He filled the tea chests with kitchen equipment and cups and plates and cutlery, with books, with those clothes of his he had left behind him a year before. Studiously, and with a certain grim pleasure, he avoided everything Betsy might have insisted was hers—the poor cheap things, the stainless steel spoons and forks, the Woolworth pottery, the awful colored sheets, red and orange and olive, that he had always loathed. He and Patricia would sleep in white linen.

Betsy didn't help him. She watched, chain-smoking. He nailed the lids on the chests and on each lid he wrote in white paint his address in Australia. But he didn't paint in the letters of his own name. He painted Patricia's. This wasn't done to needle Betsy but he was glad to see it was needling her.

He hadn't come back to the flat till one that morning, and of course he didn't have a key. Betsy had refused to let him in, had left him down there in the street, and he had to sit in the car he'd hired till seven. She looked as if she hadn't slept either. Miss Patricia Gordon, he wrote, painting fast and skillfully.

"Don't forget your ginger jar," said Betsy. "I don't want it."

"That's for the trunk." Miss Patricia Gordon, 23 Burwood Park Avenue, Kew, Victoria, Australia 3101. "All the pretty things are going in the trunk. I intend it as a special present for Patricia."

The Lowry came down and was carefully padded and wrapped. He wrapped the onyx ashtray and the pen jar, the alabaster bowl, the bronze paperknife, the tiny Chinese cups, the tall hock glasses. The china figurine, alas . . . he opened the lid of the trunk.

"I hope the customs open it!" Betsy shouted at him. "I hope they confiscate things and break things! I'll pray every night for it to go to the bottom of the sea before it gets there!"

"The sea," he said, "is a risk I must take. As for the customs—" He smiled. "Patricia works for them, she's a customs officer—didn't I tell you? I very much doubt if they'll even glance inside." He wrote a label and pasted it on the side of the trunk. Miss Patricia Gordon, 23 Burwood Park Avenue, Kew . . . "And now I'll have to go out and get a padlock. Keys, please. If you try to keep me out this time, I'll call the police. I'm still the legal tenant of this flat, remember."

She gave him the keys. When he had gone she put her letter in the ginger jar. She hoped he would close the trunk at once, but he didn't. He left it open, the lid thrown back, the new padlock dangling from the gold-colored clasp.

"Is there anything to eat?" he said.

"Go and find your own bloody food! Go and find some other woman to feed you!"

He liked her to be angry and fierce; it was her love he feared. He came back at midnight to find the flat in darkness, and he lay down on the sofa with the tea chests standing about him like defenses, like barricades, the white paint showing faintly in the dark. Miss Patricia Gordon . . .

Presently Betsy came in. She didn't put on the light. She wound her way between the chests, carrying a candle in a saucer which she set down on the trunk. In the candlelight, wearing a long white nightgown, she looked like a ghost, like some wandering madwoman, a Mrs. Rochester, a Woman in White.

"Maurice."

"Go away, Betsy, I'm tired."

"Maurice, please. I'm sorry I said all those things. I'm sorry I locked you out."

"OK, I'm sorry too. It's a mess, and maybe I shouldn't have done it the way I did. But the best way is for me just to go and my things to go and make a clean split. Right? And now will you please be a good girl and go away and let me get some sleep?"

What happened next he hadn't bargained for. It hadn't crossed his mind. Men don't understand about women and sex. She threw herself on him, clumsily, hungrily. She pulled his shirt open and began kissing his neck and his chest, holding his head, crushing her mouth to his mouth, lying on top of him and gripping his legs with her knees.

He gave her a savage push. He kicked her away, and she fell and struck her head on the side of the trunk. The candle fell off, flared and died in a pool of wax. In the darkness he cursed floridly. He put on the light and she got up, holding her head where there was a little blood.

"Oh, get out, for God's sake," he said, and he manhandled her out, slamming the door after her.

In the morning, when she came into the room, a blue bruise on her forehead, he was asleep, fully clothed, spreadeagled on his back. She shuddered at the sight of him. She began to get breakfast but she couldn't eat anything. The coffee made her gag and a great nauseous shiver went through her. When she went back to him he was sitting up on the sofa, looking at his plane ticket to Paris.

"The men are coming for the stuff at ten," he said as if nothing had happened, "and they'd better not be late. I have to be at the airport at noon."

She shrugged. She had been to the depths and she thought he couldn't hurt her anymore.

"You'd better close the trunk," she said absentmindedly.

"All in good time." His eyes gleamed. "I've got a letter to put in yet."

Her head bowed, the place where it was bruised sore and swollen, she looked loweringly at him. "You never write letters."

"Just a note. One can't send a present without a note to accompany it, can one?"

He pulled the ginger jar out of the trunk, screwed up her letter without even glancing at it, and threw it on the floor. Rapidly yet ostentatiously and making sure that Betsy could see, he scrawled across a sheet of paper: *All this is for you, darling Patricia, forever and ever.*

"How I hate you," she said.

"You could have fooled me." He took a large angle lamp out of the trunk and set it on the floor. He slipped the note into the ginger jar, rewrapped it, tucked the jar in between the towels and cushions which padded the fragile objects. "Hatred isn't the word I'd use to describe the way you came after me last night."

She made no answer. Perhaps he should have put a heavy object like that lamp in one of the chests, perhaps he should open up one of the chests now. He turned round for the lamp. It wasn't there. She was holding it in both hands.

"I want that, please."

"Have you ever been smashed in the face, Maurice?" she said breathlessly, and she raised the lamp and struck him with it full on the forehead. He staggered and she struck him again, and again and again, raining blows on his face and his head. He screamed. He sagged, covering his face with bloody hands. Then with all her strength she gave him a great swinging blow and he fell to his knees, rolled over and at last was stilled and silenced.

There was quite a lot of blood, though it quickly stopped flowing. She stood there looking at him and she was sobbing. Had she been sobbing all the time? She was covered with blood. She tore off her clothes and dropped them in a heap around her. For a moment she knelt beside him, naked and weeping, rocking backwards and forwards, speaking his name, biting her fingers that were sticky with his blood.

But self-preservation is the primal instinct, more powerful than love or sorrow, hatred or regret. The time was nine o'clock, and in an hour those men would come. Betsy fetched water in a bucket, detergent, cloths and a sponge. The hard work, the great cleansing, stopped her tears, quieted her heart and dulled her thoughts. She thought of nothing, working frenziedly, her mind a blank.

When bucket after bucket of reddish water had been poured down the sink and the carpet was soaked but clean, the lamp washed and dried and polished, she threw her clothes into the basket in the bathroom and had a bath. She dressed carefully and brushed her hair. Eight minutes to ten. Everything was clean and she had opened the window, but the dead thing still lay there on a pile of reddened newspapers.

"I loved him," she said aloud, and she clenched her fists. "I hated him."

The men were punctual. They came at ten sharp. They carried the six tea chests and the silver-colored trunk with the gold-colored clasps downstairs.

When they had gone and their van had driven away, Betsy sat down on the sofa. She looked at the angle lamp, the onyx pen jar and ashtray, the ginger jar, the alabaster bowls, the hock glasses, the bronze paperknife, the little Chinese cups, and the Lowry that was back on the wall. She was quite calm now and she didn't really need the brandy she had poured for herself.

Of the past she thought not at all and the present seemed to exist only as a palpable nothingness, a thick silence that lay around her. She thought of the future, of three months hence, and into the silence she let forth a steady, rather toneless peal of laughter. Miss Patricia Gordon, 23 Burwood Park Avenue, Kew, Victoria, Australia 3101. The pretty, greedy, hard face, the hands so eager to undo that padlock and prise open those golden clasps to find the treasure within . . .

And how interesting that treasure would be in three months' time, like nothing Miss Patricia Gordon had seen in all her life! It was as well, so that she would recognize it, that it carried on top of it a note in a familiar hand: *All this is for you, darling Patricia, forever and ever.*

THE TIGER RETURNS TO THE MOUNTAIN

"Would he knock down the door? Would he talk sweetly, like the big bad wolf? Would he maybe wear a human mask, then drop the mask just before he sank his teeth into her?"

Where is danger hiding? For women, it can be lurking in many places and not just the obvious ones. T. L. Parkinson, examining the possibilities, remembers the legend of Beauty and the Beast and transforms it into yet another modern reworking. But he is not content merely to go the vulgar route of "girl meets gorilla," nor does he simply settle for the message popularized in fairy tales and folk ballads that loathly swains are gentle at heart and that "love conquers all." Rather, in what I see as a daring act of the male psyche imagining a female dream (or nightmare), he has created a story within a story within a story—and who's to say which contains the actual beast, the true tiger?

On October 22nd the Tiger Man escaped from prison. It was front-page news for a week. He abducted a bride who was relieving herself behind a tree after her wedding. Molly figured the bride was drunk—drunk on love. Molly threw a broken lamp into a box, her mouth twisting in memory. It was a half hour before anyone knew the young girl was missing; the groom had been busy talking to his parents. It had been intimated, in the investigative news reports, that the parents did not entirely approve of his marriage to the fair-haired girl—and so the bride was out of the groom's mind for a time.

Time enough.

Two weeks after the Tiger Man's escape, Molly was preparing to move from her home on Outreach Road. Near the end of the public road, where the emptying house stood, the mountain's shadow made everything dark; she could see the prison near the top, surrounded by a circle of sticklike trees, like a fallen crown.

Fear was in the air, a greasy feel, like pollution. As the official moving day approached, Molly was too busy trying to fit everything into boxes to worry about the media sensation. The Tiger Man was a natural, a creepy special effect, something that, after a time, you got used to and could ignore, almost.

If I had to spell it out, Molly thought, closing up the box that contained broken things with cords, I feel occupied. Nothing more can come in, not even more of the same. At last, in some weird way, I'm complete.

The day finally arrived. She had marked it on the calendar with a red circle around the date. The picture on this month was Thor's Hammer, drenched in red sunlight, against an insane blue sky. Moving was awful, like an explosion. When the pieces landed, where would she be? If I am doing the right thing, Molly thought, why don't I feel good? Actually, she thought, looking about in herself as though she were a box of bric-a-brac, I don't feel anything.

Molly's daughter, Sarah, sat glumly in the corner of the spacious mountainside house—paid for by money Carl had earned through drug dealing—and glared. Her eyes were powerful brittle lights. When the movers started dropping things, Molly suggested that Sarah go visit a friend.

"What if the Tiger Man gets me?" Sarah asked, zapping Molly with her eyes. Molly was exposed, yet somehow indifferent to the beams.

"No one's going to get you, unless it's me. Now scoot."

As Sarah walked away, she stared at her feet, as if wishing them away.

"She's intense," one of the movers said. Molly didn't answer. The other mover said, "It's hard on kids to be uprooted," as if answering for her.

Molly supposed Sarah would go to the post office. The post office fascinated Sarah. Sarah said it was their only connection with the big world—whatever that was. Molly had been there this morning and picked up the stuffed-animal toy in the special P.O. box. That was the way they always sent the cocaine. Carl was long gone, but the Down-South connection couldn't get it through their heads that this end of the business was washed up.

Molly wondered what would happen when they demanded payment. She would write them to tell them the deal was off, but she didn't have an address.

When the house was empty, the movers packed up, carrying out their black blankets and swinging their arms in long tired arcs, when she had only the small house in town to look forward to, Molly sat in the empty front room, purple and black shadowed as night fell, and cried.

Carl had been awfully good-looking. He had shiny skin like well-oiled wood, marbly blue-gray eyes, and he smelled of Mennen Skin Bracer and work sweat, the sweet/bitter kind that drips down a man's sides when he is making money, or love.

His eyebrows made sharp little points, like a woman's when she plucked them just so; but his were natural, and he raised the left one when he was puzzled or feeling sexy.

He had approached her at a Playhouse-on-the-Green presentation of *Taming of the Shrew*. He had come to her softly, like a summer wind, like a cloud shadow across a field of poppies.

They went out four times before they had sex. Molly had wanted to do it on their third date, under the sycamore tree, which pelted the car with leaves in the strong wind, but he had resisted.

Carl said he was a carpenter, working mostly in Crescent City but planning to open his own contracting business soon, so he could send other men out to do the hard work and he would organize things. He was very good, he said, at organizing things.

Carl's hands were pretty smooth for a carpenter, but maybe he was just careful, or wore gloves. Anyway, Molly grew to trust him, despite some superficial doubts. She had never trusted anybody completely, not even her parents, so this was a new feeling for her. She wanted to practice it, make it a habit.

Molly didn't know about Carl-and-cocaine, at first. Sometimes they smoked a joint before going out, but that was all. One night, after a couple of bottles of cheap red wine, in a frenzy of mutual confession, Carl admitted to freebasing cocaine "a while ago." Just how long ago, Molly could not get him to say.

One night, months later, in the middle of a particularly hot and dry summer, Molly kissed Carl and her face froze.

After Sarah was born, they moved onto the hill, below the mountain where the prison had been built a few years before.

Molly did not care for symbolism, but sometimes the prison loomed like a memory of a future event. If there must be a reason for them living here, under that shadow, then let it be a reminder that everyone had something bad inside that should be kept locked up.

Carl was often away. Molly missed him. The feeling was becoming familiar. Carl had gone to Cokenders; the drug thing was in the past. He was busy with a construction project near the river.

Molly took care of Sarah, walked in the forest, and waited.

Molly picked herself up from the floor. It was night now, heavy and still. Winter was slow in coming this year; the seasons seemed to have merged together into a sort of blurry, heavy mass. She felt it on her shoulders, in her throat, pressing on her mind like a big, soft hand.

She walked to the car, down the curving cobblestone path. She had been so proud of that path: cobblestones all the way from Belgium, though they had always been hard to walk on. She sat in the car with the radio softly playing and stared at the dark house.

It looked really empty, like it had never been lived in. A

corpse whose soul had fled. Her heart felt that way too. Carl had been in prison for a year; there never had been a construction project. He had been going to Mexico to make his pickups. He had two small planes.

There was so much about him that she didn't know, that came out at the hearings. He had been in reform school, he had been in jail twice, had been accused of raping a high school girl (date rape), but the charges had been dropped by the girl's embarrassed parents. He had been arrested for beating a homosexual with a pipe, after he let the guy give him a blow job in the alley outside the bar where he and Molly had sometimes gone. One year, suspended sentence. He had been arrested twice for dealing, but had gotten off on technicalities. He couldn't drive a nail, but had once driven a purple Mercedes, until he lost it on a bad deal.

When he was released the final time—a model prisoner, they had said—Molly tried to make a go of it, for Sarah's sake. It lasted about six months. Molly was sure he was dealing again. Like a moth to the flame. She found three thousand dollars, in hundred-dollar bills, in his wallet.

One day, as her love for him died slowly, fading away into a memory, then into amnesia, she went to his closet and opened the door. All his clothes were gone and so was his alligator suitcase. There was his pair of dirty Keds he did the gardening in, lying on the floor, a hole in the toe of the left one.

There was no note, nothing. Molly felt it inside, like a bubble of gas the size of her heart: this time he was gone for good.

The new house was in a cul-de-sac. The windows were aluminum, the frames thin and clattering in the faintest wind. Molly hated the place immediately.

She had too much furniture, so she had a yard sale the next Sunday. It was sunny, humid, and chilly, and she met several of her neighbors, a young Japanese man, an Irish gentleman who talked a lot about his dislike of holidays, especially Christmas, an older woman who had a dog she said had been abused. Molly wondered if the woman had not been abused in some way too; she walked as if an invisible hand were constantly swatting her. Molly thought it was a mistake to identify too much with animals.

Sarah was in school, third grade, the same school she had gone to before, so she had that to hold onto and adjusted fairly quickly. After a four-day glaring session that should have melted the walls, she got up one morning and went about her business as if nothing had changed. This made Molly's depression seem even more apparent, and humbling.

Sarah came home one day with some news of her own about the Tiger Man. "Mom," she said, chewing noisily on purple bubble gum, "some of the kids at school have started a club. A Tiger Man fan club. Boys mostly." There was one school: grade school in one building, high school in another, connected by a narrow hallway of dirty glass, like a greenhouse.

"Oh, really," Molly said. She was pretty open-minded about kids, but this gave her a little shock.

"Yeah, older boys, seventh grade and up," Sarah said. "Anything in the paper today?" When Molly shook her head, Sarah wandered up to her bedroom, dragging her books, which were tied with a belt.

In the next few weeks the news about the Tiger Man died down. The consensus was that he was either dead, satisfied, or moved off to another area to stalk fresh game. He had been spotted only once recently, by a teenager who, it was later reported, was in one of those clubs that were springing up all around. So the boy's credibility was in question. He said he had seen the Tiger Man running naked into a forest. The Tiger Man had looked over his shoulder, showing his face, and that was why the boy knew it just wasn't some crazy person who liked to run through the forest naked.

One Sunday afternoon when Sarah was over at Patricia's— Sarah's slightly retarded friend, who was two years older but in the same grade—Molly started sorting out some odds and ends that she couldn't unload at the garage sale, and found a stack of Carl's letters, some of which she had not read.

She had gone through phases when he had been in prison: full, empty, then full again. It had been dizzying. Sometimes she had read the letters, sometimes she filed them away, unopened. She did a lot of filing away the six months before his return.

She opened the unopened letters, laid them in a neat stack. Carl always wrote to her on the best paper, silky, with the fine weave visible, like veins through healthy skin. She arranged them in chronological order and began to read.

Somehow the day had gotten away from her. She sat in the dark, the letters gleaming like dying fluorescent lights. She couldn't believe it. She pinched herself. Even the hair on her arms hurt.

Carl had been in jail with the Tiger Man, who had been his cellmate for a while, until they put him (the Tiger Man) in solitary, for mauling a guard with his very human, very sharp fingernails.

Carl wrote that he thought maybe an accident had destroyed the Tiger Man's face, although that didn't account for the fur, or the eyes. Carl was a great one for improbable theories. "It seems right, once you get used to him. There are a lot stranger animals in this place." Carl said he would have asked the Tiger Man how it had happened, but the right time just never came.

Molly remembered a man she had seen in the rain, who appeared under her umbrella suddenly and disappeared: a man without a face, with the features ripped off.

Funny, Carl hadn't mentioned the Tiger Man to her when he had gotten out of jail. Molly guessed it was probably the same old story with Carl: nothing made much of an impression on him.

Carl had confided in the Tiger Man those dull evenings in the cell, if Carl's account was to be believed. Sex, drug addiction, women past present and future, and love. Carl had confessed his guilt about lying to Molly. He spoke of her innocence, which nothing he did seemed to change. "He likes to think about you. He is kind of a philosopher, and is trying to figure out what trust is, if love is blind, that sort of thing."

He wrote to me religiously, Molly thought, picking up the letters and dropping them into the wastebasket. I should have read those letters when they came and thrown them out then. Molly took the letters from the wastebasket and put them in the green plastic trash can in the side alley, fastening the lid tightly. In a week they'd be ashes in the dump. "He doesn't believe in you," Carl had written. "When he gets out, he wants to meet you. He's in for life, three lifetimes actually, but I didn't say anything. He is kind of sad, you know, when he talks about you, so I keep my mouth shut." Whatever you said about Carl, he was not the sort to put out another's hope.

Molly turned on a light, feeling like a weak caribou that a predator had spotted for his dinner.

She sat down again, staring at the blotter, imagining Carl writing in his cell, his green eyes frosted with emotion. The light was dim and shadows were everywhere. She slammed the empty drawer and nicked her thumb.

Cursing, sucking the blood, which tasted like metal, she thought: Be reasonable, Molly. He's long gone, clear into another county. There's no reason to think he'd really come here. Yet she could feel those yellow eyes staring up from her depths, staring out.

As she turned, the front door burst open. Something entered on a wave of darkness.

Molly clenched her fists, backed against the desk, let out her breath.

The something came into the light.

"Hi, Mom," Sarah said, throwing her new book bag onto the rocking chair. "I came home early."

Molly sat up nights in the cold damp bed, the cover pulled over her knees, and thought of what she'd say. Would he knock down the door? Would he talk sweetly, like the big bad wolf? Would he maybe wear a human mask, then drop the mask just before he sank his teeth into her? There was a breeze blowing in the room, though the windows were closed. Molly got up and checked the window fastenings, but the chill wind did not stop. She crawled under the covers and waited.

She woke in the dead of night with his breath on her neck, settling on her like hot fog.

It was a Friday afternoon. The doorbell rang. Sarah was due home from school shortly. She must have forgotten her key. Molly, munching a chicken sandwich, opened the thin pine door, not bothering to look.

"Sarah," she said crankily, standing behind the door and wiping at the tarnished doorknob with her apron. "I hate the tinny sound of that bell. When we get some money, I'm going to get it fixed, chimes, something nice."

The Tiger Man was a wind from a heated plain.

He flowed into the cold room, filling it up. He thrust Molly aside with his sweaty palms. She could feel the blood roaring in them. She fell against the door, in a kind of blank shock.

He slammed the door closed and Molly against it, in one fluid motion.

Molly opened her mouth and no sound came out. She was looking into the middle of the room; if she looked at him, then he would be real. She would not look. They would both be unreal. But she couldn't help herself. The eyes drew her, commanded her.

They were like a golden mirror, which reflected her frightened face back to her. She was small and black in there, against a field of gold. Yet there was the appearance of immense depth in the eyes, behind her shaking image, of mysterious roads traveled and forgotten.

He made no threatening moves. He stood there still as stone. She watched him, like a soldier at attention, moving only her eyes, because she thought if she moved anything else, her fear would show and he would hurt her.

His face was twice as big as a human's, big as a plate. It was completely covered with fur, deep fur that sparkled with an animal effervescence, even in the shadowy foyer. Not a human face distorted by some sort of industrial accident. Carl had been wrong in trying to find a logical explanation. The fur was deep, like grass on the plains in the rainy season; there were great black lines, like war paint on a backdrop of billowy white and sunshine yellow. It was all sharpness, one color and then another, with no in-between; beautiful and terrible. Molly was reminded of Carl's arching eyebrows.

For a minute, as her eyes swam and she tried to keep herself from swooning, she thought it might really be Carl, wearing a mask and playing a trick, so he could get back into her life.

"Down," the Tiger Man said. There had been a noise outside, maybe the mailman, who always came late on Friday. Molly dropped to her knees. The floor felt sticky. Not Carl, not anything she had met before, yet oddly familiar: animal breath, ferny, fetid. His words poured out damply, embedded in a growl. Something about being tired of running, always running toward her, not away, something like that. It was hard to tell.

She started to quiver inside, first in her stomach, which

always got the brunt of unspent feeling. Jittery and heavy, it felt like an animal running about inside her.

He had a black pack slung over his shoulder. He pulled out something white, took her hands and tied them with the soft fabric.

She started to whimper—the fear erupted from her stomach, with a small amount of bile—then stopped herself, remembering the fate of the weak caribou.

His grip kept tightening until she straightened her spine and denied her fear. Those PBS nature specials had taught her something about dealing with predators.

She wanted to speak, say something like, "What do you want? I have no money; the jewelry is upstairs," because she wanted this to be a regular robbery, not something out of her wildest dreams. Then maybe he would simply become a robber and take her jewels and leave. The mind could have that power, to transform and filter reality. But he pasted tape across her lips before she could start.

He bent down, put two arms solid as tree trunks under her, and carried her upstairs as though she were nothing.

The cool unlit room had one big window, now faced away from the sun. He dropped her onto the bed.

Was he going to rape her? Certainly, he had ulterior motives. She wished herself away, away from here, from him. Then, as she started to leave, cascading out of herself into limbo, she willed herself back into the room. Out there would be worse—a big, empty, squeaky kind of nothing. Here, she had a chance.

A few seconds passed. He did not join her on the bed. She opened her eyes and peered carefully over her shoulder. Still there, both of them. He stood back, all face and eyes, looking at her, really looking, like Italian men looked at you, she thought, really seeing you but impersonal. His gaze lingered on her bare feet, hot as sun. She had thin feet; "the bound feet of a princess," Carl had called them.

"Trust me," he said. "Don't make any noise, don't struggle, and you can trust me."

Downstairs the door opened. Molly felt a fresh uprising of panic.

"Mom, I'm home," Sarah called up the stairwell. Her voice sounded thin and hollow.

The Tiger Man moved into the shadow-striped hall, silent as a cat, though he wore army boots crusted with mud.

After the sounds of a brief struggle, like air being let out of a balloon, he returned with his prize.

Molly could see Sarah's eyes burning with fear and anger. The Tiger Man looked at the bound unmoving girl in his arms and put her down with surprising gentleness on the bedside chair, knocking Molly's underwear onto the floor.

He checked their bindings every half hour or so; Molly guessed the time by counting her heartbeats.

He made a phone call downstairs. She could hear uncannily well. My child is threatened; I have new senses now, heightened and sharp. I could lift this house from the foundations if my hands weren't tied.

Molly's mind raced. Sarah whispered, "Mom, what's going on?" but Molly could only moan through the surgical tape, a wounded animal sound, which she immediately stifled.

She silenced Sarah with her eyes.

Molly turned over, wrestling with her bindings, and as she was about to turn back again, she remembered the letters. Should she have read them? Maybe the knowledge had brought this down on her. Maybe not. But something Carl had said leapt to the foreground. The Tiger Man had been fascinated by the idea of innocence, a quality Molly could dimly remember in herself.

She rolled over. The tired old bedsprings sounded like mice. Could she bring the glow of innocence to her face, drown the Tiger Man in her sincerity?

She heard him padding up the stairs as she decided that she could do it, she could remember. Things went round and round in her and never left. Finally, an opportunity to put that curse to good use.

He opened the door. He stood in the doorway, a massive shape, still as a mountain. She looked up at him, her eyes filling with what she thought she had lost, trust and the blind need to hope. He is stone, he is majestic and still. Like magic, the feeling came, rising out of nowhere. She was certain it looked good—it certainly felt real—because he came over to her when he saw her summons, and began to loosen her bindings.

Over his quite human shoulder, knotted with muscles, particularly around the neck at the hairline—his hair was brownish blond and conventionally cut—she watched Sarah silently loosen her own bindings as well.

He lay down beside her, breathing deeply. He had unbuttoned the collar of his blue work shirt.

"I won't hurt you," he said. "I just need a place to lay low, until I can figure out what to do next. I knew your husband. He told me all about you." He said this last dreamily, and looked at her with eyes like melting mirrors.

"Yes, I know. He wrote me about you too. I feel—as if I have known you for a long time." Her voice shivered.

He sighed rancidly. She wondered if he had been eating forest animals. Then wondered, horrified, if he had eaten his human victims.

But she was not his victim; she was his partner in crime. She must keep that thought in her mind, in her movements.

She rolled against him, made a soft surprised sound, then pulled quickly away, as though she had touched something molten. She let her eyes leisurely move down his body. He noticed, and his body hardened as if it were made entirely of erectile tissue.

If it weren't for the face, she thought, he has the kind of body I used to like, when I was younger and didn't know anything. He looks remarkably like Carl, all that feminine muscularity and shifting unfocused eyes. Then she remembered where she was, who she was with, and shivered.

He started to stroke her neck with a callused hand. The fingers were greenish, the veins protruded in a vaguely attractive way, the nails round and perfect. His teeth were square and yellow with large incisors.

She moaned, the hard and soft moan that used to set Carl on fire. Carl had tried to figure it out, why it worked, but never could. The more he tried, the more inexplicable it had become, and the more powerful.

The Tiger Man began slowly to remove her clothes. She tried to help, but he pushed her hands away. She fought back her revulsion. I have no hands, she thought; he is my hands. She had to go through with this, give Sarah time to free herself and call the police.

Sarah had curled up into a ball on the chair. Darkness covered her as the sun sped away across the lawn. She was easing her way out of the bindings, as expertly as a magician in a trunk might free himself.

Molly hated the thought of Sarah having to see Mommy give herself to the Tiger Man, but maybe she wouldn't look. She wasn't a morbid child and didn't even like violent cartoons.

He finished undressing her and placed her in the position he wanted, like a doll a child cherishes. A cold thin wind moved across her body and turned sweat to ice. She looked down at her body: blue and unreal. The Tiger Man rose in front of her, onto his knees, and slid out of his shirt, revealing a finely chiseled chest, shiny skin, almost metallic-looking, poreless and without hair. His yellow eyes were like the glowing dials of a clock radio.

Molly felt as though she had awakened in wet sheets after a nightmare. When she reached down to touch her belly, she found that he was drooling on her.

He grinned, leaned forward, covering her first with his shadow, then his body.

"Go slow," she whispered in his ear as he entered her. "I want it to last forever."

She heard, with her sharpened hearing, under his heavy wet movements, Sarah eventually slide from the chair and go downstairs.

It did seem to last forever. He was too big and it hurt. She said to herself: There are two things here, like oil and water. One of them is me, and one of them is him. They do not mix. They do not even live in the same universe.

She had to buy time, so she put on a good show. "Slower, baby, slower," she kept saying. She said it in a million different, mysterious ways.

When the Tiger Man came—like a huge muscle going into spasm—Molly was sure that she had kept him distracted.

She breathed a little easier when he rolled off her, and with the wavelike motion of her own breath, fear and disgust rose up in her throat, a cold sour taste.

She swallowed, and listened. Nothing. Had Sarah gone outside to wait for the police?

Molly hoped so, though she sensed something was wrong.

The Tiger Man had one green-veined, copper-skinned hand close to her throat. It held her down in what she supposed was meant to be a gesture of affection. She stared at the ceiling, searching for words, finding none.

She looked everywhere but at him. She watched a daddy longlegs lower itself from a corner, watched the last trace of sun fade from the room.

But what had happened to Sarah? Why was it so quiet? She quickly glanced at the door, which Sarah had left open a crack.

The Tiger Man's yellow eyes tracked her gaze like searchlights, found the slit of light from the door, traced it back to the empty chair.

He jumped from bed and crashed out the door. Whatever he was, he was all mass; she could feel the imprint he had left in the mattress, like a black hole.

Molly rolled from the bed and into the hall. She hit a wall of cold air. There was struggling downstairs, something tearing.

"Sarah, are you all right?" Molly shouted. "Don't you dare hurt her." She stood on the first step, ready to jump.

"The police wouldn't believe me," Sarah moaned to the floor as the Tiger Man picked her up and again brought her upstairs. "They thought I was making it up, because I'm a kid. With an active imagination. Don't believe everything you read, he said. And then he hung up."

She still held the phone, the broken wire trailing behind her like a tail.

"Go inside," the Tiger Man said. "I won't hurt her if you do what I say."

Molly reluctantly moved back into the bedroom. The Tiger Man put Sarah down on the chair, glanced at the ropes she had loosened, then smiled.

"Not bad, kid," he said. "You'll do OK."

Molly had moved slowly to the darkest corner of the room. There was only one window, through which the light from a streetlight dully gleamed.

The Tiger Man had turned his back. He was staring with a

kind of innocent rapture at the ropes, at Sarah. Molly sat down on the green armchair and braced herself. She calculated the distance, the strength of her legs.

He backed up a little, seemed about to turn around.

This was her chance. Molly lifted her feet, pulled them to her chest, then kicked directly into the small of his back. He let out a startled sound, like a mattress being jumped on, and then he was sailing through the closed window, his hands held in front of him. The broken glass showered into the blue light. For a second, as he hung suspended outside the window, Molly could see the glass piercing his flesh. He looked like the image of a man in a shattering mirror.

Molly got up, trying to stifle a sense of guilt. "Sarah, stand up," she said. "Let's get out of here." Molly rushed to the door, knocking over a vase of old flowers. Foul-smelling water darkened the rug. Stepping over it, she pulled on her clothes. She didn't go to the window to see if he was dead. Somehow, she didn't want to know.

Molly grabbed Sarah's arm and they ran.

The sun was gone entirely. There was no moon. Milky haze hid the stars. Outside was like waking up under a blanket, all turned around.

"We'll go to the police station," Molly said. "He might not be dead. And he can run faster than us."

When they were halfway down the street, they turned around, looked back at the rickety house. There was no movement, but Molly wasn't convinced.

"Run," Molly said. "Run like he's after us."

They raced down the street. There was no one out tonight. It was like a ghost town. You can't count on luck to get you out of scrapes, Molly thought; I have to keep my wits about me. I can fall apart later if I need to.

They rounded a corner, into the dim glow of a street lamp that flickered brightly, then died, then came back on. A car spun around the corner, out of nowhere. A dull brick-red VW. Molly waved her arms in the air, and the car pulled over.

A square-faced young man, cool green eyes, reddish brown hair cut boyishly, leaned out the window. "You two in some kind of trouble?"

"Thank God you stopped," Molly said. "Please take us to the police station. We've had an intruder."

"Sure, get in." Sarah climbed in back, Molly in front. The seats were tattered and there was a funny smell; the man probably had a dog.

The man seemed satisfied to wait for Molly to offer an explanation. Molly was panting from the run. She should say something, but every time she started, she stopped. It seemed private, what had happened. This man was a stranger.

Sarah's damp hand was on Molly's shoulder. Molly glanced into the back seat. Her own shoulder smelled like the Tiger Man, like a cage at the zoo in need of cleaning.

"Stop here, please," Molly told the young man after they had gone a few blocks. They were in front of Mary's house, a close friend of Molly's. The light was on and Molly could see movement inside.

"Sarah, go on in and tell Mary I'll call from the police station." The car stopped, the door rattled open. Sarah got out reluctantly. "Hurry along now."

The young man reached over Molly to close the door; the door handle fell off. "Got to get this fixed," he said, and threw the handle into the back seat. Then he started up again, silent as a stone, though he smiled a little, a strange half smile on the right side only.

"It's only a little way now," he said. His voice was older than his face; his hands curled whitely about the wheel.

The drive seemed to go on and on, but it took her a while to realize something was wrong. Her time sense was in a state of shock. She had started to drift. The windows were tightly closed, though they rattled as if they might fall out any minute. The musty smell began to get to her, to rouse her suspicions.

"You have a dog?" she asked finally, the first two words sharp, the last two blurry.

"No, not exactly," he said.

"Could you open a window?" she said. "I have allergies."

"Windows are broken too."

Then she noticed they were nearing the outskirts of town, going down into the valley, the valley beneath the mountain and the prison. It was dark in the cleft of the valley, thick and tangled with trees.

"We're going in the wrong direction!" Molly shouted. Adrenaline snapped through her. "Turn around."

She reached toward the door and he stepped on the gas.

"Don't try it."

They roared past the church where the bride had been abducted by the Tiger Man. The windows gleamed in the headlights; the steeple was dark and ragged against the sky. Molly recognized it from the newspaper photos.

"I have a place I want to show you," the young man said.

The car gathered speed as they moved into the valley, roaring through the tunnel of trees, scattering leaves like escaping birds.

Molly clung to the door, her fingers in the hole where the handle had been, just in case. Maybe they'd come up behind another car and he'd slow down and she could get the door open somehow. She waited. She could run into the woods. She gave him a sideways glance; he looked big, square, clunky.

He reached into the back seat with his right hand, keeping his eye on the road.

Her heart jumped. Was he going to kill her? She braced herself, stomping on the floor with her right foot, as though the brake pedal were on her side.

But what he pulled from the back seat was not a knife or a gun. It was a mask, a cheap plastic tiger's mask, the kind you can get at Woolworth's for Halloween.

He put it on.

"I am the Tiger Man," he said. "You've read about me in the papers."

Somehow, Molly thought, this is a little pathetic.

He turned off the main road onto an unpaved back road. Her head kept hitting the low roof of the car, and feathery dust fell down.

"Got to go slower now," he said. "Don't want to bust my car in a pothole. You just sit tight. We'll get there soon enough."

After a couple more minutes, he pulled over into a turnout for logging trucks, under trees blacker than the night sky. There was a little hollow further in, which he followed until they had lost sight of the road. Molly looked around, trying to figure out where they were. An overturned trash can had spilled its contents. The garbage glowed like night-blooming flowers.

The man grabbed Molly roughly by the shoulder. "Over there." He grabbed her head and made her look. "See that space between the trees, sort of a tunnel? Well, that's where I dragged my first victim, the bride you probably read about."

He looked at her to see her reaction. Her face felt blank; she was boiling inside, and when she boiled, her expression got as flat as a skillet.

Molly knew it was hopeless to try to get the door open on her side without a handle. She was fishing around with her right hand under the seat, but didn't think she could reach the handle he had thrown into the back without his noticing. She would have to climb over him if she were to get out.

She looked where he told her to look, so she had time to think, without his glassy bird's eyes staring at her, distracting her. There was a dark hole in the woods, an empty space, and she felt convinced that part of the young man's story was true: that the Tiger Man had dragged his first victim through there. There were bits of phosphorescent stuff hanging from the vines that might have been part of a bridal veil.

She wondered how the young man had come upon the spot. She looked at him. He turned and leered at her with perfect teeth white as the moon, not yellow and square and fearsome.

But he *was* frightening, in a dry insect way. She felt his papery skin against her arm and shuddered.

Could she use innocence against him, or charm? If he thought she was being sincere, he would probably go crazy and kill her. The thought of seducing him was completely repugnant. It was impossible even to hold the thought for long.

Besides, she felt he had a somewhat colder fate in mind for her.

"Tell me the truth," Molly said, her voice as even as a blade. "Are you a fan of his? Did you read about him in the papers?"

He looked startled by her forthrightness, as Molly had hoped. "My husband, who is a crack dealer, knew the real Tiger Man in prison. They were close, like brothers. The Tiger Man is at my house right now." She paused to let the words sink in. The story sounded good and shocking, even to her.

"I've slept with him."

The young man looked at her, eyes downcast and disbelieving. "You're crazy," he said, his voice shivering like a bird on a bare branch. "You couldn't—I'm—"

Had she found the key?

His face went blank, then twisted around the edges as though he were coming apart. For a moment, she wondered if she should have said anything so challenging. If you exposed someone's weakness, sometimes they got violent. But he continued to crumble and sputter.

"I did," Molly said, stubbornly. "You're not." She was still fishing around under the seat for the door handle when her hand came upon something cold, greasy, hard. She grabbed it, coughed, so he would look at her face, and then pulled out a wrench.

He saw it, but there was nowhere to go. Molly's arms were pretty strong, from all the packing and moving boxes. She hit him on the side of the head, a hard crack, the sound of an egg breaking. She felt nothing, really. Was this a human, or one in a line of deteriorating images? The mask fell from his face and he slumped onto the wheel. The black gash along his skull looked like a winding mountain road. It took a long time to bleed.

Molly had a hard time climbing over him to get out of the car. She tried moving him but could not.

It was amazing how heavy a dead man could be.

Molly stretched the cramps from her legs and looked around. She smelled beer, rusty metal, the moldering sting of the forest. Leaves dropped to the ground, whirled about, then grew still. Somewhere above, hidden by the dark wall of trees, was the prison on the mountainside, spinning out webs of barbed wire and light.

Why had the Tiger Man chosen this spot, so near the prison, to drag his first victim? Had he been unable to get free, even in his mind?

Molly could understand that, not being able even to imagine freedom.

She walked over to the hole in the forest wall, reached down and pulled a piece of the torn bridal veil from a tangle of thorns. She put it in her pocket. The police would need to see this.

She went back to the car. The young man was crumpled and

small, like dirty clothes. She touched his head, which was black with blood, the gash having opened wide, exposing bone. His lips were gray. She could feel the cold pouring out of him.

She straightened up, holding out her hands. They looked as though they belonged to someone else. Blood dripped from her fingers, slow thick drops. A fly landed on her nose and she wiped at it, not thinking, then let her fingers fall.

She leaned over and looked at her reflection in the dirty window of the VW. Her face was striped with blood, larger than life in the warped glass. Like war paint, strange and sinister.

Was the Tiger Man's lair in the forest, under the looming mountain and the stone walls of the prison? It seemed reasonable. If she followed the tunnel through the forest, up to the prison, what would she find on the way? A pile of bones, a mirror, a book of newspaper clippings? She must be quick about it.

She paused for a moment. Maybe she should go to the police station. But it was miles away, and she wasn't sure she could find it. The road here had been long and dark and she might get lost. The prison was closer, and she knew where it was, because even now the searchlights passed over the tops of the trees. She could follow the lights, and the trail the Tiger Man had made.

The path lay that way, into the forest. She looked behind her one last time and plunged into the fragrant dark.

"Hello," he said.

CONSANGUINITY

"Sometimes desire found its own desperation."

Ronald Duncan was a man of exceptionally varied talents: poet, playwright, librettist, translator, disciple of Gandhi. But here, in a little-known, deceptively quiet story, he also revealed himself as an excellent practitioner of ambiguous horror fiction. In the great tradition of James or Wharton, this is a haunting work which tilts our moral universe and surely provokes more questions than it will answer.

The setting is wartime Britain—a moment when, as Duncan tells us, "events moved quickly . . . and nobody looked too closely." And in a first-class railway compartment en route to Edinburgh, a chance encounter between two officers home on leave leads to an impromptu invitation. One of them has a sister. One may or may not have had a wife. These facts are hardly sinister, but what follows is. However, let me say only that a single reading is not enough, and a second may lead to a third, or however many it takes until Duncan's design, with its inexorably advancing carnality, can be completely perceived.

The *Flying Scotsman* was two hours late. That used to happen frequently during the war, especially when the Heinkels had been over during the night. The train was blacked out, the lights were dim; two officers sat opposite each other in a first-class compartment. One of them was reading *The Idiot*; the other, a major of about thirty-five, sat huddled in a corner staring intently in front of him as though examining a scene which lay behind his eyes. He smoked continuously. Neither of the men had spoken for four hours; they had been in the train for four hours five minutes. Even then their conversation had been restricted, and omitted any introductions. Captain Maclean of the Seaforth Highlanders had permitted himself to remark that it was "a perfect bore carrying these bloody gas masks around," and in reply Major Buckle of the Black Watch had grunted. Their reticence was, however, not due to the notices displayed above their seats to the effect that "Idle chatter helps Hitler" but to the fact that neither had any curiosity about the other. Perhaps both had seen too much of their fellow men to want to get to know another. That was true of Captain Maclean at least, who had just endured nine weeks of a crowded troopship. To him, understandably, silence now seemed a luxury and solitude an indulgence.

He planned to spend his leave in complete privacy. It was unlikely that his sister, who kept house for him in Edinburgh, would do anything to spoil his brief retreat. But as a precaution he had delayed informing her of his arrival, and merely sent her a wire from King's Cross. He did not wish to be met at Waverley Station by a gathering of the clan.

The train jolted suddenly to a standstill. A cloud of steam from the vacuum brakes oozed into the compartment.

"Signals, I suppose," Maclean said, putting down his book and glancing at the blind over the window. "This will make us later than ever."

Major Buckle looked at his watch. Comment was unnecessary. A stop was unlikely to hasten their arrival.

But after about ten minutes the express edged its way forward again and eventually sidled unobtrusively into a station.

This moment always provided an opening gambit for conversation during the war, which even Captain Maclean could not resist.

"Where are we?" he asked, peering round the blind at the completely darkened platform.

"God knows," Buckle replied. "It looks like hell. Maybe it is hell. I think I recognize it. I used to go to the St. Leger occasionally. This will be Doncaster."

They both remarked almost simultaneously that they should have been eighty miles nearer Edinburgh by this time, after which observation they felt almost old friends. Nothing joins people together so quickly as a mutual complaint.

"It's bloody rough," Maclean muttered, "catching a train that's half a day late when you've only got a fortnight's leave."

"Been overseas?" Buckle asked, without the slightest interest.

"Singapore." The reply was curt but not rude.

"Tough." The comment was sympathetic without sentiment.

Not a word more was said. The fact that Maclean's regiment had retreated for four months through the Malayan jungle, only to be practically annihilated on the docks at Singapore, and that he was the only officer of his brigade alive to tell the tale, was no excuse for him to do so. It was not shame that kept him silent; he would have been just as reticent if he had taken part in a victory. One did not talk shop.

"Seen any good shows in London recently?" he asked.

"Rattigan's play wasn't bad."

"But that came off months ago."

"Did it?"

"Yes. Time passes."

"Does it?" Buckle asked pointedly.

Maclean looked embarrassed, sensing some philosophical edge behind the question. Then suddenly he smiled with relief.

"Ah, of course, I see what you mean. Time certainly does drag in a train."

"That's not what I meant."

"Oh."

Maclean picked up his book. Within five minutes, both officers were sleeping. The train tore through the night, carrying its ungainly passengers forward while they crawled back into their dreams. Dreams of a severed hand like a glove on the floor. Dreams of a Negress with a necklace of breasts. But Maclean remembered neither when he awoke in the half light with a crick in his neck. Quickly he straightened his tie and combed his hair.

"What we need is a cup of char," he said.

"We've just passed through Peebles," Buckle told him. "We should be in in about half an hour."

One could not say that the two officers had slept together, but the fact that they had sprawled within the same compartment seemed to ease their relationship. The morning found them much more talkative than they had been the night before.

"Do you live in Edinburgh too?" Maclean asked.

"No, but I used to. That's why I'm going there."

Paradoxes always annoyed Maclean. He was afraid that somebody was pulling his leg.

"You mean you live just outside the city?" he asked, hoping to clear up the apparent contradiction.

"No, I don't live anywhere now," Buckle answered without a note of regret.

Immediately three garish pictures floated into the Captain's mind: First, he visualized the Major standing beside a bombed-out house, smoldering in ruins, where lay the bodies of his entire family. For some reason a rocking horse and a teddy bear were to the fore in this image. The second visual headline showed the Major driving his tank through the approaches to Benghazi. A dispatch rider hands him a cable. It is from his wife. Maclean could read it clearly over Major Buckle's shoulder. "I am sleeping occasionally with the postman, but I am pregnant by the milkman. When you get this I shall be living with the dustman. Your loving wife."

"War's a bloody bore, the way it uproots chaps," he said.

Then the third picture came into his mind. He saw his sister Angela standing waiting on the platform, her mouth as full of questions as his nanny's used to be of pins.

"If you've nowhere to stay in Edinburgh, my sister and I would be awfully pleased to put you up."

"Thank you. I should be glad of your hospitality for a night or two."

"And, of course, your wife, if . . ."

"No, I am alone."

The second image flashed like a film trailer across Maclean's mind.

"I am not married."

It faded. And the third picture, of his sister standing on the platform, came into focus. He had not the slightest doubt that she was there waiting.

Everything about Angela was a compromise, even her sex. With her cairn puppy waiting beside her and her smart crocodile handbag tucked under her arm, she looked completely unobtrusive. Her whole appearance was a compromise, for though Angela knew that her looks were striking, and wished to be the center of attraction, yet she dressed so tastefully and stood so demurely that you would not pause as you passed her or notice what she wore. Her rather chic hat suggested a femininity and gaiety which the severity of her tweeds contradicted. In one hand she twirled a pretty French parasol, but her stance was that of a man. Nobody had ever told her that she had beautiful legs and a pretty instep, but she knew. Perhaps that was why she wore the sheerest silk stockings and the flattest and heaviest of brogues to ruin the effect. Just as Nature had failed to make up its mind, giving her straight, dull hair (whereas her brother's was naturally curly) and the prettiest eyes and mouth above a rather too heavy chin. Her hips were distinctly boyish, but not even the tightest bra could hide her breasts. Though Angela was nearly thirty she was as embarrassed by her breasts as she had been when they first leaned out from their boyish tree. Alex had laughed at her then; she still feared his derision and wished her womanhood away. For it was that which confused their relationship. Ever since their mother's death she had been both mother and sister to Alex. For the last ten years she had been wife in all but shame. She was, of course, quite unaware of any incestuous leanings; she merely liked Alex more than any other man, and had turned away the attentions of several admirers because any surrender to them had made her feel unfaithful to him. They were happy living together in the old house in Randal Crescent. They could read books at table, they could sit on the edge of each other's bed.

She had counted the days, the hours, till this train should bring him back to her. And as it steamed into the platform and she saw him stepping down from his compartment, she felt entire again for the first time in twelve months. First her eyes, then her feet, ran to meet him, as though she would embrace him and erase the months of anxiety she had endured but dared not show. He was all the world to her—or almost. For the rest, perhaps one day she would adopt one.

"Alex!" she cried. But there was no embrace. The cairn on the lead took one hand and her parasol the other. "Here's Boxer to see you. He's awfully patient. Your train's hours late."

Alex was both officer and gentleman. He gave his sister a smile, but kissed and fondled the dog.

Then, turning, he introduced her to the Major. But Angela had no eyes for him; she was wholly absorbed in her brother. Like any woman, though, she was more observant than she was curious, and noticed detail even when she was not looking for it. In the cursory but polite glance she gave Major Buckle as he shook her hand, Angela formed an indelible impression. She saw him as a lonely, shy, and pathetic figure, and was not in the least taken in by his strong build and hearty manner. His light-blue eyes gave him a remoteness, a coldness that attracted her, while his lips, which seemed unnaturally red against the pallor of his skin, gave his mouth a sensuousness and warmth that repelled her. She also noticed that his batman had ironed the wrong side of his tie.

Buckle, on the other hand, had every opportunity to look at Angela while she chatted away so excitedly to her brother. And though his eyes grazed over her closely, he saw only her wet lower lip, her breasts, and her narrow hips, and was quite unaware of the color of her eyes and hair, or what she was wearing. By the time they had reached the ticket barrier, he knew that he wanted to sleep with her. It was a bore that he would be her brother's guest.

The next few days were the happiest in Angela's life. She did not know why. Historians maintain that wars are caused by economics. They are wrong. Economics is their excuse; the reason for war is that it destroys that which we all want destroyed: the status quo, with which we identify our own inhibitions. War alone releases our personal relationships. It is not a necessary evil but a necessary pleasure. If we were honest, we would admit that all the slaughter, cruelty, and suffering that war entails remain for us merely a matter of regrettable statistics. What means something to us is that war provides us with that sense of insecurity which is life, when peace has seemed as respectable and as dull as death. It is true that a drunken orgy might provide a similar release, but it is quite difficult to remain completely drunk for several years and impossible to indulge in the briefest fling without some curious sense of remorse. In war, we can release ourselves without guilt; indeed, our excuses become duties and any behavior is condoned under the blanket of the great sacrifice which we curse publicly but enjoy privately. National disasters can be borne with comfortable fortitude: it is personal sorrow, not grief for another but a lack in our own life, which is so unbearable. It is a burden we would put down though a million men fall with it.

Angela sang as she skipped about the kitchen in dressing gown and mules getting the breakfast. Angela sang as she carried first one tray and then the other up to the two men's rooms. She had got up early and done all the housework and prepared a picnic. Now as she ran her bath and admired her figure in the mirror above it, she was radiant with happiness. It was nice having two men to fuss over again. She had not felt so useful since her father had died. It was nice getting up early to cut sandwiches, make a salad, and iron shirts; and what doubled her pleasure was that she could now indulge her affection for her brother with a certain sense of virtue, or even sacrifice. His leave was short: it was right he should have breakfast in bed. And the presence of a guest in the house gave another excuse for any of the luxuries she planned. As she stepped into the bath she decided she would give them salmon for supper. Then she remembered she had not locked the bathroom door. She got out of the bath to do so. Still singing gaily, she stepped into the water again. The door remained ajar.

"I'll sling this sponge at you, Alex, if you rinse your razor in my bath. It's a filthy trick."

There was a note of soft petulance in her voice, the tone women use when they complain about those masculine habits which are so endearing to them.

"Hurry up and get out of that. Buckle will want a bath too." Alex dipped his razor beside her, and turned to lather his face.

Angela lay full length, swishing the water together with her legs so that it flopped up over her flat tummy. It was a sort of aid to meditation she had employed since childhood.

"Alex, do you like him?"

Her casual voice betrayed the fact that the question meant a great deal to her.

"Immensely," he replied.

Angela sat up, relieved, and began soaping herself energetically. His answer had meant everything to her.

"We seem to get on so well together," she said. "I can hardly believe you only met him in a train three days ago. And yet he's so reticent. I hardly know a thing about him."

"Do you need to?" Alex mumbled, his face contorted beneath his blade.

"Not if you like him."

The trio passed the next few days very idly, without plan or purpose, driving out for a picnic during the day and pub crawling in the evening. This was to please Alex, who still had literary aspirations. Edinburgh is probably the only city in the British Isles where writers still congregate at their regular tavern, and not even the war dispersed this coterie of affable but garrulous codgers. Angela liked to hear her brother talk; after a couple of whiskeys she, too, was convinced of his talent. She felt as proud as a mother, and listened as indulgently as a wife while he told the synopsis of a play he intended to write one fine day to a Scotch Nationalist poet who accepted Drambuie and beer in strict rotation. Angela knew the plot better than Alex, prompted him here and there, and remarked that a scene reminded her of a play by Bridie she had seen years ago at the Kings. After all, she was his sister.

Throughout these sessions Major Buckle sat content, yet contributed little to the conversation beyond an admission that he had not read whatever book they happened to be discussing. But he seldom took his eyes off Alex, and though he himself had no literary pretensions and did nothing to express his own personality, he was plainly impressed by that of his friend. It was the shadowlike loyalty to her brother that made Angela warm to Peter Buckle. He didn't attract her physically. Both his appearance and her responses were far too vague, nebulous, and undefined for her to have any feeling as precise as that. On the other hand, his features were regular and inconspicuous and his personality so passive that she could not possibly find him objectionable. It was, she felt, as if she now had two brothers, and the better they got on together, the fonder she became of each.

As they walked home after the third evening spent in the Green Dragon, Angela slipped her right arm through her brother's and, since Buckle was on her left, she gave him the other. After the fifth evening, she kissed her brother good night, and since Buckle was sitting beside Alex, she gave him a peck too. They seemed such good friends it was only right they should share her favors. After the seventh evening spent in precisely the same fashion, and following the consumption of half a dozen whiskeys, Angela and Buckle found themselves alone in the back of a car. Sometimes the suggestive environment can be mistaken for personal feeling. Major Buckle took the initiative. He smudged her lips and undid the buttons of her blouse, only withdrawing when the intricacies of her bra defeated his fumbling fingers. By the end of a fortnight, it was agreed that there was some sort of understanding between them, though neither could have told precisely what was understood. It certainly was not love; it looked dangerously like the imminence of marriage. Events moved quickly in war and nobody looked too closely. It was agreed that the three of them should go to London and see a few shows.

As her relationship with Buckle developed, Angela relaxed. She took to wandering in and out of her brother's bedroom clad in her undies, or precariously swathed in a bath towel. Their rooms in the hotel adjoined; she used to sit for hours gossiping to Alex as he lay in bed. Buckle's room was only across the corridor, but he remained undisturbed. Nevertheless, his presence there was an indispensable catalyst. Angela felt that, now she had a man of her own as it were, there was nothing to inhibit her enjoying such harmless intimacies with her brother. Another factor, of course, was that she knew her brother's leave would soon be over. No one knew then when or whether they would see each other again. In those circumstances, when there were air raids every night to remind people how transient their moment was, despair was often mistaken for desire. Sometimes desire found its own desperation.

Buckle proposed to Angela while she lay beside him on the platform of Lancaster Gate tube station. It seemed the decent thing to do, though even Major Buckle, who was not sufficiently a realist to have a sense of humor, recognized something slightly inappropriate in making plans for the future in the middle of a series of air raids which had already destroyed several square miles of the city. Perhaps their horizontal position on the asphalt floor compensated for the less romantic aspects of the occasion. They had been forced to seek shelter in the tube on their way back to their hotel from the Mercury Theatre. That was four hours ago. The all clear had not sounded. Alex lay beside them sleeping. The rest of the platform was covered with ungainly bodies slunk in sleep and each covered by a single blanket. These were the regulars, timid termites who had taken to sleeping in the tubes every night. Trains did not wake them, passengers walking by did not disturb them, nothing embarrassed them. Couples old and young lay under the slot machines and wire refuse baskets, and even on the stairs, as though in the privacy of their own bedrooms. Though the English are supposed to be prudes, once they are horizontal, in parks or on the beach, they lose all modesty and have less inhibitions in public than they have in the privacy of their homes. Many a man now walking in the sun was begotten on the steps of an escalator in the full glare of a neon light.

In such an environment, Angela could hardly have refused. Death was in the air and birth, or something extraordinarily like it, lay all about her. She snuggled up to Buckle and smiled over his shoulder at her brother. They were joined in holy wedlock two days later by special license at Caxton Hall. Alex gave her away and Buckle received her, both slightly hilarious and a little drunk. Only Angela was serious or sober.

After the sordid civic ceremony, where the officializing bureaucrat apes a clergyman by intoning the regulations with his hands clasped together, and gives you a receipt with all the unction of handing you a sacrament, the couple drove straight to Victoria Station. Alex accompanied them on to the platform to put them in the train to Brighton. He stood by the window talking to his sister. There were tears in her eyes. Only four days of his leave remained. She could not bear to leave him.

"Couldn't Alex come too?" she pleaded, turning to her husband.

Together they dragged him into the carriage just as the train started. Alex felt rather an intruder and a little foolish, holding a bag of confetti in his pocket. He could scarcely open it now and fling it over them before sitting beside them for the rest of the journey.

"I've only got a platform ticket," he said.

"Let's go along to the bar and have a drink," Buckle suggested.

The two friends immediately left the compartment. Angela smiled indulgently after them, they glared into her compact and powdered her nose. It all seemed a dream to her. She glanced at the ring on her finger. Like any virgin, she was terribly frightened. She knew she was going to lose something she had preserved but did not want. It was like going to the dentist. But it was nice that Alex had come too. She used her lipstick with deliberation, then crossed her legs and looked out of the window, counting the telegraph posts that passed in a minute. She knew that they stood fifty-five yards apart, and from those data could compute the speed of the train. It was a trick she had learned from her father.

Angela awoke the next morning, but before she was conscious of the light she was aware of her dream. Before opening her eyes, she tried to recall it. . . .

She had been out hunting, but instead of riding a horse she had dreamed she was sitting astride a giraffe. The animal had galloped, quite out of control, through a forest where every tree was on fire, each separate limb of timber blossoming with a flame. Having recalled her dream, she remembered, and raising her thighs, removed the bath towel beneath her. She got out of bed and carried it into the bathroom. Buckle was not in bed; neither was he in the bath. She frowned, then dimly remembered that he had said something or other about going downstairs to get an evening paper. But that, she realized, must have been last night. He must have returned since then. There was proof of that. She rang for her coffee, got back into bed, and lit a cigarette. Probably her husband and Alex had gone for a dip.

The hotel was by the beach. At any rate she did not feel like bathing: she felt very refreshed. She had never slept so deeply or woken so well. For an hour she lay enjoying the sensation of heaviness in her limbs. It was to her as if her youth had been a drought and now it had rained and she was the rain and she was the river. But for all that she could recall nothing of the storm, nor did she try. It was enough to lie there enjoying the sensation of being quenched. Her limbs had drunk from her own desire. Her thighs and her breasts felt heavy, and yet it was this that at the same time made her feel so light as though she might float. It was the first time that Angela had been aware of her own body as an instrument of pleasure. She had previously regarded it as a vehicle for health.

She had her breakfast and then decided for once in her life not to take a bath. She did not want to wash this feeling away. She looked carefully at her nakedness in the mirror. She looked just the same.

Appearance can be deceptive, she thought, and stretched like a cat.

She dressed quickly and went along the corridor to her brother's room, expecting to find her husband jawing to him. Alex was alone; he lay in bed reading.

"Have you and Peter been out for a bathe?" Angela asked him.

Alex shook his head.

"I wonder where he's gone."

"Probably for a walk?"

Angela nodded.

For the next hour, neither gave Buckle a thought. But when they went downstairs Angela asked the hotel porter if he had seen Major Buckle. The man was not helpful. He had not seen anyone go out, and since he had not been on duty the previous evening when Angela and her husband had arrived, he would not have recognized him anyhow.

"If he didn't have breakfast with you upstairs he must have been into the dining room," Alex suggested.

But the headwaiter assured them that nobody had been to Angela's table that morning.

They decided that Buckle had gone for a bathe or taken a walk, and set out to wander along the front. At first they tried to see if they could spot him among the bathers who already sported themselves on the beach, but after a few moments their own conversation became absorbing; they forgot their search, thinking they would find Buckle at the hotel when they got back. They walked for about three miles along the front, stopped and had coffee and then returned leisurely to their hotel.

"Have you seen my husband?" Angela asked the porter as he handed her the key to her room.

"No, madam," the man replied cheerfully, as if reassuring her.

"That fool thinks we're having an affair, and that you're frightened your husband will come and catch us red-handed," Alex joked as they went up in the lift.

Angela said nothing. She was not amused.

Her room was empty. There was no note or message from Buckle. For some reason, neither Angela nor her brother thought of looking in the bathroom or on the dressing table to see whether Buckle's shaving kit or hairbrushes were still there. But when he did not appear for lunch, or turn up during the afternoon, they decided that he had probably been called up to London by the War Office on some urgent business and had been delayed longer than he expected.

"That sort of thing often happens these days," Alex told his sister. "A chap in our regiment got called off on some secret mission the first day of his leave."

"He could have phoned."

"Maybe he did when we were out."

"Then there'd have been a message."

"If he's in London, he's bound to have lunched at the club. I'll ring and ask if they've seen him."

Alex shook his head as he returned. They sat for a few minutes in silence.

"I'll go and pack," Angela said.

She was now very worried. So was her brother, but with more reason. He had not told her that when he had inquired for her husband, the secretary of the club had blandly replied that Buckle was dead. Of course Alex realized that there must have been two members with the same name. Still, it had been a shock to him.

*　　*　　*

Early next morning, Alex accompanied his sister to the War Office. A Colonel Hutchison received them. Alex explained: if Buckle had been recalled to his unit or dispatched on some mission, it was only fair that his wife should be told of his whereabouts, especially in these circumstances. . . .

"What circumstances?" the Colonel asked sympathetically.

"We were on our honeymoon," Angela said; "we were only married yesterday afternoon."

"You did say Major Peter Buckle of the Black Watch?" the Colonel asked.

"Yes, sir," Alex replied rather shortly.

"Are you sure there's not some mistake?"

"A woman's hardly likely to forget her husband's name," Angela said.

The Colonel rang a bell on his desk.

"Bring me the army list of the Black Watch," he told the secretary.

When this was handed to him he glanced rapidly down the list of names. Then he got up and looked out of the window.

"I thought it was unlikely. But there was just a chance that there were two officers of the same name and rank in the same regiment."

He turned and faced the brother and sister.

"As I said, there must be some mistake. Major Buckle was blown to pieces before my eyes six months ago."

"Impossible!" Angela blurted out.

"A mine exploded under his car. Very little was left of Buckle, but quite enough to identify him. The man whom you married yesterday must have been masquerading as Major Buckle."

"I'm sure he was genuine," Maclean said. "I'd have spotted it if he wasn't."

"I'm sorry, Captain, but I doubt it. There are plenty of these people who pass themselves off as officers these days. We must trace this Major Buckle of yours. Intelligence will want to question him. I suppose you've got a photograph of him? Did he look remotely like this?"

The Colonel produced a photograph from the drawer of his desk.

"Yes, that's Peter," Angela said.

"That's impossible I'm afraid, madam. If you have a photograph of your husband you can compare it with this. I am sure you will see that the likeness is only enough to justify the imposter in his attempt. Have you such a photograph?"

Angela shook her head sadly, and then remembered.

"Oh yes, I took several snaps of my brother and my husband at a picnic we had outside Edinburgh a couple of weeks ago."

"May I see them?"

"The film hasn't been developed yet," Alex explained.

"Then go and get it immediately, Captain, and we'll have it developed here."

Half an hour later, Alex returned with the camera and handed it to the Colonel. Then he took his sister into the canteen while the film was developed. They waited.

Colonel Hutchison looked hopelessly embarrassed as he placed the six prints on the table before them.

"Your brother looks quite a film star," he muttered, then immediately regretted the remark.

Angela stared at the prints. There were six photographs of her brother, but no trace of any figure, however dim, standing beside him.

KEEPING HOUSE

MICHAEL BLUMLEIN

"In the mirror my face was becoming less and less distinct, its individual features being drained of life by a darkness whose origin I had yet to guess."

In a story that evokes shuddering memories of both Shirley Jackson's masterpiece, The Haunting of Hill House, *and that earlier classic of a woman's descent into madness, "The Yellow Wallpaper," by Charlotte Perkins Gilman, Michael Blumlein puts us, along with his nameless heroine, into a situation of encroaching dread. Yet as we watch her, trapped in an increasingly isolated struggle against the insistent forces advancing to claim her, we sense what she, beset by fits of lewdness and compelled to acts of ritual purification, cannot—that the disturbance must have a source other than suspected malign emanations from an adjoining building. Wrote Jackson, "No human eye can isolate the unhappy coincidence of line and place which suggests evil in the face of a house . . . ," and yet she herself was slyly playing tricks on us, misdirecting our attention, just as Blumlein wishes to. And as she succeeded, so he does, as well, leaving us suspended somewhere between shock and pity.*

I am here alone. Curtis left last week, was driven out, I should say. I have no regrets, except perhaps that I waited so long. If I am to preserve what we have, I need this detachment. I must be able to concentrate. Now more than ever I have to focus my will.

When I think how it all began, I want to laugh at our innocence. We were in the market for a house and were taken by our agent to a block where two were for sale, one next to the other. They had been built together at the turn of the century and were nearly identical. Each was two stories and shingled, with large bay windows facing east. The house to the north was in a poorer state of repair than the other, and when I queried various neighbors, I found that this had been the case for years. From what I gathered, its paint seemed to weather and its shingles to split faster than its twin, and the sidewalk in front always seemed to be cracked and filled with weeds. Curtis pointed out that it was by far the cheaper of the two, and whatever its deficiencies of structure or façade could easily be repaired for the difference in price. I reminded him that as an assistant professor of classics at the university I received a healthy stipend, and it seemed both unnecessary and absurd to suffer the inconvenience of renovation when the house next to it had been recently painted and was clean and ready for occupancy. Moreover, I was already experiencing antipathies, which, though vague, were sufficient to dissuade me. Curtis remonstrated that I was making decisions based on superstition, an allegation I did not dignify with a reply. Shortly after, we purchased the one I favored.

I believe now that neither of us was right, and we should have avoided the neighborhood altogether. The house next door affects other houses, ours perhaps most of all. Its walls abut ours, a contact whose intimacy is impossible to escape. Like Siamese twins we share a circulation, the stealthy paths of mice and ants; between us lies shelter for cockroaches and termites. I do not imagine these things, for I have seen the severed paws and death grins of mice caught in our traps. There are days when I have sat for hours at my desk awaiting some

invasion, other times when I am certain that the steady drip I
hear in the pipes is the prodromal surge of a vile and infested
sewage being directed at us from next door. During the rains
last year I began to notice thin and shiny trails across the
carpet in our daughter's room. One night I rose to her crying,
and upon entering her room touched with my sole something
fleshy and cold. My throat convulsed, and at that moment I
saw two beady eyes peering from within the bars of her crib.
Monstrous fantasies seized me as I slapped frantically at the
wall, searching for the light switch. When finally I found it and
threw back the night, I saw immediately how far my imagination had flown. My daughter was lying in her crib, already back
asleep. Next to her was a stuffed bear with radiant eyes, and on
the floor were two dark specks. I touched them, and recoiled.
Slugs. Trapped in the green fluid on my sole was the partial
body of another. Somehow I made it to the bathroom where,
after retching into the toilet, I disrobed and smothered myself
in soap and hot water.

For the next few weeks I dreamed about doing battle with
limbless creatures whose flesh dripped when punctured. I was
never vanquished, but neither was I ever victorious. The battles
were nightmarishly everlasting.

Curtis suggested that I act upon the source of these dreams,
meaning, as I understood, that I get rid of the slugs that infested
our daughter's room. I accepted the advice and plugged up a
large space I found where the wall should have been snug
against the flooring. It was a northern wall, and as I repaired it,
I sensed that the crack would open again, that it was an entry
being created by the pressure of the house next door. The fact
that it was into Tanya's room—toward, that is, the most vulnerable member of our family—occurred to me, but I quickly
smothered the thought. Clearly, the dreams had upset me, and
I tried to think with a mind like Curtis's, one that believes that
nightmares can be stopped by plugging holes. My husband is as
pragmatic as he is strong-willed. He is the kind of man a
woman can trust when she can no longer trust herself.

Sometime in March we planted our garden, and when the
lettuce broke through the ground a few weeks later, we began
our nightly snail and slug raids. With flashlight and spade
Curtis and I picked and crushed the slimy creatures. The task

was never a delight, but as our slaughter climbed into the hundreds, my nausea did abate. Shortly thereafter, the nightmares stopped.

In the middle of May, Tanya entered her third year. Chirpy and ebullient, she was a bright and lovely child, testing limits, seeking forever to turn the world upside down. The garden flourished, despite weeds and thick blackberry brambles from the adjoining plot. I accepted a summer position with the university that provided child care for Tanya and allowed me to escape the house. As June approached, I have to say I was as content as ever. Buoyed by new responsibilities away from home, by a daughter fighting and laughing down the corridors of childhood, by a husband who at last was beginning to find satisfaction at work, I became genuinely cheerful. I began to believe in myself and my power to overcome obstacles, and as a first step, I turned on the house next door.

At first I allowed it to remain, using my will simply to transform it to a thing of little consequence. When I passed the house in the morning, I blurred my eyes, imagining it to be less solid than a cloud, less real than a dream. I turned its roof into the feathered back of a small bird, its shingles into the bird's tufted belly. And when the wind blew, it was not so hard to pretend that the house had taken flight.

Later, I devised an even more powerful technique. I found a way in my mind to merge one wall of the house with another, eliminating perspective and the lessons of vision. Solid forms I deconstructed, melting their complex geometries into simpler dimensions. Little by little the house came to subtend but a single plane, composed of two intersecting lines. I fused the two into one, and then the one line into a single point. I wrestled with this point for nearly a week before, after a supreme effort, I caused it to disappear.

The house had gone. I had eliminated my chief foe. When I passed it now, I saw nothing, not even an absence. I felt finally safe from the waves that used to press me into panic and make me doubt my sanity. With relief I turned my mind homeward.

Despite our happiness that summer I knew that I had more to give. Freed from the preoccupation that had fed unnaturally within me, I vowed to show Curtis the love I knew I was capable of.

I began to pay more attention to our own house, cleaning it in the hours after work, trying to keep it tidy. I started a program of daily mopping of the kitchen and bathrooms, and every two or three days I vacuumed the rugs in the other rooms. The dirty dishes and glasses, which had always irritated me, now became constant reminders of failure. The demands of work, a child, married life, and the new regime on which I had embarked kept me forever in the position of trying to catch up. I had to make a change, and after weeks of turmoil I made a decision: with money we had saved for our yearly vacation I went out and purchased a dishwasher. Certainly I regretted having to lose our vacation, but the disappointment was more than compensated for by my satisfaction. The glasses were finally spotless, the counters clean, and I was once again in command.

After a few weeks of this routine I began to notice things about the house that had never occurred to me. For instance, even though we were adjoined on both north and south by other homes and thus had windows facing only east and west, the light in all the rooms sat distinctly on the southern walls. By this I do not mean the actual sunlight, which in the late fall and winter when the sun is to the south slants northward, but rather the radiance, the luminosity of the air. There seemed to be a glow, an enhancement, that hung upon the austral walls, and I could not account for it by any difference in the texture of the plaster or color of the paint. Conversely, the northern sides of the rooms seemed in perpetual penumbra, as though some substance around them were absorbing free light, trapping it, as it were, in shadow. This was manifest in morning as well as afternoon. With some consternation I discovered that it obtained even at night when the rooms were illumined artificially.

I removed the pictures and posters that hung on the darkened walls, transferring what I could to the south side of the rooms. For several days I mentally juggled the furniture, trying to rearrange it so that it lay beyond the border that shadowed the north. I finally settled on a position several feet from the wall, which placed it in an area of adequate illumination and seemed at the same time to preserve the symmetry of the room. Curtis expressed doubts as to the new arrangement but allowed to give it a try, reaffirming my feeling of self-confidence and trust in our relationship. I remember that a wave of gratitude passed through me, and I decided to do something special.

The next day, after dropping Tanya at her day-care, I went shopping. I had in mind to buy a pair of slacks that Curtis had recently admired on a friend of ours. I found them in the window of a downtown store, and after the sales clerk had assured me that no one else had tried the pair on, I entered a booth and stepped into them. They were rose-colored and cut tight, clinging like another skin so that I had to suck in my breath to fasten them. At the mirror I was amazed at how they transformed me, as though the fabric were infused with a vitality of its own. The sales clerk coyly said nothing, though I am certain she must have known. On the bus home I clutched the pants to my lap with a rising excitement.

I coaxed Tanya to bed early and made quick rounds of the house, tidying and cleaning up. Several pictures seemed slightly askew, and as I straightened them, I noticed that the windows needed washing. Resolving to do it the next day, I went to the bathroom and drew a bath. While it was running, I wrapped myself in a robe and rounded the bedroom, picking up the dust balls that had accumulated since morning.

Normally I do not like baths, but before the sexual act they seem appropriate. Somehow the touch of the water, its shapelessness and transparency, prepares me for what is to come. This time, however, the water seemed less than clean. I spied oily spots and strands of hair floating on the surface, and beneath them I sensed the pull of unsanitary currents. I began to feel that I was being covered by a coat of grime and quickly stood up, pulling the plug and watching to make sure the water drained fully. Only when it had did I dare step back in the tub and turn on the faucets for the shower. At once I felt relieved of the burden of uncleanliness, and I scrubbed thoroughly, until my skin was red.

When I had dried, I went to the bedroom to dress. The slacks were folded on the bed, and I eyed them several times, feeling skittish and excited. I slipped them on, carefully closing the zipper against my skin and smoothing the fabric down my thighs. I pulled the big mirror out of the closet, leaned it against the wall and stepped back.

Something flitted behind me, and I whirled around, too late

to catch sight of it. I returned to the image in front of me, unable to take my eyes from the slacks. Their color had darkened from rose to scarlet, and what at first had been attractive now seemed lewd. Again something flickered in the background, and when I turned I thought I glimpsed a serpentine shape, but it disappeared before I could determine its source. The bedroom was growing dimmer, and I switched on a lamp. The slacks seemed now an even deeper red, and I thought I could see tiny hairs on the surface. A moment later these hairs began to beat in time with my heart.

I wondered if this were an effect of the light, which, despite the lamp, seemed inexorably to be failing. At the same time, the room was getting stuffy, and I found that even deep breaths were catching in my throat. In the mirror my face was becoming less and less distinct, its individual features being drained of life by a darkness whose origin I had yet to guess. This darkness grew until all else in the room was on the verge of extinction. I wrenched myself from the mirror, seeking an escape beyond the opacity of the room and its oppressive walls. But all was in shadow, and suddenly I realized the source of the darkness. I had placed the mirror against the north wall, inadvertently making it a window through which the menace from next door could pass. My preoccupation with the pants had made me forget, and I was in grave jeopardy.

I forced a laugh, but it was a cry of panic that echoed in the room. Nocturnal beasts lay in corners, and I began to sense thready digits groping for my flesh. The cloth on my skin was alive, the hairs glowing in the darkness, and in a siege of terror I leapt at the mirror, the gate, striking it with the heel of a shoe I had torn from my foot. There was a hiss, an instant of violence, and then the glass screeched and shattered. Splintered eyes flew through the air, settling to the ground in dangerous patterns. The room seemed momentarily to brighten, but then the darkness became total and I collapsed to the floor.

I forget much of what happened after that, except that by the time Curtis arrived home I had disposed of the glass and the mirror casing. I was wearing a different pair of slacks, and even now am not quite sure what became of the others. I tried to explain what had happened but was hardly coherent: large pieces of the afternoon had somehow vanished from my memory. I felt self-conscious and not a little embarrassed. Curtis was grumpy from a bad day at work, and it was easiest to forget the whole matter. We had a quick dinner and went to bed early. That night the nightmares returned.

Over the course of the next weeks the situation at home deteriorated. Curtis's job became more and more demanding, and many evenings passed when I ate dinner alone. Tanya reacted by clinging more to me, though whether this was due to Curtis's absence or the other pressures that were building, I'm not sure. Regardless, her newfound insecurity came at a time when I had little extra to give. I was engaged in a battle of my own.

Shortly after the episode with the mirror I quit my summer post with the university. It had become too difficult to concentrate on even minor tasks when the safety of my home and family was at stake. I resolved to do what was necessary to eliminate the threat.

As I began to spend more time at home, I realized how timely my decision had been. New intrusions were coming daily from the neighboring house, and it took every effort to neutralize them. After removing all mirrors and reflecting glass, I scrubbed the walls with cleanser. Even so, discolored areas remained, and there were cracks through which cold drafts blew even on windless days. On the floor I found several patches of rug that had been unnaturally frayed and a carpet tack that had somehow worked its way loose. Dust and lint seemed to accumulate ever faster, and I had to begin vacuuming twice daily. That, I think, was in October. Two weeks ago the smell began.

It started in the basement but after a day or two came to occupy the whole house. I presumed at first an impaction of unusually thick waste in one of the sewage lines, but neither toilet nor sink in all the house was affected. Next I imagined that some hitherto unknown septic system, only now discovered, liberated, perhaps, by the deep burrowing of some rodent, had been disrupted. The supposition was preposterous, but at the time I was quite willing to go to any length of self-deception. And yet even then I suppose I knew the source.

The stench was constant, though its quality varied by location. In our bedroom it hung like a vast and sulphurous cloud, impossibly foul, such that I could not enter without convulsions taking my stomach. In the living room it hovered acridly along the edges, waiting until I was well inside to gag me. And on the lower level of the house the air was fetid and moist, a rank breeding ground for mildew and other malodorous fungi.

Night and day the odors remained, assaulting me and poisoning the air. By this time I had no doubt as to their source, and the willfulness of the attack I took as a test of my resolve. I doubled, then redoubled, my cleaning efforts. No longer was it sufficient to have the floors clean; the walls too had to be washed, as well as ceilings, closets, and windows. I bought scents to freshen each room and several times daily sprayed the air with pungent aerosols. I began to change my clothes more frequently to prevent the odors from staying on the fabrics, and my own body I washed morning, afternoon, and evening. My determination had an effect, for I was able at length to eliminate the stench, though success depended on my constant and unyielding vigilance. I deemed such an expense small, and became infused with renewed vigor and hope. At last I was recovering my powers and would soon again be in control.

At these prospects I began to feel better, and for a few days believed even that the problems were solved. In retrospect, I see how hope had replaced reality, but I can hardly be blamed for wanting a respite from the turmoil of those days. Not only was I fighting the battle for our home, but I was drawn increasingly into conflicts with Tanya and Curtis. Neither seemed to share my concerns for our safety. On the contrary, they seemed to withdraw, leaving me more and more isolated, and this at a time when I needed their support more than ever. I tried at first to understand, reasoning that Curtis was under pressure at work and could not be burdened by other problems. And Tanya was just a child. How could she possibly be held responsible for this deterioration?

Nonetheless, my suspicions grew, and in an act of near desperation I decided to confront them, beginning with my daughter.

The next day I kept her home from the sitter, forcing her to stand against the north wall of her bedroom. I did not spray that morning and waited until the stench had become unbearable. Then I asked if she noticed the bad smell.

She shook her head, a false look of innocence on her face.

"Don't lie to me," I said, and grabbed her, pressing her nose to the wall. "Smell it."

Deliberately, she began to cry, and I slapped her. She cried more, but by then I could no longer bear it and rushed from the room. That night Curtis told me I was sick.

I suppose I should have expected it, realizing the distrust in which we now seemed to hold each other, but it struck me as a heartless and untimely jibe. Had he been laboring as I had, struggling moment by moment to maintain a semblance of order in our home, I might have dismissed his judgment as rash but unavoidable. But this was not the case, and clearly his comment was intended to provoke and isolate me further. It had its desired effect, and the verbal fight that ensued turned physical, then violent. Hard blows were struck, and in a sudden flash I recognized the true face of an enemy. Crying, clawing, I drove it from the house.

That was days ago. Now I am here alone. At times I think Tanya is with me, other times not. There is a shape in her crib that moves subtly. Perhaps it is trying to speak. At night it glows faintly . . . indeed, is the single luminosity within the ever-darkening shadow. I bring food, saving what is not eaten for myself. She has become a good child and no longer cries. Perhaps the tongue has been taught by the other worms.

The house next door has come back, and I realize how shallow my understanding has been. Wood and plaster, nails, glass, none of these carries a threat to my person. Nor does the house itself, for in truth it is but an agent. What opposes me is the realm of which it is born, its past, present, and future. What lives resides in the earth, in the deformed seeds of plants and weeds, sprouting and sending roots against me, malicious tendrils like earthworms burrowing through the soil to penetrate my walls and sully.

I have covered the windows with linoleum. I attempt to keep my house clean.

Yesterday I devised a way to defeat the odors. With the long-stemmed matches Curtis keeps beside our fireplace I cauterized my nostrils. There was a brief slice of pain, but now I am immune to nasal challenge. My will hardens. Daily I am growing more potent.

This morning I found the red pants. They were lying in the closet beneath dirty linens. Their color has somehow faded, and along the legs are glistening trails. Spots of mold dot the seams in obvious patterns.

With dawning recognition I slip them on, fastening them at the waist. I extinguish all lights. The fabric clings like a web to my skin as I go to lie in the closet. In a dark as dense as my will I pull Curtis's remaining clothes from the hangers, settling among them without fear. Thus reposed, a beacon now, a bait, I offer myself in sacrifice.

THE VILLA DÉSIRÉE

MAY SINCLAIR

"She *liked* that strangeness that kept other people away and left him to her altogether. He was more her own that way."

I have chosen to include "The Villa Désirée," first published in 1926, over an earlier, favorite May Sinclair story, "Where Their Fire Is Not Quenched" (1923), because the latter, though a brilliantly chilling conceptualization of the banality of lust without love, has been far too frequently anthologized. "The Villa Désirée," on the other hand, is a curious little exploration of a similar theme that, so far as I can tell, has not been readily available since the mid-1930s.

The setting is the South of France, the place a sun-drenched house with a view of the sea, where the intensely golden light seems to draw up "a faint powdery smell from the old floor." A virginal young woman, Mildred Eve, has arrived here to await her fiancé, Louis Carson, a suave, almost indecently handsome rich man given to extravagant romantic gestures, whose courtship of her has been impulsively brief. There, amidst the unfamiliar but delightfully luxurious atmosphere, Mildred is happy in anticipation of his arrival and only just a bit unsettled by the knowledge that his last bride died in the very room she is to occupy. . . .

He had arranged it all for her. She was to stay a week in Cannes with her aunt and then to go on to Roquebrune by herself, and he was to follow her there. She, Mildred Eve, supposed he could follow her anywhere, since they were engaged now.

There had been difficulties, but Louis Carson had got over all of them by lending her the Villa Désirée. She would be all right there, he said. The caretakers, Narcisse and Armandine, would look after her—Armandine was an excellent cook—and she wouldn't be five hundred yards from her friends the Derings. It was so like him to think of it, to plan it all out for her. And when he came down? Oh, when he came down he would go to the Cap Martin Hotel, of course.

He understood everything without any tiresome explaining. She couldn't afford the hotels at Cap Martin and Monte Carlo; and though the Derings had asked her to stay with them, she really couldn't dump herself down on them like that, almost in the middle of their honeymoon.

Their honeymoon—she could have bitten her tongue out for saying it, for not remembering. It was awful of her to go talking to Louis Carson about honeymoons, after the appalling tragedy of *his*.

There were things she hadn't been told, that she hadn't liked to ask: Where it had happened? And how? And how long ago? She only knew it was on his wedding night, that he had gone in to the poor little girl of a bride and found her dead there, in the bed.

They said she had died in a sort of fit.

You had only to look at him to see that something terrible had happened to him at some time. You saw it when his face was doing nothing: a queer, agonized look that made him strange to her while it lasted. It was more than suffering; it was almost as if he could be cruel, only he never was, he never could be. *People* were cruel, if you liked; they said his face put them off. Mildred could see what they meant. It might have put *her* off, perhaps, if she hadn't known what he had gone through. But the first time she had met him he had been pointed out to her as the man to whom just that appalling thing had happened. So far from putting her off, that was what had drawn her to him from the beginning, made her pity him first, then love him. There engagement had come quick, in the third week of their acquaintance.

When she asked herself: After all, what do I know about him? she had her answer: I know *that*. She felt that already she had entered into a mystical union with him through compassion. She *liked* the strangeness that kept other people away and left him to her altogether. He was more her own that way.

There was (Mildred Eve didn't deny it) his personal magic, the fascination of his almost abnormal beauty. His black, white, and blue. The intensely blue eyes under the straight black bars of the eyebrows, the perfect pure white face suddenly masked by the black mustache and small black pointed beard. And the rich vivid smile he had for her, the lighting up of the blue, the flash of white teeth in the black mask.

He had smiled then at her embarrassment as the awful word leaped out at him. He had taken it from her and turned the sharp edge of it.

"It would never do," he had said, "to spoil the *honeymoon*. You'd much better have my villa. Someday, quite soon, it'll be yours too. You know I like anticipating things."

That was always the excuse he made for his generosities. He had said it again when he engaged her seat in the *train de luxe* from Paris and wouldn't let her pay for it. (She had wanted to travel third class.) He was only anticipating, he said.

He was seeing her off now at the Gare de Lyons, standing on the platform with a great sheaf of blush roses in his arms. She, on the high step of the railway carriage, stood above him, swinging in the open doorway. His face was on a level with her feet; they gleamed white through the fine black stockings. Suddenly he thrust his face forward and kissed her feet. As the train moved he ran beside it and tossed the roses into her lap.

And then she sat in the hurrying train, holding the great sheaf of blush roses in her lap, and smiling at them as she dreamed. She was on the Riviera Express; the Riviera Express. Next week she would be in Roquebrune, at the Villa Désirée. She read the three letters woven into the edges of the gray cloth cushions: P.L.M.: Paris—Lyons—Mediterranée, Paris—Lyons—Mediterranée, over and over again. They sang themselves to the rhythm of the wheels; they wove their pattern into her dream. Every now and then, when the other passengers weren't looking, she lifted the roses to her face and kissed them.

She hardly knew how she dragged herself through the long dull week with her aunt at Cannes.

And now it was over and she was by herself at Roquebrune.

The steep narrow lane went past the Derings' house and up the face of the hill. It led up into a little olive wood, and above the wood she saw the garden terraces. The sunlight beat in and out of their golden yellow walls. Tier above tier, the blazing terraces rose, holding up their ranks of spindle-stemmed lemon and orange trees. On the topmost terrace the Villa Désirée stood white and hushed between two palms, two tall poles each topped by a head of dark-green, curving, sharp-pointed blades. A gray scrub of olive trees straggled up the hill behind it and on each side.

Rolf and Martha Dering waited for her with Narcisse and Armandine on the steps of the veranda.

"Why on earth didn't you come to us?" they said.

"I didn't want to spoil your honeymoon."

"Honeymoon, what rot! We've got over *that* silliness. Anyhow, it's our third week of it."

They were detached and cool in their happiness.

She went in with them, led by Narcisse and Armandine. The caretakers, subservient to Mildred Eve and visibly inimical to the Derings, left them together in the salon. It was very bright and French and fragile and worn, all faded gray and old greenish gilt, the gilt chairs and settees carved like picture frames round the gilded cane. The hot light beat in through the long windows open to the terrace, drawing up a faint powdery smell from the old floor.

Rolf Dering stared at the room, sniffing, with fine nostrils in a sort of bleak disgust.

"You'd much better have come to us," he said.

"Oh, but—it's charming."

"Do you *think* so?" Martha said. She was looking at her intently.

Mildred saw that they expected her to feel something, she

wasn't sure what, something that they felt. They were subtle and fastidious.

"It does look a little queer and—unlived in," she said, straining for the precise impression.

"I should say," said Martha, "it had been too much lived in, if you ask me."

"Oh, no. That's only dust you smell. I think, perhaps, the windows haven't been open very long."

She resented this criticism of Louis's villa.

Armandine appeared at the doorway. Her little slant Chinesey eyes were screwed up and smiling. She wanted to know if Madame wouldn't like to go up and look at her room.

"We'll all go up and look at it," said Rolf.

They followed Armandine up the steep, slender, curling staircase. A closed door faced them on the landing. Armandine opened it, and the hot golden light streamed out to them again.

The room was all golden white; it was like a great white tank filled with blond water where things shimmered, submerged in the stream—the white-painted chairs and dressing table, the high white-painted bed, the pink-and-white striped ottoman at its foot, all vivid and still, yet quivering in the stillness, with the hot throb, throb of the light.

"*Voilà*, Madame," said Armandine.

They didn't answer. They stood, fixed in the room, held by the stillness, staring, all three of them, at the high white bed that rose up, enormous, with its piled mattresses and pillows, the long white counterpane hanging straight and steep, like a curtain, to the floor.

Rolf turned to Armandine.

"Why have you given Madame this room?"

Armandine shrugged her fat shoulders. Her small Chinesey eyes blinked at him, slanting, inimical.

"Monsieur's orders, Monsieur. It is the best room in the house. It was Madame's room."

"I know. That's *why*—"

"But no, Monsieur. Nobody would dislike to sleep in Madame's room. The poor little thing, she was so pretty, so sweet, so young, Monsieur. Surely Madame will not dislike the room."

"Who *was*—Madame?"

"But Monsieur's wife, Madame. Madame Carson. Poor Monsieur, it was so sad—"

"Rolf," said Mildred, "did he bring her here—on their honeymoon?"

"Yes."

"Yes, Madame. She died here. It was so sad. Is there anything I can do for Madame?"

"No, thank you, Armandine."

"Then I will get ready the tea."

She turned again in the doorway, crooning in her thick Provençal voice. "*Madame* does not dislike her room?"

"No, Armandine. No. It's a beautiful room."

The door closed on Armandine. Martha opened it again to see whether she was listening on the landing. Then she broke out:

"Mildred—you know you loathe it. It's beastly. The whole place is beastly."

"You can't stay in it," said Rolf.

"Why not? Do you mean, because of Madame?"

Martha and Rolf were looking at each other, as if they were both asking what they should say. They said nothing.

"Oh, her poor little ghost won't hurt me, if that's what you mean."

"Nonsense," Martha said. "Of course it isn't."

"What is it, then?"

"It's so beastly lonely, Mildred," said Rolf.

"Not with Narcisse and Armandine."

"Well, I wouldn't sleep a night in the place," Martha said, "if there wasn't any other on the Riviera. I don't like the look of it."

Mildred went to the open lattice, turning her back on the high, rather frightening bed. Down there below the terraces she saw the gray flicker of the olive woods and, beyond them, the sea. Martha was wrong. The place was beautiful; it was adorable. She wasn't going to be afraid of poor little Madame. Louis had loved her. He loved the place. That was why he had lent it to her.

She turned. Rolf had gone down again. She was alone with Martha. Martha was saying something.

"Mildred—where's Mr. Carson?"

"In Paris. Why?"

"I thought he was coming here."

"So he is, later on."

"To the villa?"

"No. Of course not. To Cap Martin." She laughed. "So *that's* what you're thinking of, is it?"

She could understand her friend's fear of haunted houses, but not these previsions of impropriety.

Martha looked shy and ashamed.

"Yes," she said. "I suppose so."

"How horrid of you! You might have trusted me."

"I do trust you." Martha held her a minute with her clear loving eyes. "Are you sure you can trust *him*?"

"Trust him? Do *you* trust Rolf?"

"Ah—if it was like that, Mildred—"

"It *is* like that."

"You're really not afraid?"

"What is there to be afraid of? Poor little Madame?"

"I didn't mean Madame. I meant Monsieur."

"Oh—wait till you've seen him."

"Is he *very* beautiful?"

"Yes. But it isn't *that*, Martha. I can't tell you what it is."

They went downstairs, hand in hand, in the streaming light. Rolf waited for them on the veranda. They were taking Mildred back to dine with them.

"Won't you let me tell Armandine you're stopping the night?" he said.

"No, I won't. I don't want Armandine to think I'm frightened."

She meant she didn't want Louis to think she was frightened. Besides, she was not frightened.

"Well, if you find you don't like it, you must come to us," he said.

And they showed her the little spare room next to theirs with its camp bed made up, the bedclothes turned back, all ready for her, any time of the night, in case she changed her mind. The front door was on the latch.

"You've only to open it, and creep in here and be safe," Rolf said.

I I

Armandine—subservient and no longer inimical, now that the Derings were not there—Armandine had put the candle and matches on the night table and the bell which, she said, would summon her if Madame wanted anything in the night. And she had left her.

As the door closed softly behind Armandine, Mildred drew in her breath with a light gasp. Her face in the looking glass, between the tall lighted candles, showed its mouth half open, and she was aware that her heart shook slightly in its beating. She was angry with the face in the glass with its foolish mouth gaping. She said to herself: Is it possible I'm frightened? It was not possible. Rolf and Martha had made her walk too fast up the hill, that was all. Her heart always did that when she walked too fast uphill, and she supposed that her mouth always gaped when it did it.

She clenched her teeth and let her heart choke her till it stopped shaking.

She was quiet now. But the test would come when she had blown out the candles and had to cross the room in the dark to the bed.

The flame bent backward before the light puff she gave, and righted itself. She blew harder, twice, with a sense of spinning out the time. The flame writhed and went out. She extinguished the other candle at one breath. The red point of the wick pricked the darkness for a second and died, too, with a small crackling sound. At the far end of the room the high bed glimmered. She thought: Martha was right. The bed *is* awful.

She could feel her mouth set in a hard grin of defiance as she went to it, slowly, too proud to be frightened. And then suddenly, halfway, she thought about Madame.

The awful thing was, climbing into that high funeral bed that Madame had died in, your back felt so undefended. But once she was safe between the bedclothes it would be all right. It would be all right so long as she didn't think about Madame. Very well, then, she wouldn't think about her. You could frighten yourself into anything by thinking.

Deliberately, by an intense effort of her will, she turned the

sad image of Madame out of her mind and found herself thinking about Louis Carson.

This was Louis's house, the place he used to come to when
he wanted to be happy. She made out that he had sent her there
because he wanted to be happy in it again. She was there to
drive away the unhappiness, the memory of poor little Madame. Or, perhaps, because the place was sacred to him; because they were both so sacred, she and the young dead bride
who hadn't been his wife. Perhaps he didn't think about her as
dead at all; he didn't want her to be driven away. The room she
had died in was not awful to him. He had the faithfulness for
which death doesn't exist. She wouldn't have loved him if he
hadn't been faithful. You could be faithful and yet marry again.

She was convinced that whatever she was there for, it was for
some beautiful reason. Anything that Louis did, anything he
thought or felt or wanted, would be beautiful. She thought of
Louis standing on the platform in the Paris station, his beautiful face looking up at her; its sudden darting forward to kiss her
feet. She drifted again into her happy hypnotizing dream, and
was fast asleep before midnight.

She woke with a sense of intolerable compulsion, as if she
were being dragged violently up out of her sleep. The room was
gray in the twilight of the unrisen moon.

And she was not alone.

She knew that there was something there. Something that
gave up the secret of the room and made it frightful and obscene. The grayness was frightful and obscene. It gathered itself
together; it became the containing shell of the horror.

The thing that had waked her was there with her in the
room.

For she knew she was awake. Apart from her supernatural
certainty, one physical sense, detached from the horror, was
alert. It heard the ticking of the clock on the chimney piece,
the hard sharp shirring of the palm leaves outside, as the wind
rubbed their knife blades together. These sounds were witnesses
to the fact that she was awake, and that therefore the thing
that was going to happen would be real. At the first sight of the
grayness she had shut her eyes again, afraid to look into the
room, because she knew that what she would see there was
real. But she had no more power over her eyelids than she had

had over her sleep. They opened under the same intolerable compulsion. And the supernatural thing forced itself now on her sight.

It stood a little in front of her by the bedside. From the breasts downward its body was unfinished, rudimentary, not quite born. The gray shell was still pregnant with its loathsome shapelessness. But the face—the face was perfect in absolute horror. And it was Louis Carson's face.

Between the black bars of the eyebrows and the black pointed beard she saw it, drawn back, distorted in an obscene agony, corrupt and malignant. The face and the body, flesh and yet not flesh, they were the essence made manifest of untold, unearthly abominations.

It came on to her, bending over her, peering at her, so close that the piled mattresses now hid the lower half of its body. And the frightful thing about it was that it was blind, parted from all controlling and absolving clarity, flesh and yet not flesh. It looked for her without seeing her; and she knew that, unless she could save herself that instant, it would find what it looked for. Even now, behind the barrier of the piled-up mattresses, the unfinished form defined and completed itself; she could feel it shake with the agitation of its birth.

Her heart staggered and stopped in her breast, as if her breast had been clamped down onto her backbone. She struggled against wave after wave of faintness; for the moment that she lost consciousness the appalling presence there would have its way with her. All her will rose up against it. She dragged herself upright in the bed, suddenly, and spoke to it:

"Louis! What are you doing there?"

At her cry it went, without moving; sucked back into the grayness that had borne it.

She thought: It'll come back. It'll come back. Even if I don't see it I shall know it's in the room.

She knew what she would do. She would get up and go to the Derings. She longed for the open air, for Rolf and Martha, for the strong earth under her feet.

She lit the candle on the night table and got up. She still felt that It was there, and that standing upon the floor she was more vulnerable, more exposed to it. Her terror was too extreme for her to stay and dress herself. She thrust her bare feet into her shoes, slipped her traveling coat over her nightgown, and went downstairs and out through the house door, sliding back the bolts without a sound. She remembered that Rolf had left a lantern for her in the veranda, in case she should want it—as if they had known.

She lit the lantern and made her way down the villa garden, stumbling from terrace to terrace, through the olive wood and the steep lane to the Derings' house. Far down the hill she could see a light in the window of the spare room. The house door was on the latch. She went through and on into the lamp-lit room that waited for her.

She knew again what she would do. She would go away before Louis Carson could come to her. She would go away tomorrow and never come back again. Rolf and Martha would bring her things down from the villa; he would take her into Italy in his car. She would get away from Louis Carson forever. She would get away up through Italy.

I I I

Rolf had come back from the villa with her things and he had brought her a letter. It had been sent up that morning from Cap Martin.

It was from Louis Carson.

> My Darling Mildred,
>   You see I couldn't wait a fortnight without seeing you. I *had* to come. I'm here at the Cap Martin Hotel.
>   I'll be with you sometime between half-past ten and eleven—

Below, at the bottom of the lane, Rolf's car waited. It was half-past ten. If they went now they would meet Carson coming up the lane. They must wait till he had passed the house and gone up through the olive wood.

Martha had brought hot coffee and rolls. They sat down at the other side of the table and looked at her with kind, anxious eyes as she turned sideways, watching the lane.

"Rolf," she said suddenly, "do you know anything about Louis Carson?"

She could see them looking now at each other.

"Nothing. Only the things the people here say."

"What sort of things?"

"Don't tell her, Rolf."

"Yes. He *must* tell me. I've got to know."

She had no feeling left but horror, horror that nothing could intensify.

"There's not much. Except that he was always having women with him up there. Not particularly nice women. He seems," Rolf said, "to have been rather an appalling beast."

"Must have been," said Martha, "to have brought his poor little wife there, after—"

"Rolf, what did Mrs. Carson die of?"

"Don't ask *me*," he said.

But Martha answered. "She died of fright. She saw something. I told you the place was beastly."

Rolf shrugged his shoulders.

"Why, you said you felt it yourself. We both felt it."

"Because we knew about the beastly things he did there."

"*She* didn't know. I tell you, she saw something."

Mildred turned her white face to them.

"I saw it too."

"You?"

"What? What did you see?"

"Him. Louis Carson."

"He must be dead then, if you saw his ghost."

"The ghosts of poor dead people don't kill you. It was what he *is*. All that beastliness in a face. A face."

She could hear them draw in their breath short and sharp. "Where?"

"There. In that room. Close by the bed. It was looking for me. I saw what *she* saw."

She could see them frown now, incredulous, forcing themselves to disbelieve. She could hear them talking, their voices beating off the horror.

"Oh, but she couldn't. He wasn't there."

"He heard her scream first."

"Yes. He was in the other room, you know."

"*It* wasn't. He can't keep it back."

"Keep it back?"

"No. He was waiting to go to her."

Her voice was dull and heavy with realization. She felt herself struggling, helpless, against their stolidity, their unbelief.

"Look at that," she said. She pushed Carson's letter across to them.

"He was waiting to go to her," she repeated. "And—last night—he was waiting to come to me."

They stared at her, stupefied.

"Oh, can't you *see?*" she cried. "It didn't wait. It got there before him."

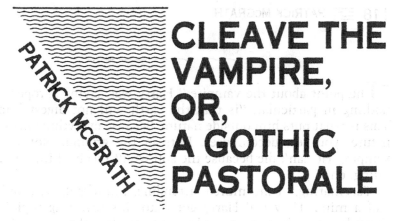

CLEAVE THE VAMPIRE, OR, A GOTHIC PASTORALE

PATRICK McGRATH

"All very tranquil, all very pastoral, hearts at peace under an English heaven and so on; why then did I have such an awful feeling of *dread?*"

If there is anything that you can be sure about when it comes to Patrick McGrath, a writer of more surprises than two sleeves could possibly hold, it's this: he is incapable of producing "just" another vampire story. But, in one major respect, McGrath is upholding a grand tradition, for those scenes in vampire literature that most slow our heartbeat and bring a flush—of terror! of excitement!—to our faces are the ones of intimate contact between monster and prey. One might even observe that there's often a peculiar letdown felt stirring in an audience when a vampire is robbed of his moment of fangish triumph, and must slink away into the night. And it's a provocative thought that the only thing worse than a vampire's advances could be a vampire's indifference.

Noting this phenomenon, McGrath spins it around a bit, drops it off in the English countryside, and allows us to watch the increasingly unsuitable behavior of an undermedicated upper-class matron with sex on the brain and a vampire on the lawn.

———————〜〜〜〜〜———————

"The point about the vampire," Harry was saying apropos of nothing in particular, "is that the earth will not digest him. This is what puts him outside nature. Because everything *inside* nature, you see, decomposes. Rots in the ground. Not your vampire. He can't die because the soil won't receive him. Interesting, eh?"

"Fascinating," I murmured, attending, I'm afraid, with only half a mind. How had Harry got onto this revolting topic? I think he must have seen a film. But my thoughts were elsewhere, with Hilary, our daughter; I hadn't taken my medication for days, I was so worried about the girl. She was only nineteen, but already she'd shown a quite alarming propensity for falling in love with utterly unsuitable men. There was that dreadful business with the plumbers last year, and before that—I shudder at the very thought of it—the scandalous "arrangement" she made with two of the gardeners at her boarding school. If only, I said to her before breakfast, she'd settle down with someone solid, someone like Tony Piker-Smith, for example.

"But Mummy," she said—she was sitting at her dressing table, brushing her hair—"you can't want me to marry such a drip. You didn't marry a drip."

I sighed. "Your father," I said, "is a man of"—I groped for the word—"*predictable* passions. This is why I married him. One knows what to expect from him; one has elbow room, so to speak."

Hilary snorted. "But I don't *want* elbow room, Mummy! Not with the man I marry!" She turned to face me. I was sitting on the edge of the bed. Suddenly an expression of mild alarm appeared in her eyes. "Mummy," she said, "have you stopped taking your pills again?"

I am Lady Hock, of Wallop Hall, and Hilary is my daughter. When we reached the dining room a few minutes later Harry was already deep in the *Times* crossword. It was a bright sunny morning in August, I remember, and I asked Stoker, our butler, a corpulent man, to serve me kidneys. My son Charles was standing at the french windows and gazing out over the croquet lawn. "Perfect day for cricket," he said. "Couldn't have hoped for a better day."

I was in no mood to talk to Charles about the weather, for Charles, you see, was the cause of my present anxiety about Hilary. Always an impulsive boy, he had now, without consulting anyone, invited an entire cricket team down for the weekend. Stoker wasn't very happy about it, but I was less concerned about him than I was about Hilary. An entire cricket team! I wouldn't be able to let the girl out of my sight until they'd all been safely packed off back to London on Sunday night. It was dreadfully tiresome, the whole thing, and I was beginning to feel one of my headaches coming on. It was then that Harry started talking about rotting vampires; just what I needed. The problem with young men, you see, is that they tend to *prey* upon me—it was that way with the plumbers, and the gardeners too. Not that their attentions aren't delightful, but Hilary is a girl of nineteen, after all, and whatever my own feelings in the matter I felt it my duty, as a mother, to protect her. I don't think that's abnormal, do you?

Wallop Hall is situated deep in the rolling farmland of the Berkshire Downs, about five miles from the village of Wallop, a sleepy cluster of ancient, crumbling cottages with honeysuckle and dog rose twining about the doorways, and dampness and mildew within. There's a shop or two, a church, an inn—and the village green, a fine stretch of greensward with a wood on the far side and a cricket pavilion. This is a Victorian structure replete with spires and gargoyles, and according to Harry it's a fine example of Rustic Gothic. I think it a monstrosity myself, but the point is, two hours later I was sitting in a deck chair beside my old friend Olive Babblehump, perspiring gently and waiting for the cricket to begin. The sun was warm, and a few white clouds, puffy affairs, fleecy at the edges, drifted across a deep blue sky. The smell of fresh-mown grass was rank in our nostrils, and I was telling Olive that though Tony Piker-Smith had an extremely limited imagination, he was just the type, if only Hilary would listen to me, to give a wife *elbow room.*

Now Olive is a dear woman, but not to be trusted. "I think, my dear," she said, "that if you try to clip that girl's wings she'll run off with someone impossible just to spite you. I nearly made that mistake with Diana."

Well! I didn't say anything to that, and you'll understand why when I tell you that Diana Babblehump, Olive's eldest, had been in a lunatic asylum for the past three years after murdering the parish priest with a blunt ax in a moment of delusional psychosis. But Olive was unaware of just how jarringly inappropriate her comment was; she hauled out her knitting and began to hum.

It was a nice day for it, anyway. Quite a large crowd had turned out, some, like ourselves, in deck chairs, others sprawled on blankets on the grass. Insects murmured, and over on the far side of the green, by Gibbet's Wood, a fat cow stood in a patch of sunlight and flicked at the flies with its tail. All very tranquil, all very pastoral, hearts at peace under an English heaven and so on; why then did I have such an awful feeling of *dread*? A few of the village cricketers, young sheep farmers mostly, were knocking a ball about, but the opposition had not yet arrived. "Whatever do you suppose has happened to them?" I asked Olive.

"Search me," she said, not even looking up from her knitting. But then she did lift her eyes. "My dear," she said, "you really should be wearing a hat in this sunshine, with the medicine you take."

I said nothing. How could I keep a proper eye on Hilary if I was all doped up like a zombie? And then the most peculiar thing happened: I could suddenly see hundreds of worms crawling in and out of Olive's head! Her skin had gone an awful yellowy-green color, and little clotted lumps of rotting flesh began to drip from her bones and into her knitting. The smell was *foul*. It only lasted a moment, I'm happy to say, but what a very nasty moment it was. And then, thank God, Harry arrived.

Harry's arrival somewhere is almost always an anticlimax. His presence is warmly anticipated, for he is, after all, the squire, but once he actually gets there the performance never varies: a moment of robust hilarity, and then he makes for the bar. This morning was no exception, though he did pause to say how d'ye do to Olive and me, and inquire, bless him, what our poison was. "Gin," we both replied with some alacrity.

Harry's one true passion in life is hunting foxes on horseback. Harry would hunt every day if he could, and often does. The villagers love him for it. They see him out on the Downs with his hounds, riding a big brown mare, red-faced, portly, in loud tweeds, and panting with the sheer animal exhilaration of the chase. It makes them feel secure. This, they know, is England. He comes home at the end of the day splattered with mud and blood, and deeply happy. He stamps into the house and takes off his boots by the fire. Stoker will already have drawn his bath. He drinks a great deal of claret at dinner, and passes out shortly afterward in the library. Stoker puts him to bed, locks the doors, and turns out the lights. Wallop Hall sleeps. The routine is immutable, and any disturbance of it makes Harry sulky and explosive, so I try to make sure that no disturbance occurs.

All of which suits me nicely. I am, as I hinted earlier, an adherent of the "elbow-room" theory of marital relations. I need not, I think, elaborate; suffice it to say that Harry and I are perfectly happy with our arrangement, and have been for many years. Unfortunately I can't talk to him about Hilary, and as you've observed Olive isn't very sympathetic either, which leaves me to fret alone; but that, I suppose, is what it means to be a mother. But I must say, I was never so glad in all my life to see Harry as I was then, after the awful way Olive turned into that *thing* right in front of my eyes.

I don't suppose I shall ever forget the first glimpse I had of the creature. The other team had all arrived and Charles, who captained the Wallop eleven, had won the toss and elected to bat. I cast an idle glance at the opening bowler—and sat up rigid in my deck chair, for I instantly realized why I had been feeling so odd all morning! I trembled all over—I could feel my blood grow hot, and a deep flush suffused my features. It was going to be bad, this I knew immediately, very bad indeed, and I sank back into my deck chair gasping for breath and attempting to disguise from Olive my excitement. There was a vampire among us.

I was surprised, at first, at how small he was—just an inch over five feet, I'd guess, no taller than Olive herself. He was very thin, with a disproportionately long face dominated by a huge, cadaverous jaw, deeply sunken eyes, and a fierce shock of jet-black hair, thickly oiled, that was brushed straight back from a sharp peak dead in the center of a low cliff of overhanging forehead. He was very elegantly turned out, little and horrible though he was, in sharply creased cream-colored trousers and a spotlessly white shirt. But this did not deceive me, for though he was supposedly here for the cricket I recognized him straightaway for a thing that lived outside nature. Having recovered my poise I turned to Olive—and found her staring at him with rapt and shameless fascination! My heart sank. If he had this effect on Olive, what would he do to poor Hilary?

A hush fell over the green and he began his run to the wicket. I must say, he did present a graceful figure, in a diabolical sort of a way, as he came cantering in at what was, given his size, remarkable speed. His hair was tossing, and even from where I sat a sort of red glow was discernible deep in each of his eye sockets. Charles, at the other end, gazed at him undaunted and briefly tapped his bat in the crease. And then another peculiar thing happened: in mid-stride the creature seemed suddenly to freeze, and hung there, suspended in the air, as though he were a photograph, with his little legs rearing well off the ground, his head thrown back, hair wild, eyes blazing redly and one arm lifted straight and rigid from the shoulder and clutching in its long, bony fingers the ball itself. But only for a moment; then *down* came his arm, and the ball, little more than a red blur, screamed toward Charles, evaded his cautious poke, shaved his offside stump, and finished with a loud *smack!* in the wicket keeper's glove. All around the green, people breathed again. "Well," said Olive, resuming her knitting, "he's certainly a quick one." I turned to look for Hilary; she was sitting on the veranda of the pavilion, next to Tony Piker-Smith, and her eyes, like Olive's, were positively shining. I felt as though a serpent had wormed its way into our Eden.

The rest of the morning was difficult, to say the least. I watched with an increasingly sick and hollow feeling as the creature—his name, I learned, was Cleave—began to demolish our batting. Ted Dung was the first to go: a loud crack, and the farmer was gazing on stupidly as his wicket was torn clean out of the soil and sent cartwheeling wildly away. There was one incident that particularly horrified me, and that was the removal of Tony Piker-Smith. He took a very fast ball full in the groin, and went down with a cry of pain. "How was that?!" cried Cleave, whirling about to appeal to the umpire for leg before wicket. The umpire was Len Grace, the undertaker. Slowly he straightened up. He transferred a penny from his left hand to his right, and shook his head. Tony's groin had not, in his opinion, been directly shielding his wicket. Had the ball continued on its way, it would have missed the leg stump. Len Grace, everyone agreed, had a very nice eye.

But Cleave had no respect for Len's nice eye. He snarled, he positively snarled—and I shuddered, for I saw quite clearly, as they gleamed in the sunshine, that his canines were much too long, and sharpened at the ends to a fine point. I turned to Olive, but her eyes were on her knitting. "Did you see that?" I whispered.

"What's that?" she murmured, simulating abstraction. "Oh good Lord, poor Tony"—for the young man was by this point being helped off the field by a couple of our chaps, and his plump pink face was all scrunched up with pain. Hilary had risen to her feet and was pressing her fist to her mouth, as she does in moments of stress. This, at least, I took to be a good sign.

Charles continued to play very elegant cricket, however, and was soon clipping loose balls gracefully through the slips. In this way the score slowly mounted, and by lunchtime we were forty-nine for seven, most of those having come from Charles's bat. We warmly applauded as he led the field back to the pavilion for lunch, which had, as usual, been prepared by a number of the farmers' wives and was laid out on trestle tables. The high spirits that generally attended these affairs were some-what dampened by Tony's absence—still in terrible pain, he'd been driven to the doctor's by Hilary. Harry, however, was genial, and appeared to harbor no suspicions of Cleave. "Have a drink," he said, "sherry, gin, scotch." And then: "No beer, I'm afraid"—and this struck me as rather a sinister development—"it all seems to have *soured* for some reason. Storm coming, perhaps."

"I wonder," said the other, in those deep, cultured tones of his, "if I might have a Bloody Mary?"

Olive managed to seat herself next to him at lunch, and

immediately began to chatter. She found out that his mother was Hungarian; her eldest girl, Diana, she said, once knew a deaf nun from Dubrovnik, and this got her onto the lunatic asylum, and what a nice man the medical superintendent was, even if he was Irish—and so it went, and the little creature merely grinned his cold, dead grin at her and said almost nothing, and between those bloodless lips of his I saw the teeth shining with a nasty, yellowish luster. Then Hilary returned from the doctor, and with an expression of great concern Cleave rose to his feet and inquired after the injured man. A rather subdued Hilary said that the doctor had taken him to the Royal Berkshire Hospital for detailed X rays, as his testicles were very badly bruised, and possibly fractured. Cleave—the monster! —murmured how desperately sorry he was, and sat down. Such was his demeanor that Charles—warm, goodhearted Charles— felt constrained to tell him that he shouldn't blame himself, that it was a freak accident, and Tony, he was sure, wasn't seriously hurt.

"I fear the worst," said Cleave. "I bowl too fast, I always have."

"Nonsense," said Charles, "you bowl magnificently." The murmur of support this statement garnered was, however, dutiful rather than warm. But you see how effectively Tony had been taken out of the picture?

The cricket resumed. I was unable to concentrate on the play, however, because Cleave had begun to produce some very uncanny visual effects, their function doubtless being to unhinge my mind and thus remove the last obstacle to his ravishment of Hilary. The most unsettling of these disturbances was his transformation of that pleasant and tranquil scene from positive to negative. For an instant all that was light—sky, cricketers, etc.—became impenetrably black, and all that was dark—trees, grass—was bleached to a ghostly white. But only for an instant. Then it would be normal again, then back to the negative, and it would flash like this for about half a minute. It was most bizarre to watch the cow, which was black and white, during one of these "storms," for the animal appeared to blink off and on like a light bulb. It was some sort of electrical interference, produced telepathically, I presume, and it was, as I say, aimed directly at me. If Olive experienced it, she said nothing; and I began then to suspect that she understood Cleave's designs— understood and *approved* them!

The players came in for tea. I decided at last that I must act. I drew Charles aside. "Darling," I whispered—the tone I adopted was one of extreme gravity—"do you really think we want all these characters for the night?"

"But Mother!" he said.

"Quietly, darling," I murmured.

"Mother, I've *invited* them. I can't just—"

"I know, darling. But all the same—" I broke off. A shadow had fallen between us. It was Cleave.

"Lady Hock," he began—and oh, he had a voice like old port, rich, smooth, full-bodied—"forgive me for interrupting."

I assumed a mask of chilly politeness. "Not at all, Mr. Cleave."

"Lady Hock, I really feel that we cannot impose upon you to house and feed eleven total strangers, despite your son's most cordial invitation."

"But I say!" cried Charles.

Cleave laid a hand on his shoulder. "I think it would be better for all concerned if you permitted us to fend for ourselves at the Wallop Arms."

Oh, this was difficult. Something in me weakened. The charm of the creature was overpowering, irresistible almost—but I held firm. To Charles's dismay I made no attempt to dissuade him. "If you're sure you won't be too uncomfortable?" I said.

"We shall be very comfortable, Lady Hock," he said. I felt relieved and grateful—and quite inexplicably disappointed! His eyes were burning upon me, and, like a chicken before a fox, I could not avert my gaze. With a sudden surge of some powerful but involuntary emotion I blurted out: "But *you* must dine with us, Mr. Cleave, and," I added, "be our guest."

No sooner were the words out of my mouth than I regretted them, regretted them bitterly—but I could not help myself. Oh, you stupid woman, I thought—having just been safely delivered of the creature, here you are inviting him right back in again! He bowed his assent.

Charles was somewhat appeased. I turned to go; it was at that moment that Hilary appeared. "Hilary," I said, "Mr. Cleave will be joining us for dinner, and staying in the Rose Room, but the rest of the team will put up at the Wallop Arms."

"Oh good," said Hilary. "Good, I mean," she added, flushing slightly, "about Mr. Cleave."

"So darling," I said, "perhaps you'd run back to the Hall and let Stoker know."

"Of course," she said. "Pip pip, Mr. Cleave."

"Pip pip," said the vampire, dryly; and Hilary was gone.

Play ended at half past six. All the villagers went home to their cottages. Birds chattered in Gibbet's Wood, and the pavilion grew shadowy, its gargoyles standing out sharp and black against the twilight. A pale mist drifted across the green, subtly tinted with the odors of opened graves, but no nostril lingered to sniff it, and so, by slow and imperceptible degrees, night fell.

Dinner. Tony wasn't there, as he'd been admitted to the Royal Berks by this time, but Olive was. Oh yes, Olive was there, and if my suspicions about her had been merely tentative during the day, they hardened to certainty that evening, and by means of an incident that I shall now describe.

I'd heard Harry inviting Cleave to have a look at the sporting prints in the library. Now, this invitation was made while Harry was on his way upstairs for his bath, and Cleave, already dressed for dinner, was on his way down—doubtless hoping to work on Hilary before anyone else appeared. I myself was dressed by this time; and on hearing Harry's invitation I slipped down the back stairs and made my way round the side of the house to the library window, the curtains of which had not, fortunately, been completely closed. I was thus able to watch Cleave from a place of concealment.

For some minutes he glanced at Harry's prints; then he took a book from the shelves and began idly turning the pages. Stoker entered with a scotch and soda on a silver tray; as he retired I heard a car pull up at the front door. That would be Olive, I thought. Sure enough, a few moments later Stoker showed Olive Babblehump into the library.

Cleave looked extremely handsome in evening clothes. His dinner jacket was impeccably tailored, and brought out, as his cricketing whites did not, the darkness of his hair and eyes, so striking against the chalky pallor of his skin. He turned, then, his long white face, his blackly smoldering eyes, upon Olive, and the old trout positively melted. Olive, dressed for dinner, I should remark here, is a quite alarming sight—with bare shoulders, bare throat, and bare arms, there seem to be simply *acres* of slackly withered, pinkly powdered, diamond-dripping flesh; she heaves and wobbles about the place like a prize turkey, glittering richly from a hundred stones—but Cleave did not back off in alarm, as I'd seen other young men do when Olive took a fancy to them, nor did he merely stand his ground; he *advanced*, rather, he moved in, and I almost cried out to the silly woman to beware, beware—but that would have ruined everything.

Olive has only one breast, but that was enough for Cleave. I could not hear what was said, but something was said, and whatever it was it did for poor Olive. To my utter incredulity at the sheer brazenness of the creature, Cleave took her in his arms and nuzzled her throat with apparent ardor. Olive threw her head back. She was soon, I could tell, uttering small moans, a clawlike hand clutching each of Cleave's shoulders (for they were, as I've said, exactly the same height). The next thing was, he was after her breast! Then he had it right out of her gown, and was *at it* with his teeth—while Olive, with an *almighty* shudder, rolled her head from side to side, and heaved and panted, clutching at him as her withered flesh wobbled and rippled with grotesque lust. But then, quite suddenly, she clicked her head into an upright position and opened her eyes—and what a shock she gave me! For her eyes were *red*—not merely bloodshot, as I've often seen them of a morning, but a furious, incandescent red, just as Cleave's were when he was bowling at Charles. But what was worse, much worse, was the fact that those horrible eyes of hers were gazing *straight at me*—for in my distraction I was standing in full view outside the window, in the gap between the curtains!

Olive and I stared at one another as though the window were a mirror—and she and I were one, identical, the same! Thus we stood for a timeless moment, frozen in guilty complicity as the monster went about his foul and carnal work. When at last he lifted his head I slipped away, and he did not see me. I let myself in by the back door, and stole up to my room by the back stairs, and leaned against my bedroom door with my heart pounding fit to burst.

There was a slightly uncomfortable moment when I met Olive in the drawing room ten minutes later. Her eyes were back to their usual color, and her breast was back in her gown, but the change in her was obvious to me. She behaved quite normally (insofar as Olive Babblehump could ever be said to behave normally) but nonetheless I knew. And she knew I knew. It was, I think you'll agree, a rather delicate situation.

Cricket, quite naturally, was the topic of conversation at table. We had a very nice side of roast beef which Harry, after removing the skewer, carved and served with his usual skill and joviality. Stoker was kept busy with the claret as we all, for one reason or another, were drinking deeply that night. The new potatoes were very tasty, and so were the peas, which came from the garden. A simple meal, but I like to think—and Harry is with me on this—that it can be favorably compared to anything the French might produce. Was Cleave, I suddenly wondered, a *Frenchman*? No; I remembered then that he was a Hungarian. God alone knows what they eat.

Hilary was looking very lovely in a pale blue gown that nicely complemented her slender figure and set off her fair complexion to advantage. I'd talked to her before we came down, and tried to warn her about Cleave. I'm afraid I wasn't very successful; I didn't want to terrify the child, and to my rather veiled warnings she responded with a brisk impatience and told me I must take my pills. As if this were any time for pills!

Stoker served us with his usual stately phlegm, and Harry appeared to be in good form. Harry was actually quite a good talker, once upon a time; his mind has a distinctly metaphysical cast, but unfortunately it has rarely had a chance to assert itself this last decade or so, what with the hunting and the claret. But for Cleave's benefit he tossed out a few ideas, and they were sufficient to get the talk going, and permitted Harry gradually to shift his attention from the conversation, to the roast beef, to the wine, where it lingered for the remainder of the meal. "Cricket," he rumbled at one stage, "is much more than a game, of course. I should call it an idyll, myself—a rural scene of peace, simplicity, and goodness."

There was a moment's silence; nobody, as I say, had heard Harry say such a thing for at least fifteen years. "What do you think of that, Olive?" he boomed, his face growing red. Olive and Harry, you see, have this running charade; when they're drinking, which they usually are, unless Harry's on his horse, he acts the dashing chevalier, she the belle dame. It's pathetic, really, but it gives him pleasure. This evening, however, Olive wasn't playing. She only had eyes for Cleave, which wasn't really fair to Harry.

"Oh, I quite agree, Sir Harry," said Cleave. "Cricket symbolizes human activity in an ideal society, a society bound by love, where law provides merely a frame. All else is art—harmony—the civilized struggle of man and man in a spirit entirely ludic. It's how the Greeks made war."

"Fancy," said Olive, with some vulgarity, her eyes still burning upon the clever little monster. Oh, I know you, Olive Babblehump, I thought, you only want to be *feasted upon* by this creature. But there was a flaw in his argument, and the flaw was this: there is an evil that can play the game too, and you, Cleave, I said to myself, are it. I did not announce this, of course; perhaps I should have. The idea would have been alien to Harry, and even more so to Hilary and Charles. Olive alone would know what I meant by *an evil that plays the game*—but she had already succumbed.

I crept into his room late that night after everyone had gone to bed. I half expected to find him wide awake and preparing for his nocturnal depredations. What I should have done then I have no idea; something, I trusted, would have occurred to me. I had a few religious artifacts with me but no garlic, as we don't use it in the kitchen; and for the rest, I thought, well, maybe I can *talk* him out of it. Promise him my silence if he'll simply prey on some other family. I was even prepared, I'm not ashamed to admit it, to offer *myself* to him, if only he'd spare Hilary. To such lengths will a mother go when danger threatens. Fortunately it did not come to that; he was asleep.

How beautiful he was in sleep! One could understand why Olive had succumbed so quickly. I myself was tempted, I was sorely tempted, but my resolve held. I hit him extremely hard on the head with a piece of metal piping that the plumbers had left behind, and then with a croquet mallet I hammered the meat skewer right through his heart. What a horrible mess it made.

Harry found me there about half an hour later. Poor Harry, he was quite distressed. He thought it a bit "off." Not quite "the thing," he said. Not cricket.

I'm in the asylum now, for killing Cleave the vampire, and *that's* not cricket if you ask me. Still, it's not so bad. They've put me on the same ward as Diana Babblehump and we've started a bridge club. Olive visits regularly and smuggles in gin, bless her. But she's not to be trusted, not since Cleave got at her. I've tried to warn Hilary about her, but she thinks I'm mad. Poor girl, she does make me fret. I haven't taken my medication for days, I'm so worried about her. Olive was wrong about the medical superintendent; he's not a nice man, not a nice man at all. He's Irish, and he plays golf, and I noticed yesterday that his eyes turn red when he thinks nobody's looking.

THE SWORDS

ROBERT AICKMAN

"You know how, at the best, a tiny thing can make all the difference in your feeling about a woman, and I was far from sure that this thing was tiny at all."

It is with extreme pleasure that I find myself in the position of introducing perhaps even one new reader to the work of Robert Aickman. For he is a modern writer, revered by aficionados of horror and yet almost unknown to the world at large, whom I find personifies all the seductive power of Strangeness, of that state of not-knowing—of never knowing, in fact—that causes us to hunger, always, for more. And what he accomplishes with each of his elegantly wrought stories is to make us believe utterly in a sort of immediately recognizable parallel universe where one often has more to fear from the pathetically grotesque than the hugely monstrous.

Here, a young commercial traveler, putting up for the night in an English provincial town, discovers a shabby touring carnival in which a bizarre sideshow invites audience participation. However, his inability to resist the lure of a private performance proves his downfall; afterward, I'm afraid, one's notion of sexual penetration can never be quite the same.

Meanwhile, Aickman, employing his usual carefully offhand style, coolly delights in the reader's astonishment and in his own perversity.

———————————————

Corazón malherido
Por cinco espadas

FEDERICO GARCÍA LORCA

My first experience?

My first experience was far more of a test than anything that has ever happened to me since in that line. Not more agreeable, but certainly more testing. I have noticed several times that it is to beginners that strange things happen, and often, I think, to beginners only. When you know about a thing, there's just nothing to it. This kind of thing included—anyway, in most cases. After the first six women, say, or seven, or eight, the rest come much of a muchness.

I was a beginner all right; raw as a spring onion. What's more, I was a real mother's boy: scared stiff of life, and crass ignorant. Not that I want to sound disrespectful to my old mother. She's as good as they come, and I still hit it off better with her than with most other females.

She had a brother, my Uncle Elias. I should have said that we're all supposed to be descended from one of the big pottery families, but I don't know how true it is. My gran had little bits of pot to prove it, but it's always hard to be sure. After my dad was killed in an accident, my mother asked my Uncle Elias to take me into his business. He was a grocery salesman in a moderate way—and nothing but cheap lines. He said I must first learn the ropes by going out on the road. My mother was thoroughly upset because of my dad having died in a smash, and because she thought I was bound to be in moral danger, but there was nothing she could do about it, and on the road I went.

It was true enough about the moral danger, but I was too simple and too scared to involve myself. As far as I could, I steered clear even of the other chaps I met who were on the road with me. I was pretty certain they would be bad influences, and I was always bound to be the baby of the party anyway. I was dead rotten at selling and I was utterly lonely—not just in a manner of speaking, but truly lonely. I hated the life but Uncle Elias had promised to see me all right and I couldn't think of what else to do. I stuck it on the road for more than two years, and then I heard of my present job with the building society—read about it, actually, in the local paper—so that I was able to tell Uncle Elias what he could do with his cheap groceries.

For most of the time we stopped in small hotels—some of them weren't bad either, both the room and the grub—but in a few towns there were special lodgings known to Uncle Elias, where I and Uncle Elias's regular traveler, a sad chap called Bantock, were ordered by Uncle Elias to go. To this day I don't know exactly why. At the time I was quite sure that there was some kickback for my uncle in it, which was the obvious thing to suppose, but I've come since to wonder if the old girls who kept the lodgings might not have been my uncle's fancy women in the more or less distant past. At least once, I got as far as asking Bantock about it, but he merely said he didn't know what the answer was. There was very little that Bantock admitted to knowing about anything beyond the current prices of soap flakes and scotch. He had been forty-two years on the road for my uncle when one day he dropped dead of a thrombosis in Rochdale. Mrs. Bantock, at least, had been one of my uncle's women off and on for years. That was something everyone knew.

These women who kept the lodgings certainly behaved as if what I've said was true. You've never seen or heard such dives. Noises all night so that it was impossible to sleep properly, and often half-dressed tarts beating on your door and screaming that they'd been swindled or strangled. Some of the travelers even brought in boys, which is something I have never been able to understand. You read about it and hear about it, and I've often seen it happen, as I say, but I still don't understand it. And there was I in the middle of it all, pure and unspotted. The woman who kept the place often cheeked me for it. I don't know how old Bantock got on. I never found myself in one of these places at the same time as he was there. But the funny part was that my mother thought I was extra safe in one of these special lodgings, because they were all particularly guaranteed by her brother, who made Bantock and me go to them for our own good.

Of course it was only on some of the nights on the road. But always it was when I was quite alone. I noticed that at the time when Bantock was providing me with a few introductions and openings, they were always in towns where we could stay in commercial hotels. All the same, Bantock had to go to these special places when the need arose, just as much as I did, even though he never would talk about them.

One of the towns where there was a place on Uncle Elias's list was Wolverhampton. I fetched up there for the first time after I had been on the job for perhaps four or five months. It was by no means my first of these lodgings, but for that very reason my heart sank all the more as I set eyes on the place and was let in by the usual bleary-eyed cow in curlers and a dirty overall.

There was absolutely nothing to do. Nowhere even to sit and watch the telly. All you could think of was to go out and get drunk, or bring someone in with you from the pictures. Neither idea appealed very much to me, and I found myself just wandering about the town. It must have been late spring or early summer, because it was pleasantly warm, though not too hot, and still only dusk when I had finished my tea, which I had to find in a café, because the lodging did not even provide tea.

I was strolling about the streets of Wolverhampton, with all the girls giggling at me, or so it seemed, when I came upon a sort of small fair. Not knowing the town at all, I had drifted into the run-down area up by the old canal. The main streets were quite wide, but they had been laid out for daytime traffic to the different works and railway yards, and were now quiet and empty, except for the occasional lorry and the boys and girls playing around at some of the corners. The narrow streets running off contained lines of small houses, but a lot of the houses were empty, with windows broken or boarded up, and holes in the roof. I should have turned back, but for the sound made by the fair; not pop songs on the amplifiers, and not the pounding of the old steam organs, but more a sort of high tinkling, which somehow fitted in with the warm evening and the rosy twilight. I couldn't at first make out what the noise was, but I had nothing else to do, very much not, and I looked around the empty back streets, until I could find what was going on.

It proved to be a very small fair indeed; just half a dozen stalls, where a few kids were throwing rings or shooting off toy rifles, two or three covered booths, and, in the middle, one very small roundabout. It was this that made the tinkling music. The roundabout *looked* pretty too; with snow queen and icing sugar effects in the center, and different colored sleighs going round, each just big enough for two, and each, as I remember, with a colored light high up at the peak. And in the middle was a very pretty blond girl dressed as some kind of Pierrette. Anyway she seemed very pretty at that time to me. Her job was to collect the money from the people riding in the sleighs, but the trouble was that there weren't any. Not a single one. There weren't many people about at all, and inevitably the girl caught my eye. I felt I looked a charley as I had no one to ride with, and I just turned away. I shouldn't have dared to ask the girl herself to ride with me, and I imagine she wouldn't have been allowed to in any case. Unless, perhaps, it was her roundabout.

The fair had been set up on a plot of land which was empty simply because the houses which had stood on it had been demolished or just fallen down. Tall, blank factory walls towered up on two sides of it, and the ground was so rough and uneven that it was like walking on lumpy rocks at the seaside. There was nothing in the least permanent about the fair. It was very much here today and gone tomorrow. I should not have wondered if it had had no real business to have set up there at all. I doubted very much if it had come to any kind of agreement for the use of the land. I thought at once that the life must be a hard one for those who owned the fair. You could see why fairs like that have so largely died out from what things used to be in my gran's day, who was always talking about the wonderful fairs and circuses when she was a girl. Such customers as there were, were almost all mere kids, even though kids do have most of the money nowadays. These kids were doing a lot of their spending at a tiny stall where a drab-looking woman was selling ice cream and toffee apples. I thought it would have been much simpler and more profitable to concentrate on that, and enter the catering business rather than trying to provide entertainment for people who prefer to get it in their houses. But very probably I was in a gloomy frame of mind that evening. The fair was pretty and old-fashioned, but no one could say it cheered you up.

The girl on the roundabout could still see me, and I was sure was looking at me reproachfully—and probably contemptuously as well. With that layout, she was in the middle of things and impossible to get away from. I should just have mooched off, especially since the people running the different stalls were all beginning to shout at me, as pretty well the only full adult in sight, when, going round, I saw a booth in more or less the farthest corner, where the high factory walls made an angle. It was a square tent of very dirty red and white striped canvas, and over the crumpled entrance flap was a rough-edged, dark-painted, horizontal board, with written on it in faint gold capital letters THE SWORDS. That was all there was. Night was coming on fast, but there was no light outside the tent and none shining through from inside. You might have thought it was a store of some kind.

For some reason, I put out my hand and touched the hanging flap. I am sure I should never have dared actually to draw it aside and peep in. But a touch was enough. The flap was pulled back at once, and a young man stood there, sloping his head to one side so as to draw me in. I could see at once that some kind of show was going on. I did not really want to watch it, but felt that I should look a complete imbecile if I just ran away across the fairground, small though it was.

"Two bob," said the young man, dropping the dirty flap and sticking out his other hand, which was equally dirty. He wore a green sweater, mended but still with holes, grimy gray trousers, and grimier sandals. Sheer dirt was so much my first impression of the place that I might well have fled after all, had I felt it possible. I had not noticed this kind of griminess about the rest of the fair.

Running away, however, wasn't on. There were so few people inside. Dotted about the bare, bumpy ground, with bricks and broken glass sticking out from the hard earth, were twenty or thirty wooden chairs, none of them seeming to match, most of them broken or defective in one way or another, all of them chipped and off-color. Scattered among these hard chairs was an audience of seven. I know it was seven, because I had no difficulty in counting, and because soon it mattered. I made the eighth. All of them were in single units and all were men: this time men and not boys. I think that I was the youngest among them, by quite a long way.

And the show was something I have never seen or heard of since. Nor even read of. Not exactly.

There was a sort of low platform of dark and discolored wood up against the back of the tent—probably right onto the factory walls outside. There was a burly chap standing on it, giving the spiel, in a pretty rough delivery. He had tight yellow curls, the color of cheap lemonade but turning gray, and a big red face, with a splay nose, and very dark red lips. He also had small eyes and ears. The ears didn't seem exactly opposite one another, if you know what I mean. He wasn't much to look at, though I felt he was very strong and could probably have taken on all of us in the tent single-handed and come out well on top. I couldn't decide how old he was—either then or later. (Yes, I did see him again—twice.) I should imagine he was nearing fifty, and he didn't look in particularly good condition, but it seemed as though he had just been made with more thew and muscle than most people are. He was dressed like the youth at the door, except that the sweater of the chap on the platform was not green but dark blue, as if he were a seaman, or perhaps acting one. He wore the same dirty gray trousers and sandals as the other man. You might almost have thought the place was some kind of boxing booth.

But it wasn't. On the chap's left (and straight ahead of where I sat at the edge of things and in the back row) a girl lay sprawled out facing us in an upright canvas chair, as faded and battered as everything else in the outfit. She was dressed up like a French chorus, in a tight and shiny black thing, cut low, and black fishnet stockings, and those shiny black shoes with super high heels that many men go for in such a big way. But the total effect was not particularly sexy, all the same. The different bits of costume had all seen better days, like everything else, and the girl herself looked more sick than spicy. Under other conditions, I thought to begin with, she might have been pretty enough, but she had made herself up with green powder, actually choosing it, apparently, or having it chosen for her, and her hair, done in a tight bun, like a ballet dancer's, was not so much mousy as plain colorless. On top of all this, she was lying over the chair, rather than sitting in it, just as if she was feeling faint or about to be ill. Certainly she was doing nothing at all to lead the chaps on. Not that I myself should have wanted to be led. Or so I thought at the start.

And in front of her, at the angle of the platform, was this pile of swords. They were stacked crisscross, like cheese straws, on top of a low stool, square and black, the sort of thing they make in Sedgeley and Wednesfield and sell as Japanese, though this specimen was quite plain and undecorated, even though more than a bit chipped. There must have been thirty or forty swords, as the pile had four corners to it, where the hilts of the swords were set diagonally above one another. It struck me later that perhaps there was one sword for each seat, in case there was ever a full house in the tent.

If I had not seen the notice outside, I might not have realized they *were* swords, or not at first. There was nothing gleaming about them, and nothing decorative. The blades were a dull gray, and the hilts were made of some black stuff, possibly even plastic. They looked thoroughly mass-produced and industrial, and I could not think where they might have been got. They were not fencing foils but something much solider, and the demand for real swords nowadays must be mainly ceremonial, and less and less even of that. Possibly these swords came from suppliers for the stage, though I doubt that too. Anyway, they were thoroughly dingy swords, no credit at all to the regiment.

I do not know how long the show had been going on before I arrived, or if the man in the seaman's sweater had offered any explanations. Almost the first thing I heard was him saying, "And now, gentlemen, which of you is going to be the first?"

There was no movement or response of any kind. Of course there never is.

"Come *on*," said the seaman, not very politely. I felt that he was so accustomed to the backwardness of his audiences that he was no longer prepared to pander to it. He did not strike me as a man of many words, even though speaking appeared to be his job. He had a strong accent, which I took to be Black

Country, though I wasn't in a position properly to be sure at that time of my life, and being myself a Londoner.

Nothing happened.

"What you think you've paid your money for?" cried the seaman, more truculent, I thought, than sarcastic.

"You tell us," said one of the men on the chairs. He happened to be the man nearest to me, though in front of me.

It was not a very clever thing to say, and the seaman turned it to account.

"You," he shouted, sticking out his thick, red forefinger at the man who had cheeked him. "Come along up. We've got to start somewhere."

The man did not move. I became frightened by my own nearness to him. I might be picked on next, and I did not even know what was expected of me, if I responded.

The situation was saved by the appearance of a volunteer. At the other side of the tent, a man stood up and said, "I'll do it."

The only light in the tent came from a single Tilley lamp hissing away (none too safely, I thought) from the crosspiece of the roof, but the volunteer looked to me exactly like everyone else.

"At last," said the seaman, still rather rudely. "Come on then."

The volunteer stumbled across the rough ground, stepped onto my side of the small platform, and stood right in front of the girl. The girl seemed to make no movement. Her head was thrown so far back that, as she was some distance in front of me, I could not see her eyes at all clearly. I could not even be certain whether they were open or closed.

"Pick up a sword," said the seaman sharply.

The volunteer did so, in a rather gingerly way. It looked like the first time he had ever had his hand on such a thing, and, of course, I never had either. The volunteer stood there with the sword in his hand, looking an utter fool. His skin looked gray by the light of the Tilley, he was very thin, and his hair was failing badly.

The seaman seemed to let him stand there for quite a while, as if out of devilry, or perhaps resentment at the way he had to make a living. To me the atmosphere in the dirty tent seemed full of tension and unpleasantness, but the other men in the audience were still lying about on their hard chairs looking merely bored.

After quite a while, the seaman, who had been facing the audience, and speaking to the volunteer out of the corner of his mouth, half-turned on his heel, and still not looking right at the volunteer, snapped out: "What are you waiting for? There are others to come, though we could do with more."

At this, another member of the audience began to whistle "Why Are We Waiting?" I felt he was getting at the seaman or showman, or whatever he should be called, rather than at the volunteer.

"Go on," shouted the seaman, almost in the tone of a drill instructor. "Stick it in."

And then it happened, this extraordinary thing.

The volunteer seemed to me to tremble for a moment, and then plunged the sword right into the girl on the chair. As he was standing between me and her, I could not see where the sword entered, but I could see that the man seemed to press it right in, because almost the whole length of it seemed to disappear. What I could have no doubt about at all was the noise the sword made. A curious thing was that we were so used to at least the idea of people being stuck through with swords that, even though, naturally, I had never before seen anything of the kind, I had no doubt at all of what the man had done. The noise of the sword tearing through the flesh was only what I should have expected. But it was quite distinct even above the hissing of the Tilley. And quite long drawn out too. And horrible.

I could sense the other men in the audience gathering themselves together on the instant and suddenly coming to life. I could still see little of what precisely had happened.

"Pull it out," said the seaman, quite casually, but as if speaking to a moron. He was still only half-turned toward the volunteer, and still looking straight in front of him. He was not looking at anything; just holding himself in control while getting through a familiar routine.

The volunteer pulled out the sword. I could again hear that unmistakable sound.

The volunteer still stood facing the girl, but with the tip of the sword resting on the platform. I could see no blood. Of course I thought I had made some complete misinterpretation, been fooled like a kid. Obviously it was some kind of conjuring.

"Kiss her if you want to," said the seaman. "It's included in what you've paid."

And the man did, even though I could only see his back. With the sword drooping from his hand, he leaned forward and downward. I think it was a slow and loving kiss, not a smacking and public kiss, because this time I could hear nothing.

The seaman gave the volunteer all the time in the world for it, and, for some odd reason, there was no whistling or catcalling from the rest of us; but in the end, the volunteer slowly straightened up.

"Please put back the sword," said the seaman, sarcastically polite.

The volunteer carefully returned it to the heap, going to some trouble to make it lie as before.

I could now see the girl. She was sitting up. Her hands were pressed together against her left side, where, presumably, the sword had gone in. But there was still no sign of blood, though it was hard to be certain in the bad light. And the strangest thing was that she now looked not only happy, with her eyes very wide open and a little smile on her lips, but, in spite of that green powder, beautiful too, which I was far from having thought in the first place.

The volunteer passed between the girl and me in order to get back to his seat. Even though the tent was almost empty, he returned to his original place religiously. I got a slightly better look at him. He still looked just like everyone else.

"Next," said the seaman, again like a sergeant numbering off.

This time there was no hanging back. Three men rose to their feet immediately, and the seaman had to make a choice.

"You then," he said, jabbing out his thick finger toward the center of the tent.

The man picked was elderly, bald, plump, respectable-looking, and wearing a dark suit. He might have been a retired railway foreman or electricity inspector. He had a slight limp, probably taken in the way of his work.

The course of events was very much the same, but the second comer was readier and in less need of prompting, including about the kiss. His kiss was as slow and quiet as the first man's had been: paternal perhaps. When the elderly man stepped away, I saw that the girl was holding her two hands against the center of her stomach. It made me squirm to look.

And then came the third man. When he went back to his seat, the girl's hands were to her throat.

The fourth man, on the face of it a rougher type, with a cloth cap (which, while on the platform, he never took off) and a sports jacket as filthy and worn out as the tent, apparently drove the sword into the girl's left thigh, straight through the fishnet stocking. When he stepped off the platform, she was clasping her leg, but looking so pleased that you'd have thought a great favor had been done her. And still I could see no blood.

I did not really know whether or not I wanted to see more of the details. Raw as I was, it would have been difficult for me to decide.

I didn't have to decide, because I dared not shift in any case to a seat with a better view. I considered that a move like that would quite probably result in my being the next man the seaman called up. And one thing I knew for certain was that whatever exactly was being done, I was not going to be one who did it. Whether it was conjuring, or something different that I knew nothing about, I was not going to get involved.

And, of course, if I stayed, my turn must be coming close in any case.

Still, the fifth man called was not me. He was a tall, lanky, perfectly black Negro. I had not especially spotted him as such before. He appeared to drive the sword in with all the force you might expect of a black man, even though he was so slight, then threw it on the floor of the platform with a clatter, which no one else had done before him, and actually drew the girl to her feet when kissing her. When he stepped back, his foot struck the sword. He paused for a second, gazing at the girl, then carefully put the sword back on the heap.

The girl was still standing, and it passed across my mind that the Negro might try to kiss her again. But he didn't. He went quietly back to his place. Behind the scenes of it all, there appeared to be some rules, which all the other men knew about. They behaved almost as though they came quite often to the show, if a show was what it was.

Sinking down once more into her dilapidated canvas chair,

the girl kept her eyes fixed on mine. I could not even tell what color her eyes were, but the fact of the matter is that they turned my heart right over. I was so simple and inexperienced that nothing like that had ever happened to me before in my whole life. The incredible green powder made no difference. Nothing that had just been happening made any difference. I wanted that girl more than I had ever wanted anything. And I don't mean I just wanted her body. That comes later in life. I wanted to love her and tousle her and all the other, better things we want before the time comes when we know that however much we want them, we're not going to get them.

But, in justice to myself, I must say that I did not want to take my place in a queue for her.

That was about the last thing I wanted. And it was one chance in three that I should be next to be called. I drew a deep breath and managed to scuttle out. I can't pretend it was difficult. I was sitting near the back of the tent, as I've said, and no one tried to stop me. The lad at the entrance merely gaped at me like a fish. No doubt he was quite accustomed to the occasional patron leaving early. I fancied that the bruiser on the platform was in the act of turning to me at the very instant I got up, but I knew it was probably imagination on my part. I don't think he spoke, nor did any of the other men react. Most men at shows of that kind prefer to behave as if they were invisible. I did get mixed up in the greasy tent flap, and the lad in the green sweater did nothing to help, but that was all. I streaked across the fairground, still almost deserted, and still with the roundabout tinkling away, all for nothing, but very prettily. I tore back to my nasty bedroom and locked myself in.

On and off, there was the usual fuss and schemozzle in the house, and right through the hours of darkness. I know, because I couldn't sleep. I couldn't have slept that night if I'd been lying between damask sheets in the Hilton Hotel. The girl on the platform had got deep under my skin, green face and all: the girl and the show too, of course. I think I can truly say that what I experienced that night altered my whole angle on life, and it had nothing to do with the rows that broke out in the other bedrooms, or the cackling and bashing on the staircase, or the constant pulling the plug, which must have been the noisiest in the Midlands, especially as it took six or seven pulls or more for each flush. That night I really grasped the fact that most of the time we have no notion of what we really want, or we lose sight of it. And the even more important fact that what we really want just doesn't fit in with life as a whole, or very seldom. Most folk learn slowly, and never altogether learn at all. I seemed to learn all at once.

Or perhaps not quite, because there was very much more to come.

The next morning I had calls to make, but well before the time arrived for the first of them I had sneaked back to that tiny, battered, little fairground. I even skipped breakfast, but breakfast in Uncle Elias's special lodging was very poor anyway, though a surprising number turned up for it each day. You wondered where so many had been hiding away all night. I don't know what I expected to find at the fair. Perhaps I wasn't sure I should find the fair there at all.

But I did. In full daylight, it looked smaller, sadder, and more utterly hopeless for making a living even than the night before. The weather was absolutely beautiful, and so many of the houses in the immediate area were empty, to say nothing of the factories, that there were very few people around. The fair itself was completely empty, which took me by surprise. I had expected some sort of Gypsy scene and had failed to realize that there was nowhere on the lot for even Gypsies to sleep. The people who worked the fair must have gone to bed at home, like the rest of the world. The plot of land was surrounded by a wire-mesh fence, put up by the owner to keep out tramps and meth drinkers, but by now the fence wasn't up to much, as you would expect, and, after looking round, I had no difficulty in scrambling through a hole in it, which the lads of the village had carved out for fun and from having nothing better to do. I walked over to the dingy booth in the far corner and tried to lift the flap.

It proved to have been tied up at several places and apparently from the inside. I could not see how the person doing the tying had got out of the tent when he had finished, but that was the sort of trick of the trade you would expect of fairground folk. I found it impossible to see inside the tent at all without using my pocketknife, which I should have hesitated to do at the best of times, but while I was fiddling around, I heard a voice just behind me.

"What's up with you?"

There was a very small, old man standing at my back. I had certainly not heard him come up, even though the ground was so rough and lumpy. He was hardly more than a dwarf, he was as brown as a horse chestnut or very nearly, and there was not a hair on his head.

"I wondered what was inside," I said feebly.

"A great big python, two miles long, that don't even pay its rent," said the little man.

"How's that?" I asked. "Hasn't it a following?"

"Old-fashioned," said the little man. "Old-fashioned and out of date. Doesn't appeal to the women. The women don't like the big snakes. But the women have the money these times, *and* the power and the glory too." He changed his tone. "You're trespassing."

"Sorry, old man," I said. "I couldn't hold myself back on a lovely morning like this."

"I'm the watchman," said the little man. "I used to have snakes too. Little ones, dozens and dozens of them. All over me, and every one more poisonous than the next. Eyes darting, tongues flicking, scales shimmering: then *in*, right home, then back, then in again, then back. Still in the end, it wasn't a go. There's a time and a span for all things. But I like to keep around. So now I'm the watchman. While the job lasts. While anything lasts. Move on then. Move on."

I hesitated.

"This big snake you talk of," I began, "this python—"

But he interrupted quite shrilly.

"There's no more to be said. Not to the likes of you, any road. Off the ground you go, and sharply. Or I'll call the police constable. He and I work hand in glove. I take care to keep it that way. You may not have heard that trespass is a breach of the peace. Stay here and you'll be sorry for the rest of your life."

The little man was actually squaring up to me, even though the top of his brown skull (not shiny, by the way, but matte and patchy, as if he had some trouble with it) rose hardly above my waist. Clearly, he was daft.

As I had every kind of reason for going, I went. I did not even ask the little man about the times of performances that that evening, or if there were any. Inside myself, I had no idea whether I should be back, even if there were performances, as there probably were.

I set about my calls. I'd had no sleep, and, since last night's tea, no food, and my head was spinning like a top, but I won't say I did my business any worse than usual. I probably felt at the time that I did, but now I doubt it. Private troubles, I have since noticed, make very little difference to the way most of us meet the outside world, and as for food and sleep, they don't matter at all until weeks and months have passed.

I pushed on then, more or less in the customary way (though, in my case, the customary way, at that job, wasn't up to very much at the best of times), and all the while mulling over and around what had happened to me, until the time came for dinner. I had planned to eat in the café where I had eaten the night before, but I found myself in a different part of the city, which, of course, I didn't know at all, and, feeling rather faint and queer, fell instead into the first place there was.

And there, in the middle of the floor, believe it or not, sitting at a Formica-topped table, was my girl with the green powder, and, beside her, the seaman or showman, looking more than ever like a run-down boxer.

I had not seriously expected ever to set eyes on the girl again. It was not, I thought, the kind of thing that happens. At the very most I might have gone again to the queer show, but I don't think I really would have, when I came to think out what it involved.

The girl had wiped off the green powder, and was wearing a black coat and skirt and a white blouse, a costume you might perhaps have thought rather too old for her, and the same fishnet stockings. The man was dressed exactly as he had been the night before, except that he wore heavy boots instead of dirty sandals, heavy and mud-caked, as if he had been walking through fields.

Although it was the dinner hour, the place was almost empty, with a dozen unoccupied tables, and these two sitting in the center. I must almost have passed out.

But I wasn't really given time. The man in the jersey recognized me at once. He stood up and beckoned to me with his thick arm. "Come and join us." The girl had stood up too.

There was nothing else I could do but what he said.

The man actually drew back a chair for me (they were all painted in different, bright colors, and had been reseated in new leatherette), and even the girl waited until I had sat down before sitting down herself.

"Sorry you missed the end of last night's show," said the man.

"I had to get back to my lodgings, I suddenly realized." I made it up quite swiftly. "I'm new to the town," I added.

"It can be difficult when you're new," said the man. "What'll you have?"

He spoke as if we were on licensed premises, but it was pretty obvious we weren't, and I hesitated.

"Tea or coffee?"

"Tea, please," I said.

"Another tea, Berth," called out the man. I saw that the two of them were both drinking coffee, but I didn't like the look of it, any more than I usually do.

"I'd like something to eat as well," I said, when the waitress brought the tea. "Thank you very much," I said to the man.

"Sandwiches: York ham, salt beef, or luncheon meat. Pies. Sausage rolls," said the waitress. She had a very bad stye on her left lower eyelid.

"I'll have a pie," I said, and, in due course, she brought a cold one, with some salad on the plate, and the bottle of sauce. I really required something hot, but there it was.

"Come again tonight," said the man.

"I'm not sure I'll be able to."

I was finding it difficult even to drink my tea properly, as my hands were shaking so badly, and I couldn't think how I should cope with a cold pie.

"Come on the house, if you like. As you missed your turn last night."

The girl, who had so far left the talking to the other, smiled at me very sweetly and personally, as if there was something quite particular between us. Her white blouse was open very low, so that I saw more than I really should, even though things are quite different today from what they once were.

Even without the green powder, she was a very pale girl, and her body looked as if it might be even whiter than her face, almost as white as her blouse. Also I could now see the color of her eyes. They were green. Somehow I had known it all along.

"In any case," went on the man, "it won't make much difference with business like it is now."

The girl glanced at him as if she were surprised at his letting out something private, then looked at me again and said, "Do come." She said it in the friendliest, meltingest way, as if she really cared. What's more, she seemed to have some kind of foreign accent, which made her even more fascinating, if that were possible. She took a small sip of coffee.

"It's only that I might have another engagement that I couldn't get out of. I don't know right now."

"We mustn't make you break another engagement," said the girl, in her foreign accent, but sounding as if she meant just the opposite.

I managed a bit more candor. "I might get out of my engagement," I said, "but the truth is, if you don't mind my saying so, that I didn't greatly care for some of the others in the audience last night."

"I don't blame you," said the man very dryly, and rather to my relief, as you can imagine. "What would you say to a private show? A show just for you?" He spoke quite quietly, suggesting it as if it had been the most normal thing in the world, or as if I had been Charles Clore.

I was so taken by surprise that I blurted out, "What! Just me in the tent?"

"In your own home, I meant," said the man, still absolutely casually, and taking a noisy pull on his pink earthenware cup. As the man spoke, the girl shot a quick, devastating glance. It was exactly as if she softened everything inside me to water. And, absurdly enough, it was then that my silly pie arrived, with the bit of green salad, and the sauce. I had been a fool to ask for anything at all to eat, however much I might have needed it in theory.

"With or without the swords," continued the man, lighting a cheap-looking cigarette. "Madonna has been trained to do anything else you want. Anything you may happen to think of." The girl was gazing into her teacup.

I dared to speak directly to her. "Is your name really Madonna? It's nice."

"No," she said, speaking rather low. "Not really. It's my working name." She turned her head for a moment, and again our eyes met.

"There's no harm in it. We're not Catholics," said the man, "though Madonna was once."

"I like it," I said. I was wondering what to do about the pie. I could not possibly eat.

"Of course a private show would cost a bit more than two bob," said the man. "But it would be all to yourself, and, under those conditions, Madonna will do anything you feel like." I noticed that he was speaking just as he had spoken in the tent: looking not at me or at anyone else, but straight ahead into the distance, and as if he were repeating words he had used again and again and was fed up with but compelled to make use of.

I was about to tell him I had no money, which was more or less the case, but didn't.

"When could it be?" I said.

"Tonight, if you like," said the man. "Immediately after the regular show, and that won't be very late, as we don't do a ten or eleven o'clock house at a date like this. Madonna could be with you at a quarter to ten, easy. And she wouldn't necessarily have to hurry away either, not when there's no late-night matinée. There'd be time for her to do a lot of her novelties if you'd care to see them. Items from her repertoire, as we call them. Got a good place for it, by the way? Madonna doesn't need much. Just a room with a lock on the door to keep out the nonpaying patrons, and somewhere to wash her hands."

"Yes," I said. "As a matter of fact, the place I'm stopping at should be quite suitable, though I wish it was brighter, and a bit quieter too."

Madonna flashed another of her indescribably sweet glances at me. "I shan't mind," she said softly.

I wrote down the address on the corner of a paper I had found on my seat, and tore it off.

"Shall we call it ten pounds?" said the man, turning to look at me with his small eyes. "I usually ask twenty and sometimes fifty, but this is Wolverhampton not the Costa Brava, and you belong to the refined type."

"What makes you say that?" I asked, mainly in order to gain time for thinking what I could do about the money.

"I could tell by where you sat last night. At pretty well every show there's someone who picks that seat. It's a special seat for the refined types. I've learnt better now than to call them up, because it's not what they want. They're too refined to be called up, and I respect them for it. They often leave before the end, as you did. But I'm glad to have them in at any time. They raise the standard. Besides, they're the ones who are often interested in a private show, as you are, and willing to pay for it. I have to watch the business of the thing too."

"I haven't got ten pounds ready in spare cash," I said, "but I expect I can find it, even if I have to fiddle it."

"It's what you often have to do in this world," said the man. "Leastways if you like nice things."

"You've still got most of the day," said the girl, smiling encouragingly.

"Have another cup of tea?" said the man.

"No, thanks very much."

"Sure?"

"Sure."

"Then we must move. We've an afternoon show, though it'll probably be only for a few kids. I'll tell Madonna to save herself as much as she can until the private affair tonight."

As they were going through the door on to the street, the girl looked back to throw me a glance over her shoulder, warm and secret. But when she was moving about, her clothes looked much too big for her, the skirt too long, the jacket and blouse too loose and droopy, as if they were not really her clothes at all. On top of everything else, I felt sorry for her. Whatever the explanation of last night, her life could not be an easy one.

They'd both been too polite to mention my pie. I stuffed it into my attaché case, of course without the salad, paid for it, and dragged off to my next call, which proved to be right across the town once more.

I didn't have to do anything dishonest to get the money.

It was hardly to be expected that my mind would be much on my work that afternoon, but I stuck to it as best I could, feeling that my life was getting into deep waters and that I had better keep land of some kind within sight, while it was still possible.

It was as well that I did continue on my proper round of calls, because at one of the shops my immediate problem was solved for me without my having to lift a finger. The owner of the shop was a nice old gentleman with white hair, named Mr. Edis, who seemed to take to me the moment I went through the door. He said at one point that I made a change from old Bantock with his attacks of asthma (I don't think I've so far mentioned Bantock's asthma, but I knew all about it), and that I seemed a good lad, with a light in my eyes. Those were his words, and I'm not likely to make a mistake about them just yet, seeing what he went on to. He asked me if I had anything to do that evening. Rather pleased with myself, because it was not an answer I should have been able to make often before, not if I had been speaking the truth, I told him *Yes*, I had a date with a girl.

"Do you mean with a Wolverhampton girl?" asked Mr. Edis.

"Yes. I've only met her since I've been in the town." I shouldn't have admitted that to most people, but there was something about Mr. Edis that led me on and made me want to justify his good opinion of me.

"What's she like?" asked Mr. Edis, half closing his eyes, so that I could see the red all round the edges of them.

"Gorgeous." It was the sort of thing people said, and my real feelings couldn't possibly have been put into words.

"Got enough small change to treat her properly?"

I had to think quickly, being taken so much by surprise, but Mr. Edis went on before I had time to speak.

"So that you can cuddle her as you want?"

I could see that he was getting more and more excited.

"Well, Mr. Edis," I said, "as a matter of fact, not quite enough. I'm still a beginner in my job, as you know."

I thought I might get a pound out of him, and quite likely only as a loan, the Midlands people being what we all know they are.

But on the instant he produced a whole fiver. He flapped it in front of my nose like a kipper.

"It's yours on one condition."

"I'll fit in if I can, Mr. Edis."

"Come back tomorrow morning after my wife's gone out—

she works as a traffic warden, and can't hardly get enough of it—come back here and tell me all about what happens."

I didn't care for the idea at all, but I supposed that I could make up some lies, or even break my word and not go back at all, and I didn't seem to have much alternative.

"Why, of course, Mr. Edis. Nothing to it."

He handed over the fiver at once.

"Good boy," he said. "Get what you're paying for out of her, and think of me while you're doing it, though I don't expect you will."

As for the other five pounds, I could probably manage to wangle it out of what I had, by scraping a bit over the next week or two, and cooking the cash book a trifle if necessary, as we all do. Anyway, and being the age I was, I hated all this talk about money. I hated the talk about it much more than I hated the job of having to find it. I did not see Madonna in that sort of way at all, and I should have despised myself if I had. Nor, to judge by how she spoke, did it seem the way in which she saw me. I could not really think of any other way in which she would be likely to see me, but I settled that one by trying not to think about the question at all.

My Uncle Elias's special lodging in Wolverhampton was not the kind of place where visitors just rang the bell and waited to be admitted by the footman. You had to know the form a bit if you were to get in at all, not being a resident, and still more if, once inside, you were going to find the exact person you were looking for. At about half past nine I thought it best to start lounging around in the street outside. Not right on top of the house door, because that might have led to misunderstanding and trouble of some kind, but moving up and down the street, keeping both eyes open and an ear cocked for the patter of tiny feet on the pavement. It was almost dark, of course, but not quite. There weren't many people about but that was partly because it was raining gently, as it does in the Midlands: a soft, slow rain that you can hardly see, but extra wetting, or so it always feels. I am quite sure I should have taken up my position earlier if it hadn't been for the rain. Needless to say, I was like a cat on hot bricks. I had managed to get the pie inside me between calls during the afternoon. I struggled through it on a bench just as the rain was beginning. And at about half past six

I'd had a cup of tea and some beans in the café I'd been to the night before. I didn't want any of it. I just felt that I ought to eat something in view of what lay ahead of me. Though, of course, I had precious little idea of what that was. When it's truly your first experience, you haven't; no matter how much you've been told and managed to pick up. I'd have been in a bad state if it had been any woman that was supposed to be coming, let alone my lovely Madonna.

And there she was, on the dot, or even a little early. She was dressed in the same clothes she had worn that morning. Too big for her and too old for her; and she had no umbrella and no raincoat and no hat.

"You'll be wet," I said.

She didn't speak, but her eyes looked, I fancied, as if she were glad to see me. If she had set out in that green powder of hers, it had all washed off.

I thought she might be carrying something, but she wasn't, not even a handbag.

"Come in," I said.

Those staying in the house were lent a key (with a deposit to pay on it), and, thank God, we got through the hall and up the stairs without meeting anyone, or hearing anything out of the way, even though my room was at the top of the building.

She sat down on my bed and looked at the door. After what had been said, I knew what to do and turned the key. It came quite naturally. It was the sort of place where you turned the key as a matter of course. I took off my raincoat and let it lie in a corner. I had not turned on the light. I was not proud of my room.

"You must be soaked through," I said. The distance from the fairground was not all that great, but the rain was of the specially wetting kind, as I've remarked.

She got up and took off her outsize black jacket. She stood there holding it until I took it and hung it on the door. I can't say it actually dripped, but it was saturated, and I could see a wet patch on the eiderdown where she had been sitting. She had still not spoken a word. I had to admit that there seemed to have been no call for her to do so.

The rain had soaked through to her white blouse. Even with almost no light in the room I could see that. The shoulders were sodden and clinging to her, one more than the other. Without the jacket, the blouse looked quainter than ever. Not only was it loose and shapeless, but it had sleeves that were so long as to droop down beyond her hands when her jacket was off. In my mind I had a glimpse of the sort of woman the blouse was made for, big and stout, not my type at all.

"Better take that off too," I said, though I don't now know how I got the words out. I imagine that instinct looks after you even the first time, provided it is given a chance. Madonna did give me a chance, or I felt that she did. Life was sweeter for a minute or two than I had ever thought possible.

Without a word, she took off her blouse and I hung it over the back of the single bedroom chair.

I had seen in the café that under it she had been wearing something black, but I had not realized until now that it was the same tight, shiny sheath that she wore in the show, and that made her look so French.

She took off her wet skirt. The best I could do was to drape it over the seat of the chair. And there she was, super high heels and all. She looked ready to go onstage right away, but that I found rather disappointing.

She stood waiting, as if for me to tell her what do do.

I could see that the black sheath was soaking wet, anyway in patches, but this time I didn't dare to suggest that she take it off.

At last Madonna opened her mouth. "What would you like me to begin with?"

Her voice was so beautiful, and the question she asked so tempting, that something got hold of me and, before I could stop myself, I had put my arms round her. I had never done anything like it before in my whole life, whatever I might have felt.

She made no movement, so that I supposed at once I had done the wrong thing. After all, it was scarcely surprising, considering how inexperienced I was.

But I thought too that something else was wrong. As I say, I wasn't exactly accustomed to the feel of a half-naked woman, and I myself was still more or less fully dressed, but all the same I thought at once that the feel of her was disappointing. It came as a bit of a shock. Quite a bad one, in fact. As often, when facts replace fancies. Suddenly it had all become rather like a nightmare.

I stepped back.

"I'm sorry," I said.

She smiled in her same sweet way. "I don't mind," she said.

It was nice of her, but I no longer felt quite the same about her. You know how, at the best, a tiny thing can make all the difference in your feeling about a woman, and I was far from sure that this thing was tiny at all. What I was wondering was whether I wasn't proving not to be properly equipped for life. I had been called backward before now, and perhaps here was the reason.

Then I realized that it might all be something to do with the act she put on, the swords. She might be some kind of freak, or possibly the man in the blue jersey did something funny to her, hypnotized her, in some way.

"Tell me what you'd like," she said, looking down at the scruffy bit of rug on the floor.

I was a fool, I thought, and merely showing my ignorance.

"Take that thing off," I replied. "It's wet. Get into bed. You'll be warmer there."

I began taking off my own clothes.

She did what I said, squirmed out of the black sheath, took her feet gently out of the sexy shoes, rolled off her long stockings. Before me for a moment was my first woman, even though I could hardly see her. I was still unable to face the idea of love by that single, dim electric light, which only made the draggled room look more draggled.

Obediently, Madonna climbed into my bed and I joined her there as quickly as I could.

Obediently, she did everything I asked, just as the man in the blue sweater had promised. To me she still felt queer and disappointing—flabby might almost be the word—and certainly quite different from what I had always fancied a woman's body would feel like if ever I found myself close enough to it. But she gave me my first experience nonetheless, the thing we're concerned with now. I will say one thing for her: from first to last she never spoke an unnecessary word. It's not always like that, of course.

But everything had gone wrong. For example, we had not

even started by kissing. I had been cram full of romantic ideas about Madonna, but I felt that she was not being much help in that direction, for all her sweet and beautiful smiles and her soft voice and the gentle things she said. She was making herself almost too available, and not bringing out the best in me. It was as if I had simply acquired new information, however important, but without any exertion of my feelings. You often feel like that, of course, about one thing or another, but it seemed dreadful to feel it about this particular thing, especially when I had felt so differently about it only a little while before.

"Come on," I said to her. "Wake up."

It wasn't fair, but I was bitterly disappointed, and all the more because I couldn't properly make out why. I only felt that everything in my life might be at stake.

She moaned a little.

I heaved up from on top of her in the bed and threw back the bedclothes behind me. She lay there flat in front of me, all gray—anyway in the dim twilight. Even her hair was colorless, in fact pretty well invisible.

I did what I suppose was rather a wretched thing. I caught hold of her left arm by putting both my hands round her wrist, and tried to lug her up toward me, so that I could feel her thrown against me, and could cover her neck and front with kisses, if only she would make me want to. I suppose I might under any circumstances have hurt her by dragging at her like that, and that I shouldn't have done it. Still no one could have said it was very terrible. It was quite a usual sort of thing to do, I should say.

But what actually happened was very terrible indeed. So simple and so terrible that people won't always believe me. I gave this great, bad-tempered, disappointed pull at Madonna. She came up toward me and then fell back again with a sort of wail. I was still holding onto her hand and wrist with my two hands, and it took me quite some time to realize what had happened. What had happened was that I had pulled her left hand and wrist right off.

On the instant, she twisted out of the bed and began to wriggle back into her clothes. I was aware that even in the almost nonexistent light she was somehow managing to move very swiftly. I had a frightful sensation of her beating round in my room with only one hand, and wondered in terror how she could possibly manage. All the time, she was weeping to herself, or wailing might be the word. The noise she made was very soft, so soft that but for what was happening I might have thought it was inside my own head.

I got my feet onto the floor with the notion of turning on the light. The only switch was of course by the door. I had the idea that with some light on the scene, there might be certain explanations. But I found that I couldn't get to the switch. In the first place, I couldn't bear the thought of touching Madonna, even accidentally. In the second place, I discovered that my legs would go no farther. I was too utterly scared to move at all. Scared, repelled, and that mixed-up something else connected with disappointed sex for which there is no exact word.

So I just sat there, on the edge of the bed, while Madonna got back into her things, crying all the while, in that awful, heartbreaking way I shall never forget. Not that it went on for long. As I've said, Madonna was amazingly quick. I couldn't think of anything to say or do. Especially with so little time for it.

When she had put on her clothes, she made a single appallingly significant snatch in my direction, caught something up, almost as if she, at least, could see in the dark. Then she had unlocked the door and bolted.

She had left the door flapping open off the dark landing (we had time switches, of course), and I could hear her pat-patting down the staircase, and so easily and quietly through the front door that you might have thought she lived in the place. It was still a little too early for the regulars to be much in evidence.

What I felt now was physically sick. But I had the use of my legs once more. I got off the bed, shut and locked the door, and turned on the light.

There was nothing in particular to be seen. Nothing but my own clothes lying about, my sodden-looking raincoat in the corner, and the upheaved bed. The bed looked as if some huge monster had risen through it, but nowhere in the room was there blood. It was all just like the swords.

As I thought about it, and about what I had done, I suddenly vomited. They were not rooms with hot and cold running water, and I half-filled the old-fashioned washbowl, with its faded flowers at the bottom and big thumbnail chippings round the rim, before I had finished.

I lay down on the crumpled bed, too fagged to empty the basin, to put out the light, even to draw something over me, though I was still naked and the night getting colder.

I heard the usual sounds beginning on the stairs and in the other rooms. Then, there was an unexpected, businesslike rapping at my own door.

It was not the sort of house where it was much use first asking who was there. I got to my feet again, this time frozen stiff, and, not having a dressing gown with me, put on my wet raincoat, as I had to put on something and get the door open, or there would be more knocking, and then complaints, which could be most unpleasant.

It was the chap in the blue sweater—the seaman or showman or whatever he was. Somehow I had known it might be.

I can't have looked up to much, as I stood there shaking, in only the wet raincoat, especially as all the time you could hear people yelling and beating it up generally in the other rooms. And of course I hadn't the slightest idea what line the chap might choose to take.

I needn't have worried. Not at least about that.

"Show pass off all right?" was all he asked; and looking straight into the distance as if he were on his platform, not at anyone or anything in particular, but sounding quite friendly notwithstanding, provided everyone responded in the right kind of way.

"I think so," I replied.

I daresay I didn't appear very cordial, but he seemed not to mind much.

"In that case, could I have the fee? I'm sorry to disturb your beauty sleep, but we're moving on early."

I had not known in what way I should be expected to pay, so had carefully got the ten pounds into a pile, Mr. Edis's fiver and five single pounds of my own, and put it into the corner of a drawer, before I had gone out into the rain to meet Madonna.

I gave it to him.

"Thanks," he said, counting it, and putting it into his trousers pocket. I noticed that even his trousers seemed to be seaman's trousers, now that I could see them close to, with him standing just in front of me. "Everything all right then?"

"I think so," I said again. I was taking care not to commit myself too far in any direction I could think of.

I saw that now he was looking at me, his small eyes deep-sunk.

At that exact moment, there was a wild shriek from one of the floors below. It was about the loudest human cry I had heard until then, even in one of those lodgings.

But the man took no notice.

"All right then," he said.

For some reason, he hesitated a moment, then he held out his hand. I took it. He was very strong, but there was nothing else remarkable about his hand.

"We'll meet again," he said. "Don't worry."

Then he turned away and pressed the black time switch for the staircase light. I did not stop to watch him go. I was sick and freezing.

And so far, despite what he said, our paths have not recrossed.

SALON SATIN

CAROLYN BANKS

"Tell me about your husband," he insisted.
"There is nothing to tell."
This amused him. "I suspected," he said finally.

_____

In a wicked, wicked tale that should remind some readers just a bit of Stephen King's "Quitters Inc." and still others of the diabolically clever fiction of the great John Collier, Carolyn Banks takes on the all-American, all-consuming subject of weight loss. It is our gain.

_____

"**O**h, my God!" Libby hit the BMW's brakes so hard that both women were jolted against their seat harnesses. "Sorry," she said, laughing apologetically. "But look." She swerved toward the curb so that Joyce could follow the direction in which she was pointing.

"What?" Joyce said. "I don't see a thing."

"There," Lib emphasized, "in that doorway."

"Oh." Joyce put an arch in her voice. "*That* doorway."

It was Salon Satin, the total beauty facility that was touted endlessly on television and in the local press. Salon Satin, which seemed to most of the women of Westlake Hills to be the gaudiest, most outrageous place they'd ever seen.

Consider the Salon Satin logo, made up of seven gothic windows side by side. And in the worst color combination imaginable: blue, purple, green, orange, white, violet, red. "I mean, really," was all that most of the women could muster to say.

Certainly none of them would ever set foot inside the place, no matter what Salon Satin might promise.

"I see her," Joyce said now, finally catching the point Libby had been trying to make. "I see her!"

It was their friend Shelley, easily the most queen-sized of the group. Or at least she had been.

"She's skinny," Lib almost whispered.

"Maybe it's someone else," Joyce prayed, "not Shelley at all."

But it was Shell, and she came shrieking over to their car. "Are you going to try it?" she asked. "Salon Satin?"

Libby and Joyce exchanged bewildered glances, but they listened to Shelley as she ran through her spiel. She'd dropped twenty pounds. Twenty pounds! And quickly, too. Hadn't they seen her just last month?

"Salon Satin is not for me." Lib was emphatic. She, somewhere between a five and a seven, could afford to be. Joyce, on the other hand, whose jeans had recently become too tight, perked up and really considered it. Why not? She'd tried acupuncture, hypnosis, and a thousand diets. She'd put her aesthetics aside temporarily and give Salon Satin a try. Who knew? Maybe even Emmet, her anerotic husband, would revive.

"If you ask me," Libby said as they drove home, "Shell looks like a hooker."

"Maybe," Joyce said. But really she was thinking: Yes, but a *thin* hooker. Shelley had been recently widowed. Joyce found herself wondering if that was what it took.

Salon Satin was worse inside than she could have imagined, but then, Joyce and Emmet's own quarters were done in an almost industrial gray and muted tweed. Still, it was hard for anyone of reasonable taste to take: the way the rooms spilled into each other, blue into purple into green and so on, complete with stained-glass windows in those hues. Needless to add, there were satin-clad attendants, each dressed to match the room in which he or she was working. And some of the rooms—the blue, the green, the white and the violet—had dishes of candies in exactly those colors as well.

Oy, Joyce thought as she smiled through the tour.

There was one room left. Its door was covered in black satin and it was locked. The girl who led the tour apologized and led Joyce back to reception: the blue.

"Your reason for coming here?" The girl with the pad wore blue polish on her nails.

"Weight loss."

"And exactly how many pounds?"

Joyce's first instinct was to lie, but then she caught sight of herself in the blue-tinged mirror, caught sight of her midriff and belly merging as she sat. Emmet, Emmet, it had been two years since he'd tried to touch her. "Thirty," she admitted.

"That will take three visits," the girl said, smiling. "You'll go to the orange room today, then the green, and if you're losing sufficiently . . ." She trailed off, looking at Joyce expectantly. When no questions came, she snapped her pad shut and rang for an orange-clad attendant. "We're required by law to tell you"—her voice became mechanical—"that not everyone reaches the weight-loss goals she's set."

"How many do?" Joyce asked.

"Oh—" The girl with blue nails looked around the room. "One in a blue moon."

Joyce lay on the orange satin sheet and stared up at the ceiling. She saw a lizard—a chameleon, she guessed, since it too was orange—above her. Its eyes seemed like colored glass, hard, rigid.

She turned her head to the side and was startled to see three young children, two boys and a girl, dressed in orange harlequin suits. They juggled oranges, tossing them in bold arcs each to each.

Joyce laughed. There was a strange sound, part rattle, part swish, as though a beaded curtain had been parted. The children, letting the oranges fall to the floor, backed respectfully from the room. Joyce turned to see what they saw: a tall, slender black man. There was something serpentine about him, though he wasn't in any way repulsive. On the contrary. Joyce felt her insides quiver, turn gooshy and liquid.

He came closer. Joyce's eyes were riveted upon his. It was as though, so long as he stared, she would be unable to turn her own gaze away.

Finally he blinked and Joyce was able not only to look away but to breathe. She closed her eyes now, afraid to lock upon his again. She felt him leaning over her, felt his fingers just inches from her breast. Her eyes flew open. But he wasn't near her, wasn't near at all. He laughed softly, as if he knew what she had been thinking.

That evening, she declined a scotch and soda. When dinner came, she passed the French bread without taking any. Her husband didn't notice, but Libby, dining with them, did. "Salon Satin?" Lib whispered. Joyce told her yes.

Joyce sat in a green satin box. She was naked now, and the box forced her to sit cross-legged, exposing herself, as it were. But she wasn't the performer, she was the audience. Four green-clad ballerinas whirled and vaulted to soft, tender strains. There was something green about the music, too.

When the performance was over, he came again, the black man. He was naked, too. Joyce found herself unable to keep from staring at his groin. His penis, even in repose, was solid and long. Joyce yearned to take it in her hand.

He bent down, almost as if bowing, and reached for her, helped her to her feet. She stood unashamed, her head tilted back so that she could look at him and with that look say, yes, that she was ready, neither shy nor coy. . . .

Again, his knowing laugh. He cupped her chin with his hands and his teeth gleamed in the green streaming light. "Later," he said. "In a week, perhaps. When you are"—his fingers left her and his voice grew faraway and dim—"thinner."

Joyce looked down at her feet. A young serpent essed across her toes and away, under the green satin door. Joyce hadn't been afraid, hadn't pulled away. The serpent was beautiful, like a satin ribbon looped and drawn across the floor.

* * *

That night and the next Joyce and Emmet were forced to entertain Emmet's clients, to eat in restaurants. Joyce always looked forward to these occasions, as if the desserts and rich sauces so consumed were calorically innocent. Both nights, however, Joyce was able to look appreciatively but without any hint of yearning at the pastry tray's luxurious creations of puff pastry and whipped cream. "None for me, thanks," she said.

She had lost fourteen pounds. Later, in bed, she turned to Emmet and ran her fingers along the fringes of his hair.

"I'm tired, Joyce," he told her. "Come on, what are we, kids?"

"I have sixteen pounds to lose," Joyce told the girl with blue fingernails. "I'll do anything."

"Anything?"

"Yes."

The girl rang, and six young men in tuxedos—they looked rather like pallbearers, Joyce thought—came out and beckoned to Joyce.

She looked questioningly at the girl with blue nails, but had no hope, she saw, of even getting the girl's attention.

Something made her hesitate, however.

"Tut tut," came a voice. She turned and saw the black man. "You did," he reminded her, "say you'd do anything."

Joyce smiled, nodded, and went willingly now, following the six down the corridors as the light shifted, blue to purple to green to orange to white. In the white room, the six men started to undress, leaning upon one another at first to remove their shoes, their socks, their trousers. Their voices were loud, but the satin on the walls and the floors and the furniture seemed to absorb the shock of the sound.

They made love to each other, their limbs tangled, their mouths continually engaged. Joyce leaned back against the wall—they were totally unaware of her—and watched until they seemed to have sated themselves. One of them finally noticed her. He stood, went to his trousers to retrieve a key, and led her through the violet room to the black satin door.

"You did say anything," he reminded her.

"Yes," Joyce said.

With that, he unlocked the door and gave it a push.

It rocked back on its hinges and held itself open. Joyce walked boldly in. It closed behind her, and she heard the unmistakable sound of the key again in the lock.

The pace of her breathing increased. She was sweating, too, though the room was quite cold. She touched her forehead and her fingers came away wet.

The room was blacker than any she had ever been in. Then there was a gonglike sound and an immediate hiss accompanied by bright red flame. He, the black man, was silhouetted before her.

"Undress," he said.

"I'm cold," she told him. Her hand, however, went to the buttons of her blouse. She began to undo them.

He threw something, a fine gold powder of some sort, on the brazier and the flame grew instantly hot. He watched as Joyce stripped.

Joyce smiled. "I am, as you requested, thinner," she said.

He walked about her, inspecting her as if she were a piece of fine statuary. "So you are," he agreed. He took her hand and placed it on his penis. She felt it swell, lifting her hand a foot or more.

Joyce laughed delightedly. Her thumb sought the delicate knob at the end.

"Tell me about your husband," he insisted.

"There is nothing to tell."

This amused him. "I suspected," he said finally. He knelt at her feet. She felt his breath on her thighs, felt his lips on her belly. Emmet had never done that to her, never once.

He pulled back. "You aren't quite thin enough," he said, standing, searching for his clothes.

"No, please," Joyce said, "please."

"I'm sorry," he said, sliding one leg into his trousers. "It's Salon Satin policy. Unless . . ." He pondered.

"I told you." Joyce fought to keep from sounding shrill. "I'll do—"

"Oh, yes." His teeth gleamed at her again. "Anything."

He sent her home. She walked through the breezeway with the weapon that he had given her. It was as if it had materialized in his hand.

Sure enough, just as he'd said, there they were: Libby and

Emmet, writhing, their bodies glistening with sweat. They didn't even see her, something Joyce regretted. She did as she was told, however, showering them with bullets until neither of them would ever move again.

She went directly to the black satin door, no one barring her way. He was there. He took the weapon from her, lifted her skirt, stroked her bottom.

"No one saw you?" he asked.

"No."

"Good. But before we proceed, do you know who I am?"

"You are Satin," Joyce said, gesturing at the words, Salon Satin, in vermeil on the black satin wall.

"Very good," he said. "Very good," white teeth gleaming, ebony body rock hard and muscled taut. "And do you know . . ."

"Yes, yes," Joyce interrupted, taking his hand and guiding it under the waistband of her new black satin panties.

"You are thinner," he said, momentarily distracted.

"Thirty pounds so." She had stepped through the bedroom where Libby and Emmet lay, stepped through the bloodspray so that she might reach the bathroom scale.

"Then you do know?"

Joyce was coquettish for the first time in her life, rolling his penis between the palms of her hands and fawning up at him. "About the, uh, typographical error?" She knelt now, about to close her lips upon him. "Yes, Satin. Yes, yes, I know."

"Mmmmm," he answered.

HOW LOVE CAME TO PROFESSOR GUILDEA

ROBERT HITCHENS

"Men are differently made. To me the watchful eye of affection would be abominable."

At the turn of the century, when this famous story was written, its unhurried pace would have been unremarkable, as would, also, have been the life of scholarly celibacy chosen by its title character. Today, both may seem a trifle unreal, but I suggest, as you read, simply to imagine yourself back in the London of that bygone era, caught in a moment when Queen Victoria was nearing the end of her reign, when flower girls still stood outside of railway stations offering nosegays for sale, and when a respectable butler had no expectation that his employer would regard "him as a human being."

Myself, I first encountered Professor Guildea and his cursed dilemma over three decades ago, in the pages of that most wonderful anthology, Dorothy L. Sayers's Omnibus of Crime. *Along with practically every other tale in that book, I read it so often I had almost committed it to memory by the time I entered college. Today, however, with a larger experience of human nature and years of amateur psychologizing under my belt, this insidious haunting spawned by one man's "defi-*

*ciency of affection" seems to me as poignant as it is truly
horrible.*

Dull people often wondered how it came about that Father
Murchison and Professor Frederic Guildea were intimate friends.
The one was all faith, the other all skepticism. The nature of
the Father was based on love. He viewed the world with an
almost childlike tenderness above his long black cassock; and
his mild, yet perfectly fearless, blue eyes seemed always to be
watching the goodness that exists in humanity, and rejoicing at
what they saw. The Professor, on the other hand, had a hard
face like a hatchet, tipped with an aggressive black goatee. His
eyes were quick, piercing and irreverent. The lines about his
small, thin-lipped mouth were almost cruel. His voice was
harsh and dry, sometimes, when he grew energetic, almost
soprano. It fired off words with a sharp and clipping utterance.
His habitual manner was one of distrust and investigation. It
was impossible to suppose that, in his busy life, he found any
time for love, either of humanity in general or of an individual.

Yet his days were spent in scientific investigations which
conferred immense benefits upon the world.

Both men were celibates. Father Murchison was a member of
an Anglican order which forbade him to marry. Professor Guildea
had a poor opinion of most things, but especially of women. He
had formerly held a post as lecturer at Birmingham. But when
his fame as a discoverer grew he removed to London. There, at
a lecture he gave in the East End, he first met Father Murchison. They spoke a few words. Perhaps the bright intelligence of
the priest appealed to the man of science, who was inclined, as
a rule, to regard the clergy with some contempt. Perhaps the
transparent sincerity of this devotee, full of common sense,
attracted him. As he was leaving the hall he abruptly asked the
Father to call on him at his house in Hyde Park Place. And the
father, who seldom went into the West End, except to preach,
accepted the invitation.

"When will you come?" said Guildea.

He was folding up the blue paper on which his notes were
written in a tiny, clear hand. The leaves rustled dryly in accompaniment to his sharp, dry voice.

"On Sunday week I am preaching in the evening at St. Saviour's, not far off," said the Father.

"I don't go to church."

"No," said the Father, without any accent of surprise or condemnation.

"Come to supper afterward?"

"Thank you. I will."

"What time will you come?"

The Father smiled.

"As soon as I have finished my sermon. The service is at six-thirty."

"About eight then, I suppose. Don't make the sermon too long. My number in Hyde Park Place is a hundred. Good night to you."

He snapped an elastic band round his papers and strode off without shaking hands.

On the appointed Sunday, Father Murchison preached to a densely crowded congregation at St. Saviour's. The subject of his sermon was sympathy, and the comparative uselessness of man in the world unless he can learn to love his neighbor as himself. The sermon was rather long, and when the preacher, in his flowing black cloak and his hard round hat, with a straight brim over which hung the ends of a black cord, made his way toward the Professor's house, the hands of the illuminated clock disk at the Marble Arch pointed to twenty minutes past eight.

The Father hurried on, pushing his way through the crowd of standing soldiers, chattering women, and giggling street boys in their Sunday best. It was a warm April night, and, when he reached Number 100 Hyde Park Place, he found the Professor bareheaded on his doorstep, gazing out toward the Park railings and enjoying the soft, moist air in front of his lighted passage.

"Ha, a long sermon!" he exclaimed. "Come in."

"I fear it was," said the Father, obeying the invitation. "I am that dangerous thing—an ex-tempore preacher."

"More attractive to speak without notes, if you can do it. Hang your hat and coat—oh, cloak—here. We'll have supper at once. This is the dining room."

He opened a door on the right and they entered a long, narrow room, with a gold paper and a black ceiling, from which hung an electric lamp with a gold-colored shade. In the room stood a small oval table with covers laid for two. The Professor rang the bell. Then he said:

"People seem to talk better at an oval table than at a square one."

"Really. Is that so?"

"Well, I've had precisely the same party twice, once at a square table, once at an oval table. The first dinner was a dull failure, the second a brilliant success. Sit down, won't you?"

"How d'you account for the difference?" said the Father, sitting down and pulling the tail of his cassock well under him.

"H'm. I know how you'd account for it."

"Indeed. How then?"

"At an oval table, since there are no corners, the chain of human sympathy—the electric current—is much more complete. Eh! Let me give you some soup."

"Thank you."

The Father took it, and, as he did so, turned his beaming blue eyes on his host. Then he smiled.

"What!" he said, in his pleasant, light tenor voice. "You do go to church sometimes, then?"

"Tonight is the first time for ages. And, mind you, I was tremendously bored."

The Father still smiled, and his blue eyes gently twinkled.

"Dear, dear!" he said. "What a pity!"

"But not by the sermon," Guildea added. "I don't pay a compliment. I state a fact. The sermon didn't bore me. If it had, I should have said so, or said nothing."

"And which would you have done?"

The Professor smiled almost genially.

"Don't know," he said. "What wine d'you drink?"

"None, thank you. I'm a teetotaler. In my profession and *milieu* it is necessary to be one. Yes, I will have some soda water. I think you would have done the first."

"Very likely, and very wrongly. You wouldn't have minded much."

"I don't think I should."

They were intimate already. The Father felt most pleasantly at home under the black ceiling. He drank some soda water and seemed to enjoy it more than the Professor enjoyed his claret.

"You smile at the theory of the chain of human sympathy, I see," said the Father. "Then what is your explanation of the failure of your square party with corners, the success of your oval party without them?"

"Probably on the first occasion the wit of the assembly had a chill on his liver, while on the second he was in perfect health. Yet, you see, I stick to the oval table."

"And that means—"

"Very little. By the way, your omission of any allusion to the notorious part liver plays in love was a serious one tonight."

"Your omission of any desire for close human sympathy in your life is a more serious one."

"How can you be sure I have no such desire?"

"I divine it. Your look, your manner, tell me it is so. You were disagreeing with my sermon all the time I was preaching. Weren't you?"

"Part of the time."

The servant changed the plates. He was a middle-aged, blond, thin man, with a stony white face, pale, prominent eyes, and an accomplished manner of service. When he had left the room the Professor continued:

"Your remarks interested me, but I thought them exaggerated."

"For instance?"

"Let me play the egoist for a moment. I spend most of my time in hard work, very hard work. The results of this work, you will allow, benefit humanity."

"Enormously," assented the Father, thinking of more than one of Guildea's discoveries.

"And the benefit conferred by this work, undertaken merely for its own sake, is just as great as if it were undertaken because I loved my fellow man and sentimentally desired to see him more comfortable than he is at present. I'm as useful precisely in my present condition of—in my present nonaffectional condition—as I should be if I were as full of gush as the sentimentalists who want to get murderers out of prison, or to put a premium on tyranny—like Tolstoy—by preventing the punishment of tyrants."

"One may do great harm with affection; great good without it. Yes, that is true. Even *le bon motif* is not everything, I know. Still I contend that, given your powers, you would be far more useful in the world with sympathy, affection for your kind, added to them than as you are. I believe even that you would do still more splendid work."

The Professor poured himself out another glass of claret.

"You noticed my butler?" he said.

"I did."

"He's a perfect servant. He makes me perfectly comfortable. Yet he has no feeling of liking for me. I treat him civilly. I pay him well. But I never think about him, or concern myself with him as a human being. I know nothing of his character except what I read of it in his last master's letter. There are, you may say, no truly human relations between us. You would affirm that his work would be better done if I had made him personally like me as man—of any class—can like man—of any other class?"

"I should, decidedly."

"I contend that he couldn't do his work better than he does it at present."

"But if any crisis occurred?"

"What?"

"Any crisis, change in your condition. If you needed his help, not only as a man and a butler, but as a man and a brother? He'd fail you then, probably. You would never get from your servant that finest service which can only be prompted by an honest affection."

"You have finished?"

"Quite."

"Let us go upstairs then. Yes, those are good prints. I picked them up in Birmingham when I was living there. This is my workroom."

They came into a double room lined entirely with books, and brilliantly, rather hardly, lit by electricity. The windows at one end looked onto the Park, at the other onto the garden of a neighboring house. The door by which they entered was concealed from the inner and smaller room by the jutting wall of the outer room, in which stood a huge writing table loaded with letters, pamphlets, and manuscripts. Between the two windows of the inner room was a cage in which a large gray parrot was clambering, using both beak and claws to assist him in his slow and meditative peregrinations."

"You have a pet," said the Father, surprised.

"I possess a parrot," the Professor answered dryly. "I got him for a purpose when I was making a study of the imitative powers of birds, and I have never got rid of him. A cigar?"

"Thank you."

They sat down. Father Murchison glanced at the parrot. It had paused in its journey and, clinging to the bars of its cage, was regarding them with attentive round eyes that looked deliberately intelligent but by no means sympathetic. He looked away from it to Guildea, who was smoking, with his head thrown back, his sharp, pointed chin, on which the small black beard bristled, upturned. He was moving his under lip up and down rapidly. This action caused the beard to stir and look peculiarly aggressive. The Father suddenly chuckled softly.

"Why's that?" cried Guildea, letting his chin drop down on his breast and looking at his guest sharply.

"I was thinking it would have to be a crisis indeed that could make you cling to your butler's affection for assistance."

Guildea smiled too.

"You're right. It would. Here he comes."

The man entered with coffee. He offered it gently and retired like a shadow retreating on a wall.

"Splendid, inhuman fellow," remarked Guildea.

"I prefer the East End lad who does my errands in Bird Street," said the Father. "I know all his worries. He knows some of mine. We are friends. He's more noisy than your man. He even breathes hard when he is specially solicitous, but he would do more for me than put the coals on my fire, or black my square-toed boots."

"Men are differently made. To me the watchful eye of affection would be abominable."

"What about that bird?"

The Father pointed to the parrot. It had got up on its perch and, with one foot uplifted in an impressive, almost benedictory manner, was gazing steadily at the Professor.

"That's the watchful eye of imitation, with a mind at the back of it, desirous of reproducing the peculiarities of others. No, I thought your sermon tonight very fresh, very clever. But I have no wish for affection. Reasonable liking, of course, one desires"—he tugged sharply at his beard, as if to warn himself against sentimentality—"but anything more would be most irksome, and would push me, I feel sure, toward cruelty. It would also hamper one's work."

"I don't think so."

"The sort of work I do. I shall continue to benefit the world without loving it, and it will continue to accept the benefits without loving me. That's all as it should be."

He drank his coffee. Then he added, rather aggressively:

"I have neither time nor inclination for sentimentality."

When Guildea let Father Murchison out, he followed the Father onto the doorstep and stood there for a moment. The Father glanced across the damp road into the Park.

"I see you've got a gate just opposite you," he said idly.

"Yes. I often slip across for a stroll to clear my brain. Good night to you. Come again someday."

"With pleasure. Good night."

The Priest strode away, leaving Guildea standing on the step.

Father Murchison came many times again to Number 100 Hyde Park Place. He had a feeling of liking for most men and women whom he knew, and of tenderness for all, whether he knew them or not, but he grew to have a special sentiment toward Guildea. Strangely enough, it was a sentiment of pity. He pitied this hardworking, eminently successful man of big brain and bold heart, who never seemed depressed, who never wanted assistance, who never complained of the twisted skein of life or faltered in his progress along its way. The Father pitied Guildea, in fact, because Guildea wanted so little. He had told him so, for the intercourse of the two men, from the beginning, had been singularly frank.

One evening, when they were talking together, the Father happened to speak of one of the oddities of life, the fact that those who do not want things often get them, while those who seek them vehemently are disappointed in their search.

"Then I ought to have affection poured upon me," said Guildea, smiling rather grimly. "For I hate it."

"Perhaps someday you will."

"I hope not, most sincerely."

Father Murchison said nothing for a moment. He was drawing together the ends of the broad band round his cassock. When he spoke he seemed to be answering someone.

"Yes," he said slowly, "yes, that *is* my feeling—pity."

"For whom?" said the Professor.

Then, suddenly, he understood. He did not say that he understood, but Father Murchison felt, and saw, that it was quite unnecessary to answer his friend's question. So Guildea, strangely enough, found himself closely acquainted with a man—his opposite in all ways—who pitied him.

The fact that he did not mind this, and scarcely ever thought about it, shows perhaps as clearly as anything could the peculiar indifference of his nature.

I I

One autumn evening, a year and a half after Father Murchison and the Professor had first met, the Father called in Hyde Park Place and inquired of the blond and stony butler—his name was Pitting—whether his master was at home.

"Yes, sir," replied Pitting. "Will you please come this way?"

He moved noiselessly up the rather narrow stairs, followed by the Father, tenderly opened the library door, and in his soft, cold voice, announced:

"Father Murchison."

Guildea was sitting in an armchair before a small fire. His thin, long-fingered hands lay outstretched upon his knees, his head was sunk down on his chest. He appeared to be pondering deeply. Pitting very slightly raised his voice.

"Father Murchison to see you, sir," he repeated.

The Professor jumped up rather suddenly and turned sharply round as the Father came in.

"Oh," he said. "It's you, is it? Glad to see you. Come to the fire."

The Father glanced at him and thought him looking unusually fatigued.

"You don't look well tonight," the Father said.

"No?"

"You must be working too hard. That lecture you are going to give in Paris is bothering you?"

"Not a bit. It's all arranged. I could deliver it to you at this moment verbatim. Well, sit down."

The Father did so, and Guildea sank once more into his chair and stared hard into the fire without another word. He seemed to be thinking profoundly. His friend did not interrupt him, but quietly lit a pipe and began to smoke reflectively. The eyes of Guildea were fixed upon the fire. The Father glanced about the room, at the walls of soberly bound books, at the crowded writing table, at the windows, before which hung heavy, dark-blue curtains of old brocade, at the cage, which stood between them. A green baize covering was thrown over it. The Father wondered why. He had never seen Napoleon—so the parrot was named—covered up at night before. While he was looking at the baize, Guildea suddenly jerked up his head, and, taking his hands from his knees and clasping them, said abruptly:

"D'you think I'm an attractive man?"

Father Murchison jumped. Such a question coming from such a man astounded him.

"Bless me!" he ejaculated. "What makes you ask? Do you mean attractive to the opposite sex?"

"That's what I don't know," said the Professor gloomily, and staring again into the fire. "That's what I don't know."

The Father grew more astonished.

"Don't know!" he exclaimed.

And he laid down his pipe.

"Let's say—d'you think I'm attractive, that there's anything about me which might draw a—a human being, or an animal, irresistibly to me?"

"Whether you desired it or not?"

"Exactly—or—no, let us say definitely—if I did not desire it."

Father Murchison pursed up his rather full, cherubic lips, and little wrinkles appeared about the corners of his blue eyes.

"There might be, of course," he said, after a pause. "Human nature is weak, engagingly weak, Guildea. And you're inclined to flout it. I could understand a certain class of lady—the lion-hunting, the intellectual lady, seeking you. Your reputation, your great name—"

"Yes, yes," Guildea interrupted, rather irritably, "I know all that, I know."

He twisted his long hands together, bending the palms outward till his thin, pointed fingers cracked. His forehead was wrinkled in a frown.

"I imagine," he said—he stopped and coughed dryly, almost shrilly—"I imagine it would be very disagreeable to be liked, to be run after—that is the usual expression, isn't it—by anything one objected to."

And now he half-turned in his chair, crossed his legs one over the other, and looked at his guest with an unusual, almost piercing interrogation.

"Anything?" said the Father.

"Well—well, anyone. I imagine nothing could be more unpleasant."

"To you—no," answered the Father. "But—forgive me, Guildea, I cannot conceive of you permitting such intrusion. You don't encourage adoration."

Guildea nodded his head gloomily.

"I don't," he said, "I don't. That's just it. That's the curious part of it, that I—"

He broke off deliberately, got up and stretched.

"I'll have a pipe too," he said.

He went over to the mantelpiece, got his pipe, filled it and lighted it. As he held the match to the tobacco, bending forward with an inquiring expression, his eyes fell upon the green baize that covered Napoleon's cage. He threw the match into the grate and puffed at the pipe as he walked forward to the cage. When he reached it he put out his hand, took hold of the baize and began to pull it away. Then suddenly he pushed it back over the cage.

"No," he said, as if to himself, "no."

He returned rather hastily to the fire and threw himself once more into his armchair.

"You're wondering," he said to Father Murchison. "So am I. I don't know at all what to make of it. I'll just tell you the facts and you must tell me what you think of them. The night before last, after a day of hard work—but no harder than usual—I went to the front door to get a breath of air. You know I often do that."

"Yes, I found you on the doorstep when I first came here."

"Just so. I didn't put on hat or coat. I just stood on the step as I was. My mind, I remember, was still full of my work. It was rather a dark night, not very dark. The hour was about eleven, or a quarter past. I was staring at the Park, and presently I found that my eyes were directed toward somebody who was sitting, back to me, on one of the benches. I saw the person—if it was a person—through the railings."

"If it was a person!" said the Father. "What do you mean by that?"

"Wait a minute. I say that because it was too dark for me to know. I merely saw some blackish object on the bench, rising into view above the level of the back of the seat. I couldn't say it was man, woman, or child. But something there was, and I found that I was looking at it."

"I understand."

"Gradually, I also found that my thoughts were becoming fixed upon this thing or person. I began to wonder, first, what it was doing there; next, what it was thinking; lastly, what it was like."

"Some poor creature without a home, I suppose," said the Father.

"I said that to myself. Still, I was taken with an extraordinary interest about this object, so great an interest that I got my hat and crossed the road to go into the Park. As you know, there's an entrance almost opposite my house. Well, Murchison, I crossed the road, passed through the gate in the railings, went up to the seat, and found that there was—nothing on it."

"Were you looking at it as you walked?"

"Part of the time. But I removed my eyes from it just as I passed through the gate, because there was a row going on a little way off, and I turned for an instant in that direction. When I saw that the seat was vacant I was seized by a most absurd sensation of disappointment, almost of anger. I stopped and looked about me to see if anything was moving away, but I could see nothing. It was a cold night and misty, and there were few people about. Feeling, as I say, foolishly and unnaturally disappointed, I retraced my steps to this house. When I got here I discovered that during my short absence I had left the hall door open—half open."

"Rather imprudent in London."

"Yes. I had no idea, of course, that I had done so, till I got back. However, I was only away three minutes or so."

"Yes."

"It was not likely that anybody had gone in."

"I suppose not."

"Was it?"

"Why do you ask me that, Guildea?"

"Well, well!"

"Besides, if anybody had gone in on your return you'd have caught him, surely."

Guildea coughed again. The Father, surprised, could not fail to recognize that he was nervous and that his nervousness was affecting him physically.

"I must have caught cold that night," he said, as if he had read his friend's thought and hastened to contradict it. Then he went on:

"I entered the hall, or passage, rather."

He paused again. His uneasiness was becoming very apparent.

"And you did catch somebody?" said the Father.

Guildea cleared his throat.

"That's just it," he said, "now we come to it. I'm not imaginative, as you know."

"You certainly are not."

"No, but hardly had I stepped into the passage before I felt certain that somebody had got into the house during my absence. I felt convinced of it, and not only that, I also felt convinced that the intruder was the very person I had dimly seen sitting upon the seat in the Park. What d'you say to that?"

"I begin to think you are imaginative."

"H'm! It seemed to me that the person—the occupant of the seat—and I had simultaneously formed the project of interviewing each other, had simultaneously set out to put that project into execution. I became so certain of this that I walked hastily upstairs into this room, expecting to find the visitor awaiting me. But there was no one. I then came down again and went into the dining room. No one. I was actually astonished. Isn't that odd?"

"Very," said the Father, quite gravely.

The Professor's chill and gloomy manner and uncomfortable, constrained appearance kept away the humor that might well have lurked round the steps of such a discourse.

"I went upstairs again," he continued, "sat down and thought the matter over. I resolved to forget it, and took up a book. I might perhaps have been able to read, but suddenly I thought I noticed—"

He stopped abruptly. Father Murchison observed that he was staring toward the green baize that covered the parrot's cage.

"But that's nothing," he said. "Enough that I couldn't read. I resolved to explore the house. You know how small it is, how easily one can go all over it. I went all over it. I went into every room without exception. To the servants, who were having supper, I made some excuse. They were surprised at my advent, no doubt."

"And Pitting?"

"Oh, he got up politely when I came in, stood while I was there, but never said a word. I muttered 'Don't disturb yourselves,' or something of the sort, and came out. Murchison, I found nobody new in the house—yet I returned to this room entirely convinced that somebody had entered while I was in the Park."

"And gone out again before you came back?"

"No, had stayed, and was still in the house."

"But, my dear Guildea," began the Father, now in great astonishment. "Surely—"

"I know what you want to say—what I should want to say in your place. Now, do wait. I am also convinced that this visitor has not left the house and is at this moment in it."

He spoke with evident sincerity, with extreme gravity. Father Murchison looked him full in the face and met his quick, keen eyes.

"No," he said, as if in reply to an uttered question. "I'm perfectly sane, I assure you. The whole matter seems almost as incredible to me as it must to you. But, as you know, I never quarrel with facts, however strange. I merely try to examine into them thoroughly. I have already consulted a doctor and been pronounced in perfect bodily health."

He paused, as if expecting the Father to say something.

"Go on, Guildea," he said, "you haven't finished."

"No. I felt that night positive that somebody had entered the house and remained in it, and my conviction grew. I went to bed as usual, and, contrary to my expectation, slept as well as I generally do. Yet directly I woke up yesterday morning I knew that my household had been increased by one."

"May I interrupt you for one moment? How did you know it?"

"By my mental sensation. I can only say that I was perfectly conscious of a new presence within my house, close to me."

"How very strange," said the Father. "And you feel absolutely certain that you are not overworked? Your brain does not feel tired? Your head is quite clear?"

"Quite. I was never better. When I came down to breakfast that morning I looked sharply into Pitting's face. He was as coldly placid and inexpressive as usual. It was evident to me that his mind was in no way distressed. After breakfast I sat down to work, all the time ceaselessly conscious of the fact of this intruder upon my privacy. Nevertheless, I labored for several hours, waiting for any development that might occur to clear away the mysterious obscurity of this event. I lunched. About half past two I was obliged to go out to attend a lecture. I therefore took my coat and hat, opened my door, and stepped onto the pavement. I was instantly aware that I was no longer intruded upon, and this although I was now in the street surrounded by people. Consequently, I felt certain that the thing in my house must be thinking of me, perhaps even spying upon me."

"Wait a moment," interrupted the Father. "What was your sensation? Was it one of fear?"

"Oh, dear no. I was entirely puzzled—as I am now—and keenly interested, but not in any way alarmed. I delivered my lecture with my usual ease and returned home in the evening. On entering the house again I was perfectly conscious that the intruder was still there. Last night I dined alone and spent the hours after dinner in reading a scientific work in which I was deeply interested. While I read, however, I never for one moment lost the knowledge that some mind—very attentive to me—was within hail of mine. I will say more than this—the sensation constantly increased, and, by the time I got up to go to bed, I had come to a very strange conclusion."

"What? What was it?"

"That whoever—or whatever—had entered my house during my short absence in the Park was more than interested in me."

"More than interested in you?"

"Was fond, or was becoming fond, of me."

"Oh!" exclaimed the Father. "Now I understand why you asked me just now whether I thought there was anything about you that might draw a human being or an animal irresistibly to you."

"Precisely. Since I came to this conclusion, Murchison, I will confess that my feeling of strong curiosity has become tinged with another feeling."

"Of fear?"

"No, of dislike, of irritation. No—not fear, not fear."

As Guildea repeated unnecessarily this asseveration he looked again toward the parrot's cage.

"What is there to be afraid of in such a matter?" he added. "I'm not a child to tremble before bogeys."

In saying the last words he raised his voice sharply; then he walked quickly to the cage and, with an abrupt movement, pulled the baize covering from it. Napoleon was disclosed, apparently dozing upon his perch with his head held slightly on one side. As the light reached him, he moved, ruffled the feathers about his neck, blinked his eyes, and began slowly to sidle to and fro, thrusting his head forward and drawing it back with an air of complacent, though rather unmeaning, energy. Guildea stood by the cage, looking at him closely, and indeed with an attention that was so intense as to be remarkable, almost unnatural.

"How absurd these birds are!" he said at length, coming back to the fire.

"You have no more to tell me?" asked the Father.

"No. I am still aware of the presence of something in my house. I am still conscious of its close attention to me. I am still irritated, seriously annoyed—I confess it—by that attention."

"You say you are aware of the presence of something at this moment?"

"At this moment—yes."

"Do you mean in this room, with us, now?"

"I should say so—at any rate, quite near us."

Again he glanced quickly, almost suspiciously, toward the cage of the parrot. The bird was sitting still on its perch now. Its head was bent down and cocked sideways, and it appeared to be listening attentively to something.

"That bird will have the intonations of my voice more correctly than ever by tomorrow morning," said the Father, watching Guildea closely with his mild blue eyes. "And it has always imitated me very cleverly."

The Professor started slightly.

"Yes," he said. "Yes, no doubt. Well, what do you make of this affair?"

"Nothing at all. It is absolutely inexplicable. I can speak quite frankly to you, I feel sure."

"Of course. That's why I have told you the whole thing."

"I think you must be overworked, overstrained, without knowing it."

"And that the doctor was mistaken when he said I was all right?"

"Yes."

Guildea knocked his pipe out against the chimney piece.

"It may be so," he said, "I will not be so unreasonable as to deny the possibility, although I feel as well as I ever did in my life. What do you advise then?"

"A week of complete rest away from London, in good air."

"The usual prescription. I'll take it. I'll go tomorrow to Westgate and leave Napoleon to keep house in my absence."

For some reason, which he could not explain to himself, the pleasure Father Murchison felt in hearing the first part of his friend's final remark was lessened, was almost destroyed, by the last sentence.

He walked toward the City that night, deep in thought, remembering and carefully considering the first interview he had with Guildea in the latter's house a year and a half before.

On the following morning Guildea left London.

I I I

Father Murchison was so busy a man that he had little time for brooding over the affairs of others. During Guildea's week at the sea, however, the Father thought about him a great deal, with much wonder and some dismay. The dismay was soon banished, for the mild-eyed priest was quick to discern weakness in himself, quicker still to drive it forth as a most undesirable inmate of the soul. But the wonder remained. It was destined to reach a crescendo. Guildea had left London on a Thursday. On a Thursday he returned, having previously sent a note to Father Murchison which mentioned that he was leaving Westgate at a certain time. When his train ran in to Victoria Station, at five o'clock in the evening, he was surprised to see the cloaked figure of his friend standing upon the gray platform behind a line of porters.

"What, Murchison!" he said. "You here! Have you seceded from your order that you are taking this holiday?"

They shook hands.

"No," said the Father. "It happened that I had to be in this neighborhood today, visiting a sick person. So I thought I would meet you."

"And see if I were still a sick person, eh?"

The Professor glanced at him kindly, but with a dry little laugh.

"Are you?" replied the Father gently, looking at him with interest. "No, I think not. You appear very well."

The sea air had, in fact, put some brownish red into Guildea's always thin cheeks. His keen eyes were shining with life and energy, and he walked forward in his loose gray suit and fluttering overcoat with a vigor that was noticeable, carrying easily in his left hand his well-filled Gladstone bag.

The Father felt completely reassured.

"I never saw you look better," he said.

"I never was better. Have you an hour to spare?"

"Two."

"Good. I'll send my bag up by cab, and we'll walk across the Park to my house and have a cup of tea there. What d'you say?"

"I shall enjoy it."

They walked out of the station yard, past the flower girls and newspaper sellers toward Grosvenor Place.

"And you have had a pleasant time?" the Father said.

"Pleasant enough, and lonely. I left my companion behind me in the passage at Number 100, you know."

"And you'll not find him there now, I feel sure."

"H'm!" ejaculated Guildea. "What a precious weakling you think me, Murchison!"

As he spoke he strode forward more quickly, as if moved to emphasize his sensation of bodily vigor.

"A weakling—no. But anyone who uses his brain as persistently as you do yours must require an occasional holiday."

"And I required one very badly, eh?"

"You required one, I believe."

"Well, I've had it. And now we'll see."

The evening was closing in rapidly. They crossed the road at Hyde Park Corner and entered the Park, in which were a number of people going home from work; men in corduroy trousers, caked with dried mud, and carrying tin cans slung over their shoulders, and flat panniers in which lay their tools. Some of the younger ones talked loudly or whistled shrilly as they walked.

"Until the evening," murmured Father Murchison to himself.

"What?" asked Guildea.

"I was only quoting the last words of the text, which seems written upon life, especially upon the life of pleasure: 'Man goeth forth to his work, and to his labor.' "

"Ah, those fellows are not half bad fellows to have in an audience. There were a lot of them at the lecture I gave when I first met you, I remember. One of them tried to heckle me. He had a red beard. Chaps with red beards are always hecklers. I laid him low on that occasion. Well, Murchison, and now we're going to see."

"What?"

"Whether my companion has departed."

"Tell me—do you feel any expectation of—well—of again thinking something is there?"

"How carefully you choose language. No, I merely wonder."

"You have no apprehension?"

"Not a scrap. But I confess to feeling curious."

"Then the sea air hasn't taught you to recognize that the whole thing came from overstrain."

"No," said Guildea, very dryly.

He walked on in silence for a minute. Then he added:

"You thought it would?"

"I certainly thought it might."

"Make me realize that I had a sickly, morbid, rotten imagination —eh? Come now, Murchison, why not say frankly that you packed me off to Westgate to get rid of what you considered an acute form of hysteria?"

The Father was quite unmoved by this attack.

"Come now, Guildea," he retorted, "what did you expect me to think? I saw no indication of hysteria in you. I never have.

One would suppose you the last man likely to have such a malady. But which is more natural—for me to believe in your hysteria or in the truth of such a story as you told me?"

"You have me there. No, I mustn't complain. Well, there's no hysteria about me now, at any rate."

"And no stranger in your house, I hope."

Father Murchison spoke the last words with earnest gravity, dropping the half-bantering tone which they had both assumed.

"You take the matter very seriously, I believe," said Guildea, also speaking more gravely.

"How else can I take it? You wouldn't have me laugh at it when you tell it to me seriously?"

"No. If we find my visitor still in the house, I may even call upon you to exorcise it. But first I must do one thing."

"And that is?"

"Prove to you, as well as to myself, that it is still there."

"That might be difficult," said the Father, considerably surprised by Guildea's matter-of-fact tone.

"I don't know. If it has remained in my house I think I can find a means. And I shall not be at all surprised if it is still there—despite the Westgate air."

In saying the last words the Professor relapsed into his former tone of dry chaff. The Father could not quite make up his mind whether Guildea was feeling unusually grave or unusually gay. As the two men drew near to Hyde Park Place their conversation died away and they walked forward silently in the gathering darkness.

"Here we are!" said Guildea at last.

He thrust his key into the door, opened it and let Father Murchison into the passage, following him closely and banging the door.

"Here we are!" he repeated in a louder voice.

The electric light was turned on in anticipation of his arrival. He stood still and looked round.

"We'll have some tea at once," he said. "Ah, Pitting!"

The pale butler, who had heard the door bang, moved gently forward from the top of the stairs that led to the kitchen, greeted his master respectfully, took his coat and Father Murchison's cloak, and hung them on two pegs against the wall.

"All's right, Pitting? All's as usual?" said Guildea.

"Quite so, sir."

"Bring us up some tea to the library."

"Yes, sir."

Pitting retreated. Guildea waited till he had disappeared, then opened the dining-room door, put his head into the room, and kept it there for a moment, standing perfectly still. Presently he drew back into the passage, shut the door, and said:

"Let's go upstairs."

Father Murchison looked at him inquiringly, but made no remark. They ascended the stairs and came into the library. Guildea glanced rather sharply round. A fire was burning on the hearth. The blue curtains were drawn. The bright gleam of the strong electric light fell on the long rows of books, on the writing table—very orderly in consequence of Guildea's holiday—and on the uncovered cage of the parrot. Guildea went up to the cage. Napoleon was sitting humped up on his perch with his feathers ruffled. His long toes, which looked as if they were covered with crocodile skin, clung to the bar. His round and blinking eyes were filmy, like old eyes. Guildea stared at the bird very hard and then clucked with his tongue against his teeth. Napoleon shook himself, lifted one foot, extended his toes, sidled along the perch to the bars nearest to the Professor, and thrust his head against them. Guildea scratched it with his forefinger two or three times, still gazing attentively at the parrot; then he returned to the fire just as Pitting entered with the tea tray.

Father Murchison was already sitting in an armchair on one side of the fire. Guildea took another chair and began to pour out tea as Pitting left the room closing the door gently behind him. The Father sipped his tea, found it hot, and set the cup down on a little table at his side.

"You're fond of that parrot, aren't you?" he asked his friend.

"Not particularly. It's interesting to study sometimes. The parrot mind and nature are peculiar."

"How long have you had him?"

"About four years. I nearly got rid of him just before I made your acquaintance. I'm very glad now I kept him."

"Are you? Why is that?"

"I shall probably tell you in a day or two."

The Father took his cup again. He did not press Guildea for

an immediate explanation, but when they had both finished their tea he said:

"Well, has the sea air had the desired effect?"

"No," said Guildea.

The Father brushed some crumbs from the front of his cassock and sat up higher in his chair.

"Your visitor is still here?" he asked, and his blue eyes became almost ungentle and piercing as he gazed at his friend.

"Yes," answered Guildea calmly.

"How do you know it, when did you know it—when you looked into the dining room just now?"

"No. Not until I came into this room. It welcomed me here."

"Welcomed you! In what way?"

"Simply by being here, by making me feel that it is here, as I might feel that a man was if I came into the room when it was dark."

He spoke quietly, with perfect composure in his usual dry manner.

"Very well," the Father said, "I shall not try to contend against your sensation, or to explain it away. Naturally, I am in amazement."

"So am I. Never has anything in my life surprised me so much. Murchison, of course I cannot expect you to believe more than that I honestly suppose—imagine, if you like—that there is some intruder here, of what kind I am totally unaware. I cannot expect you to believe that there really is anything. If you were in my place, I in yours, I should certainly consider you the victim of some nervous delusion. I could not do otherwise. But—wait. Don't condemn me as a hysteria patient, or as a madman, for two or three days. I feel convinced that—unless I am indeed unwell, a mental invalid, which I don't think is possible—I shall be able very shortly to give you some proof that there is a newcomer in my house."

"You don't tell me what kind of proof?"

"Not yet. Things must go a little farther first. But, perhaps even tomorrow I may be able to explain myself more fully. In the meanwhile, I'll say this: that if, eventually, I can't bring any kind of proof that I'm not dreaming I'll let you take me to any doctor you like, and I'll resolutely try to adopt your present view—that I'm suffering from an absurd delusion. That is your view, of course?"

Father Murchison was silent for a moment. Then he said, rather doubtfully:

"It ought to be."

"But isn't it?" asked Guildea, surprised.

"Well, you know, your manner is enormously convincing. Still, of course, I doubt. How can I do otherwise? The whole thing must be fancy."

The Father spoke as if he were trying to recoil from a mental position he was being forced to take up.

"It must be fancy," he repeated.

"I'll convince you by more than my manner, or I'll not try to convince you at all," said Guildea.

When they parted that evening, he said:

"I'll write to you in a day or two probably. I think the proof I am going to give you has been accumulating during my absence. But I shall soon know."

Father Murchison was extremely puzzled as he sat on the top of the omnibus going homeward.

I V

In two days' time he received a note from Guildea asking him to call, if possible, the same evening. This he was unable to do as he had an engagement to fulfill at some East End gathering. The following day was Sunday. He wrote saying he would come on the Monday, and got a wire shortly afterward: "Yes Monday come to dinner seven-thirty Guildea." At half past seven he stood on the doorstep of Number 100.

Pitting let him in.

"Is the Professor quite well, Pitting?" the Father inquired as he took off his cloak.

"I believe so, sir. He has not made any complaint," the butler formally replied. "Will you come upstairs, sir?"

Guildea met them at the door of the library. He was very pale and somber, and shook hands carelessly with his friend.

"Give us dinner," he said to Pitting.

As the butler retired, Guildea shut the door rather cautiously. Father Murchison had never before seen him look so disturbed.

"You're worried, Guildea," the Father said. "Seriously worried."

"Yes, I am. This business is beginning to tell on me a good deal."

"Your belief in the presence of something here continues then?"

"Oh, dear, yes. There's no sort of doubt about the matter. The night I went across the road into the Park something got into the house, though what the devil it is I can't yet find out. But now, before we go down to dinner, I'll just tell you something about that proof I promised you. You remember?"

"Naturally."

"Can't you imagine what it might be?"

Father Murchison moved his head to express a negative reply.

"Look about the room," said Guildea. "What do you see?"

The Father glanced round the room, slowly and carefully.

"Nothing unusual. You do not mean to tell me there is any appearance of—"

"Oh, no, no, there's no conventional white-robed, cloudlike figure. Bless my soul, no! I haven't fallen so low as that."

He spoke with considerable irritation.

"Look again."

Father Murchison looked at him, turned in the direction of his fixed eyes, and saw the gray parrot clambering in its cage, slowly and persistently.

"What?" he said, quickly. "Will the proof come from there?"

The Professor nodded.

"I believe so," he said. "Now let's go down to dinner. I want some food badly."

They descended to the dining room. While they ate and Pitting waited upon them, the Professor talked about birds, their habits, their curiosities, their fears, and their powers of imitation. He had evidently studied this subject with the thoroughness that was characteristic of him in all that he did.

"Parrots," he said presently, "are extraordinarily observant. It is a pity that their means of reproducing what they see are so limited. If it were not so, I have little doubt that their echo of gesture would be as remarkable as their echo of voice often is."

"But hands are missing."

"Yes. They do many things with their heads, however. I once knew an old woman near Goring on the Thames. She was afflicted with the palsy. She held her head perpetually sideways and it trembled, moving from right to left. Her sailor son brought her home a parrot from one of his voyages. It used to reproduce the old woman's palsied movement of the head exactly. Those gray parrots are always on the watch."

Guildea said the last sentence slowly and deliberately, glancing sharply over his wine at Father Murchison, and, when he had spoken it, a sudden light of comprehension dawned in the Priest's mind. He opened his lips to make a swift remark. Guildea turned his bright eyes toward Pitting, who at the moment was tenderly bearing a cheese meringue from the lift that connected the dining room with the lower regions. The Father closed his lips again. But presently, when the butler had placed some apples on the table, had meticulously arranged the decanters, brushed away the crumbs and evaporated, he said, quickly:

"I begin to understand. You think Napoleon is aware of the intruder?"

"I know it. He has been watching my visitant ever since the night of that visitant's arrival."

Another flash of light came to the priest.

"That was why you covered him with green baize one evening?"

"Exactly. An act of cowardice. His behavior was beginning to grate upon my nerves."

Guildea pursed up his thin lips and drew his brows down, giving to his face a look of sudden pain.

"But now I intend to follow his investigations," he added, straightening his features. "The week I wasted at Westgate was not wasted by him in London, I can assure you. Have an apple."

"No, thank you; no, thank you."

The Father repeated the words without knowing that he did so. Guildea pushed away his glass.

"Let us come upstairs, then."

"No, thank you," reiterated the Father.

"Eh?"

"What am I saying?" exclaimed the Father, getting up. "I was thinking over this extraordinary affair."

"Ah, you're beginning to forget the hysteria theory?"

They walked out into the passage.

"Well, you are so very practical about the whole matter."

"Why not? Here's something very strange and abnormal come into my life. What should I do but investigate it closely and calmly?"

"What, indeed?"

The Father began to feel rather bewildered, under a sort of compulsion which seemed laid upon him to give earnest attention to a matter that ought to strike him—so he felt—as entirely absurd. When they came into the library his eyes immediately turned, with profound curiosity, toward the parrot's cage. A slight smile curled the Professor's lips. He recognized the effect he was producing upon his friend. The Father saw the smile.

"Oh, I'm not won over yet," he said in answer to it.

"I know. Perhaps you may be before the evening is over. Here comes the coffee. After we have drunk it we'll proceed to our experiment. Leave the coffee, Pitting, and don't disturb us again."

"No, sir."

"I won't have it black tonight," said the Father. "Plenty of milk, please. I don't want my nerves played upon."

"Suppose we don't take coffee at all?" said Guildea. "If we do you may trot out the theory that we are not in a perfectly normal condition. I know you, Murchison, devout priest and devout skeptic."

The Father laughed and pushed away his cup.

"Very well, then. No coffee."

"One cigarette, and then to business."

The gray-blue smoke curled up.

"What are we going to do?" said the Father.

He was sitting bolt upright as if ready for action. Indeed there was no suggestion of repose in the attitudes of either of the men.

"Hide ourselves, and watch Napoleon. By the way—that reminds me."

He got up, went to a corner of the room, picked up a piece of green baize, and threw it over the cage.

"I'll pull that off when we are hidden."

"And tell me first if you have had any manifestation of this supposed presence during the last few days?"

"Merely an increasingly intense sensation of something here, perpetually watching me, perpetually attending to all my doings."

"Do you feel that it follows you about?"

"Not always. It was in this room when you arrived. It is here now—I feel. But in going down to dinner, we seemed to get away from it. The conclusion is that it remained here. Don't let us talk about it just now."

They spoke of other things till their cigarettes were finished. Then, as they threw away the smoldering ends, Guildea said:

"Now, Murchison, for the sake of this experiment, I suggest that we should conceal ourselves behind the curtains on either side of the cage, so that the bird's attention may not be drawn toward us and so distracted from that which we want to know more about. I will pull away the green baize when we are hidden. Keep perfectly still, watch the bird's proceedings, and tell me afterward how you feel about them, how you explain them. Tread softly."

The Father obeyed, and they stole toward the curtains that fell before the two windows. The Father concealed himself behind those on the left of the cage, the Professor behind those on the right. The latter, as soon as they were hidden, stretched out his arm, drew the baize down from the cage, and let it fall on the floor.

The parrot, which had evidently fallen asleep in the warm darkness, moved on its perch as the light shone upon it, ruffled the feathers round its throat, and lifted first one foot and then the other. It turned its head round on its supple, and apparently elastic, neck, and, diving its beak into the down upon its back, made some searching investigations with, as it seemed, a satisfactory result, for it soon lifted its head again, glanced around its cage, and began to address itself to a nut which had been fixed between the bars for its refreshment. With its curved beak it felt and tapped the nut, at first gently, then with severity. Finally it plucked the nut from the bars, seized it with its rough, gray toes, and, holding it down firmly on the perch, cracked it and pecked out its contents, scattering some on the floor of the cage and letting the fractured shell fall into the china bath that was fixed against the bars. This accomplished, the bird paused meditatively, extended one leg backward, and went through an elaborate process of wing-stretching that made it look as if it were lopsided and deformed. With its head reversed, it again applied itself to a subtle and exhaustive search among the feathers of its wing. This time its investigation seemed interminable, and Father Murchison had time to realize the absurdity of the whole position, and to wonder why he had lent himself to it. Yet he did not find his sense of humor laughing at it. On the contrary, he was smitten by a sudden gust of horror. When he was talking to his friend and watching him, the Professor's manner, generally so calm, even so prosaic, vouched for the truth of his story and the well-adjusted balance of his mind. But when he was hidden this was not so. And Father Murchison, standing behind his curtain, with his eyes upon the unconcerned Napoleon, began to whisper to himself the word *madness*, with a quickening sensation of pity and of dread.

The parrot sharply contracted one wing, ruffled the feathers around its throat again, then extended its other leg backward, and proceeded to the cleaning of its other wing. In the still room the dry sound of the feathers being spread was distinctly audible. Father Murchison saw the blue curtains behind which Guildea stood tremble slightly, as if a breath of wind had come through the window they shrouded. The clock in the far room chimed, and a coal dropped into the grate, making a noise like dead leaves stirring abruptly on hard ground. And again a gust of pity and of dread swept over the Father. It seemed to him that he had behaved very foolishly, if not wrongly, in encouraging what must surely be the strange dementia of his friend. He ought to have declined to lend himself to a proceeding that, ludicrous, even childish in itself, might well be dangerous in the encouragement it gave to a diseased expectation. Napoleon's protruding leg, extended wing, and twisted neck, his busy and unconscious devotion to the arrangement of his person, his evident sensation of complete loneliness, most comfortable solitude, brought home with vehemence to the Father the undignified buffoonery of his conduct, the more piteous buffoonery of his friend. He seized the curtains with his hands and was about to thrust them aside and issue forth when an abrupt movement of the parrot stopped him. The bird, as if sharply attracted by something, paused in its pecking, and, with its head still bent backward and twisted sideways on its neck, seemed to listen intently. Its round eye looked glistening and strained like the eye of a disturbed pigeon. Contracting its wing, it lifted its head and sat for a moment erect on its perch, shifting its feet mechanically up and down, as if a dawning excitement produced in it an uncontrollable desire of movement. Then it thrust its head forward in the direction of the further room and remained perfectly still. Its attitude so strongly suggested the concentration of its attention on something immediately before it that Father Murchison instinctively stared about the room, half expecting to see Pitting advance softly, having entered through the hidden door. He did not come, and there was no sound in the chamber. Nevertheless, the parrot was obviously getting excited and increasingly attentive. It bent its head lower and lower, stretching out its neck until, almost falling from the perch, it half extended its wings, raising them slightly from its back, as if about to take flight, and fluttering them rapidly up and down. It continued this fluttering movement for what seemed to the Father an immense time. At length, raising its wings as far as possible, it dropped them slowly and deliberately down to its back, caught hold of the edge of its bath with its beak, hoisted itself on to the floor of the cage, waddled to the bars, thrust its head against them, and stood quite still in the exact attitude it always assumed when its head was being scratched by the Professor. So complete was the suggestion of this delight conveyed by the bird that Father Murchison felt as if he saw a white finger gently pushed among the soft feathers of its head, and he was seized by a most strong conviction that something, unseen by him but seen and welcomed by Napoleon, stood immediately before the cage.

The parrot presently withdrew its head, as if the coaxing finger had been lifted from it, and its pronounced air of acute physical enjoyment faded into one of marked attention and alert curiosity. Pulling itself up by the bars it climbed again upon its perch, sidled to the left side of the cage, and began apparently to watch something with profound interest. It bowed its head oddly, paused for a moment, then bowed its head again. Father Murchison found himself conceiving—from this elaborate movement of the head—a distinct idea of a personality. The bird's proceedings suggested extreme sentimentality combined with that sort of weak determination which is often the most persistent. Such weak determination is a very common attribute of persons who are partially idiotic. Father Murchison was moved to think of these poor creatures who will often, so strangely and unreasonably, attach themselves with persistence to those who love them least. Like many priests, he had had some experience of them, for the amorous idiot is peculiarly sensitive to the attraction of preachers. This bowing movement of the parrot recalled to his memory a terrible, pale woman who for a time haunted all churches in which he ministered, who was perpetually endeavoring to catch his eye, and who always bent her head with an obsequious and cunningly conscious smile when she did so. The parrot went on bowing, making a short pause between each genuflection, as if it waited for a signal to be given that called into play its imitative faculty.

"Yes, yes, it's imitating an idiot," Father Murchison caught himself saying as he watched.

And he looked again about the room, but saw nothing; except the furniture, the dancing fire, and the serried ranks of the books. Presently the parrot ceased from bowing, and assumed the concentrated and stretched attitude of one listening very keenly. He opened his beak, showing his black tongue, shut it, then opened it again. The Father thought he was going to speak, but he remained silent, although it was obvious that he was trying to bring out something. He bowed again two or three times, paused, and then, again opening his beak, made some remark. The Father could not distinguish any words, but the voice was sickly and disagreeable, a cooing and, at the same time, querulous voice, like a woman's, he thought. And he put his ear nearer to the curtain, listening with almost feverish attention. The bowing was resumed, but this time Napoleon added to it a sidling movement, affectionate and affected, like the movement of a silly and eager thing, nestling up to someone, or giving someone a gentle and furtive nudge. Again the Father thought of that terrible, pale woman who had haunted churches. Several times he had come upon her waiting for him after evening services. Once she had hung her head smiling, had lolled out her tongue and pushed against him sideways in the dark. He remembered how his flesh had shrunk from the poor thing, the sick loathing of her that he could not banish by remembering that her mind was all astray. The parrot paused, listened, opened his beak, and again said something in the same dovelike, amorous voice, full of sickly suggestion and yet hard, even dangerous, in its intonation. A loathsome voice, the Father thought it. But this time, although he heard the voice more distinctly than before, he could not make up his mind whether it was like a woman's voice or a man's—or perhaps a child's. It seemed to be a human voice, and yet oddly sexless. In order to resolve his doubt he withdrew into the darkness of the curtains, ceased to watch Napoleon and simply listened with keen attention, striving to forget that he was listening to a bird, and to imagine that he was overhearing a human being in conversation. After two or three minutes' silence the voice spoke again, and at some length, apparently repeating several times an affectionate series of ejaculations with a cooing emphasis that was unutterably mawkish and offensive. The sickliness of the voice, its falling intonations and its strange indelicacy, combined with a die-away softness and meretricious refinement, made the Father's flesh creep. Yet he could not distinguish any words, nor could he decide on the voice's sex or age. One thing alone he was certain of as he stood still in the darkness—that such a sound could only proceed from something peculiarly loathsome, could only express a personality unendurably abominable to him, if not to everybody. The voice presently failed, in a sort of husky gasp, and there was a prolonged silence. It was broken by the Professor, who suddenly pulled away the curtains that hid the Father and said to him:

"Come out now, and look."

The Father came into the light, blinking, glanced towards the cage, and saw Napoleon poised motionless on one foot with his head under his wing. He appeared to be asleep. The Professor was pale, and his mobile lips were drawn into an expression of supreme disgust.

"Faugh!" he said.

He walked to the windows of the further room, pulled aside the curtains and pushed the glass up, letting in the air. The bare trees were visible in the gray gloom outside. Guildea leaned out for a minute drawing the night air into his lungs. Presently he turned round to the Father, and exclaimed abruptly:

"Pestilent! Isn't it?"

"Yes—most pestilent."

"Ever hear anything like it?"

"Not exactly."

"Nor I. It gives me nausea, Murchison, absolute physical nausea."

He closed the window and walked uneasily about the room.

"What d'you make of it?" he asked over his shoulder.

"How d'you mean exactly?"

"Is it man's, woman's, or child's voice?"

"I can't tell, I can't make up my mind."

"Nor I."

"Have you heard it often?"

"Yes, since I returned from Westgate. There are never any words that I can distinguish. What a voice!"

He spat into the fire.

"Forgive me," he said, throwing himself down in a chair. "It turns my stomach—literally."

"And mine," said the Father, truly.

"The worst of it is," continued Guildea, with a high, nervous accent, "that there's no brain with it, none at all—only the cunning of idiocy."

The Father started at this exact expression of his own conviction by another.

"Why d'you start like that?" asked Guildea, with a quick suspicion which showed the unnatural condition of his nerves.

"Well, the very same idea had occurred to me."

"What?"

"That I was listening to the voice of something idiotic."

"Ah! That's the devil of it, you know, to a man like me. I could fight against brain—but this!"

He sprang up again, poked the fire violently, then stood on the hearth rug with his back to it and his hands thrust into the high pockets of his trousers.

"That's the voice of the thing that's got into my house," he said. "Pleasant, isn't it?"

And now there was really horror in his eyes, and in his voice.

"I must get it out," he exclaimed. "I must get it out. But how?"

He tugged at his short black beard with a quivering hand.

"How?" he continued. "For what is it? Where is it?"

"You feel it's here—now?"

"Undoubtedly. But I couldn't tell you in what part of the room."

He stared about, glancing rapidly at everything.

"Then you consider yourself haunted?" said Father Murchison.

He, too, was much moved and disturbed, although he was not conscious of the presence of anything near them in the room.

"I have never believed in any nonsense of that kind, as you know," Guildea answered. "I simply state a fact which I cannot understand, and which is beginning to be very painful to me. There is something here. But whereas most so-called hauntings have been described to me as inimical, what I am conscious of is that I am admired, loved, desired. This is distinctly horrible to me, Murchison, distinctly horrible."

Father Murchison suddenly remembered the first evening he had spent with Guildea, and the latter's expression almost of disgust, at the idea of receiving warm affection from anyone. In the light of that long-ago conversation the present event seemed supremely strange, and almost like a punishment for an offense committed by the Professor against humanity. But, looking up at his friend's twitching face, the Father resolved not to be caught in the net of his hideous belief.

"There can be nothing here," he said. "It's impossible."

"What does that bird imitate, then?"

"The voice of someone who has been here."

"Within the last week then. For it never spoke like that before, and mind, I noticed that it was watching and striving to imitate something before I went away, since the night that I went into the Park, only since then."

"Somebody with a voice like that must have been here while you were away," Father Murchison repeated, with a gentle obstinacy.

"I'll soon find out."

Guildea pressed the bell. Pitting stole in almost immediately.

"Pitting," said the Professor, speaking in a high, sharp voice, "did anyone come into this room during my absence at the sea?"

"Certainly not, sir, except the maids—and me, sir."

"Not a soul? You are certain?"

"Perfectly certain, sir."

The cold voice of the butler sounded surprised, almost resentful. The Professor flung out his hand toward the cage.

"Has the bird been here the whole time?"

"Yes, sir."

"He was not moved, taken elsewhere, even for a moment?"

Pitting's pale face began to look almost expressive, and his lips were pursed.

"Certainly not, sir."

"Thank you. That will do."

The butler retired, moving with a sort of ostentatious rectitude. When he had reached the door, and was just going out, his master called,

"Wait a minute, Pitting."

The butler paused. Guildea bit his lips, tugged at his beard uneasily two or three times, and then said,

"Have you noticed—er—the parrot talking lately in a—a very peculiar, very disagreeable voice?"

"Yes, sir—a soft voice like, sir."

"Ha! Since when?"

"Since you went away, sir. He's always at it."

"Exactly. Well, and what did you think of it?"

"Beg pardon, sir?"

"What do you think about his talking in this voice?"

"Oh, that it's only his play, sir."

"I see. That's all, Pitting."

The butler disappeared and closed the door noiselessly behind him.

Guildea turned his eyes on his friend.

"There, you see!" he ejaculated.

"It's certainly very odd," said the Father. "Very odd indeed. You are certain you have no maid who talks at all like that?"

"My dear Murchison! Would you keep a servant with such a voice about you for two days?"

"No."

"My housemaid has been with me for five years, my cook for seven. You've heard Pitting speak. The three of them make up my entire household. A parrot never speaks in a voice it has not heard. Where has it heard that voice?"

"But we hear nothing?"

"No. Nor do we see anything. But it does. It feels something too. Didn't you observe it presenting its head to be scratched?"

"Certainly it seemed to be doing so."

"It was doing so."

Father Murchison said nothing. He was full of increasing discomfort that almost amounted to apprehension.

"Are you convinced?" said Guildea, rather irritably.

"No. The whole matter is very strange. But till I hear, see, or feel—as you do—the presence of something, I cannot believe."

"You mean that you will not?"

"Perhaps. Well, it is time I went."

Guildea did not try to detain him, but said, as he let him out:

"Do me a favor, come again tomorrow night."

The Father had an engagement. He hesitated, looked into the Professor's face and said:

"I will. At nine I'll be with you. Good night."

When he was on the pavement he felt relieved. He turned round, saw Guildea stepping into his passage, and shivered.

V

Father Murchison walked all the way home to Bird Street that night. He required exercise after the strange and disagreeable evening he had spent, an evening upon which he looked back already as a man looks back upon a nightmare. In his ears, as he walked, sounded the gentle and intolerable voice. Even the memory of it caused him physical discomfort. He tried to put it from him, and to consider the whole matter calmly. The Professor had offered his proof that there was some strange presence in his house. Could any reasonable man accept such proof? Father Murchison told himself that no reasonable man could accept it. The parrot's proceedings were, no doubt, extraordinary. The bird had succeeded in producing an extraordinary illusion of an invisible presence in the room. But that there really was such a presence the Father insisted on denying to himself. The devoutly religious, those who believe implicitly in the miracles recorded in the Bible, and who regulate their lives by the messages they suppose themselves to receive directly from the Great Ruler of a hidden World, are seldom inclined to accept any notion of supernatural intrusion into the affairs of daily life. They put it from them with anxious determination. They regard it fixedly as hocus-pocus, childish if not wicked.

Father Murchison inclined to the normal view of the devoted churchman. He was determined to incline to it. He could not—so he now told himself—accept the idea that his friend was being supernaturally punished for his lack of humanity, his deficiency in affection, by being obliged to endure the love of some horrible thing, which could not be seen, heard, or handled. Nevertheless, retribution did certainly seem to wait upon Guildea's condition. That which he had unnaturally dreaded and shrunk from in his thought he seemed to be now forced unnaturally to suffer. The Father prayed for his friend that night before the little, humble altar in the barely furnished, cell-like chamber where he slept.

On the following evening, when he called in Hyde Park Place, the door was opened by the housemaid, and Father Murchison mounted the stairs, wondering what had become of Pitting. He was met at the library door by Guildea and was painfully struck by the alteration in his appearance. His face was ashen in hue, and there were lines beneath his eyes. The eyes themselves looked excited and horribly forlorn. His hair and dress were disordered and his lips twitched continually, as if he were shaken by some acute nervous apprehension.

"What has become of Pitting?" asked the Father, grasping Guildea's hot and feverish hand.

"He has left my service."

"Left your service!" exclaimed the Father in utter amazement.

"Yes, this afternoon."

"May one ask why?"

"I'm going to tell you. It's all part and parcel of this—this most odious business. You remember once discussing the relations men ought to have with their servants?"

"Ah!" cried the Father, with a flash of inspiration. "The crisis has occurred?"

"Exactly," said the Professor, with a bitter smile. "The crisis has occurred. I called upon Pitting to be a man and a brother. He responded by declining the invitation. I upbraided him. He gave me warning. I paid him his wages and told him he could go at once. And he has gone. What are you looking at me like that for?"

"I didn't know," said Father Murchison, hastily dropping his eyes, and looking away. "Why," he added. "Napoleon is gone too."

"I sold him today to one of those shops in Shaftesbury Avenue."

"Why?"

"He sickened me with his abominable imitation of—his intercourse with—well, you know what he was at last night. Besides, I have no further need of his proof to tell me I am not dreaming. And, being convinced as I now am, that all I have thought to have happened has actually happened, I care very little about convincing others. Forgive me for saying so, Murchison, but I am now certain that my anxiety to make you believe in the presence of something here really arose from some faint doubt on that subject—within myself. All doubt has now vanished."

"Tell me why."

"I will."

Both men were standing by the fire. They continued to stand while Guildea went on.

"Last night I felt it."

"What?" cried the Father.

"I say that last night, as I was going upstairs to bed, I felt something accompanying me and nestling up against me."

"How horrible!" exclaimed the Father involuntarily.

Guildea smiled drearily.

"I will not deny the horror of it. I cannot, since I was compelled to call on Pitting for assistance."

"But—tell me—what was it, at least what did it seem to be?"

"It seemed to be a human being. It seemed, I say; and what I mean exactly is that the effect upon me was rather that of human contact than of anything else. But I could see nothing, hear nothing. Only, three times, I felt this gentle, but determined, push against me, as if to coax me and to attract my attention. The first time it happened I was on the landing outside this room, with my foot on the first stair. I will confess to you, Murchison, that I bounded upstairs like one pursued. That is the shameful truth. Just as I was about to enter my bedroom, however, I felt the thing entering with me, and, as I have said, squeezing, with loathsome, sickening tenderness, against my side. Then—"

He paused, turned toward the fire and leaned his head on his arm. The Father was greatly moved by the strange helplessness and despair of the attitude. He laid his hand affectionately on Guildea's shoulder.

"Then?"

Guildea lifted his head. He looked painfully abashed.

"Then, Murchison, I am ashamed to say I broke down, suddenly, unaccountably, in a way I should have thought wholly impossible to me. I struck out with my hands to thrust the thing away. It pressed more closely to me. The pressure, the contact became unbearable to me. I shouted out for Pitting. I—I believe I must have cried—'Help.' "

"He came, of course?"

"Yes, with his usual soft, unemotional quiet. His calm—its opposition to my excitement of disgust and horror—must, I suppose, have irritated me. I was not myself, no, no!"

He stopped abruptly. Then—

"But I need hardly tell you that," he added, with most piteous irony.

"And what did you say to Pitting?"

"I said that he should have been quicker. He begged my pardon. His cold voice really maddened me, and I burst out into some foolish, contemptible diatribe, called him a machine, taunted him, then—as I felt that loathsome thing nestling once more to me—begged him to assist me, to stay with me, not to leave me alone—I meant in the company of my tormentor. Whether he was frightened, or whether he was angry at my unjust and violent manner and speech a moment before, I don't know. In any case he answered that he was engaged as a butler, and not to sit up all night with people. I suspect he thought I had taken too much to drink. No doubt that was it. I believe I swore at him as a coward—I! This morning he said he wished to leave my service. I gave him a month's wages, a good character as a butler, and sent him off at once."

"But the night? How did you pass it?"

"I sat up all night."

"Where? In your bedroom?"

"Yes—with the door open—to let it go."

"You felt that it stayed?"

"It never left me for a moment, but it did not touch me again. When it was light I took a bath, lay down for a little while, but did not close my eyes. After breakfast I had the explanation with Pitting and paid him. Then I came up here. My nerves were in a very shattered condition. Well, I sat down, tried to write, to think. But the silence was broken in the most abominable manner."

"How?"

"By the murmur of that appalling voice, that voice of a lovesick idiot, sickly but determined. Ugh!"

He shuddered in every limb. Then he pulled himself together, assumed, with a self-conscious effort, his most determined, most aggressive, manner, and added:

"I couldn't stand that. I had come to the end of my tether; so I sprang up, ordered a cab to be called, seized the cage, and drove with it to a bird shop in Shaftesbury Avenue. There I sold the parrot for a trifle. I think, Murchison, that I must have been nearly mad then, for, as I came out of the wretched shop, and stood for an instant on the pavement among the cages of rabbits, guinea pigs, and puppy dogs, I laughed aloud. I felt as if a load was lifted from my shoulders, as if in selling that voice I had sold the cursed thing that torments me. But when I got back to the house it was here. It's here now. I suppose it will always be here."

He shuffled his feet on the rug in front of the fire.

"What on earth am I to do?" he said. "I'm ashamed of myself, Murchison, but—but I suppose there are things in the world that certain men simply can't endure. Well, I can't endure this, and there's an end of the matter."

He ceased. The Father was silent. In the presence of this extraordinary distress he did not know what to say. He recognized the uselessness of attempting to comfort Guildea, and he sat with his eyes turned, almost moodily, to the ground. And while he sat there he tried to give himself to the influences within the room, to feel all that was within it. He even, half unconsciously, tried to force his imagination to play tricks with him. But he remained totally unaware of any third person with them. At length he said:

"Guildea, I cannot pretend to doubt the reality of your misery here. You must go away, and at once. When is your Paris lecture?"

"Next week. In nine days from now."

"Go to Paris tomorrow then. You say you have never had any

consciousness that this—this thing pursued you beyond your own front door!"

"Never—hitherto."

"Go tomorrow morning. Stay away till after your lecture. And then let us see if the affair is at an end. Hope, my dear friend, hope."

He had stood up. Now he clasped the Professor's hand.

"See all your friends in Paris. Seek distractions. I would ask you also to seek—other help."

He said the last words with a gentle earnest gravity and simplicity that touched Guildea, who returned his handclasp almost warmly.

"I'll go," he said. "I'll catch the ten o'clock train, and tonight I'll sleep at a hotel, at the Grosvenor—that's close to the station. It will be more convenient for the train."

As Father Murchison went home that night he kept thinking of that sentence: "It will be more convenient for the train." The weakness in Guildea that had prompted its utterance appalled him.

VI

No letter came to Father Murchison from the Professor during the next few days, and this silence reassured him, for it seemed to betoken that all was well. The day of the lecture dawned and passed. On the following morning, the Father eagerly opened the *Times* and scanned its pages to see if there were any report of the great meeting of scientific men which Guildea had addressed. He glanced up and down the columns with anxious eyes, then suddenly his hands stiffened as they held the sheets. He had come upon the following paragraph:

> We regret to announce that Professor Frederic Guildea was suddenly seized with severe illness yesterday evening while addressing a scientific meeting in Paris. It was observed that he looked very pale and nervous when he rose to his feet. Nevertheless, he spoke in French fluently for about a quarter of an hour. Then he appeared to become uneasy. He faltered and glanced about like a man appre-

hensive, or in severe distress. He even stopped once or twice, and seemed unable to go on, to remember what he wished to say. But, pulling himself together with an obvious effort, he continued to address the audience. Suddenly, however, he paused again, edged furtively along the platform, as if pursued by something which he feared, struck out with his hands, uttered a loud, harsh cry, and fainted. The sensation in the hall was indescribable. People rose from their seats. Women screamed, and, for a moment, there was a veritable panic. It is feared that the Professor's mind must have temporarily given way owing to overwork. We understand that he will return to England as soon as possible, and we sincerely hope that necessary rest and quiet will soon have the desired effect, and that he will be completely restored to health and enabled to prosecute further the investigations which have already so benefited the world.

The Father dropped the paper, hurried out into Bird Street, sent a wire of inquiry to Paris, and received the same day the following reply: "Returning tomorrow. Please call evening. Guildea." On that evening the Father called in Hyde Park Place, was at once admitted, and found Guildea sitting by the fire in the library, ghastly pale, with a heavy rug over his knees. He looked like a man emaciated by a long and severe illness, and in his wide-open eyes there was an expression of fixed horror. The Father started at the sight of him, and could scarcely refrain from crying out. He was beginning to express his sympathy when Guildea stopped him with a trembling gesture.

"I know all that," Guildea said, "I know. This Paris affair—" He faltered and stopped.

"You ought never to have gone," said the Father. "I was wrong. I ought not to have advised your going. You were not fit."

"I was perfectly fit," he answered, with the irritability of sickness. "But I was—I was accompanied by that abominable thing."

He glanced hastily round him, shifted his chair and pulled the rug higher over his knees. The Father wondered why he was thus wrapped up. For the fire was bright and red and the night was not very cold.

"I was accompanied to Paris," he continued, pressing his upper teeth upon his lower lip.

He paused again, obviously striving to control himself. But the effort was vain. There was no resistance in the man. He writhed in his chair and suddenly burst forth in a tone of hopeless lamentation.

"Murchison, this being, thing—whatever it is—no longer leaves me even for a moment. It will not stay here unless I am here, for it loves me, persistently, idiotically. It accompanied me to Paris, stayed with me there, pursued me to the lecture hall, pressed against me, caressed me while I was speaking. It has returned with me here. It is here now"—he uttered a sharp cry—"now, as I sit here with you. It is nestling up to me, fawning upon me, touching my hands. Man, man, can't you feel that it is here?"

"No," the Father answered truly.

"I try to protect myself from its loathsome contact," Guildea continued, with fierce excitement, clutching the thick rug with both hands. "But nothing is of any avail against it. Nothing. What is it? What can it be? Why should it have come to me that night?"

"Perhaps as a punishment," said the Father, with a quick softness.

"For what?"

"You hated affection. You put human feelings aside with contempt. You had, you desired to have, no love for anyone. Nor did you desire to receive any love from anything. Perhaps this is a punishment."

Guildea stared into his face.

"D'you believe that?" he cried.

"I don't know," said the Father. "But it may be so. Try to endure it, even to welcome it. Possibly then the persecution will cease."

"I know it means me no harm," Guildea exclaimed, "it seeks me out of affection. It was led to me by some amazing attraction which I exercise over it ignorantly. I know that. But to a man of my nature that is the ghastly part of the matter. If it would hate me, I could bear it. If it would attack me, if it would try to do me some dreadful harm, I should become a man again. I should be braced to fight against it. But this gentleness, this abominable solicitude, this brainless worship of an idiot, persistent, sickly, horribly physical, I cannot endure. What does it want of me? What would it demand of me? It nestles to me. It leans against me. I feel its touch, like the touch of a feather, trembling about my heart, as if it sought to number my pulsations, to find out the inmost secrets of my impulses and desires. No privacy is left to me." He sprang up excitedly. "I cannot withdraw," he cried, "I cannot be alone, untouched, unworshiped, unwatched for even one half second. Murchison, I am dying of this, I am dying."

He sank down again in his chair, staring apprehensively on all sides, with the passion of some blind man, deluded in the belief that by his furious and continued effort he will attain sight. The Father knew well that he sought to pierce the veil of the invisible and have knowledge of the thing that loved him.

"Guildea," the Father said, with insistent earnestness, "try to endure this—do more—try to give this thing what it seeks."

"But it seeks my love."

"Learn to give it your love and it may go, having received what it came for."

"T'sh! You talk as a priest. Suffer your persecutors. Do good to them that despitefully use you. You talk as a priest."

"As a friend I spoke naturally, indeed, right out of my heart. The idea suddenly came to me that all this—truth or seeming, it doesn't matter which—may be some strange form of lesson. I have had lessons—painful ones. I shall have many more. If you could welcome—"

"I can't! I can't!" Guildea cried fiercely. "Hatred! I can give it that—always that, nothing but that—hatred, hatred."

He raised his voice, glared into the emptiness of the room, and repeated, "Hatred!"

As he spoke the waxen pallor of his cheeks increased, until he looked like a corpse with living eyes. The Father feared that he was going to collapse and faint, but suddenly he raised himself upon his chair and said, in a high and keen voice, full of suppressed excitement:

"Murchison, Murchison!"

"Yes. What is it?"

An amazing ecstasy shone in Guildea's eyes.

"It wants to leave me," he cried. "It wants to go! Don't lose a moment! Let it out! The window—the window!"

The Father, wondering, went to the near window, drew aside the curtains, and pushed it open. The branches of the trees in the garden creaked dryly in the light wind. Guildea leaned forward on the arms of his chair. There was silence for a moment. Then Guildea, speaking in a rapid whisper, said:

"No, no. Open this door—open the hall door. I feel—I feel that it will return the way it came. Make haste—ah, go!"

The Father obeyed—to soothe him, hurried to the door and opened it wide. Then he glanced back at Guildea. He was standing up, bent forward. His eyes were glaring with eager expectation, and, as the Father turned, he made a furious gesture toward the passage with his thin hands.

The Father hastened out and down the stairs. As he descended in the twilight he fancied he heard a slight cry from the room behind him, but he did not pause. He flung the hall door open, standing back against the wall. After waiting a moment—to satisfy Guildea—he was about to close the door again, and had his hand on it, when he was attracted irresistibly to look forth toward the park. The night was lit by a young moon, and, gazing through the railings, his eyes fell upon a bench beyond them.

Upon this bench something was sitting, huddled together very strangely.

The Father remembered instantly Guildea's description of that former night, that night of Advent, and a sensation of horror-stricken curiosity stole through him.

Was there then really something that had indeed come to the Professor? And had it finished its work, fulfilled its desire, and gone back to its former existence?

The Father hesitated a moment in the doorway. Then he stepped out resolutely and crossed the road, keeping his eyes fixed upon this black or dark object that leaned so strangely upon the bench. He could not tell yet what it was like, but he fancied it was unlike anything with which his eyes were acquainted. He reached the opposite path and was about to pass through the gate in the railings when his arm was brusquely grasped. He started, turned round, and saw a policeman eyeing him suspiciously.

"What are you up to?" said the policeman.

The Father was suddenly aware that he had no hat upon his

head, and that his appearance, as he stole forward in his cassock, with his eyes intently fixed upon the bench in the Park, was probably unusual enough to excite suspicion.

"It's all right, policeman," he answered, quickly, thrusting some money into the constable's hand.

Then, breaking from him, the Father hurried toward the bench, bitterly vexed at the interruption. When he reached it nothing was there. Guildea's experience had been almost exactly repeated; and, filled with unreasonable disappointment, the Father returned to the house, entered it, shut the door, and hastened up the narrow stairway into the library.

On the hearthrug, close to the fire, he found Guildea lying with his head lolled against the armchair from which he had recently risen. There was a shocking expression of terror on his convulsed face. On examining him the Father found that he was dead.

The doctor who was called in said that the cause of death was failure of the heart.

When Father Murchison was told this, he murmured:

"Failure of the heart! It was that then!"

He turned to the doctor and said:

"Could it have been prevented?"

The doctor drew on his gloves and answered:

"Possibly, if it had been taken in time. Weakness of the heart requires a great deal of care. The Professor was too much absorbed in his work. He should have lived very differently."

The Father nodded.

"Yes, yes," he said, sadly.

WINGS

HARRIET ZINNES

"You little witch," he said without any animosity, "you've tired me out: and I don't believe it, yes, you've given me pleasure. But what play are we in, what play?"

Imagine noticing as you walk through your front door that your possessions are just slightly disarranged ... yet at first glance, nothing is missing. Where is the intruder now—gone? Or perhaps lying in wait? How should you prepare yourself for the encounter, or is it possible that nothing you can do or say will matter in the slightest?

There are some stories that, even if you are expecting to be surprised, succeed in catching you off guard. Harriet Zinnes's tale of an extremely unusual and very demanding uninvited guest is one of them.

He opened the door and saw the chair in the center of the little room. He was surprised of course. What visitor had displaced that chair, his Eames chair that never, simply never, was moved from in front of his desk? He looked quickly around the room to see whether anything else had been moved. Had his apartment been broken into? He walked over to the desk itself, quickly glanced at his books and typewriter, then opened the top drawer, shut that, opened the drawers on the side. Nothing touched. Nothing seemingly removed. He walked over to the large filing cabinet and again opened drawers. Again everything in place. He left what he called his study—a mere anteroom really—and walked into the living room. Had he raised the lid of his grand piano? He couldn't remember doing that. He looked at the couch, not at all disheveled, the chairs, the little tables, lamps in order. He again walked over to the piano. He was sure John had left his Schubert notes on the ledge of the piano. Wasn't he in the midst of rehearsing? And what was Satie's *Gnossienne* doing opened on the piano bench? He went into the dining room, glanced at the neat buffet, and then opened the drawers of the little chest in which he kept his mother's silver. Everything in place.

He then walked into his bedroom. Walked directly to his bureau to look at the drawers of his chest, especially the top drawer where he kept gold cufflinks, tie pins, and those silly gold chains that he never wore but that his first love Ted Blight had given him. As he was opening the drawer, a strange voice called out to him: "Hi." He turned abruptly, his heart pounding. What he saw was more a little girl than a woman. A twelve-year-old girl (or was she a woman?) was sitting propped up on pillows. His pillows! She kept staring at him, smiling, holding him transfixed, as she casually took out a cigarette lighter and lit a cigarette. "Smoke?" she asked.

"I never smoke in my bedroom—and don't allow anyone else to," he found himself saying sharply.

She smiled at that. "Rule number one just broken."

Why didn't he retort to that or at least walk over to her, even run over, and grab the cigarette from her mouth? He was certainly capable of doing a thing like that, especially under the anger he was feeling. "I wish you'd put out that cigarette," he found himself saying quietly.

"Oh, I'm not going to do that. I always smoke in bedrooms, especially the bedrooms of the men whom I have followed."

"Followed? You've been following me?" He was stunned. Had he been so preoccupied lately about the play's possible closing that he was not aware when he was being followed? "How long have you been following me? And for God's sake why? Why have you been following me?"

"One question at a time. I've been following you since I saw you perform in *Oh! Calcutta,* and I've been following you because I like you. This morning you happened to have left your apartment door open—I gather you were late for your rehearsal—so that it was easy enough for me to get in."

"Left my apartment door open? I'm becoming absentminded. But how long have you been following me?"

"Three days. You see, it didn't take long to trap you."

"Trap me? Yes, that's it exactly. You have trapped me. Now that you are here holding me entrapped, as it were, hm, now what do you want of me? May I sit down at least?" Why on earth was he asking her permission? She wasn't holding him at gunpoint. Merely with her eyes, and that godawful cigarette. "Will you leave now, now that you have made your presence known and have found me in my own apartment? Surely that is all you want. You may get off the bed now, thank you."

"But that's exactly where I want to be. You are an idiot. Why do you suppose I've been following you if I didn't want to get into bed with you. Why?"

"You don't want to go to bed with me," he blurted out with astonishment. "Not with me. Don't you know, don't you know I don't like women!"

"I know," she said calmly, "but I like you and there's no reason after all why you can't be trained to like me. I'm not that ugly, and at first I'll make very few demands on you. I've trained men like you before. You'll be all right. Don't worry. You may be my chief star. You may require only one lesson. Come here. Let's start our first session. It may be the last, really. Don't be shy. I won't hurt you."

He couldn't believe that he was walking toward the bed. What kind of witch was she? Not only did he walk over to the bed—the wrong side; he never slept on that side of the bed with his lovers—but he began to undress: took off his shoes, his socks, his jacket, shirt, tie, and undershirt (that gorgeous pink one that Al so loved) and finally with just a little embarrassment his undershorts, pink bikinis, hot pink of course, with that daring scarlet red border.

"You're doing just fine," she said soothingly. "I'll start by giving you an encouraging kiss." Shivering, he accepted that light kiss. It was on his cheek, thank goodness, he thought. Why was he shivering, and why wasn't he running away? Why wasn't he throwing her forcibly off the bed?

"Look here," he found himself saying, "I don't want any more of your entrapment. I don't like women, and surely not little girls—are you twelve or thirteen, for heaven's sake—and this is my bed, my apartment, my life. Why why don't you get out of here, once and for all?" But his actions were belying his words. Imagine. He was kissing her on the lips and he thought he heard all sorts of mad words such as *darling dear sweetheart my love.* Whatever was happening here in his own bedroom? He wasn't chagrined or mortified. Maybe he was on the stage and just simply did not know where he was. He remembered his part in that Shaw play in which he was wooing that older woman. What was the name of the play? Wasn't he called Eugene or something like that? Maybe he was now onstage. "Are we rehearsing a play? Say, are we rehearsing a play? Tell me, what's my part like? Am I getting the leading role? Whom am I playing opposite? You're not my leading lady, are you? And what is your name? And how old are you anyway?"

At this point he recognized she had no energy for words. She was forcing him to enter her, and he was doing just that. Did the director call for the act itself? Oh God, wasn't he in a Broadway production? Was it just porn? Had he been shot into the twenty-first century where such things were permitted on the legitimate stage? What country was he in, what stage, what city, and above all, what play—and did he have the leading role? But he suddenly felt himself spent, and threw himself off the little girl—surely she was just a little girl—and stretched out his arms across the bed. "You little witch," he said without any animosity, "you've tired me out: and I don't believe it, yes, you've given me pleasure. But what play are we in, what play?"

As he picked himself up and turned to her side of the bed, he was appalled that she wasn't there. Of course she's probably gone to the john. He waited for what seemed at least ten minutes. He hardly had the strength to get off the bed to look for her. At first he decided to call out. But what was her name?

"Little girl," he began, "little girl, where are you? Are you in the john? Come out, will you? I've got to ask you more questions." No answer. "Little girl," he called again. "Where are you?" Still no answer. He'd just have to pick himself up off the bed and investigate. Entirely nude (and he never let his lovers see him nude: it was his rule NEVER TO BE TOTALLY REVEALED), he walked toward the bathroom. The door was wide open. She was not there. He made a frantic tour of the apartment. She was nowhere to be seen. Should he try to run out to find her? Without his clothes? That would never do. No, he'd better run into his room and dress quickly for the pursuit. He was dashing into his room toppling his best marble table and adorable Tiffany lamp when the crash of the lamp called him to his senses. *But this is my opportunity to get rid of her. What am I doing trying to find her? Am I so bewitched that I can't even know when I have it good?* Trembling—still with the shock of his new delight and with the equally new discovery that he could get rid of a strange creature who had bewitched him—he sat down entirely naked on his favorite leather chair, snuggled up in it, and tried to recover his senses. The only action surely was inaction. He came quickly to that conclusion. His brain apparently had not been harmed. He could think straight and hard. That little witch had followed him and had had him. He had surely been had. And it was over. Relieved he felt his back arch comfortably against the chair. He was just about to close his eyes with exhaustion and triumph, when he heard a small voice say, "Bye-bye my love. You were beautiful."

He looked up in time to see the little girl spread wings and fly directly out of his living-room window. Luckily it's a French window, he thought. John was right when he chose that.

THE BASILISK

R. MURRAY GILCHRIST

"Oh, why am I thus torn between the man and the fiend?"

There is an operatic quality to this lush nineteenth-century tale by R. Murray Gilchrist, a writer described by one critic as a sort of Aubrey Beardsley in prose. Its mood veers between frenzy and melancholy, as the two lovers, weary with frustrated longing, attempt to break a sensual enchantment. But at the same time that the language infuses our senses with its eerie vegetable torpor, it seems to hide beneath a nearly overpowering gothic richness layers of even more suggestive meaning. There is little dialogue, but of what there is, note how many of the phrases vibrate with memorably weird, tantalizing eroticism.

Marina gave no sign that she heard my protestation. The embroidery of Venus's hands in her silk picture of The Judgment of Paris was seemingly of greater import to her than the love which almost tore my soul and body asunder. In absolute despair I sat until she had replenished her needle seven times. Then impassioned nature cried aloud:

"You do not love me!"

She looked up somewhat wearily, as one debarred from rest. "Listen," she said. "There is a creature called a Basilisk, which turns men and women into stone. In my girlhood I saw the Basilisk—I am stone!"

And, rising from her chair, she departed the room, leaving me in amazed doubt as to whether I had heard aright. I had always known of some curious secret in her life: a secret which permitted her to speak of and to understand things to which no other woman had dared to lift her thoughts. But alas! it was a secret whose influence ever thrust her back from the attaining of happiness. She would warm, then freeze instantly; discuss the purest wisdom, then cease with contemptuous lips and eyes. Doubtless this strangeness had been the first thing to awaken my passion. Her beauty was not of the kind that smites men with sudden craving: it was pale and reposeful, the loveliness of a marble image. Yet, as time went on, so wondrous became her fascination that even the murmur of her swaying garments sickened me with longing. Not more than a year had passed since our first meeting, when I had found her laden with flaming tendrils in the thinned woods of my heritage. A very Dryad, robed in grass color, she was chanting to the sylvan deities. The invisible web took me, and I became her slave.

Her house lay two leagues from mine. It was a low-built mansion lying in a concave park. The thatch was gaudy with stonecrop and lichen. Amongst the central chimneys a foreign bird sat on a nest of twigs. The long windows blazed with heraldic devices; and paintings of kings and queens and nobles hung in the dim chambers. Here she dwelt with a retinue of aged servants, fantastic women and men half imbecile, who *salaamed* before her with Eastern humility and yet addressed her in such terms as gossips use. Had she given them life they could not have obeyed with more reverence. Quaint things the women wrought for her—pomanders and cushions of thistle-down; and the men were never happier than when they could tell her of the first thrush's egg in the thornbush or a sighting of the bitterns that haunted the marsh. She was their goddess and their daughter. Each day had its own routine. In the morning she rode and sang and played; at noon she read in the dusty library, drinking to the full of the dramatists and the platonists. Her own life was such a tragedy as an Elizabethan would have adored. None save her people knew her history, but there were wonderful stories of how she had bowed to tradition, and concentrated in herself the characteristics of a thousand wizard fathers. In the blossom of her youth she had sought strange knowledge, and had tasted thereof, and rued.

The morning after my declaration she rode across her park to the meditating walk I always paced till noon. She was alone, dressed in a habit of white with a loose girdle of blue. As her mare reached the yew hedge, she dismounted, and came to me with more lightness than I had ever beheld in her. At her waist hung a black glass mirror, and her half-bare arms were adorned with cabalistic jewels.

When I knelt to kiss her hand, she sighed heavily. "Ask me nothing," she said. "Life itself is too joyless to be more embittered by explanations. Let all rest between us as now. I will love coldly, you warmly, with no nearer approaching." Her voice rang full of a wistful expectancy: as if she knew that I should combat her half-explained decision. She read me well, for almost ere she had done I cried out loudly against it: "It can never be so—I cannot breathe—I shall die."

She sank to the low moss-covered wall. "Must the sacrifice be made?" she asked, half to herself. "Must I tell him all?" Silence prevailed awhile, then turning away her face she said: "From the first I loved you, but last night in the darkness, when I could not sleep for thinking of your words, love sprang into desire."

I was forbidden to speak.

"And desire seemed to burst the cords that bound me. In that moment's strength I felt that I could give all for the joy of being once utterly yours."

I longed to clasp her to my heart. But her eyes were stern, and a frown crossed her brow.

"At morning light," she said, "desire died, but in my ecstasy I had sworn to give what must be given for that short bliss, and to lie in your arms and pant against you before another midnight. So I have come to bid you fare with me to the place where the spell may be loosed, and happiness bought."

She called the mare; it came whinnying, and pawed the

ground until she had stroked its neck. She mounted, setting in my hand a tiny, satin-shod foot that seemed rather child's than woman's. "Let us go together to my house," she said. "I have orders to give and duties to fulfill. I will not keep you there long, for we must start soon on our errand." I walked exultantly at her side, but, the grange in view, I entreated her to speak explicitly of our mysterious journey. She stooped and patted my head. " 'Tis but a matter of buying and selling," she answered.

When she had arranged her household affairs, she came to the library and bade me follow her. Then, with the mirror still swinging against her knees, she led me through the garden and the wilderness down to a misty wood. It being autumn, the trees were tinted gloriously in dusky bars of coloring. The rowan, with his amber leaves and scarlet berries, stood before the brown black-spotted sycamore; the silver beech flaunted his golden coins against my poverty; firs, green and fawn-hued, slumbered in hazy gossamer. No bird caroled, although the sun was hot. Marina noted the absence of sound, and without prelude of any kind began to sing from the ballad of the Witch Mother: about the nine enchanted knots, and the trouble-comb in the lady's knotted hair, and the master-kid that ran beneath her couch. Every drop of my blood froze in dread, for whilst she sang her face took on the majesty of one who traffics with infernal powers. As the shade of the trees fell over her, and we passed intermittently out of the light, I saw that her eyes glittered like rings of sapphires. Believing now that the ordeal she must undergo would be too frightful, I begged her to return. Supplicating on my knees—"Let me face the evil alone!" I said, "I will entreat the loosening of the bonds. I will compel and accept any penalty." She grew calm. "Nay," she said, very gently, "if aught can conquer, it is my love alone. In the fervor of my last wish I can dare everything."

By now, at the end of a sloping alley, we had reached the shores of a vast marsh. Some unknown quality in the sparkling water had stained its whole bed a bright yellow. Green leaves, of such a sour brightness as almost poisoned to behold, floated on the surface of the rush-girdled pools. Weeds like tempting veils of mossy velvet grew beneath in vivid contrast with the soil. Alders and willows hung over the margin. From where we stood a half-submerged path of rough stones, threaded by deep swift channels, crossed to the very center. Marina put her foot upon the first step. "I must go first," she said. "Only once before have I gone this way, yet I know its pitfalls better than any living creature."

Before I could hinder her she was leaping from stone to stone like a hunted animal. I followed hastily, seeking, but vainly, to lessen the space between us. She was gasping for breath, and her heartbeats sounded like the ticking of a clock. When we reached a great pool, itself almost a lake, that was covered with lavender scum, the path turned abruptly to the right, where stood an isolated grove of wasted elms. As Marina beheld this, her pace slackened, and she paused in momentary indecision; but, at my first word of pleading that she should go no further, she went on, dragging her silken mud-bespattered skirts. We climbed the slippery shores of the island (for island it was, being raised much above the level of the marsh), and Marina led the way over lush grass to an open glade. A great marble tank lay there, supported on two thick pillars. Decayed boughs rested on the crust of stagnancy within, and frogs, bloated and almost blue, rolled off at our approach. To the left stood the columns of a temple, a round, domed building, with a closed door of bronze. Wild vines had grown athwart the portal; rank, clinging herbs had sprung from the overteeming soil; astrological figures were chiseled on the broad stairs.

Here Marina stopped. "I shall blindfold you," she said, taking off her loose sash, "and you must vow obedience to all I tell you. The least error will betray us." I promised, and submitted to the bandage. With a pressure of the hand, and bidding me neither move nor speak, she left me and went to the door of the temple. Thrice her hand struck the dull metal. At the last stroke a hissing shriek came from within, and the massive hinges creaked loudly. A breath like an icy tongue leaped out and touched me, and in the terror my hand sprang to the kerchief. Marina's voice, filled with agony, gave me instant pause. *"Oh, why am I thus torn between the man and the fiend? The mesh that holds life in will be ripped from end to end! Is there no mercy?"*

My hand fell impotent. Every muscle shrank. I felt myself

turn to stone. After a while came a sweet scent of smoldering wood: such an oriental fragrance as is offered to Indian gods. Then the door swung to, and I heard Marina's voice, dim and wordless, but raised in wild deprecation. Hour after hour passed so, and still I waited. Not until the sash grew crimson with the rays of the sinking sun did the door open.

"Come to me!" Marina whispered. "Do not take off your blindfold. Quick—we must not stay here long. He is glutted with my sacrifice."

Newborn joy rang in her tones. I stumbled across and was caught in her arms. Shafts of delight pierced my heart at the first contact with her warm breasts. She turned me round, and bidding me look straight in front, with one swift touch untied the knot. The first thing my dazed eyes fell upon was the mirror of black glass which had hung from her waist. She held it so that I might gaze into its depths. And there, with a cry of amazement and fear, *I saw the shadow of the Basilisk.*

The Thing was lying prone on the floor, the presentiment of a sleeping horror. Vivid scarlet and sable feathers covered its gold-crowned cock's-head, and its leathern dragon-wings were folded. Its sinuous tail, capped with a snake's eyes and mouth, was curved in luxurious and delighted satiety. A prodigious evil leaped in its atmosphere. But even as I looked a mist crowded over the surface of the mirror: the shadow faded, leaving only an indistinct and wavering shape. Marina breathed upon it, and, as I peered and pored, the gloom went off the plate and left, where the Thing had lain, the prostrate figure of a man. He was young and stalwart, a dark outline with a white face, and short black curls that fell in tangles over a shapely forehead, and eyelids languorous and red. His aspect was that of a weariéd demon-god.

When Marina looked sideways and saw my wonderment, she laughed delightedly in one rippling running tune that should have quickened the dead entrails of the marsh. "I have conquered!" she cried. "I have purchased the fullness of joy!" And with one outstretched arm she closed the door before I could turn to look; with the other she encircled my neck, and, bringing down my head, pressed my mouth to hers. The mirror fell from her hand, and with her foot she crushed its shards into the dank mold.

The sun had sunk behind the trees now, and glittered through the intricate leafage like a charcoal burner's fire. All the nymphs of the pools arose and danced, gray and cold, exulting at the absence of the divine light. So thickly gathered the vapors that the path grew perilous. "Stay, love," I said. "Let me take you in my arms and carry you. It is no longer safe for you to walk alone." She made no reply, but, a flush arising to her pale cheeks, she stood and let me lift her to my bosom. She rested a hand on either shoulder, and gave no sign of fear as I bounded from stone to stone. The way lengthened deliciously, and by the time we reached the plantation the moon was rising over the further hills. Hope and fear fought in my heart: soon both were set at rest. When I set her on the dry ground she stood a-tiptoe, and murmured with exquisite shame: "Tonight, then, dearest. My home is yours now."

So, in a rapture too subtle for words, we walked together, arm-enfolded, to her house. Preparations for a banquet were going on within: the windows were ablaze, and figures passed behind them bowed with heavy dishes. At the threshold of the hall we were met by a triumphant crash of melody. In the musicians' gallery bald-pated veterans played with flute and harp and viol-de-gamba. In two long rows the antic retainers stood, and bowed, and cried merrily: "Joy and health to the bride and groom!" And they kissed Marina's hands and mine, and, with the players sending forth that half-forgotten tenderness which threads through ancient songbooks, we passed to the feast, seating ourselves on the dais, whilst the servants filled the tables below. But we made little feint of appetite. As the last dish of confections was removed a weird pageant swept across the further end of the banqueting room: Oberon and Titania with Robin Goodfellow and the rest, attired in silks and satins gorgeous of hue, and bedizened with such late flowers as were still with us. I leaned forward to commend, and saw that each face was brown and wizened and thin haired: so that their motions and their wedding paean felt goblin and discomforting; nor could I smile till they departed by the further door. Then the tables were cleared away, and Marina, taking my fingertips in hers, opened a stately dance. The servants followed, and in the second maze, a shrill and joyful laughter proclaimed that the bride had sought her chamber. . . .

Ere the dawn I wakened from a troubled sleep. My dream had been of despair: I had been persecuted by a host of devils, thieves of a priceless jewel. So I leaned over the pillow for Marina's consolation; my lips sought hers, my hand crept beneath her head. My heart gave one mad bound—then stopped.

A QUARTER PAST YOU

JONATHAN CARROLL

"He became an entirely different person in the dark. She couldn't see him so he could have been anyone."

Between any two people, the sharing of a sexual fantasy is an exhibition of trust. It is also, however, an opening for vulnerability, and what is whispered in the safety of the dark can return to haunt one in the daylight hours. Jonathan Carroll understands this possibility only too well, and he recognizes how innocently—at first—we hurt one another in the name of love.

It began innocently enough, sort of. They loved each other. They wanted to grow old together, and that is the only real proof of great love. But recently there had been one thing, one large speck of dust on their otherwise clear lens: sex. It had always been fine with them, and there *were* times when they reveled in each other. But sleep with another person a thousand nights and some of sex's phosphorescence rubs off under the touch of familiar fingers.

One time, as they worked to catch each other's rhythms, she'd uttered something inadvertently that made him smile and want to talk about later, during those fading soft moments before sleep.

"You shouldn't!" was what she'd suddenly said.

He hadn't been doing anything new or special, so he had to assume she was fantasizing a naughty scene with someone else! The thought excited him, particularly because he himself had often done the same thing.

Afterward in the blue dark, he touched her hand and asked if he was right.

"I'm embarrassed." But then she giggled—her sign she was willing to talk.

"Come on, don't be embarrassed. I've done it too. I promise! It's just another way."

"You promise you won't misunderstand?"

"I promise."

"OK, but I'm really embarrassed."

He squeezed her hand and knew not to say anything or else she would shut right up.

"Well, it's not anyone in particular. Just this man. It's a fantasy. I see him on a subway and can't stop looking at him."

"How's he dressed?"

"The way I like—jacket and tie, maybe in a nice suit. But he's also wearing fresh white tennis sneakers, which throws the whole thing off in a great way. It's a touch of humor that says he wears what he wants and doesn't give a damn what others think."

"OK. So what happens then?"

She took a deep breath and let it all out slowly before continuing. "I see him and can't stop looking, as I said. He's sexy and that's part of it, sure, but there are other things that make him more special than just that.

"He has these great Frenchman's eyes, and is carrying a book I've been meaning to read for a long time. Finally he looks at me and I'm hooked completely. The best part is, he doesn't check out my body or anything. Just looks at me and I know he's interested. I love that. He doesn't go over me like I'm a new car in the showroom."

Her story was much more detailed than he'd have thought. In

his own fantasies, he'd make eyes at waitresses in high heels or shopgirls with thick lips. Things were arranged. They'd go back to her apartment. Once there, they'd leap to it with instant heat and curiosity.

Moments pass before he realizes she's begun speaking again.

". . . follows me when I get off the subway. Knowing he's there behind makes me incredibly excited. I know what's going to happen and I know I'll do it, no matter what."

She talked on, giving the most minute, loving details. She and Mr. White Sneakers never speak, not once. As things get more intense, they slow down until it's all movement under water.

The single sentence ever said aloud is the line "You shouldn't!" This is something she says each time, but only once it's actually happening and she feels a momentary pang of guilt. But that passes quickly because the experience is simply too rare and extreme for guilt to enter into it at all.

When she was finished, there was a silence thick as fur between them. Under her breath, she mumbled something about its not being a very original fantasy.

"Don't say that! Don't degrade it! What do you care, so long as it excites *you*? What difference does it make how original it is? I bet three-quarters of most people's sexual fantasies are either about taking or being taken.

"What's his name?" He helped her.

"Who, the man? I have no idea. We don't talk. He never tells me."

"What do you *want* his name to be?"

"I never thought about it. What a funny question."

He went into the kitchen for some wine. When he returned, the light on her side of the bed was on and she was sitting with her arms wrapped around her knees.

"Peter Copeland." She smiled at him and shrugged as if a little embarrassed.

"Peter Copeland? Sounds like a Yalie."

She shrugged again. "I don't know. It's just the kind of name he would have."

"OK. Is it always the same fantasy? Do you ever make up others about him?"

She took a sip of wine and thought about it. She no longer seemed uncomfortable talking about Peter Copeland now that the fact of him was out in the open and had a name.

"Usually the same— The subway, what he wears . . . How he follows me. It's enough."

That last phrase hit him hard. He'd had so many different fantasies with so many different predictable faces and settings. "It's enough." He knew then he was jealous of her and her Peter Copeland, content with each other and their silent, mutual fever.

The next day walking to work, he stopped in the middle of the street and started to smirk. At a florist, he bought ten tulips, her favorite flower, and arranged to have them sent over to their apartment. On the enclosed card he wrote, "I hope you like tulips. They're my favorite. Thanks for putting the comet over last night's sky. Peter."

And in bed that night, he changed everything. He became an entirely different person in the dark. She couldn't see him so he could have been anyone. He wanted to be Peter Copeland but didn't know how.

Usually they spoke, but in this half hour when they owned each other, he said nothing. From the beginning she understood and responded eagerly. Whenever they sailed toward something familiar, their own from their years together, he steered them away. Then she took over and was strong or passive when he least expected it.

It was all better than he had imagined and once again he grew so jealous of Peter Copeland. No stranger, however wonderful, deserved what she offered now. The only things he had ever given *his* dream lovers were both anonymous and forgettable.

At the end, when she again said, "You shouldn't!" he was thrilled she was saying it both to him and someone else. A moment later he wished it were only him.

The next day he bought the book he knew she had been wanting to read. Inside he wrote, "I think you'll like this. Peter." She discovered it under her pillow. Sitting down on the bed, she held it on her lap, both hands on top of it and very still. What was he doing? Did she like it?

Their electricity and willingness to go in so many new directions both awed and scared them a little. Both wondered who they were doing this for—themselves or the other?

That week their nights were long exhausting experiments. He couldn't ask her what she liked because it all had to remain silent: spoken only through touch and movement. By eight every night they were excited and looking at the clock. Whatever they'd been used to doing before was unimportant and forgotten. Now they would slip into their new second skins and whatever was left of the day would hide because it did not know them.

On Thursday she was out walking and decided to buy him a present. In a store, a salesman spread beautiful cashmere sweaters over a glass counter. Lilac. Taupe. Black. She couldn't decide. Only after leaving the store did she realize she'd chosen one that would look better on Peter Copeland than on her husband. That startled her, but she made no move to return it. She simply wouldn't tell him.

At work he realized he'd written the name PETER COPELAND three times on a pad of paper in front of him. He didn't even know he was doing it. Each time the script was completely different. As if he were trying to forge rather than invent the other man's signature.

"What's for dinner?"
"Your favorite—chili."
He didn't like chili.

There was no chili—her little joke—but the tulips he sent were in a new black and yellow vase on the dining table between them. They were like a third person in the room. He wanted to tell her about writing Copeland's name but the vivid flowers were enough of the other's presence for the moment.

He looked at them again and realized he was not looking at

the same ones he'd bought: Those were pink, these are deep
red. Where did she put his?

"It's tulip season again, huh?"

She smiled and nodded.

"I saw some great pink ones the other day. I knew I should
have gotten them for you. Somebody beat me to it, huh?"

Her smile remained. It said nothing different from a moment
ago. Or was it the slightest bit pitying?

He liked to shave before going to bed—a personal quirk.
Standing in front of the bathroom mirror scraping off the
last bits of snowy foam, he suddenly pointed his razor at the
mirror.

"I heard what you two are doing. Don't think I don't know,
you bastard!"

"Are you talking to me?" she called from the bedroom.

"No, Peter Copeland."

He smiled his own weird smile when she didn't say anything
to *that*.

Her fingers were moving lightly across his face when he saw
how to break it. Pushing her hand away, he took over and
started touching her much too hard, hurting her. To his surprise, she jerked and twisted but remained silent. It was always
silent now. Somewhere in these recent days they had both
accepted that. But why wasn't she protesting? Why didn't she
tell him to stop? Did she like it? How could she? She had said a
million times she couldn't understand how people could like
hurting each other in bed. Or was Peter Copeland allowed
everything? Worse, was the pain he gave pleasant to her now?
That was insane! It meant he knew nothing about his wife. It
made him breathe too fast. What parts of her did he know, for
sure? What else had she held back from him over the years?

He started saying brutal, dirty things to her. It was something they both disliked. Their sexy words to each other were
always funny and flattering, loving.

"Don't!" It was the first time she had spoken. She was looking
straight at him, real alarm on her face.

"Why? I'll do what I want."

He continued talking. Touching her too hard, talking, ruining everything. He told her where he worked, how much money he made, what his hobbies were. He told her where he'd gone to college, where he grew up, how he liked his eggs done.

Soon she was crying and stopped moving altogether. He was in the middle of explaining to her that he wore white sneakers because he had this bad foot infection. . . .

THE MASTER BUILDER

CHRISTOPHER FOWLER

"But then, of course, there were other reasons for the glowing testimonials of his clients. . . . Smiling to herself, Alison picked up the phone and dialed."

Laurie Fischer, the outwardly self-assured heroine of this modern metropolitan Grand Guignol, is, unfortunately, about to learn just how fragile are anyone's illusions of control. No matter what walls we build around ourselves, they can, under insistent, insidious pressure, be breached.

A move is the catalyst: Laurie used to live in Manhattan, but, acting on unaccustomed impulse, she's crossed the Hudson and gentrifying, "semi-fashionable" Hoboken is now home—or it will be as soon as the renovations on her new co-op are completed. The extensive work is being done by a lone builder, a jack-of-all-trades suggested by her best friend. She's heard of his rather unusual reputation and imagines that he will help Laurie get a new lease on life in more ways than one.

But since this is a story by Christopher Fowler, who specializes in the art of urban anxiety, who loves to expose for us the potential for peril in those seemingly insignificant choices we make each day, Laurie's troubles are hardly over after she's been presented with the final bill.

———~~~~~———

"The place I went to see on West Forty-fourth?"

"Mmm—I'm lighting a cigarette—go on."

"It turned out to be a miniature attic with a small circular window and a sloping ceiling. The kind of room you couldn't even lock up a small child in. Although of course you can lock a small child up in almost anything."

"You're not going to be single all your life, Laurie. Then you might feel different about having children."

"I doubt it. My favorite story is still the one about the princes in the tower."

"Tell me the rest. There's obviously more, otherwise you wouldn't be dragging this out for so long."

"OK . . ."

"I mean, of course you're not going to find another place in midtown Manhattan, for God's sake. You should have made Jerry move out."

"Alison, it was his apartment!"

"Then you guys should have stayed together. It was worth it just for the location."

"Shut up, Allie, and let me finish. So, this was the fifth apartment I'd checked out since noon, and it was raining, and naturally there was as much chance of finding a cab as there was locating the Ark of the Covenant, and I find myself in Herald Square so I jump on the PATH train—"

"Oh my God, you're moving to New Jersey."

"Well, Hoboken. It's—"

"I know, I know, only ten minutes from town and half the rent. But you know what they say: once you move off the island you never get back on. Still, I guess it's kind of semi-fashionable to live there now. Go on."

"OK, so Hoboken. Well, I was walking along a street somewhere off Washington, right down by the river, and I saw a 'For Sale' notice in this window."

"Wait, you're gonna *buy*?"

"I figure, why pay rent all your life? The point is, I put in a bid and it's been accepted."

"Can you afford it?"

Laurie laughed. "No, of course not. It's on the second floor, above a Korean deli, and it needs a hell of a lot of work, but it has a View. I mean, there's just the river straight ahead, then the lights of the city are spread out before you."

"Sounds perfect. What's the catch?"

"No catch, at least I don't think so. I want you to come out and see it with me before I start alterations. You're so good with design ideas, and you know I've no sense of color coordination."

On the other end of the line, Alison sighed. "Yeah, I guess I owe it to your future boyfriends to make sure that your apartment doesn't end up looking like you won it on *Wheel of Fortune*. Name a date and we'll go check it out."

"How about Saturday?"

"Fine by me."

The September wind that blew across from the Hudson felt humid and unhealthy. It swirled around the old ferry buildings and down into the entrance of the subway as Alison rebuttoned her coat and left the station. She checked the address on the slip of paper and headed up along Third Street, past a clutch of smart new restaurants that characterized Hoboken's reborn status as a desirable neighborhood. She quickly located the delicatessen near the corner and looked up at the windows above. The building itself appeared to be rather nondescript, its gray brickwork fascia blending with the slight architectural variations on either side. She looked back down in time to see her friend striding along the sidewalk toward her. As always, Laurie looked immaculate. Glossy dark hair brushed her shoulders as she turned her head and smiled. The expensively simple black suit she wore emphasized her tiny waist. She had a figure that only a dedicated career woman could afford to keep.

"I'm not late, am I?" Laurie hiked up her coat sleeve and checked her watch, revealing a slender white wrist.

"No, I was early. Looks like you'll have all the stores you need right here." Alison gestured along the street.

"Hey, don't knock it." Laurie stepped into the doorway beside the deli and searched her purse for keys. "I mean, have you seen the Stylish Modes Beauty Parlor two doors along? How could I ever think of getting my hair done anywhere else?" She unlocked the outer door and beckoned Alison inside.

"It still smells a little funky in here," she said, wrinkling her nose. "The old lady who had the place kept cats."

A second door admitted them to a gloomy narrow hallway and a flight of gray-carpeted stairs. Laurie gestured dismissively at the bare walls as they ascended.

"At the moment this is just so—*hallway*. Don't look at it."

"I guess you could brighten it up by bolting some prints to the wall."

"Allie, this is not Manhattan, it's a much safer neighborhood." She had to fit three separate keys to the door locks before they could enter the apartment. "Oh, sure," said Alison, studying the burglar bolts as she passed them.

The room before them was presumably intended to be a combined sitting area and kitchen. The faded purple carpets released a pungent and unmistakably feline odor. Stained brown wallpaper revealed the shapes of recently removed paintings and light fixtures. Against the farthest wall a broken-backed sofa slumped, its corduroy covering worn smooth with use.

The two women moved into the adjoining room, turning around as they did so. The cramped kitchen alcove consisted of a mustard-yellow counter and a number of cheaply finished wooden cupboards. Mouse droppings lay scattered on most of the work surfaces.

"Admittedly the place doesn't look like it's been cleaned since the fifties," said Laurie, running a manicured finger along the top of a shelf.

"Hygiene Hell," agreed Alison, moving gingerly, careful not to touch anything. "If you're serious about this, all I can say is that you must have more design vision than I gave you credit for."

"I have more than vision," said Alison. "I have a View." She tugged on a dirty gray curtain draped across the far doorway, and there it was. A huge, spectacular room with double windows and an unspoiled view of the Hudson and the city beyond.

Any objections Alison could have raised about her friend's planned purchase were felled at a stroke. Watery sunlight streaked the sides of the distant skyscrapers that filled the room's horizons like a living fresco. Barges could be glimpsed passing the shoreside buildings, their horns sounding in forlorn cadence against the cries of wheeling gulls.

"Can you believe the previous owner had actually boarded over the windows?" said Laurie, pointing to a stack of planks standing in a corner.

"Why would anyone do that?" asked Alison, moving to the glass.

"I don't know. I guess she must have been a little crazy. I believe she was very old."

"So when did she move out?"

"She didn't. She died. The apartment went to her nephew, but he lives in the Midwest and just wants to sell it."

Laurie turned from the window and led the way to a far door across the room. Beyond lay a short flight of steps leading to the first of two bedrooms. Alison took a step inside and halted. The room was dark and musty with the smell of stale blankets. Here the windows were still nailed shut with sheets of plywood. Laurie reached across and switched on the overhead light, a single naked bulb that illuminated the sagging bed, an unraveled wicker chair, and an ancient, badly painted dresser.

"I think you're going to find yourself with a lot of structural alteration on your hands," said Alison. "Even the walls you keep will all need replastering. You'll never be able to live here while it's being fixed up." Alison tried to avoid looking at the bed, its bare mattress stained dark, perhaps with the secretions of the old woman's dying body. She looked over at Laurie, who seemed to be reading her mind.

"She didn't die here. She was in the hospital for a long time. The bathroom's through the hall in the far corner."

The cheap modern tub with the cracked floor seemed almost willfully misplaced in the large bathroom. A much older china sink stood against a partially tiled wall. Most of the plumbing seemed to have been connected in plain sight, with pipes jutting from every corner.

"It's going to cost a fortune to do it properly, you know that."

"Look at the outlay in terms of long-term investment," said Laurie. "I'll never get another chance like this."

"Maybe you're right. There's plenty of scope for renovation, I'll say that. And the property can only go up in value."

Laurie led the way back to the living room, passing another much smaller bedroom. "You think that's too small for a guest room?" she asked. "Maybe it should be knocked through."

"I don't know. You don't want to reduce the number of rooms too much. Suppose you decide that you want someone to live with you."

"Oh, no," said Laurie firmly. "I'm not living with anyone ever again. And I'm never going to get married, you know that."

"Yeah, you say so now, but maybe in a year or two . . ."

"In a year or two we could all be dead." She gestured at the walls, anxious to change the subject. "So, could it work? What do you think?"

"What I think is the apartment's wonderful. But you're going to need a real professional to come in and handle the renovation from start to finish."

"How do I find someone to do that?"

Alison smiled. "I know a master builder," she said.

Laurie Fischer worked for a large publishing house on East Fiftieth Street. She had been employed there as an acquisitions editor for nearly four years, and in that time had lived up to her reputation as a formidably bullish negotiator. Three years before, on her twenty-seventh birthday and against her better judgment, she had moved into an apartment with an advertising executive named Jerry, but her relationship with him—never once referred to by either party as a romance—had all too quickly degenerated into a series of uncomfortable power plays.

On the surface, things had seemed perfect. If the idea of cohabiting with such a man had been presented to Laurie in the form of a business deal, she would have jumped at it.

Jerry had an inquiring mind, great plans for the future, perfect teeth, and a house in the Hamptons. Unfortunately, he also had an ego the size of his real-estate holdings and a lump of rock where his heart should have been. He was a grown man of thirty-four who wanted to live with a beautiful, independent woman and still be allowed to play the field.

When the strains on the relationship started to affect Laurie's work, she moved out. The final parting was recriminatory and messy. Now she was single again, still the subject of longing glances from colleagues and friends, still the woman whose private life remained a delicious mystery to all but a few.

Allison had known her for more years than she cared to admit. The two of them had gone to high school together, had shared most secrets. The only remaining uncharted territory of their friendship was that part concerning love and sex. Even at school, Laurie had never dated. Her academic success had been qualified by her lack of popularity with other students, most of whom had felt threatened by such a noticeably superior combination of beauty and brains. Boys had quickly christened her The Icicle, and she gave them no cause to reconsider the title.

In Alison's opinion, her friend was a biological time bomb waiting to explode. Surely nobody could hold back so much for so long. Years earlier, she had forced friendship onto her glacial classmate when everyone else at school had given up trying to do so, and she had never been sorry for making the effort. Laurie, once you got to know her, was an extraordinarily kind person, a generous friend, irascible and acid-tongued at times to be sure, but always true. And although Alison considered herself to be much the less attractive of the pair, she had never felt her personality eclipsed by Laurie. After all, hadn't she been the one with all the dates, and wasn't she now still enjoying a long-term romance, albeit with a married man, while Laurie dressed for success and worked late most nights?

Alison reminded herself to call Laurie and give her the telephone number of the builder. She had never met the man personally, but friends were unable to praise him highly enough. Last year he had apparently transformed an apartment belonging to an opera singer at the Met into an award-winning *House & Garden* photo spread, yet his fees remained low and his daily rate was considered—by New York standards at least—to be very reasonable. But then, of course, there were other reasons for the glowing testimonials of his clients. . . . Smiling to herself, Alison picked up the telephone and dialed.

After half an hour of sitting in the empty apartment with a sketchpad, Laurie gave up. She rose and smoothed out the legs of her jeans, laying the pad on a pile of crumpled-up paper balls. Alison had been right. Her design sense just wasn't up to the task that faced her. The deal on the property had gone through quickly enough, and the deposit had now been paid. The mortgage loan had been handled with almost supernatural efficiency, and she saw no reason why the closing date should not be kept. What bothered her more was that she would have to continue staying with friends until the work on the apartment was completed, and who knew just how long that would take?

She looked around the room. The day's dying sunlight glanced from the river onto the walls in soft golden hues, investing the apartment with a hint of the grandeurs to come. She checked the ancient bakelite telephone to see if the line was still connected, then dialed the number Alison had given her that morning and asked to speak to the master builder.

He answered the phone himself, in a voice that was deep and slow, and gave the impression that he was weighing and judging each word before committing it to use. The job provided marvelous scope for creativity, Laurie explained, but would have to be finished before Christmas. Could he possibly come and take a look at the property before the weekend? He reckoned he could. She gave him the address and fixed a time for the meeting. After she had hung up, she wrote the number for Ray Bellano in her Filofax under "Service: Builder."

"You gonna do this properly, you gotta take it back to scratch and start again." He ran a broad hand across the living-room wall, knocked on it with his knuckle, picked at a loose edge of wallpaper that lifted away from the plaster with alarming ease. "This here is a support wall. Reckon you could replace it with a couple of central pillars, but for what? It's a big apartment. Taking out the walls'll make the living room look out of proportion to the rest of the place. Now you can do that if you want, but you're gonna be sorry you did."

In the half hour since Laurie had opened the door to the builder, he had torn down every idea she had presented. A simple yes or no didn't seem to suffice with him; there was always an adverse comment to be made. The man was downright rude.

"Sure, I can do that if you want me to, Miss, but it'll look real ugly." "We can put a window in through there, but I'm telling you it'll look kind of stupid." *We* can put a window in, as if he and Laurie were buying the apartment together. She stepped back against the far wall with her arms folded across her chest and watched as he lumbered between the rooms, digging into the plaster with the end of a metal ruler, stooping to pry up a broken section of floorboard. He was well over six feet tall, broad-chested and ugly-handsome, clad in boots and dirty jeans, dark hair curling from the neck of his sweatshirt. When he passed her, he trailed a smell of Brylcreem and sweat.

"Come in here a minute." He was calling to her from the main bedroom, as familiar as if they were newlyweds. Well, she would quickly put a stop to this.

"Mr. Bellano," she began in her coldest business voice, "let's get one thing straight around here." She walked to the doorway and waited for him to stand and look at her.

"Please, call me Ray," he said, turning slowly and rising to his full height. "All my good friends do. And as it looks like this job is gonna take some time to get right, I figure we're gonna become good friends." Then he smiled, a dangerous white smile that squared his jaw and ran from one side to the other of his bristle-shaded face. Laurie stopped in her tracks, suddenly aware that she was alone in the apartment with a complete stranger.

"I suppose you're right," she said in a careful, clear voice. "Although as I'll be staying with friends in Manhattan until the work is completed, I don't suppose we will be meeting very often." She gestured at the bedroom walls. "I'd like you to submit plans within ten working days, together with a quote for your time, building materials, and so forth."

"Now wait just a minute," said the builder, raising a broad palm. "I haven't said I'll take the job yet." He wandered from the room, leaving Laurie to fume at the man's arrogance. Who the hell did he think he was? OK, so he'd made a good job of some hot-shot opera singer's apartment, but that didn't make him Andy Warhol. If he was so great, how come his prices were so low? She stormed after him and was about to deliver a frank sermon on male arrogance when he strode out of the bathroom, almost bumping into her, and said, "I'll do it." And that was the end of that.

Or rather, the beginning.

Because two weeks later Ray Bellano delivered his plans and his estimate, and another argument developed between them.

The master builder had ignored her instructions, and had designed the apartment entirely to his own specifications. Only the finest materials were to be used, but this would force the final bill to the limit of her financial allowance.

"I cannot let you do this," said Laurie as she studied the plans in her office. "Why do the walls have to be so thick? And why use hardwood when you could use pine? This is going to clean me out, Ray, and I still have to buy furniture once it's finished."

"Look, Ms. Fischer," said Ray, "I'm sure you're great at your job—whatever it is you do—but I guess you're gonna have to trust me a little bit. I'll tell you what I want you to do. Take down this number. I want you to call one of my previous clients and ask them about me. Check it out. Then call me back and approve the fee." After he had hung up, Laurie decided to call his bluff. She telephoned the number he had given her and asked to speak to Mrs. Irene Bloom.

"Ray Bellano? The man's simply a genius. He changed my life. He rebuilt my duplex with a selection of the oddest materials, things I would never have dreamed of using, but it worked! Inlaid redwoods and fumed ash in the kitchen! After that I commissioned him to completely rebuild my other properties. If you'd like to see some pictures of his work I could get them over to you. . . ."

"That won't be necessary, thanks," replied Laurie. After hanging up, she sat by her office window and watched the teeming life in the city streets far below. It looked hot down there. Sometimes, working alone in the air-conditioned silence of her office, she felt completely cut off from the outside world. Perhaps it was just an aftereffect of leaving Jerry, but she was beginning to question the point of working so hard and sharing so little with other people. The couple she was staying with were being terrific to her, cooking almost every night and filling her spare evenings with easy conversation. Still, she knew that there would be a limit to Peter and Fran's hospitality. At dinner she made the seating numbers odd. She was a single that others were forever trying to pair up. She knew that despite all protestations to the contrary, there would be sighs of relief on both sides when she eventually moved into her own apartment. Without further hesitation, Laurie called the master builder and gave him the order to start work immediately.

A week later, she pushed open the door of the Hoboken apartment and stepped into a nightmarish explosion of brick and plaster debris. A dull thudding shook the room as she lifted her high-heeled shoes across the planks that covered gaping holes in the floor. The reverberations were coming from the bathroom, where, cocooned within a storm of plaster dust, the builder stood swinging a sledgehammer at a network of twisted pipes. Coughing, Laurie stepped back and watched from a safe distance as he lifted the hammer above his head and slammed it down into the plumbing again and again. Finally he saw her and approached, wiping rivers of sweat from his forehead and flicking it to the floor. He was stripped to the waist, and wore only his faded Levis and cowboy boots. Although it was unintentional, Laurie could not help noticing the powerfully defined pectoral muscles of his chest and the thick line of darkly curled hair that trailed across a hard tanned stomach into his jeans.

"I wouldn't advise you to come in here, Miss," he cautioned. "These walls ain't too safe at the moment."

Laurie avoided his gaze and concentrated on brushing a smudge of plaster dust from her suit. "You don't seem to have anyone helping you, Mr. Bellano," she said stiffly. "I felt sure that you'd employ a team. You can't possibly handle the job by yourself."

"I think you'll find that I'm more than capable of handlin' this alone, ma'am," he replied, a smile playing on his lips. Did she imagine it, or was there a hint of sexual suggestion in his voice? Could it be that she was acting the uptight New Yorker with this amiable Midwesterner whose gaze was as direct and unflinching as his attitude? Not caring to analyze her feelings any further, she left the chaotic apartment with a promise to return in a week's time. He was to call her office if he needed to pay cash for any builders' deliveries. The complexity of her current work schedule made it necessary for her to ask him to limit his calls to emergencies and requests for money. She was sure he understood.

When she returned to the office, she found herself in the middle of a crisis. Her secretary had been frantically trying to contact her. Where had she been? Laurie was suddenly aware that she had slipped away to the apartment without telling anyone where she was going. The motive for this course of action still proved elusive to her as she headed back to Peter and Fran's at the end of the day.

"It's really not too soon to start thinking about dating again, you know," said Fran as she ladled linguini onto her plate. "You don't need to be told what a terrific catch you'd make for someone."

"God, Fran, you make me sound like a teenager." Laurie started to carefully wrap pasta around her fork. "Dating is not a fun activity for a thirty-year-old woman, believe me. You had the taste and good grace to marry Peter when you were twenty-six. I'm past that point and moving into the Twilight Zone as far as males are concerned."

"I think you're just being cynical," said Peter, who had the annoying mealtime habit of holding his wife's hand under the table as he ate.

"It's not just cynicism. After a while you get to know all the types and their variations. The divorced guys who are either looking for reincarnations of their ex-wives or want to tell you about their plans for getting back custody of the kids. The ones who admit that they only beat up on their girlfriends when they step out of line or make eyes at someone in a restaurant. The late-starters, the Peter Pan Syndromers, the holistic health nuts, grown men who still go to discos, for Christ's sake . . ." She fell silent, toying with her pasta, embarrassed.

"Do you know when the apartment will be completed?" asked Peter in an attempt to change the conversation which looked exactly like an attempt to change the conversation. "Before Christmas, right?"

"This side of Thanksgiving, hopefully," said Laurie. "I have to get furniture in before Christmas, but it's going very slowly at the moment."

"You know," said Fran carefully, "if you were staying there you could keep a much more watchful eye on the work, and maybe speed things up."

Laurie realized then that her friends were anxious for her to name a departure date. She finished her meal in forced good humor and went to bed early. When she arrived at the office the next morning, the first thing she did was speak to Mr. Bellano.

"I guess I could finish one of the bedrooms in the next week or so," he said in that infuriatingly half-asleep voice of his. "You wouldn't disturb me by moving in."

That's nice to know, thought Laurie, angrily shoving a disk into her P.C. Jeez, I'd hate to inconvenience you. She shoved the silky black hair from her eyes and stared hard at the computer screen, not seeing the pale green paragraphs that unrolled before her.

That night, Laurie Fischer visited the Slum Club with a young, supposedly hot new novelist from Los Angeles who went by the unlikely name of Dig. She picked her way home through the garment district at five the next morning with little more than a business card and a hangover to remember the evening by, although she was sure that nothing very interesting had happened.

The following Saturday afternoon she moved into the Hoboken apartment. As Ray had promised, the bedroom was at least habitable. The room had been cleared of planks, bricks, and plasterboard, and the door closed as far as a door without a lock and handle could. The light in the room was a soft yellow, the color and smell of light pine, the walls awaiting fresh paint or clean bright wallpaper. She lay on the mattress and gazed up at the ceiling as the afternoon sun fell below the water and threw slivers of light across the ceiling.

She could hear Ray working—quietly, for once—in the next room. It sounded as if he was planing wood. She could hear the metal edge dragging lightly and then lifting as he inspected his work, running his fingers across the grain, checking the finish. The man was a fifties caricature. He probably took women to bed by throwing them over his shoulder. She wondered where he lived, who his friends were. She had forgotten that there were men like him, straight-arrow guys who worked with their hands and didn't spend their time smart-talking women around in circles. How had Alison come to meet him? The slow back-and-forth of the plane on the wood gradually lulled her into light, warm sleep.

She awoke to find the room half in darkness and the builder's backlit silhouette filling the bedroom doorway. He was standing very still and looking on, plane in hand, still stripped to the waist. She raised her hand to her forehead, shielding the remaining light from her eyes. He was watching her with a content half smile on his face.

"What is it?" She raised herself on one elbow and smiled back.

"You called out. I think you was dreaming."

"Really? What did I say?" Laurie was intrigued. The builder looked down at his boots, embarrassed.

"Oh, nothin' much."

"Come on, what did I say?"

"You called my name."

"I wonder why I did that."

Suddenly he walked to the bed and dropped down onto her, his broad, fleshy lips flitting over hers in a powerful kiss that forced her head back into the pillows. His right hand found her forearm and pinned it beside her head as he used his free hand to tear open the front of her shirt. She twisted in protest, raising her leg to find it met by his powerful thighs as he lowered himself on top of her, the heavy base of his erect penis pressing a denim-clad column into her crotch. With her free hand she tried to prevent his hairy chest from pushing down onto her breasts, but found her fingers digging into his back and sliding down into the waistband of his tattered jeans. In a single swift movement he tore open her thin silk brassiere, cupping her right breast with his broad, warm fingers, tweaking the small nipple between thumb and forefinger. Lowering his head, he ran his tongue into her cleavage, leaving a broad band of saliva between her breasts, continuing down to her flat, pale stomach. Feeling no resistance now, he freed her arm and used both hands to lift her buttocks and rip open the seam at the back of her skirt, pulling it to one side and allowing it to slide from the bed. The wide palm of his hand covered her pubic area as his fingers probed inside her panties, forcing them down around her thighs.

His eyes, darkly glittering, caught hers and held them as he fumbled with the opening of his jeans, freeing himself from within. She felt his hands exploring her, forcing her open as his pelvis pressed down and the head of his organ slowly entered her. She cried out, the builder's thick shaft following the rhythm of her ragged breath as inch by inch its entire length was enclosed by her shuddering body. The weight of his torso eased as he partly withdrew, holding himself aloft for a moment before pressing down hard into her, retreating and plunging again and again, the muscles in his dark arms lifting and broadening with each stroke until she felt their powerful mutual climax reach flashpoint within her and flood out in streaming neural pulses, causing her to scream now in involuntary spasms of pain and gratification.

"It was weird."

"Weird? *Weird?* The greatest sexual experience of your life, and all you can say is it was weird?"

"That's right," Laurie thought for a moment, her elbows on the table, the coffee cup poised between her hands. The restaurant was almost empty, but she still spoke softly. "Dangerous."

Alison lit a Virginia Slim and gestured impatiently with it. "Explain what you mean."

"He barely kissed me. Once I think, hard. It was sex at the most basic level. No small talk, no protection, just a fast hard ... fuck. Afterwards, he sat on the end of the bed rebuttoning his shirt, refusing to even catch my eye. I was lying there with my clothes in shreds around me, feeling like I'd been in a serious car crash, and he wasn't even out of breath. He rose and walked to the mirror, flicked his hair into place, shoved the comb into the pocket of his jeans, then went straight back to work."

"You're kidding. What did you do?"

"I guess I went a little crazy, called him a few names. He just looked up from his carpentry and smiled, so I left the apartment, took a walk around and tried to cool off. I felt so ashamed."

"Have you seen him since?"

"Sure. The next day he turned up at the apartment, on time as usual, and began work as if nothing had happened."

"So what are you going to do now?"

"I'm not sure. Obviously, the situation can't be allowed to repeat itself."

"But you need him."

"To finish the job, I guess I do."

Alison studied the end of her cigarette, a slim smile slowly forming on her face.

*   *   *

Two days later, despite Laurie's promises and protestations, it happened again. Through the master builder she allowed herself to enter a world of sexual experience that she had never before encountered. She tried to understand her willingness to take part in the increasingly furious bouts of lovemaking, which left her bruised and exhausted, but she knew that the key to explaining her behavior lay with first understanding her enigmatic partner. Ray Bellano rarely spoke, was barely civil to her, but made love with a passion and intensity that shocked Laurie to her core. Each performance became a display of power more violent than the last, but afterward he always dressed and left the apartment at once, returning home to who knew where. She managed to establish that he was single, and that he originally came from a town in southern Texas. Beyond this, she knew nothing.

That week, colleagues at work began to pass comments. She had started arriving at the office less than immaculately dressed. Her hair was often out of place, her blouse not quite so well pressed. She seemed a little wilder now, a little less composed. Her attention seemed harder to hold. She explained the reason for the change to no one. Perhaps, though, some of them guessed when she was forced to use makeup to cover the bite marks that the builder frequently left on her throat.

And the apartment started to take shape.

Electrical circuits were laid, pipes were plumbed, walls were erected, then plasterboarded and painted. The kitchen was to become a bedroom, the bedroom a bathroom. Imported Italian tiles were to be juxtaposed with inlaid parquet blocks. And in the debris of the apartment, in the shavings and woodchips and wiring and plaster and brickdust, lay Laurie, with the builder towering above, dripping sweat onto her upturned face as he thrust into her more powerfully than he had ever done before.

One rainy Sunday afternoon late in October, as she sat on the floor of the bare guest room watching the rain sweep in from the river and spatter against the windows, she asked him why he made love to her so fiercely. He thought for a moment, his fingers tracing the delicate red scratches that embroidered her back. It was the closest she ever got to an explanation.

Laurie decided it was time to discuss her situation with someone she could trust. With a high-collared jacket of stiff gray linen covering the smarting welts on her shoulder blades, she left the office and went to lunch with Alison.

As she picked her way through her spinach salad, she told her old school friend about the bizarre relationship she now found herself involved in.

"What I fail to understand," she concluded, "is why I'm doing this. It just isn't like me."

"Sex is a great release," said Alison. "Sounds to me like you're getting your ashes hauled without having to worry about any responsibility. If you were a man, you wouldn't think twice."

"Well, I'm not, and I am." Laurie pushed the half-eaten salad aside.

"Laurie, I have a confession to make," said Alison slowly. "I kind of expected this to happen."

Laurie frowned. "You kind of expected what to happen?"

"Well, let me explain. A few months back there was a woman at the office whose apartment had been rebuilt by Bellano, and she kept going on about his brilliant craftsmanship. But I got the feeling that she meant something else entirely. It transpired that among her female friends he was very popular for . . . giving great decor." Alison ground out the cigarette, coloring with embarrassment. "Let's say that the guy has a reputation for being more than just a terrific builder."

Laurie sat in dumbstruck silence for a moment. Then she rose to her feet, unclipped her handbag, and threw some money onto the table.

"You booked me a stud?" she asked, her voice taut. "I looked that desperate to you?"

"But I didn't mean any—"

"I'm sure you probably thought you were doing the right thing, but believe me it wasn't, Allie. It really wasn't." She turned on her heel and left the restaurant.

That evening, Laurie worked late. At nine-thirty, seated on the PATH train going home, she considered her options. One, she could dismiss Ray from the job and hire someone else. But would she be able to find someone who could take over from his plans? Two, she could confront him and settle the matter out in the open. Then she would face the risk of his walking out, leaving the place unfinished. Three, she could act as if nothing was wrong and let him complete his work in peace. But what would happen when he made a move to continue their liaison? Carrying on with someone who had turned out to be little more than a male prostitute was unthinkable.

As Laurie alighted from the train, she knew that the affair was over. When she arrived back at the apartment, she found the builder still there. Ray Bellano was sitting in the middle of the living-room floor surrounded by blueprints, panels of plasterboard, and sawn-off lengths of plank. The room smelled of shaved wood and fresh paint.

"I'm glad you're back," he began slowly, climbing to his feet and dusting down his jeans. "I need to talk to you about the resiting of the kitchen." His unruly black hair was greased neatly back as if, in anticipation of her anger, he was now anxious to make a good impression. "You look real good." He gestured at her suit. "Kind of severe, though."

"Listen, Ray," she said coolly, "I have to know something. What's been happening between us, is that all part of the service? When you decorate a place, do you usually get to sleep with the mistress of the house? Was I supposed to be thrown in as part of the deal?"

"I don't know what you mean." He took a step toward her, but she backed away behind the low wooden counter he had built along one side of the room.

"No," she agreed, "I don't suppose you do. I'm talking about sexual liberties."

"Hey, I don't take liberties. You wanted it." He suddenly moved around to the other side of the counter and reached out his hand, grabbing the hem of her skirt and pulling her toward him.

"Let me go," she said firmly, disentangling herself and moving away. The last thing she wanted to do was provoke him into leaving the apartment, but at the same time it was important to establish the new boundary lines between them. "You've been employed to do a job of work, and it doesn't involve giving the kind of service you're used to providing. Just leave out that side of it from now on, and we'll get along fine."

Ray stared down at his boots, as if he had been caught betraying a trust. "You just made a mistake," he said finally. "But if that's the way you want it, you got it." He returned to work without another word.

After that, she tried to spend as little time in the apartment as possible. Chance meetings with Ray merely invoked injured looks and uncomfortable silences. She left him money to purchase the materials he needed, and passed long evenings working late at the office. At the beginning of November, she took a two-week vacation to visit her parents in Florida. When she returned she found the apartment finished and a set of neatly labeled keys on the new kitchen counter, along with a final handwritten bill for labor. There was no sign of the builder. She wrote a check and forwarded it to an address in Queens. Then, as a peacemaking gesture, she invited Alison over to inspect the property and come up with a few furnishing ideas.

"It's unbelievable," Alison marveled as she passed from room to room. "I'd never have known it was the same apartment!"

Even without furniture, the transformation was nothing short of miraculous. Every lintel and surround gleamed with proud detail. Alison sat on a packing crate staring about her as Laurie made coffee in a kitchen of gray slate and black marble surfaces.

"I'm sorry for what happened between us," said Alison as she stirred her coffee. "It was all my fault." Beyond the windows, a flotilla of tugboats heralded the arrival of a large South American freighter.

Laurie came over and stood beside her friend, watching the pale sunlight sparkle against the bow of the ship as it progressed up the river. "Forget it," she said. "It was nobody's fault. I chose to let it happen." She fell silent for a moment. "Help me pick out a dining table instead."

"A dining table?" said Alison, equally eager to change the subject. "What do you need a dining table for? You don't cook."

"No, but I eat. And I may learn to cook."

"I'll believe that when I see it."

"You know, I'm going to love living here," she said, sitting down on the broad window ledge. "It feels right."

By early December most of Laurie's new furniture had been installed and the first snowstorm of the winter had clogged Manhattan streets.

In her Hoboken apartment, Laurie sat in her soft-blue living room overlooking the river, curled in her mother's old patchwork quilt watching a rented movie and eating a peanut butter sandwich. The film had almost reached the end of its running time when the picture suddenly faded and died. Laurie irritably jabbed at the remote unit, but nothing happened. The screen remained blank. The video machine refused to play or rewind.

"Goddammit." She unwrapped the quilt and walked over to the set, but there was nothing she could do to restart the tape or remove it from the machine. A minute later, the film started up by itself. By now, though, Laurie had grown tired of watching television, and prepared for bed. After she had rinsed her cup and plate, she walked into the gleaming bathroom and ran the shower. Immersing herself in the cone of steaming water, she replayed the events of the day. The publishing house was looking at ways of cutting back on personnel, and after Laurie's recent failure to secure the rights to a hotly sought-after new novel, she knew that it was time to strengthen her position in the company by putting in some extra hours.

She was just considering the best way of doing this when the shower jets slowed to a trickle, then ceased altogether. The sound of roaring water fell away to a single echoing drip as she started to shiver and reached over the frosted cubicle door for a towel.

But instead of cotton brushing her hand, something cold and slippery seized it. Yelping with fear, she pulled free and jumped back against the tiled wall. She could feel her heart pounding as she slowly pushed open the glass door. The towel lay neatly folded across the heated rail, just where she had left it.

"I tell you, that's the last time I watch a horror movie by myself," she told Alison over the telephone at work the next day. "I could have sworn there was something there."

"Don't tell me." There was a pause as Alison lit her customary cigarette. "I can't even watch the eleven o'clock news without getting goosebumps."

"You mean the mugging reports?"

"No, George Bush. Too scary. Speaking of which, did you see the news last night?"

"No, I went straight to bed and slept with the lights on. Why?"

"I guess if you're nervous I shouldn't tell you. It's in all the papers this morning."

"I don't have time to read the papers. Tell me."

"OK. Hold on." Laurie smiled, knowing that Alison was making herself comfortable on the other end of the line. "You remember all that trouble at Rockaway Beach last July when those AIDS-infected syringes washed up on the sand?"

"Didn't they find a pair of legs as well?"

"That's right, and a bunch of dead laboratory rats and a human stomach lining. Well, it's started again. Only this time they don't think it's medical waste."

"What do you mean?"

"Some woman just got washed up on shore at Rockaway last night, or rather parts of her. She'd been taken to pieces with a bone saw."

"Allie, I haven't had my lunch yet. Why are you telling me this? You know I live alone, you know how I get!"

"Sorry." Allison did not sound very sorry at all. "I thought you'd be interested. Maybe there's a book in it."

"No, thanks. We already did a children's guide called *Things to Look for on America's Coastline*."

"I'd buy you a drink after work. . . ."

"But you know I'm working late. And I am. I'll have to take a rain check. The weekend, maybe."

"OK."

Laurie worked until nine, then went home and reheated some lasagne. As she ate, she studied the freezing river from her window. The apartment was so warm that the snowflakes melted the second they touched the pane. She changed into a loosely tied kimono before heading for the television and turning it on. The screen showed a policeman being interviewed by a CNN reporter on a bleak, snowswept beach. Behind him on the sand, a pair of fat white female legs protruded from one end of a tethered tarpaulin.

"Fears are growing that another consignment of laboratory waste is being washed up on New York's beaches," said the announcer. "Last summer's outbreak saw the closure of many beaches and plunging attendance figures at nearly all of the major resorts. But with the thermometer staying at around the zero mark, that's one problem New York may avoid. This is . . ."

The picture suddenly dwindled to a point of light.

"Damn it to hell!" Laurie searched for the remote unit, but it was nowhere to be found. "This is ridiculous. . . ." She pulled out the sofa cushions and stacked them on the floor, running her hand around the back of the seat. After a fruitless search she rocked back on her heels, perplexed. "It has to be here somewhere," she said to herself. "Things don't just vanish."

Finally she gave up looking and went to bed.

That was the first time she heard the rat.

At least, it sounded like a rat. Its movements were small and sharp, and could only be heard if she kept very still and held her breath. There, behind the familiar sounds of the old building, beneath the creaking of the floorboards and the clicking of the cooling waterpipes, was another noise, like nails tickering across wood. Laurie sat up and reached for the bedside lamp switch. She clicked it on, half expecting to see a rabid laboratory rat crouching on the bedspread ready to pounce, but there was nothing unfamiliar to be found in the room. The sound continued, so faintly now that she began to wonder if it only existed in her imagination. Laurie did not sleep well that night.

"There's nothing wrong with the set."

To prove his point, the TV repairman switched it on and off several times in rapid succession. "Or the video. It has to be your supply source."

"What do you mean?" Laurie gave the television a dubious look.

"The electrical system. You've just moved in?"

"What has that got to do with it?" she asked, sharpness in her voice.

"These buildings have old wiring. Half the time it's dangerous and you don't even know it."

"I've just had new wiring installed."

"There could be a fault in that, something overloading. Are you running any other appliances while the TV is on? The iron, maybe?"

"I don't do the ironing while I watch TV," she said coldly. "I'm from New York, not Ohio."

"Well, I think it's your circuits," said the repairman, closing his tool kit and heading for the door. "Get your electrician back in to take a look."

*   *   *

The next evening, an hour before Peter and Fran came by the apartment with Chinese takeout, the bedroom lights started to misbehave. Laurie was just changing into her jeans when the room was plunged into darkness. Swearing to herself, she checked the bulb and the fuses but found nothing wrong. Ten minutes later, the lights worked again. It was a very puzzled Laurie who opened the door to her old friends that night.

"So, how are you enjoying the place?" Peter asked through a mouthful of noodles. "It really looks great."

"There are one or two teething problems."

"What kind of problems?"

"Oh, lights, plumbing." She tried to make it sound casual. "And I think there's a rat."

"You're being melodramatic," said Fran, passing a carton filled with bean sprouts across the table. "Every building has mice and roaches."

"I guess so. This sounds bigger. I hear it almost every night."

"You want me to take a look?" Peter offered, but he didn't seem too enthusiastic about the idea.

"No, it'll sort itself out. It's OK." She picked at the bean sprouts, wishing she was as confident as she sounded.

The next morning Laurie was seated at the kitchen counter dropping pieces of grapefruit into the blender when the Channel Eleven local news report began. Her mind was half on the preparation of breakfast, half on the day's planned meetings as the image on the screen changed. Lettering stripped across a beach scene: ROCKAWAY BEACH VICTIM NAMED.

"Police today identified the body of the murdered woman found on Rockaway Beach as Mrs. Irene Bloom, a forty-two-year-old CPA declared missing from her Upper West Side apartment last Thursday. . . ."

At first Laurie failed to register the name. It wasn't until she looked up at the picture that her blood ran cold. The grapefruit knife slipped in her fingers, gashing the back of her hand. Blood welled in the wound and dripped heavily onto the marble counter as she continued to stare at the photograph of Mrs. Irene Bloom displayed on the screen.

She was standing proudly in an apartment that appeared to be an exact duplicate of her own.

*   *   *

"It was the woman I spoke to, the woman he recommended I call to check his credentials. And her apartment is exactly the same as mine! He decorated it in an identical style. Don't you see what that means?"

"This is stupid, Laurie, you know that? It's just a coincidence. You want to go to the police? You want to walk in there and say Excuse me, officer, but I shared the same interior decorator as the murdered woman?"

"You know damned well that we shared more than just the decoration."

Alison sighed. She hadn't minded changing her route to work so that she could meet a near hysterical Laurie in the coffee shop on East Fiftieth, but she was bothered by the sight of a good friend seemingly falling to pieces.

"Every painter has a style," she said, trying to sound as calm and rational as possible. "The apartments he designs are bound to be similar to some extent. You're working too hard, you know that? You should get out more."

"Maybe you're right." Laurie seemed to back down suddenly. "My imagination's been a little overactive of late."

"If you're so worried, I'll set your mind at rest. After all, it was me who put you in touch with this guy in the first place. I'll call him. Do you have his number?"

"I thought you had it. You gave it to me."

"That was just a temporary one. He was moving to somewhere in Queens."

Laurie thought for a moment. "That's right," she said, remembering. "I mailed his check there." She began to rummage in her handbag. "I think I threw the piece of paper away."

"It doesn't matter. We know his name. I'll find out where he lives and give him a call. And you've got to promise me that you'll start taking things a little easier." Alison held out her hand and they shook. Laurie's fingers were freezing.

"Do we have a deal?"

"A deal."

Exactly two weeks before Christmas, Laurie's ex-boyfriend turned up at her office. He had been meaning to see her for a while now, he said, just to bury the hatchet. Coincidentally, he had just broken up with his girlfriend Carol. Laurie was surprised but hardly flattered. Still, in the spirit of Christmas she went for a drink with him and actually managed to have a good time. At the end of the evening he tried to kiss her and she pulled gently but firmly away. She did, however, give him her new home telephone number, which was certainly more than she meant to do. Jerry was a louse, but a charming one, and she figured that he deserved something for at least possessing one good quality.

The following Saturday, there was another strange occurrence in the apartment. Laurie had arrived home from work and was playing back her messages—one from Jerry suggesting dinner—when there was a thud and a bang in the next room. Clicking off the answering machine, she moved back against the wall and listened. For a minute or so there was silence. Then a weight shifted and a floorboard creaked, not from the apartment above or the one below but right in the next room, the weight falling against the wall with a sudden heart-stopping thump.

Laurie moved across to her desk and picked up the brass letter opener that lay on the blotter. Slowly she crept toward the archway into the dining room. Poised on the threshold, preparing to attack, she suddenly felt foolish. Here she was, a grown woman, acting like a child of six just because she'd heard a few unexplained bumps and thuds. With an uneasy laugh she began to lower the knife.

The apartment lights went out.

The darkness was complete and solid, like a black wall. She had always hated the dark, ever since she'd been a small child. Hurrying across the living room to the front door, she caught her shin on the edge of the coffee table and fell sprawling, her knee tearing open on its sharp steel edge. When she reached the doorway to the hall she found Jerry standing there with his finger still resting on the apartment buzzer.

Seconds later, the lights came back on.

The last thing she had intended to do was cry on his shoulder. Perhaps it was a culmination of the month's events that caused her to behave in such an uncharacteristic manner, but she hung onto Jerry and told him all her fears—about her job, her private life, and even the inexplicable problems of her apartment. When she had finished, he smiled and poured her a brandy before taking her to bed and tucking her in. He sat with her for three hours and didn't try to lay a finger on her. It was a side of him she had never seen before.

That night, for the first time in what felt like an age, she slept soundly.

The following Friday, Laurie returned late from a meeting to find that the apartment had been burgled.

"That's the whole point," she told the officer. "I'm not even sure if there's anything missing." She was standing in the living room amid the wreckage of the shattered glass coffee table and the stuffing of the slashed sofa. The young policeman picked his way from room to room with a look of distaste on his face.

"Forgive me for saying so, ma'am," he said, "but this is kind of a regular problem at the moment, and we don't have too much of a chance of catching anybody. A lot of folks resent the yuppies moving in and forcing up the local property prices."

"I understand what you're saying," said Laurie angrily, "but I've as much right to protection as the next person and I don't think it's your job to make value judgments."

"Listen, I'm just trying to tell you how it is around here." Now armed with a legitimate excuse to lose interest in the crime, the police officer moved away toward the door.

"Just make a list of the missing items and bring it down to the station, ma'am, and we'll do what we can. Also, give me the names of anyone you know who might have done this."

Halfway to the door, Laurie halted. "What makes you think I know anyone who would do something like this?" she asked.

"Well, there's no sign of a break-in. Either you forgot to lock the door or whoever it was had a key."

"Nobody has a key to this apartment except me."

"Then you left the place unlocked. If it's not one, it has to be the other."

"Terrific. You've been a great help."

After slamming the front door, she returned to the ruins of the sofa, sat down, and cried.

She found nothing missing. Her jewelry box was unopened, and some cash lay on her dressing table untouched. The damage was less serious than it had at first seemed. Even so, the coffee table and the expensive designer sofa would have to be replaced. Peter and Fran came by to help tidy the place up, and suggested that Laurie install a burglar alarm. At least, they said, it would prevent the same thing from happening again. After the last dustpan of broken glass had been emptied into the bin, they opened a bottle of red wine and toasted the coming new year.

"You have to get an entry phone to this place, you know that?"

"Jerry, what are you doing here?" Laurie stood in the doorway in her bathrobe, unprepared for visitors. To be honest though, she was glad to see her former boyfriend. She moved aside to let him enter. "You'll have to be quick, I'm getting ready to go out to dinner. But while you're here, you can do something for me."

As he walked into the living room he pulled a champagne bottle from his jacket. "To warm the new apartment," he explained. "Better late than never. What do you need me to do?"

Laurie led him down the hallway and into the strange crystal-and-mirror bathroom Ray Bellano had designed for her.

Taking the champagne bottle from him and setting it down, she positioned Jerry in the center of the room and held her finger to her lips.

"Listen," she whispered, "and then tell me what you hear."

Jerry cocked his head on one side in an exaggerated gesture of attentiveness. He listened for a while, then shook his head. "Zip," he said finally. "Nothing at all. What was I supposed to hear?"

"I don't know. There's this weird sound I keep hearing at night. Maybe I really *am* imagining it." She shook her head, then picked up the bottle and headed into the kitchen.

"What do you mean?" asked Jerry, following her through. "What are you imagining?"

"Oh, I don't know—rats, mice, you name it. Something. You need a haircut." She reached up and touched the back of his neck.

"This is the Frankie Avalon look. I happen to like it." Jerry patted his hair back in place. "So, have you had an extermina-tor in?"

"No, it doesn't seem that serious." Laurie found two glasses and opened the champagne. "It comes and goes."

"Forgive my saying so, but it looks like it's keeping you awake at night."

She poured, then touched Jerry's glass with hers. "You know how I always used to worry about little things? I'm just doing it again, that's all."

"You want me to stay with you tonight?" His smile became a smirk.

"I know it's Christmas," she said with a chuckle, "but I'm not quite that full of goodwill yet."

An hour and a half later, though, she was.

It was the first time she had made love to anyone since the departure of the master builder, and it took some getting used to. Jerry was a courteous, considerate, conservative lover. He took into account a woman's needs. He took things slowly. He massaged her body gently. In fact, she had completely forgotten how boring he was in bed.

He lay heavily on top of her, his hands kneading her breasts. His clothes were folded neatly on a nearby chair. The bedroom lights were all turned off. He was moaning softly in what he considered to be a sexy manner. Laurie felt her left leg falling asleep as he shifted his weight, pulling the sheets out again.

Suddenly, the room began reverberating with a series of deaf-ening rhythmic bangs. Jerry leapt from the bed with a cry as if he had been electrocuted. As the hammering continued, he ran to the wall and slapped on the lights. Immediately, the noise stopped as swiftly as it had begun. Laurie cautiously removed the pillow she had pulled over her ears to block out the sound.

"That's a hell of a plumbing problem you've got there," he said as soon as his heartbeat had returned to normal. "Jesus, does that happen often?"

"Quite often," replied Laurie.

"Where was it coming from?"

"The apartment," she said, still shaking. "It just comes from the apartment."

"Laurie, you *have* to meet me tonight for a Christmas drink. I've got a present for you." On the other end of the telephone,

Alison already sounded a little merry. In the background Laurie could hear an office party in full swing. She looked from the receiver to the stack of paperwork on her desk and sighed.

"Allie, I'm flying down to spend Christmas with my folks tomorrow night and I have all this work to catch up on. . . ."

"Meet you in one hour's time at 14 Christopher. If I'm there first I'll have Michael get us a table. Be there or I'll tell everyone that you rekindled an old flame last night."

"How did you know that?" asked Laurie in amazement. "Word sure gets around fast."

"You forget that Jerry still works in my department."

"Yeah, but I didn't expect him to go around telling everyone."

"Not everyone, just me. Oh, about Ray Bellano—"

"You managed to get hold of him?"

"No, I didn't. Nobody seems to have seen him alive since you had him, you man-eater. Listen, do you still have the blueprints he made up of your apartment?"

"I've got them right here in my desk drawer."

"Good, bring them with you to the restaurant. I have a little surprise for you."

The line went dead.

An hour later in the restaurant at 14 Christopher Street, Laurie and Alison exchanged gifts and drank a toast to each other. Then, at her friend's request, Laurie unfolded the plans to her apartment and laid them flat on the tablecloth.

"Remember the woman who was washed up on the beach? After she died, they put her apartment up for sale," explained Alison, fishing about in her handbag as she spoke. "I applied to the realtors and they sent me a copy of the floor layout." She found the piece of paper she was looking for and studied it carefully. "I thought it might be interesting to see if your suspicions—whatever the hell they're supposed to be—are well founded."

Laurie leaned forward and perused the two sets of plans. She was disappointed to find, however, that in blueprint form they bore little resemblance to each other.

"Kind of a letdown, huh?" said Alison, draining her glass.

"I don't know what to think anymore," replied Laurie as she reached for the wine bottle. "Let's just forget about it. Be happy I was wrong."

*   *   *

On the 28th of December, Laurie returned from her parents' condominium in Florida and climbed the stairs to her apartment. As she opened the front door, she could see the red light on her answering machine ticking on and off. She put down her bags in the hallway, then turned on the lounge radiators. While she waited for the apartment to warm up, she played back her messages.

"Laurie, call me the minute you get in. Something awful has happened. It's Allie."

Laurie raised the receiver and speed-dialed the number on the handset.

"Thank God. I didn't want you turning on the TV and hearing about it on some news show."

"Hear about what?" asked Laurie. "What are you talking about?"

"It's Jerry. I don't know how to say this any other way. He's been murdered."

The room dipped before Laurie's eyes. "No, that's not possible."

"Laurie, listen to me. Don't watch the news, OK?"

"When did this happen?" She reached out for the arm of the chair and slowly sat down.

"Yesterday. He was found in his apartment in a very bad way. I really don't want you to hear about it. Stay there, I'm on my way over."

Alison came and stayed at her friend's apartment for the next two days. The police stopped by a number of times, but only made the situation worse by describing the murder in greater detail. Jerry had been at home sitting in front of the TV when he was attacked by someone wielding a hammer, or a similarly heavy blunt instrument. By the time his attacker had finished, there hadn't been a whole lot left of Jerry to take downstairs. The door to his apartment had been torn from its hinges. There had been no witnesses to the crime, and the police had no direct leads. Was there anything at all she could tell them that would shed some light on his death? Laurie tried to think of something tangible, some concrete piece of evidence that would link the half-formed suspicions in her mind. In the end, though, she settled for promising to call the detective at the station if she remembered any further details of their final meeting.

* * *

"You sure you don't want me to stay with you again tonight?" asked Alison for the third time. "Absolutely sure?"

"Go, go, for God's sake, I'll speak to you tomorrow morning." Laurie pushed her friend to the front door and opened it for her.

"All right, but you know where I am if you need me. I'll call you before I leave and we can go to the cemetery together."

Jerry's funeral, delayed by the need for an autopsy, had finally been scheduled for eleven o'clock the following morning. Laurie was grateful for her friend's concern, but was relieved to be left alone for a while.

Beyond the windows, the river lay in darkness, ebbing sluggishly in the freezing night air.

She went to the kitchen and made herself a cup of herbal tea, then sat in the living room with a paperback novel. She felt more enervated than she had at any time since moving into the apartment. As she scanned a page and tried to concentrate on the complexities of the plot, her fingers explored the knife rips in the fabric of the sofa. Because of the Christmas rush, the new covers she had ordered had yet to arrive. The jagged striations across the material she now absently touched seemed to recall the fine red scratches which had once adorned her back like tribal markings. On a nearby table the telephone rang, making her start. She reached across and answered it.

At first she thought there was nobody on the other end of the line. Then a strange tapping sound began, like someone running a stick back and forth across the bars of a wooden cage. Behind this, she could hear a man steadily breathing, the air in his throat being forced out in a series of sexual spasms.

She hung up with a gasp of disgust. Now was not the time for someone to be playing practical jokes. She wondered if perhaps she should report the call to the police, then decided against it. She had had enough questions from them in the last two days. The only sure way to outwit cranks was to get an unlisted number. She sat back on the damaged sofa and tugged her robe more tightly over her breasts. Slowly but surely the apartment felt as if it was becoming her prison, and the containment of all the unnamed things she most dreaded.

* * *

Alison entered the claustrophobic chaos of her SoHo apartment and headed for the kitchen. Something had been bothering her on the journey back from Hoboken. She pulled out the drawers beneath the cluttered kitchen counter and began to search among the balls of twine and special-offer coupons. Finally she located what she was looking for—the blueprints Laurie had accidentally left behind in the restaurant just before Christmas.

Unfolding the plans, she held one end down with a cookie jar and began to study the geometric diagrams inch by inch. Then she took a piece of tracing paper and began to draw.

Laurie reknotted the sash around her waist and headed into the bathroom. Turning on the tap, she splashed cold water over her face in the vain hope that it would make her feel less exhausted. She was debating whether to run a bath when the telephone began to ring once more. She hesitated, her hand resting on the doorknob. Her parents sometimes liked to call her at this late hour. She walked across the darkened living room and picked up the phone.

This time the sound was clearer: a steady clicking, wood on wood, expanding and contracting. And beneath it was the rasping, quickening breath of a man fast approaching orgasm. She slammed the receiver down hard and cleared the line, her heart thudding in her chest. She was about to pick it up and dial the police when it rang again. Gingerly, she raised the earpiece and slowly moved it closer.

This time the voice was a familiar one. It was Alison, probably calling to say that she had arrived home safely.

"Laurie, thank God! Now listen carefully. You must do as I say." Laurie frowned. The voice at the other end of the line sounded taut and strange.

"Allie, what's . . ."

"Shut up and listen! You have to leave the building, right now. Just grab your bag and walk to the front door."

"Are you nuts? It must be five below out there."

"Please," pleaded the voice, "do this for me. Just get up and go."

"Why?" asked Laurie, puzzled. "Just tell me why."

"Your apartment, I checked the plans."

"So?"

"I kept thinking something was wrong. The way the place looked didn't seem to match the way it was on the blueprint." Alison sounded out of breath. Had she been running? "Ray Bellano, he built it according to the plans that he gave you, but he built it the other way around."

"What do you mean?"

"If you flip the drawing over, you get a different-shaped apartment. I tried it just now with a piece of tracing paper. There's a second wall running all the way around the place. An inner skin."

"I don't understand," said Laurie, shaking her head as if to clear away her gathering fears. "What are you saying?"

"I'm saying that he's in there with you."

Horrified, she looked up from one wall to the other. Away in the background, the clicking wooden sound had started up again. This time it was not being transmitted over the telephone but was coming from somewhere within the apartment.

"Laurie, are you there? You see what this means? He's been there with you all the time. He must be watching you right now."

The receiver slid from her hands. She knew that Alison was telling her the truth. Everything made sense. The builder had been controlling her every movement from the start, forcing her to reveal her nakedness in the sudden glare of the bedroom lights, slowly baring her body beneath the drying taps of the shower, sending her from room to room, feeding on her growing anxiety.

She rose and moved into the center of the living room, searching the walls, listening for the smallest sound. Now other details began to fall into place. She remembered forsaking her blanket and crossing naked to the TV as she tried to fix the picture, something cold touching her hand as she emerged from the shower stall, the sense of someone standing over her bed watching her as she slept, the jealous rage that hammered in the bedroom walls because Jerry had made love to her. The burglary had been nothing more than a display of anger at her leaving. How many cracks and crevices, peepholes and passageways could he have built into the apartment?

As the creaking wooden noise became more urgent, she recognized its origin. He was breaking through the slats of the living-room wall. No more sneaking from secret openings—the master builder was about to make his grand entrance.

She ran for the kitchen and the knife rack above the sink as he appeared behind her in a showering explosion of plaster and wooden staves. For a second she caught sight of him striding across the room through a spray of dust, and the madness that glittered behind his blood-streaked eyes spurred her on. "Stay away from me!" she screamed, grabbing a bread knife from the rack and holding it with both hands in front of her stomach. Ahead in the hallway, he paused. His erect penis swayed from side to side as he began to move forward once more. She backed against the counter, desperately trying to think above the noise of her racing heart. Turning, she peered ahead through the doorway of the kitchen into the hall, but now there was nothing to be seen. It was as if he had suddenly disappeared.

The apartment had fallen silent. Laurie took a step forward, then another, carefully shifting her weight as lightly as possible. She began to think clearly again. The first priority was to get out of the apartment. Her neighbor below worked nights, so she would have to go into the street for help. And to do that she would need clothes. The bedroom was at her back. Her jacket and car keys lay on the bed. She listened once more. There was still nothing to be heard from the living room or the hall. Out on the river, the sound of a barge horn was muffled by falling snow. Slowly she lowered the knife, then turned and walked into the bedroom. Into his awaiting arms.

"You'll feel better if you drink this right down." The young officer holding out the brandy to her was the same one who had called after the burglary. "Do you have someone you can stay with tonight?"

"I guess so, yes." Laurie accepted the drink and sipped at it. Although the blanket was pulled high around her shoulders she was unable to stop shivering. The doctor had told her it was shock, not cold.

The officer watched dispassionately as they removed the builder's body from the room. The handle of the breadknife thrust out above the edge of the sheet, firmly wedged between the ribs of his chest, just below his heart.

"He designed the apartment, huh?" The officer looked about approvingly. "He did a nice job. Got a real good finish on these units." He ran his hand along the edge of a shelf, then looked back at the blood-spattered body as it went through the door. "He obviously took great pride in his work."

"Ray Bellano started rebuilding the place right after I broke off with him," said Laurie, unfolding her napkin and dropping it into her lap. "I was hardly ever there, so I never noticed what he was up to. The police say he'd tried the same thing before on a smaller scale, when he rebuilt Irene Bloom's apartment. He was able to come and go as he pleased, and I was none the wiser."

"That poor woman," said Alison, burrowing her fork into a stuffed mushroom. "She obviously wasn't quick enough for him. You're lucky you didn't get washed up on the beach as well. These are delicious."

"All that time spent between the walls, watching." Laurie reached across to Alison's plate and stole a mushroom. "The police wouldn't let me see inside. They said he had—things—in there." She shuddered. "No more fixer-uppers for me. My next apartment is going to be completely ready to move into."

"Just think," said Alison through a mouthful of food, "if you hadn't slept with him in the first place, none of this would ever have happened." Laurie narrowed her eyes at her companion as she continued eating.

"He knew you'd never have sex with him again," said Alison, refusing to let the subject drop. "He must have gotten so frustrated."

"That's the worst part of it," said Laurie, slowly lowering her fork to the table. "I have a horrible feeling he never did."

They finished the rest of the meal in silence.

FESTIVAL

ERIC McCORMACK

"We slept, or tried to sleep, making the possible rigors of the festival our excuse for lying down together and not touching."

Nothing that I might say really could prepare you for what follows, nor should it. There is not a stranger story in this book. Wrote Shakespeare in Romeo and Juliet: *"All things that we ordained festival, turn from their office to black funeral." And in this account of another pair of star-crossed lovers, Eric McCormack, a master of the matter-of-fact grotesque, reaches far beyond mere tragedy to a fantastical, breath-stopping perversion of tragic fate.*

Two of us went to the festival, one came back. We took the night plane, but we didn't sleep, neither of us being great sleepers at any time, never mind on planes. Coming in over the coastline at dawn, I thought to myself: What a beautiful place, the black headlands, the long aprons of beach round green northern water, the grass and the trees greener than was possible.

* * *

"Are you all right? Are you sure you want to go through with it?"

"I'm fine."

We took a taxi from the airport. It was ancient, and so was the driver, a man who wanted to talk. Neither of us obliged. I was tired. I wasn't in the mood for small talk, and I may have been sharp with him, or at least he stopped trying and left us to ourselves.

We came down from the high moorland through a gap in the hills into the outskirts of the town (we still considered it a town, though it was more of a village, a small village). The graveyard looked as though it had no new graves, just the old ghosts. We passed the first buildings on the edge of the town, run-down looking, as though no one lived in them. Then we drove past small fieldstone houses, along deserted streets with wisps of early-morning fog still lying across the lawns.

We arrived at the bigger gray granite buildings at the center of the town, one of them the hotel. The provost had made no reservations for us (did he think we would change our minds and not come in the end?), and we were not able to find separate rooms. Even though the festival was a local affair, enough people came from the surrounding countryside to make accommodation scarce.

We slept, or tried to sleep, making the possible rigors of the festival our excuse for lying down together and not touching.

About six in the evening, we rose, ate briefly, and joined the crowds in the street walking toward the school gymnasium. The night was foggy, but not unpleasant. The children seemed impatient, but the townspeople did not hurry. They chatted to each other, and made special efforts to be polite to us. Some of them seemed to recognize us. But their avoidance of direct questions was, for me, a sure sign they knew why we were here. I thought at times I saw a glitter in their eyes, but we ourselves were excited and perhaps every one of us looked unusual.

The school gymnasium smelled like a school gymnasium. Benches on risers had been set up along the two side walls, as though we had come to watch a basketball game. Faded pennants hung from the rafters, the corners were webbed with ropes. Just inside the main doors, I could see the provost, smiling as always, a bald man with a chain of office and steel-rimmed glasses. Beside him, the school's headmaster, a young-ish man who seemed a little overawed by the occasion. They greeted everyone, the headmaster paying special attention to the children, all dressed in their best clothes, unable to hide their excitement.

The provost smiled with delight when he saw us, and he shook us warmly by the hand, saying he was so glad we'd been able to accept his invitation. He knew we'd want to sit together (we didn't contradict him), and took us by our elbows to the only two wooden chairs in the entire gymnasium. As he walked us along the front of the audience, some of the crowd who were already there applauded us courteously. We sat down and he went back to his post.

"We still have time to change our minds."
"Yes. But we won't."

At seven-thirty, the seats were filled. The lights began to dim, the audience quieted down. A cluster of spotlights shone down on a circular area of the floor covered in rope mats. A small door in the wall to our right opened and a figure, hard to make out at first, moved slowly into the circle of light. She had her back to us, a young woman with waist-length jet-black hair, wearing a white housecoat tied with a cloth belt. She walked in a very self-possessed way, in spite of occasional nervous coughs amongst the audience.

In the middle of the circle, she stopped, loosened the belt and allowed her housecoat to slip from her shoulders to the mats.

She still had her back to us as she stood there, quite naked, her shoulders heaving from deep breathing. She began to turn around slowly, allowing the audience on our side to inspect her. To see her pale face. To see that her belly, dazzling white in the glare, was swollen, that her breasts bulged.

The audience was alert. The woman lowered herself gently to the mats, letting out a gasp as she lay down.

Now her breathing became loud, deep breaths, expelled nois-ily from her throat. "Ahh! Ahh!" For a few minutes, very regularly. "Ahh! Ahh!" Then I heard additional sounds, coming this time from the audience. "Ahh! Ahh!" All round the gymnasium, voices, soft at first, perhaps the children's, then gradually louder as the adults joined in, all of them taking up the sound. "Ahh! Ahh!" Much louder now, basses, baritones, tenors, contraltos, the fluting voices of sopranos and altos, all breathing rhythmically in time with her. "Ahh! Ahh!" Her stomach convulsing in the harsh light, deflating, puffing up. "Ahh! Ahh!" In the glare, I thought that at times the shape of her belly became geometrical, rhomboid, angular. So that I wondered, I suppose we all did, what thing was struggling inside her to be born.

The heavy breathing stopped. Now she bent her knees, opening her legs wide. From where we were sitting we could see quite clearly the pressure on her cervix. She was making a new noise now, a kind of grunting. "Uugh! Uugh!" She gyrated slowly on the mats between grunts, displaying her labor to all of the audience. "Uugh! Uugh!"

After a few minutes, the accompaniment began again. "Uugh! Uugh!" Softly, then louder. "Uugh! Uugh!" I looked around and I could hear them all now, even the bald provost, the anxious headmaster. "Uugh! Uugh!" All of them grunting in cadence. "Uugh! Uugh!" Her voice still dominating, sweat running down her face now, and her breasts. Her audience sweated with her, beads of sweat glistened on every face in that gymnasium. "Uugh! Uugh!" And now we could see the waters bursting out from between her legs. "Uugh! Uugh!" And now her vulva bulging, stretching. "Uugh! Uugh!"

She began to scream, the thin scream of a trapped rabbit. "Eeeeh!" The audience took up the scream, hardly breathing. "Eeeeh!" Her white face, her white body was gradually taking on a purple tinge, her eyes stared. "Eeeeh!" The audience screaming louder with her. "Eeeeh!" We all watched the widening vulva of the black-haired woman on the gymnasium floor, she gyrating still in spite of her pain. "Eeeeh! Eeeeh!" Letting us all see the dark circle that was forming between the brilliant thighs fringed with wet black hair. "Eeeeh! Eeeeh!" I noticed I was screaming too, we were both screaming along with her.

The woman stopped moving, stopped screaming. The creature inside her would wait no longer. The crowd watched without a sound as something slithered from inside her agony onto the mat. She too was silent now, as death. I remember we turned to each other anxiously.

What was it we all expected? I ask myself that, every now and then. A demon? A monster we were looking for? A thing each one of us had brought to that place and expected to appear before us now in the flesh? I can only testify to my own fear.

But, oh, the relief, the delight, when I saw that on the gymnasium floor lay a baby, a simple, human baby, still connected to its mother. I could have cheered with joy, as most of the children around us were cheering. We smiled at each other. We smiled, and all the audience in the gymnasium seemed to be smiling too, smiles of relief at the birth of that child.

The provost stepped forward, his chain of office glittering, his glasses sparkling in the overhead lights. He looked down at the woman. She was lying unmoving on the floor, only the rhythmic movement of her breasts showing she was not dead, in spite of the blood still oozing out of her. The little heap lay between her legs, coated in blood and mucus, no sound, its arms and legs fluttering from time to time. The provost, a pair of scissors in his hand, stooped and snipped. Then he carefully picked the baby up and held it high, turning around with it so that we could all see his trophy.

At first, silence. Then murmurs of pleasure, then shouts of "YES, YES, YES," from all round the gymnasium. I joined in, we both did, hugging each other, shaking hands with our neighbors. The baby, high in the provost's arms, steadied its head, and those eyes that had never seen opened wide and looked around the gymnasium, taking us all in.

The woman on the mats lay in her pool of blood, waiting for the afterbirth. She turned her head painfully to see what it was she had delivered. She looked up at the baby just at the very moment the baby looked down at her. On the woman's face was only weariness and pain. The baby's face became a purple wrinkle and it began to scream, and its screams could be heard above all the rejoicing in the gymnasium that night.

The hotel bar was busy after the first event. Customers shook our hands and bought us drinks. They were delighted that visitors, especially visitors like us, should have witnessed the event. It was a marvelous beginning to the festival.

• • •

"Should we, one last time?"

"Why not?"

We could hardly wait to get away from the bar and up the stairs to our room. We paid no attention to the damp, we threw our clothes off and fell into bed, holding each other the way we once had so long ago. We stroked each other, hugged each other, mounted each other, writhing in pleasure. And then we slept.

Hours later, I felt the chill and drew the blankets up, and we slept with arms around each other for the rest of the night.

The second night, the fog lingered still. We walked to the gymnasium with the others. For the most part they were farmers and coal miners, with their families robust and red-cheeked, or pale and wiry. They were courteous as ever to us, but I thought I could detect more restraint than I had noticed the night before. We disagreed about that.

The gymnasium was filled by seven-thirty. Only some floodlights lit a wide strip of floor stretching between the emergency doors at each end. The provost, energetic as ever, and the headmaster, looking quite uncomfortable, walked together to the middle of the floor. They separated: the provost walked down the illuminated strip toward one set of doors, the headmaster to the other. There they turned and bowed to each other very formally. Then each pushed the doors open to the dark outside.

"Perhaps it isn't too late for us."

"Has anything changed?"

Fresh air wafted in, diluting the ingrown smell of liniment. All of us breathed gratefully and waited for the event to begin.

We didn't wait long. We heard a faint buzzing noise, distant, it might have been someone sawing down trees. The sawing noise became louder, getting nearer to the gymnasium. We looked at each other, wondering what it could be.

Then, from the open doors on our right, we noticed a black ooze spilling slowly onto the illuminated floor. The ooze was alive. It was a flood of insects spreading over the floor, its front edge straight as a ruler.

A sea with a void. Not the buzzing we had heard a few minutes before and could still hear in the background, but a rustle, a hiss, a scuttling of papery limbs, scaly bellies on the varnished wood floor. We watched the whispering advance fearfully, alert for the tide to spill over our exposed feet.

But the insects never left the illuminated strip. The leaders were, so far as I could tell, ants and silverfish: minuscule creatures in great masses, followed by larger members of their species—speckled in color, some of them—carrying their tiny pearls. They kept to tight formation though some of the ants would make brief forays toward the debris of popcorn, which they would portage back to the main armies without disrupting the march.

Cockroaches appeared, with bristling antennae and hairy legs we could plainly make out, millions of them, then slithering centipedes, and millipedes, some of them a foot long. We kept our feet tucked under our seats, ready to climb up on them at the slightest hint of disorder.

Yet already we were beginning to feel comfortable in spite of all the insects, and some of the audience were talking among themselves without any sense of fear. We had the feeling we were spectators at a parade, and that the insects were consciously showing off, aware of their role.

The PA system encouraged this notion by coughing suddenly to life, and a nasal voice began calling out the names of each species as it entered the gymnasium. I heard names I had never known. Bristletails, cockchafers, buffalo beetles, harlequins, sacred scarabs, stink bugs (I could see some of the children holding their noses, giggling), dung beetles, kissing bugs, stag beetles with their enormous antlers, and walkingstick bugs looking as though they'd come straight from some insect battlefield.

We could still hear the buzzing outside, getting louder in spite of the hissing in front of us and the noise of the audience. None of the insects had so far left the hall. They would reach the other exit and begin marching on the spot, so that after a while, much of the illuminated pathway was jammed up.

Now, a splintering sound filled the gymnasium. All the crickets within a hundred miles began hopping through the door in great chirruping masses. I could not help thinking they were Mexican jumping beans, leaping six feet in the air, or black flying fish skimming over a wooden ocean.

The last stragglers among the crickets had just made their entrance, and the entire illuminated strip of floor was full, when the buzzing noise we had heard all night exploded into the gymnasium. I put my hands over my ears to block out the pain.

Flies. Pillars of flies, twisters, cumulo-nimbuses of flies, dense fogs of flies of every kind, houseflies, black flies, midges, horse-flies, dragonflies, mosquitoes, obscuring the space above the crawling insects. They filled the air like inky water poured into a huge aquarium, so that the still leaping crickets would disap-pear up into it and drop out moments later, inverted divers. The light in the gymnasium was almost obliterated by the living, buzzing wall of flies that cut us off from the human beings on the other side.

Only about a quarter of the air space remained. In the dim light, the children cowered against their parents. They felt, as we two did, the whining presence of these flies, how they could engulf us, smother us in horror, if they once went out of control. But like the masses of crawling insects on the floor beneath them, they stayed in control, hovering in place, as though they knew exactly why they were there, the entire building vibrating with their power.

The buzzing became so loud I thought my ears would burst, even with my hands covering them. We could not speak. No ordinary human voice could have penetrated that sound. So it was that we saw, rather than heard, the entry of the bees. Bees and wasps, colorful even in the dim light, their humming causing even more vibrations, bulkier in the air than the flies, their undercarriages dangling. Platoons of them flew on the flanks of the main body, scrutinizing the audience with their multiple eyes. Behind the swarm, the vibrations were deepest, as the ponderous bodies of a million queens filled the last space above the strip, and cut off the light, like the drawing of a huge brocade curtain.

In the darkness, we all sat still, waiting. In the confined space in front of us, countless billions of insects hovered and massed, under perfect control. We were all waiting.

Suddenly, the birds were among them. We did not at first know they were there, snapping and gobbling. Then light appeared in the middle of the gymnasium as the insects, on the floor and in the air, divided and surged toward the two entrances, climbing over each other in their terror. I don't know how many escaped, for they crashed into a wall that devoured them, an enemy with a million mouths.

The calm nasal sound of the PA system intruded itself into the bedlam, identifying the predators. I could hear the names, and eventually could see the killers as the lights brightened: swallows, evil-looking horned larks and screamers, frenetic thrashers, swifts, goatsuckers, nightjars and nutcrackers pecking furiously at the floor, thousands of sparrows of every sort, shrieks and razorbills pouncing on the trapped crickets and bees. With their canny, greedy eyes, they were more frightening than all the monstrous-looking insects they gorged on.

In less than ten minutes it was over. The twittering of the predators stopped, as though on a signal, and they swooped out of the gymnasium. All that remained was a stunned audience and wastes of broken insect bodies, papery wings occasionally fluttering in the stark light.

For a time, no one spoke. The children were openly crying, leaning into the adults. Some people began to get to their feet and move toward the exits, carefully skirting past the heaps of bodies.

We followed the townspeople out into the cool night, no one talking, and walked back to the hotel.

Some of the usual customers were in the hotel bar, drinking quietly, with none of the previous night's joviality. I would have liked to ask them about the event, listen to them compare it with previous years. But I kept silent. We both were too busy, nursing our private dreads.

"Perhaps we could still . . ."
"Stop talking about it. Please stop."

In the damp bed, we lay as rigidly apart as if a sword had been set on its edge between us. For it was a damp bed that night. The sky was full of rain, and the bedroom was chilly.

That night was our last chance to talk, perhaps to agree to try again. We didn't, and there is no more to be said.

The third and last night of the festival was a clear one for that region among the hills. The fog had disappeared somewhere. I could see stars and a gibbous moon. We knew we were a little late as we walked along the road to the school gymnasium. The provost and the little headmaster were waiting anxiously at the door, to the background strains of music on the PA system, looking anxiously up the street toward us. They greeted us warmly. The provost took us both by the arm and spoke:

"You still want to go through with it?"

We both nodded.

The lights were already dimmed, and the audience was looking in our direction. The provost waved to them as he led us in. All was well.

The middle of the floor was lit by spotlights. The provost stood under the lights and spoke:

"My townspeople and my dear children. Tonight is the final night of another successful festival, and we will all see a new and very exciting event. This event takes a lot of preparation and cooperation from a lot of people, and I'd like you to join me in a big hand for everyone concerned, and especially for our two honored guests who have traveled many thousands of miles to be involved in this event for our pleasure tonight."

He paused for the applause, then went on to explain the rules of the event to the audience. I didn't listen very carefully, I knew them only too well. Before we had accepted his invitation so many months ago we had gone over the rules many times.

He finished his speech, and the audience applauded again, and hummed with anticipation while we went to our separate changing rooms, the provost himself taking charge of me. As I walked in front of the benches, people shouted, "Good luck," "Take care," and I could almost have believed them. Someone even called out, "God bless."

The preparations were simple enough. In the changing room, I took off my coat as the provost showed me the workings of the heavy wooden-handled, single-shot pistol, letting me see the bullet already in the breach. He reminded me that each of the six members of the squad would have the same kind of pistol, but that only one of them would be loaded.

"Do they know which of them has the loaded pistol?"

"No. They draw the pistols by lot—that's part of the event."

He asked me if I wanted to go out into the schoolyard and take a few practice shots. I thanked him for his concern, but assured him that we were both excellent shots, otherwise we would never have accepted his invitation.

Through the door, we could hear the PA system blaring out dramatic music with drum rolls. The overture of the final event of the festival. There was loud applause, and I knew something was happening.

The provost opened the door a crack.

"Your friend and the rest of the squad are all ready now. Shall we?"

We walked slowly out into the gymnasium, the audience clapping. The squad was lined up in place, six of them. They were all about the same height and weight, all of them covered from head to toe in white cloaks with eye holes cut out, and wearing white gloves and white shoes. I tried to spot the familiar shape, the stoop of the shoulders, the tilt of a head, the way the arms hung. I could not be sure.

Each of the six held a heavy wooden-handled pistol like my own.

I took my place on the mark ten yards away, facing the squad. Six shaded pairs of eyes measured me. I peered back at them, trying without success to find eyes I knew only too well.

The tension in the hall erodes my calm and my heart batters not just out of excitement, but because I know that you are one of the six facing me, that you may be the one with the deadly pistol. I take a deep breath.

The first figure raises its pistol slowly and takes aim at my head. The voice of the provost asks me the formal question:

"Do you wish to shoot?"

Surely they would not want to end the game so soon. I take my chance.

"No."

I see the finger begin to curl on the trigger, and I stand firm.

CLICK.

The hall fills with applause and the little provost nods, and smiles his congratulations to me.

After a moment, the crowd settles down again and I concentrate once more. The second member of the squad takes aim. I see the glint in the eyeholes, but not the color, the greenness. Not the intention. Could it be your hand aiming the weapon that might mean my death? What are you thinking?

My own hand is sweating on the handle of my pistol.

"Do you wish to shoot?"

"No."

I watch with absolute clarity the gloved finger tighten on the trigger, perhaps the last thing I will ever see.

CLICK.

The right choice. The hall resounds with applause, shouts of approval. I breathe deeply.

Silence again, more sudden this time. I suppose the audience can't wait to see how the game works itself out. The squad stands unwavering, two of them now only spectators. The third member raises an arm and aims the pistol directly at my head.

I am breathing too quickly. That steady hand, those inscrutable eyes. Could this be the pistol with the bullet? Could this be you, after all we've been through together, ready to kill me with such resoluteness?

"Do you wish to shoot?"

I need time, but there is none.

"No."

CLICK.

The audience shouts with joy. I would like to breathe deeply, not this sweaty air. But the silence falls again. The fourth figure has already raised its arm, and the pistol points at my head. I must think, analyze, figure the odds. Which of the three remaining pistols will contain the bullet? My heart is thudding with excitement I have never known. I must forget about whose hand holds the weapon. I am certain now that you will not change your mind, give yourself away. I know that, like me, you will not hesitate to fire, and I love you for it.

"Do you wish to shoot?"

Instinct gives my answer.

"YES."

I raise my pistol, keeping my arm steady, and take aim. I squeeze gently, as I have so often done in practice. The pistol bucks, and the hooded figure lifts right off the floor, a brown hole appearing where the nose would have been, and the body falls backward, the blood spurting, the pistol still snared in its hand.

The crash of the shot rings round and round and round. The stink of gunpowder overwhelms the gymnasium smells. Silence, no cheers, only the ringing in my ears. I have killed someone, but I feel nothing except that I have played the odds. I have made my choice; that part of the game is over. Now I will join all the others, a spectator. I hear my empty pistol drop to the floor.

The squad seems indifferent to the gap in its rank. The fifth figure raises its pistol.

Suddenly, I am drowning in feelings. Why, why did I fire so soon? I look toward the provost. I want to protest to him about the unfairness of the game. But I can tell nothing from his frowning face. He is too wrapped up in the game, like the crowd. I can feel their sympathies are against me. They all hope I have made a mistake, and that the bullet is in one of these last pistols. That they can enjoy another killing.

I look directly into the barrel of the pistol. My legs are weak. But I must show no fear, as we agreed. I wonder what you feel there in the squad watching me. I wonder if it is you holding the pistol. I wonder how it will feel to die.

I watch the finger tightening. I stop breathing.

CLICK.

Elation. This time, I am full of elation, alive and enjoying the game. But the audience is deadly silent, and I can't help wondering why. I have given them almost everything the game could give. We are down to the last member of the squad and my death may be seconds away. I want nothing but to get on with the game.

The pistol slowly rises in the hand of the sixth figure. There is an expertness about it that reminds me of you, when we used to practice for the festival. If only I could see the eyes. Nothing could make this moment more exciting than to know that you are the one about to fire the pistol. Please give me a signal of some kind.

The finger begins to squeeze the trigger. Will I be able to hear the blast, the first rags of sound, see the bullet winging its way toward my head, taste the metal, the shattered brain? My heart is beating wildly, I cry out.

"Is it you?"

CLICK.

Nothing has changed. Just the thud of my heartbeat, the sweaty smell of the gymnasium, the glaring lights overhead, the squad standing erect, the silence of the audience.

Vaguely I see the provost come forward. He is not smiling. He congratulates me without enthusiasm, then murmurs that perhaps I should go now. The festival is over. The silence is disturbing, the lack of approval for my survival, the hostile faces among the audience, even the children's.

I drop the provost's hand and walk toward the squad, to the crumpled body on the floor, slightly on its side in a puddle of blood. The five figures still flank it, unmoving. I stoop and pull, clumsy-fingered, at the hood, tearing it away from the head. And see your hair. The hair that spills out of the hood, the fair hair, wet with blood, I have touched morning and evening all these years. The provost takes me by the arm.

I shake off his hand. The pistol. The pistol is still clutched in your gloved hand. I bend down and loosen your fingers. I slide open the breech.

The chamber of your pistol contains no bullet.

I remember leaving the village early next morning, one of those foggy mornings that are so common in the hills at that time of the year. The provost and the keeper of the hotel helped me downstairs to the taxi with my luggage. All the rest of the village was still asleep. The provost did not invite me back, as he had two years before.

We drove north, past the gray buildings on the edge of town, past the graveyard, the gravestones poking eyes in the fog. The taxi driver was not a talkative man, but I could see how he would sneak a glance at me now and then in his rear mirror.

I did not sleep on the plane. That was something neither of us had ever been able to do.

And when I got back here, to the city, I drank a good deal. I took a long time to settle back into the humdrum life. I explained to our friends why we were no longer together, and I think, though they were shocked, they understood.

When I found out, after the last event, that all of the squad's pistols were empty, that I had the only loaded pistol, I looked at the provost and said, quite calmly, I think:

"You lied. You've made me commit murder."

He did not answer, he just looked at me. Then, in a very gentle voice, he told me that it was time to go.

Nowadays, I sleep rarely, but when I do, I sometimes dream that you are alive, and we are talking to each other. Talking, talking. Perhaps, all the long conversations we never had. And when I wake up, my eyes are wet, and I can never remember anything we said.

LADIES IN WAITING

HUGH B. CAVE

"She seemed unaware that he had touched her. Or that he even existed. She was entirely alone, still gazing into that secret world in which he had no place."

Like many lovers of weird fiction, I have a special fondness for the pulp tradition, and Hugh B. Cave certainly embodies the best of this breed of writers. At the age of twenty, he published his first story, "Corpse on the Grating"; that was sixty years ago, yet, happily for fans, he is still active today. "Ladies in Waiting," however, written in 1975, marked his return to horror after a long hiatus during which period he had done most of his work for such slick magazines as The Saturday Evening Post *and* Good Housekeeping.

There will be hardly a person who won't recognize here the tried-and-true "old dark house" and "stranded traveler" motifs upon which Cave rings his changes. But what changes! You might say this beautifully creepy narrative undulates its way to its final pounce, and if there was ever a tale that strained the limits of the possibilities for simultaneous attraction/ repulsion, this is it.

Halper, the village real-estate man, said with a squint, "You're the same people looked at that place back in April, aren't you? Sure you are. The ones got caught in that freak snowstorm and spent the night there. Mr. and Mrs. Wilkes, is it?"

"Wilkins," Norman corrected, frowning at a photograph on the wall of the old man's dingy office: a yellowed, fly-spotted picture of the house itself, in all its decay and drabness.

"And you want to look at it again?"

"Yes!" Linda exclaimed.

Both men looked at her sharply because of her vehemence. Norman, her husband, was alarmed anew by the eagerness that suddenly flamed in her lovely brown eyes and as suddenly was replaced by a look of guilt. Yes—unmistakably a look of guilt.

"I mean," she stammered, "we still want a big old house that we can do over, Mr. Halper. We've never stopped looking. And we keep thinking the Creighton place just might do."

You keep thinking it might do, Norman silently corrected. He himself had intensely disliked the place when Halper showed it to them four months ago. The sharp edge of his abhorrence was not even blunted, and time would never dull his remembrance of that shocking expression on Linda's face. When he stepped through that hundred-seventy-year-old doorway again, he would hate and fear the house as much as before, he was certain.

Would he again see that look on his wife's face? God forbid!

"Well," Halper said, "there's no need for me to go along with you this time, I guess. I'll just ask you to return the key when you're through, same as you did before."

Norman accepted the tagged key from him and walked unhappily out to the car.

It was four miles from the village to the house. One mile of narrow blacktop, three of a dirt road that seemed forlorn and forgotten even in this neglected part of New England. At three in the afternoon of an awesomely hot August day the car made the only sound in a deep green silence. The sun's heat had robbed even birds and insects of their voices.

Norman was silent too—with apprehension. Beside him his adored wife of less than two years leaned forward to peer through the windshield for the first glimpse of their destination, seeming to have forgotten he existed. Only the house now mattered.

And there it was.

Nothing had changed. It was big and ugly, with a sagging front piazza and two few windows. It was old. It was gray because almost all its white paint had weathered away. According to old Halper the Creightons had lived here for generations, having come here from Salem where one of their women in the days of witchcraft madness had been hanged for practicing demonolatry. A likely story.

As he stopped the car by the piazza steps, Norman glanced at the girl beside him. His beloved. His childhood sweetheart. Why in God's name was she eager to come here again? She had not been so in the beginning. For days after that harrowing ordeal she had been depressed, unwilling even to talk about it.

But then, weeks later, the change. Ah, yes, the change! So subtle at first, or at least as subtle as her unsophisticated nature could contrive. "Norm . . . do you remember that old house we were snowbound in? Do you suppose we might have liked it if things had been different? . . ."

Then not so subtle. "Norm, can we look at the Creighton place again? Please? Norm?"

As he fumbled the key into the lock, he reached for her hand. "Are you all right, hon?"

"Of course!" The same tone of voice she had used in Halper's shabby office. Impatient. Critical. *Don't ask silly questions!*

With a premonition of disaster he pushed the old door open.

It was the same.

Furnished, Halper had called it, trying to be facetious. There were dusty ruins of furniture and carpets and—yes—the impression that someone or something was using them; that the house had *not* been empty for eight years, as Halper claimed. Now the feeling returned as Norman trailed his wife through the downstairs rooms and up the staircase to the bedchambers above. But the feeling was strong! He wanted desperately to seize her hand again and shout, "No, no, darling! Come out of here!"

Upstairs, when she halted in the big front bedroom, turning

slowly to look about her, he said helplessly, "Hon, please—what is it? What do you *want*?"

No answer. He had ceased to exist. She even bumped into him as she went past to sit on the old fourposter with its mildewed mattress. And, seated there, she stared emptily into space as she had done before.

He went to her and took her hands. "Linda, for God's sake! What *is* it with this place?"

She looked up and smiled at him. "I'm all right. Don't worry, darling."

There had been an old blanket on the bed when they entered this room before. He had thought of wrapping her in it because she was shivering, the house was frigid, and with the car trapped in deepening snow they would have to spend the night here. But the blanket reeked with age and she had cringed from the touch of it.

Then—"Wait," he had said with a flash of inspiration. "Maybe if I could jam this under a tire! . . . Come on. It's at least worth a try."

"I'm cold, Norm. Let me stay here."

"You'll be all right? Not scared?"

"Better scared than frozen."

"Well . . . I won't be long."

How long was he gone? Ten minutes? Twenty? Twice the car had seemed about to pull free from the snow's mushy grip. Twice the wheel had spun the sodden blanket out from under and sent it flying through space like a huge yellow bird, and he'd been forced to go groping after it with the frigid wind lashing his half-frozen face. Say twenty minutes; certainly no longer. Then, giving it up as a bad job, he had trudged despondently back to the house and climbed the stairs again to that front bedroom.

And there she sat on the bed, as she was sitting now. White as the snow itself. Wide-eyed. Staring at or into something that only she could see.

"Linda! What's wrong?"

"Nothing. Nothing . . ."

He grasped her shoulders. "Look at me! Stop staring like that! What's happened?"

"I thought I heard something. Saw something."

"Saw *what?*"

"I don't know. I don't . . . remember."

Lifting her from the bed, he put his arms about her and glowered defiantly at the empty doorway. Strange. A paper-thin layer of mist or smoke moved along the floor there, drifting out into the hall. And there were floating shapes of the same darkish stuff trapped in the room's corners, as though left behind when the chamber emptied itself of a larger mass. Or was he imagining these things? One moment they seemed to be there; a moment later they were gone.

And was he also imagining the odor? It had not been present in the musty air of this room before; it certainly seemed to be now, unless his senses were playing tricks on him. A peculiarly robust smell, unquestionably male. But now it was fading.

Never mind. There *was* someone in this house, by God! He had felt an alien presence when Halper was here; even more so after the agent's departure. Someone, something, following them about, watching them.

The back of Linda's dress was unzipped, he realized then. His hands, pressing her to him, suddenly found themselves inside the garment, on her body. And her body was cold. Colder than the snow he had struggled with outside. Cold and clammy.

The zipper. He fumbled for it, found it drawn all the way down. What in God's name had she tried to do? This was his wife, who loved him. This was the girl who only a few weeks ago, at the club, had savagely slapped the face of the town's richest, handsomest playboy for daring to hint at a mate-swapping arrangement. Slowly he drew the zipper up again, then held her at arm's length and looked again at her face.

She seemed unaware he had touched her. Or that he even existed. She was entirely alone, still gazing into that secret world in which he had no place.

The rest of that night had seemed endless, Linda lying on the bed, he sitting beside her waiting for daylight. She seemed to sleep some of the time; at other times, though she said nothing even when spoken to, he sensed she was as wide awake as he. About four o'clock the wind died and the snow stopped its wet slapping of the windowpanes. No dawn had ever been more welcome, even though he was still unable to free the car and they both had to walk to the village to send a tow truck for it.

And now he had let her persuade him to come back here. He must be insane.

"Norman?"

She sat there on the bed, the same bed, but at least she was looking *at* him now, not through him into that secret world of hers. "Norman, you do like this house a little, don't you?"

"If you mean could I ever seriously think of living here—" Emphatically he shook his head. "My God, no! It gives me the horrors!"

"It's really a lovely old house, Norman. We could work on it little by little. Do you think I'm crazy?"

"If you can even imagine living in this mausoleum, I *know* you're crazy. My God, woman, you were nearly frightened out of your wits here. In this very room, too."

"Was I, Norman? Really?"

"Yes, you were! If I live to be a hundred, I'll never stop seeing that look on your face."

"What kind of look was it, Norman?"

"I don't know. That's just it—I don't know! What in heaven's name *were* you seeing when I walked back in here after my session with the car? What was that mist? That smell?"

Smiling, she reached for his hands. "I don't remember any mist or smell, Norman. I was just a little frightened. I told you—I thought I heard something."

"You *saw* something too, you said."

"Did I say that? I've forgotten." Still smiling, she looked around the room—at the garden of faded roses on shreds of time-stained wallpaper; at the shabby bureau with its solitary broken cut-glass vase. "Old Mr. Halper was to blame for what happened, Norman. His talk of demons."

"Halper didn't do that much talking, Linda."

"Well, he told us about the woman who was hanged in Salem. I can see now, of course, that he threw that out as bait, because I had told him you write mystery novels. He probably pictured you sitting in some sort of Dracula cape, scratching out your books with a quill, by lamplight, and thought this would be a marvelous setting for it." Her soft laugh was a welcome sound, reminding Norman he loved this girl and she loved him—that their life together, except for her inexplicable interest in this house, was full of gentleness and caring.

But he could not let her win this debate. "Linda, listen. If this is such a fine old house, why has it been empty for eight years?"

"Well, Mr. Halper explained that, Norman."

"Did he? I don't seem to recall any explanation."

"He said that last person to live here was a woman who died eight years ago at ninety-three. Her married name was Stanhope, I think he said, but she was a Creighton—she even had the same given name, Prudence, as the woman hanged in Salem for worshiping demons. And when she passed away there was some legal question about the property because her husband had died some years before in an asylum, leaving no will."

Norman reluctantly nodded. The truth was, he hadn't paid much attention to the real estate man's talk, but he did recall the remark that the last man of the house had been committed to an asylum for the insane. Probably from having lived in such a gloomy old house for so long, he had thought at the time.

Annoyed with himself for having lost the debate—at least, for not having won it—he turned from the bed and walked to a window, where he stood gazing down at the yard. Right down there, four months ago, was where he had struggled to free the car. Frowning at the spot now, he suddenly said aloud, "Wait. That's damn queer."

"What is, dear?" Linda said from the bed.

"I've always thought we left the car in a low spot that night. A spot where the snow must have drifted extra deep, I mean. But we didn't. We were in the highest part of the yard."

"Perhaps the ground is soft there."

"Uh-uh. It's rocky."

"Then it might have been slippery?"

"Well, I suppose—" Suddenly he pressed closer to the window glass. "Oh, damn! We've got a flat."

"What, Norman?"

"A flat! Those are new tires, too. We must have picked up a nail on our way into this stupid place." Striding back to the bed, he caught her hand. "Come on. I'm not leaving you here this time!"

She did not protest. Obediently she followed him downstairs and along the lower hall to the front door. On the piazza she hesitated briefly, glancing back in what seemed to be a moment of panic, but when he again grasped her hand, she meekly went with him down the steps and out to the car.

The left front tire was the flat one. Hunkering down beside it, he searched for the culprit nail but failed to find any. It was underneath, no doubt. Things like flat tires always annoyed him; in a properly organized world they wouldn't happen. Of course, in such a world there would not be the kind of road one had to travel to reach this place, nor would there be such an impossible house to begin with.

Muttering to himself, he opened the trunk, extracted jack, tools, and spare, and went to work.

Strange. There was no nail in the offending tire. No cut or bruise, either. The tire must have been badly made. The thought did not improve his mood as, on his knees, he wrestled the spare into place.

Then when he lowered the jack, the spare gently flattened under the car's weight and he knelt there staring at it in disbelief. "What the hell . . ." Nothing like this had *ever* happened to him before.

He jacked the car up again, took the spare off and examined it. No nail, no break, no bruise. It was a new tire, like the others. Newer, because never yet used. He had a repair kit for tubeless tires in the trunk, he recalled—bought one day on an impulse. "Repair a puncture in minutes without even taking the tire off the car." But how could you repair a puncture that wasn't there?

"Linda, this is crazy. We'll have to walk back to town, the way we did before." He turned his head. "Linda?"

She was not there.

He lurched to his feet. "Linda! Where are you?" How long had she been gone? He must have been working on the car for fifteen or twenty minutes. She hadn't spoken in that time, he suddenly realized. Had she slipped back into the house the moment he became absorbed in his task? She knew well enough how intensely he concentrated on such things. How when he was writing, for instance, she could walk through the room without his even knowing it.

"Linda, for God's sake—no!" Hoarsely shouting her name, he

stumbled toward the house. The door clattered open when he flung himself against it, and the sound filled his ears as he staggered down the hall. But now the hall was not just an ancient, dusty corridor; it was a dim tunnel filled with premature darkness and strange whisperings.

He knew where she must be. In that cursed room at the top of the stairs where he had seen the look on her face four months ago, and where she had tried so cunningly to conceal the truth from him this time. But the room was hard to reach now. A swirling mist choked the staircase, repeatedly causing him to stumble. Things resembling hands darted out of it to clutch at him and hold him back.

He stopped in confusion, and the hands nudged him forward again. Their owner was playing a game with him, he realized, mocking his frantic efforts to reach the bedroom yet at the same time seductively urging him to try even harder. And the whisperings made words, or seemed to. "Come, Norman . . . sweet Norman . . . come come come . . ."

In the upstairs hall, too, the swirling mist challenged him, deepening into a moving mass that hid the door of the room. But he needed no compass to find that door. Gasping and cursing—"Damn you, leave me alone! Get out of my way!" He struggled to it and found it open as Linda and he had left it. Hands outthrust, he groped his way over the threshold.

The alien presence here was stronger. The sense of being confronted by some unseen creature was all but overwhelming. Yet the assault upon him was less violent now that he had reached the room. The hands groping for him in the eerie darkness were even gentle, caressing. They clung with a velvet softness that was strangely pleasurable, and there was something voluptuously female about them, even to a faint but pervasive female odor.

An *odor*, not a perfume. A body scent, druglike in its effect upon his senses. Bewildered, he ceased his struggle for a moment to see what would happen. The whispering became an invitation, a promise of incredible delights. But he allowed himself only a moment of listening and then, shouting Linda's name, hurled himself at the bed again. This time he was able to reach it.

But she was not now sitting there staring into that secret

world of hers, as he had expected. The bed was empty and the seductive voice in the darkness softly laughed at his dismay. "Come, Norman . . . sweet Norman . . . come come come . . ."

He felt himself taken from behind by the shoulders, turned and ever so gently pushed. He fell floating onto the old mattress, halfheartedly thrusting up his arms to keep the advancing shadow-form from possessing him. But it flowed down over him, onto him, into him, despite his feeble resistance, and the female smell tantalized his senses again, destroying his will to resist.

As he ceased struggling he heard a sound of rusty hinges creaking in that part of the room's dimness where the door was, and then a soft thud. The door had been closed. But he did not cry out. He felt no alarm. It was good to be here on the bed, luxuriating in this sensuous, caressing softness. As he became quiescent it flowed over him with unrestrained indulgence, touching and stroking him to heights of ecstasy.

Now the unseen hands, having opened his shirt, slowly and seductively glided down his body to his belt. . . .

He heard a new sound then. For a moment it bewildered him because, though coming through the ancient wall behind him, from the adjoining bedroom, it placed him at once in his own bedroom at home. Linda and he had joked about it often, as true lovers could—the explosive little syllables to which she always gave voice when making love.

So she was content, too. Good. Everything was straightforward and aboveboard, then. After all, as that fellow at the club had suggested, mate-swapping was an in thing in this year of our Lord 1975 . . . wasn't it? All kinds of people did it.

He must buy this house, as Linda had insisted. Of course. She was absolutely right. With a sigh of happiness he closed his eyes and relaxed, no longer made reluctant by a feeling of guilt.

But—something was wrong. Distinctly, now, he felt not two hands caressing him, but more. And were they hands? They suddenly seemed cold, clammy, frighteningly eager.

Opening his eyes, he was startled to find that the misty darkness had dissolved and he could see. Perhaps the seeing came with total surrender, or with the final abandonment of his guilt feeling. He lay on his back, naked, with his nameless partner half beside him, half on him. He saw her scaly, misshapen breasts overflowing his chest and her monstrous, demonic face swaying in space above his own. And as he screamed, he saw that she did have more than two hands: she had a whole writhing mass of them at the ends of long, searching tentacles.

The last thing he saw before his scream became that of a madman was a row of three others like her squatting by the wall, their tentacles restlessly reaching toward him as they impatiently awaited their turn.

DEATH AND THE SINGLE GIRL

THOMAS M. DISCH

"Death spread his suitcoat and unzipped his fly."

There has always been a glut in the market when it comes to stories about depressed young women who see only one way out of their despair. (Think of Anna Karenina.) Thomas M. Disch, however, was writing this mordant little tale in a later era, and he was thinking of Helen Gurley Brown. Setting a scene of perfect mock misery, down to the dusty, unjacketed LPs and unemptied ashtrays, he introduces us to Jill Holzman, resident of Greenwich Village.

What's the use of going on, she asks herself, intuiting that things couldn't be worse than when you find yourself unable to watch even one more episode of "The Flintstones" alone or baking yet another batch of chocolate-chip cookies that you won't permit yourself to eat. Besides, it's been raining for five days. Faced with the dreggy horror of it all, Death suddenly seems to Jill to be just the solution . . . but since he happens to be out when she calls, well, it's a good thing he has an answering service.

At four-thirty of a rainy afternoon late in June, Jill Holzman made up her mind that she'd had it. Life was not worth living, and in any case *her* life was not an example of living. She'd come to the same decision once in her college days and taken some pills, but she'd also arranged to be discovered. This time, though, she was sincere.

She pulled a chair over to the bookshelves she'd carpentered herself, stood on it, and got down her copy of *Gestalt Therapy* from the top shelf. Inside on the blank front matter before the title page she'd written down the telephone number of Death. She'd got it from a boy she'd talked to on a bus on her way up to a World Fellowship camp in the Catskills. The boy lived at an ashram near Ashokan and was into everything occult. He gave Jill almost a full address book of organizations to get in touch with—a psychic healer in Mexico City, a Reichean therapist in the Albert Hotel, a radical-left splinter group of Scientologists—and Death.

She dialed Death's number. It was busy.

After a few pages of *Gestalt Therapy* she tried again. This time there was an answer, but it wasn't Death himself, just an answering service. She left her number.

Then, feeling rejected and thoroughly depressed, she went into the closet she called a kitchen and made a double batch of tollhouse cookies. When she'd finished washing the bowl and the tin sheets, she dumped all the warm cookies in a black plastic trash liner, sealed it, and sent it down the chute to the incinerator. Cooking always cheered her up, but the thought of having to eat those cookies was too much. Anyhow, she was trying to lose weight.

Two days later in the middle of an NBC special on drug abuse there was a phone call.

"Hello," she said, hopefully.

"Hello, I'd like to speak to Miss Jill Holzman."

"Speaking."

"Miss Holzman, this is Death. You tried to reach me two days ago, and I wasn't in."

"Oh, yes." Her knees had gone all weak, as though she'd just been elected class president and had to give an extempore speech that moment to an assembly. "Thank you for calling back."

Death said nothing. You couldn't even hear him breathing into the receiver.

"I was wondering," she began haltingly, "if you would like to come over...." The silence stretched on. She took a deep breath. "I live at 35 Barrow Street. Apartment 3-C. If you take the Seventh Avenue subway, you get off at Sheridan Square and I'm just around the corner." It occurred to her that he might have wanted her to come to him. "Or if you're too busy...?"

"No," he said, after a pause sufficiently long to make it clear that he meant yes. "I have been busy, of course, or I'd have returned your call much sooner. It's this rain. A long stretch of bad weather is always the busiest time for me."

Jill wondered if that was all that had been depressing her. The rain had gone on now for five days, the tattered edge of a hurricane that had accomplished a hundred million dollars of damage. But no, this was more than a mood. She would have stood by her decision on the sunniest day of the year.

"It is awful," Jill agreed, meaning not just the weather but existence in general.

"You still haven't mentioned, Miss Holzman, what it is, exactly, that you want."

"Oh." She tried to keep from sounding annoyed. "Do I have to come right out and say it?" Death said nothing. "What I want is to be dead."

"Fine. How's tomorrow morning? Say, ten o'clock?"

"We couldn't make it in the afternoon? Usually I don't get *up* till eleven, and I'm not wholly *conscious* till after lunch." She was about to launch into the whole sorry story of careers, of job after job lost because she couldn't wake up and go to it. Then she thought better of it. Other people just aren't interested.

"I'm afraid tomorrow afternoon is already filled. Would Thursday do?"

Jill looked at the engagement calendar on her desk. Thursday was a page away, next to a Brancusi pencil drawing. She couldn't imagine watching Lucille Ball and "The Flintstones" till then.

She gave in. "Make it tomorrow morning. I'll get up early." When he made no reply to this she panicked. I've offended him, she thought, and now he'll never come. "Really," she pleaded, "tomorrow morning would be *wonderful*. Did you say ten?"

"Yes, I'm just noting it down. Thirty-five Barrow Street?"

"Apartment 3-C."

"Ten o'clock. Very good. *A tout à l'heure.*" Which he mispronounced.

She wondered if she were making a mistake.

She woke at six A.M. with an intense realization that her apartment was squalid and unpresentable. The record cabinet was covered with stacks of dusty records out of their sleeves. The sheets were dirty, the prayer plant was languishing, a tray of butts and ashes had spilled across the bathroom tiles. Months of cooking grease filmed the mirror inside the closet, and the sight of herself in the mirror, clouded as it was, was the most discouraging datum of all.

She worked frantically, and by the time Death arrived, punctually at ten, the most obvious disorders had been disguised.

He looked down at his dripping umbrella. "Where can I put this?"

"Let me take it." She spread it open, scattering raindrops, and set it to dry in the tub, which was speckled with cleanser. Rather than let him see inside the closet, she hung his coat in the bathroom too. A London Fog.

"Well," he said, settling creakily in the painted bamboo chair.

Jill sat on the edge of the bed, her legs spread slightly apart and her hands forming a relaxed cup expressive of an open, trustful attitude. "Here we are."

For the last two years Jill had worked, when she'd worked at all, as an office temporary. It occurred to her, looking at Death, that she might well have filled in at his office sometime. She had had so many employers, and their faces had all melted together into one averagely good-looking, averagely used-up, middle-aged face that was exactly the face smiling at her now.

"You have a very attractive apartment," Death commented.

"Thank you. Actually I'm afraid I've rather let things get out of control. The view, of course, that's its best feature." No sooner were the words out of her mouth than she realized that there wasn't any view. The rain had blotted out all but the nearest rooftops. The World Trade Center had disappeared.

Or was this, she wondered, the first prefiguring of her death? Would the city shrink around her till there was nothing left but this room, this bed, her own body, and finally a single blue eye, closing?

Death spread his suitcoat and unzipped his fly. "Shall we get down to business?" he asked. He wriggled a finger inside his Jockey shorts to flip out his cock, which was limp and wrinkly and the uncertain undulant pastel of an A&P chicken.

Involuntarily Jill looked away—at Death's trouser cuffs, at the perforations in his wing-tip shoes, at his bland, self-effacing smile. "What am I supposed to do?" she asked.

"Whatever feels most natural for you, Jill."

Tentatively she took the flaccid organ in her hand and squeezed. The glans became a brighter shade of salmon. Death edged forward on the chair. The bamboo creaked.

"Perhaps," he suggested, "if you kissed it. . . ."

"You mean you want a blow job?"

Death winced. His cock shriveled with embarrassment. "If you'd rather not go on with this," he said huffily, "I can leave now."

Mentally squaring her shoulders, Jill recollected her despair, her weariness, her anomie, and all the other reasons she had for dying. It wasn't as though she were a virgin, after all, or even invincibly squeamish about the act in question, as an episode with her most recent boyfriend (Lenny Rice—he'd left for California eight months ago) had borne witness to. If Death had only been a little less perfunctory, had shown the slightest tenderness or respect for her as an individual. . . .

"No!" she protested, getting on her knees and gathering her wits. "Don't go. I was just a bit . . . taken aback. I'll do whatever you want."

"Only if *you* want to, too," Death insisted.

"Oh, I do, I do."

And, resolutely, for fifteen minutes, she did, but to no avail. Once or twice it seemed that Death might be getting it up, and Jill, responsively, would increase her efforts. However in proportion as she exerted herself, his energy diminished. It was self-defeating, a labor of Sisyphus. She began to wonder if he were impotent.

Death disengaged himself and wiped his cock dry with a Kleenex. "I suppose you're wondering if I'm impotent."

"No. No, it's my own fault."

"Well, I'm not. Usually it's a simple matter of one, two, three. It's just that, as I explained, I've been so busy. There's a limit to what one person can do."

"I'll keep trying," Jill promised wanly.

"I have another appointment at eleven-thirty on East Seventy-fourth. I'll be late as it is."

"You're not leaving! But what about me? Aren't you going to . . . to . . ." She looked out the window. There seemed to be even fewer rooftops visible than when Death had arrived. "Or am I dead already?"

Death snorted derisively. "If you were dead, my dear girl, you wouldn't know it. It's tit for tat—I come, and you go."

Jill folded her arms. "That doesn't seem fair."

"I'll tell you what. I'll return this evening—on my own time. How's that?"

What could she say but yes?

True to his word, Death returned at eight-thirty. The bottle of Almaden burgundy he'd bought at the liquor store on Christopher Street went nicely with Jill's beef bourguignon. For dessert there were parfaits of chilled vodka over pistachio ice cream. Jill wore a canvas raindress from Lord & Taylor with the bottom three buttons undone. She had debated her more provocative macramé shift but decided that the circumstances called for an appearance of compliance rather than zest.

The phonograph repeated the same six Strauss waltzes over and over and over. "Artists' Life." "The Blue Danube." "Dynamation." "Tales of the Vienna Woods." "Vienna Blood." "The Emperor Waltz." And then, returning to band one, "Artists' Life." "The Blue Danube." And so on.

Death so far relaxed as to allow her to take off his suitcoat and loosen his tie, but then, anxious to make up for that morning's failure, he took the initiative himself.

At first Jill had some hope. Initially, at least, Death evinced a larger promise of success, and they were, this time, on the bed instead of wobbling about on the bamboo chair. But this hope soon faded. At last, her make-up smudged, an eyelash lost in his pubic hair, she gave up.

"Damn," said Death.

Jill was too tired to care even that much.

"I don't know what to tell you."

"It's all right," she assured him.

"Another time?"

"Maybe I should come round to your office," she suggested.

"Good idea." He would have agreed to a tryst anywhere at that moment—a church, a graveyard, the Statue of Liberty.

After sharing a dribble of Kahlúa, the last remnant of a Twelfth Night party of two years ago, he left. Jill went over to the phonograph and lifted the needle from "Vienna Blood."

She didn't even rinse the sauce off the dishes, she was that tired. Let the roaches do their worst, she thought, and went to bed.

Death was out when she arrived. If his receptionist were to be believed he'd left only moments before, though Jill's appointment (it was written down on his calendar too, clear as a pistol shot) was for eleven o'clock, and that's what the big, businessy clock on the wall said it was, precisely eleven o'clock. For a while Jill was content to listen to the soothing not quite monotony of the receptionist transcribing from a dictaphone. The foot pedal would go *snick*, and there would be a silence about six heartbeats in duration. Then another *snick* followed by a burst of typing.

When Death was fully half an hour overdue, Jill admitted to being bored and paged through the waiting room's magazines until she'd found a nice angry article in *Cosmopolitan* to reinforce her own nice anger. It had never been an easy emotion for Jill to get to, but when she did, ah, what bliss. Her stale body would begin to tingle, to become a fountain of adrenaline that overflowed out into the weary, workaday world, every molecule of which would then begin to move a little faster until it all began to look (which it never did otherwise) as interesting as the very best Hollywood movie, starring, for instance, George C. Scott and Glenda Jackson and Liza Minnelli.

"One o'clock," Jill observed aloud, not quite accurately. "Son of a bitch."

The receptionist grimaced sympathetically. "Don't I know."

"Do you think he's going to show up at all?"

"You never can tell. Though there's one way I could guarantee it—if I go out for lunch. Then he'd be up on the next elevator. Happens every time. He's psychic or something."

"There's no one but him to relieve you?"

"The other girl left Friday. Cashed her check and disappeared."

"If you'd like to go out and grab a bite I can hold down the fort here. I mean, I'm not about to do anything else."

"*Would* you? I am famished. I'd have something delivered, but the one time I did *that*, Lord! A lousy tunafish salad sandwich—you would have thought it was the end of the world."

"Go eat."

"If anyone calls write down their name and get their number and say we'll call right back. If anyone comes in, tell them to wait. Basically, that's it."

The receptionist went off to lunch, and Death arrived on the very next elevator. He would have walked right past Jill into his office if she hadn't called attention to herself by throwing her *Cosmopolitan* at him.

"Oh! Miss Holzman!" He let go the doorknob. "You startled me."

She glowered. She had every right to.

"I thought you were my secretary."

"I said I'd relieve her so she could have lunch. You're two hours late, you know. Two *hours*."

"Some unexpected difficulties," he mumbled.

"The usual difficulties?" she asked sardonically.

He sighed.

"Once," Jill reminisced lazily as she sprawled on the vinyl couch in Death's inner office, "when I was seventeen, I had to have a root canal job. The nerve in my tooth became infected and I had to keep going back and back and back. It was weeks before the tooth was drained and sealed. The dentist told me later that I'd set a record for him—thirteen separate sessions of work on a single tooth."

"Believe me, Miss Holzman, our experience has been most atypical. I don't know what the matter is, but I assure you it isn't your fault."

"Thanks a lot."

"If you wish to come back tomorrow I'll cancel all my other appointments."

"I'm not sure I *do* wish to."

"That's perfectly understandable."

"I don't do this for my health, you know. Candidly, I regard this whole business as odious and demeaning and *medieval.* The fact that it has *also* been unsuccessful only makes for a very salty wound. For all the good *you've* been able to do I might as well have taken sleeping pills. Or arsenic, for heaven's sake!"

"If you'd like me to strangle you, or take you out in my boat. . . ."

"Don't be disgusting."

As usual, having reached the apogee of her rage, Jill found herself relenting. Death seemed truly contrite. Was he to be blamed, after all, for his failures? Rather might she pity him. She *did* pity him. It was wonderful.

So, when as a gesture of reconciliation he offered to take her to lunch at the Peking Park, she needed the merest nudge of persuasion—a "please," no more. And when, after a dilatory and scrumptious meal, he asked her to fill the vacant position at his office, it was only a matter of another nudge. It was either this, she reasoned, or going the rounds of the agencies, than which she dreaded few things in life more.

That it was life could not be denied, but there were compensations. The salary was good, the hours agreeable, and her relationship with her employer—once it was clear that her service would be strictly limited to only such tasks as the New York State Employment Board would have approved—coolly congenial. In any case, Death did not seem eager to resume their earlier intimacies. It was a job, and she did it. If you couldn't be dead, this was the next best thing.

MASTER

ANGELA CARTER

"When she had wiped the tears from her face with the back of her hand, she was herself again, and after they had been together a few weeks, she seized the opportunity of solitude to examine his guns, the instruments of his passion, and, perhaps, learn a little of Master's magic."

Deeper and deeper into the fastness of the Amazonian jungle move a pair of "ambiguous lovers"—he a veteran hunter possessed of a killing lust, she a tribal girl he's made his slave. Though he will slaughter anything—such feverish violence is meant to keep at bay an immense, soul-swallowing emptiness—it is the great patterned cats that obsess him. Once it was leopards and lynxes; now it is the jaguar, a sleekly beautiful and dangerous creature worshiped by some as a god, whose powerful aura calls to him . . . and to his companion.

Always fascinated by metamorphosis, Angela Carter also frequently has allowed her imagination to wander amidst scenes of exotic cruelty and blood-chilling barbarism. It is a fearlessness that casts a glittering enchantment over her prose, and over the reader as well.

After he discovered that his vocation was to kill animals, the pursuit of it took him far away from temperate weather until, in time, the insatiable suns of Africa eroded the pupils of his eyes, bleached his hair, and tanned his skin until he no longer looked the thing he had been but its systematic negative; he became the white hunter, victim of an exile which is the imitation of death, a willed bereavement. He would emit a ravished gasp when he saw the final spasm of his prey. He did not kill for money but for love.

He had first exercised a propensity for savagery in the acrid lavatories of a minor English public school where he used to press the heads of the new boys into the ceramic bowl and then pull the flush upon them to drown their gurgling protests. After puberty, he turned his indefinable but exacerbated rage upon the pale, flinching bodies of young women whose flesh he lacerated with teeth, fingernails, and sometimes his leather belt in the beds of cheap hotels near London's great rail termini (King's Cross, Victoria, Euston . . .). But these pastel-colored excesses, all the cool, rainy country of his birth could offer him, never satisfied him; his ferocity would attain the coloring of the fauves only when he took it to the torrid zones and there refined it until it could be distinguished from that of the beasts he slaughtered only by the element of self-consciousness it retained, for, if little of him now pertained to the human, the eyes of his self still watched him so that he was able to applaud his own depredations.

Although he decimated herds of giraffe and gazelle as they grazed in the savannahs until they learned to snuff their annihilation upon the wind as he approached, and dispatched heraldically plated hippopotami as they lolled up to their armpits in ooze, his rifle's particular argument lay with the silken indifference of the great cats, and, finally, he developed a specialty in the extermination of the printed beasts, leopards and lynxes, who carry ideograms of death in the clotted language pressed in brown ink upon their pelts by the fingertips of mute gods who do not acknowledge any divinity in humanity.

When he had sufficiently ravaged the cats of Africa, a country older by far than we are, yet to whose innocence he had always felt superior, he decided to explore the nether regions of the New World, intending to kill the painted beast, the jaguar, and so arrived in the middle of a metaphor for desolation, the place where time runs back on itself, the moist, abandoned cleft of the world whose fructifying river is herself a savage woman, the Amazon. A green, irrevocable silence closed upon him in that serene kingdom of giant vegetables. Dismayed, he clung to the bottle as if it were a teat.

He traveled by jeep through an invariable terrain of architectonic vegetation where no wind lifted the fronds of palms as ponderous as if they had been sculpted out of viridian gravity at the beginning of time and then abandoned, whose trunks were so heavy they did not seem to rise into the air but, instead, drew the oppressive sky down upon the forest like a coverlid of burnished metal. These tree trunks bore an outcrop of plants, orchids, poisonous, iridescent blossoms, and creepers the thickness of an arm with flowering mouths that stuck out viscous tongues to trap the flies that nourished them. Bright birds of unknown shapes infrequently darted past him and sometimes monkeys, chattering like the third form, leaped from branch to branch that did not move beneath them. But no motion nor sound did more than ripple the surface of the profound, inhuman introspection of the place so that, here, to kill became the only means that remained to him to confirm he himself was still alive, for he was not prone to introspection and had never found any consolation in nature. Slaughter was his only proclivity and his unique skill.

He came upon the Indians who lived among the lugubrious trees. They represented such a diversity of ethnic types they were like a living museum of man organized on a principle of regression for, the further inland he went, the more primitive they became, as if to demonstrate that evolution could be inverted. Some of the brown men had no other habitation than the sky and, like the flowers, ate insects; they would paint their bodies with the juice of leaves and berries and ornament their heads with diadems of feathers or the claws of eagles. Placid and decorative, the men and women would come softly twittering around his jeep, a mild curiosity illuminating the inward-turning, amber suns of their eyes, and he did not recognize that they were men although they distilled demented alcohol in stills of their own devising and he drank it, in order to people the inside of his head with familiar frenzy among so much that was strange.

His half-breed guide would often take one of the brown girls who guilelessly offered him her bare, pointed breasts and her veiled, limpid smile and, then and there, infect her with the clap to which he was a chronic martyr in the bushes at the rim of the clearing. Afterward, licking his chops with remembered appetite, he would say to the hunter: Brown meat, brown meat. In drunkenness one night, troubled by the prickings of a carnality that often visited him at the end of his day's work, the hunter bartered, for the spare tire of his jeep, a pubescent girl as virgin as the forest that had borne her.

She wore a vestigial slip of red cotton twisted between her thighs and her long, sinuous back was upholstered in cut velvet, for it was whorled and ridged with the tribal markings incised on her when her menses began—raised designs like the contour map of an unknown place. The women of her tribe dipped their hairs in liquid mud and then wound their locks into long curls around sticks and let them dry in the sun until each one possessed a chevelure of rigid ringlets the consistency of baked, unglazed pottery, so she looked as if her head was surrounded by one of those spiked haloes allotted to famous sinners in Sunday-school picture books. Her eyes held the gentleness and the despair of those about to be dispossessed; she had the immovable smile of a cat, which is forced by physiology to smile whether it wants to or not.

The beliefs of her tribe had taught her to regard herself as a sentient abstraction, an intermediary between the ghosts and the fauna, so she looked at her purchaser's fever-shaking, skeletal person with scarcely curiosity, for he was to her no more yet no less surprising than any other gaunt manifestation of the forest. If she did not perceive him as a man, either, that was because her cosmogony admitted no essential difference between herself and the beasts and the spirits, it was so sophisticated. Her tribe never killed; they only ate roots. He taught her to eat the meat he roasted over his campfire and, at first, she did not like it much but dutifully consumed it as though he were ordering her to partake of a sacrament for, when she saw how casually he killed the jaguar, she soon realized he was death itself. Then she began to look at him with wonder for she recognized immediately how death had glorified itself to become the principle of his life. But when he looked at her, he saw only a piece of curious flesh he had not paid much for.

He thrust his virility into her surprise and, once her wound had healed, used her to share his sleeping bag and carry his pelts. He told her her name would be Friday, which was the day he bought her; he taught her to say "master" and then let her know that was to be his name. Her eyelids fluttered for, though she could move her lips and tongue and so reproduce the sounds he made, she did not understand them. And, daily, he slaughtered the jaguar. He sent away the guide for, now he had bought the girl, he did not need him; so the ambiguous lovers went on together, while the girl's father made sandals from the rubber tire to shoe his family's feet and they walked a little way into the twentieth century in them, but not far.

Among her tribe circulated the following picturesque folk-tale. The jaguar invited the anteater to a juggling contest in which they would use their eyes to play with, so they drew their eyes out of the sockets. When they had finished, the anteater threw his eyes up into the air and back they fell—plop! in place in his head; but when the jaguar imitated him, his eyes caught in the topmost branches of a tree and he could not reach them. So he became blind. Then the anteater asked the macaw to make new eyes out of water for the jaguar and, with these eyes, the jaguar found that it could see in the dark. So all turned out well for the jaguar; and she, too, the girl who did not know her own name, could see in the dark. As they moved always more deeply into the forest, away from the little settlements, nightly he extorted his pleasure from her flesh and she would gaze over her shoulder at shapes of phantoms in the thickly susurrating undergrowth, phantoms—it seemed to her—of beasts he had slaughtered that day, for she had been born into the clan of the jaguar and, when his leather belt cut her shoulder, the magic water of which her eyes were made would piteously leak.

He could not reconcile himself to the rain forest, which oppressed and devastated him. He began to shake with malaria. He killed continually, stripped the pelts, and left the corpses behind him for the vultures and the flies.

Then they came to a place where there were no more roads.

His heart leaped with ecstatic fear and longing when he saw how nothing but beasts inhabited the interior. He wanted to destroy them all, so that he would feel less lonely, and, in order to penetrate this absence with his annihilating presence, he left the jeep behind at a forgotten township where a green track ended and an ancient whiskey priest sat all day in the ruins of a forsaken church brewing firewater from wild bananas and keening the stations of the cross. Master loaded his brown mistress with his guns and the sleeping bag and the gourds filled with liquid fever. They left a wake of corpses behind them for the plants and the vultures to eat.

At night, after she lit the fire, he would first abuse her with the butt of his rifle about the shoulders and, after that, with his sex; then drink from a gourd and sleep. When she had wiped the tears from her face with the back of her hand, she was herself again, and, after they had been together a few weeks, she seized the opportunity of solitude to examine his guns, the instruments of his passion, and, perhaps, learn a little of Master's magic.

She squinted her eye to peer down the long barrel; she caressed the metal trigger, and, pointing the barrel carefully away from her as she had seen Master do, she softly squeezed it in imitation of his gestures to see if she, too, could provoke the same shattering exhalation. But, to her disappointment, she provoked nothing. She clicked her tongue against her teeth in irritation. Exploring further, however, she discovered the secret of the safety catch.

Ghosts came out of the jungle and sat at her feet, cocking their heads on one side to watch her. She greeted them with a friendly wave of her hand. The fire began to fail but she could see clearly through the sights of the rifle since her eyes were made of water and, raising it to her shoulder as she had seen Master do, she took aim at the disc of moon stuck to the sky beyond the ceiling of boughs above her, for she wanted to shoot the moon down since it was a bird in her scheme of things and, since he had taught her to eat meat, now she thought she must be death's apprentice.

He woke from sleep in a paroxysm of fear and saw her, dimly illuminated by the dying fire, naked but for the rag that covered her sex, with the rifle in her hand; it seemed to him her clay-covered head was about to turn into a nest of birds of prey. She laughed delightedly at the corpse of the sleeping bird her bullet had knocked down from the tree and the moonlight glimmered on her curiously pointed teeth. She believed the bird she shot down had been the moon and now, in the night sky, she saw only the ghost of the moon. Though they were lost, hopelessly lost, in the trackless forest, she knew quite well where she was; she was always at home in the ghost town.

Next day, he oversaw the beginnings of her career as a marks-woman and watched her tumble down from the boughs of the forest representatives of all the furred and feathered beings it contained. She always gave the same delighted laugh to see them fall for she had never thought it would be so easy to populate her fireside with fresh ghosts. But she could not bring herself to kill the jaguar, since the jaguar was the emblem of her clan; with forceful gestures of her head and hands, she refused. But, after she learned to shoot, soon she became a better hunter than he although there was no method to her killing and they went banging away together indiscriminately through the dim, green undergrowth.

The descent of the banana spirit in the gourd marked the passage of time and they left a gross trail of carnage behind them. The spectacle of her massacres moved him and he mounted her in a frenzy, forcing apart her genital lips so roughly the crimson skin on the inside bruised and festered while the bites on her throat and shoulders oozed diseased pearls of pus that brought the blowflies buzzing about her in a cloud. Her screams were a universal language; even the monkeys under-stood she suffered when Master took his pleasure, yet he did not. As she grew more like him, so she began to resent him.

While he slept, she flexed her fingers in the darkness that concealed nothing from her and, without surprise, she discov-ered her fingernails were growing long, curved, hard and sharp.

Now she could tear his back when he inflicted himself upon her and leave red runnels in his skin; yelping with delight, he only used her the more severely and, twisting her head with its pottery appendages this way and that in pained perplexity, she gouged the empty air with her claws.

They came to a spring of water and she plunged into it in order to wash herself but she sprang out again immediately because the touch of water aroused such an unpleasant sensation on her pelt. When she impatiently tossed her head to shake away the waterdrops, her clay ringlets melted together and trickled down her shoulders. She could no longer tolerate cooked meat but must tear it raw between her fingers off the bone before Master saw. She could no longer twist her scarlet tongue around the two syllables of his name, "mas-tuh"; when she tried to speak, only a diffuse and rumbling purr shivered the muscles of her throat and she dug neat holes in the earth to bury her excrement, she had become so fastidious since she grew whiskers.

Madness and fever consumed him. When he killed the jaguar, he abandoned them in the forest with the stippled pelts still on them. To possess the clawed she was in itself a kind of slaughter, and, tracking behind her, his eyes dazed with strangeness and liquor, he would watch the way the intermittent dentellation of the sun through the leaves mottled the ridged tribal markings down her back until they seemed the demarcations of blotched areas of pigmentation subtly mimicking the beasts who mimicked the patterns of the sun through the leaves and, if she had not walked upright on two legs, he would have shot her. As it was, he thrust her down into the undergrowth, among the orchids, and drove his other weapon into her soft, moist hole while he tore her throat with his teeth and she wept, until, one day, she found she was not able to cry anymore.

The day the liquor ended, he was alone with fever. He reeled, screaming and shaking, in the clearing where she had abandoned his sleeping bag; she crouched among the lianas and crooned in a voice like soft thunder. Though it was daylight, the ghosts of innumerable jaguar crowded round to see what she would do. Their invisible nostrils twitched with the prescience of blood. The shoulder to which she raised the rifle now had the texture of plush.

His prey had shot the hunter, but now she could no longer hold the gun. Her brown and amber dappled sides rippled like water as she trotted across the clearing to worry the clothing of the corpse with her teeth. But soon she grew bored and bounded away.

Then only the flies crawling on his body were alive and he was far from home.

THE CONQUEROR WORM

STEPHEN R. DONALDSON

"Actually," she said, "I think you do like it. This way, you get to feel like a victim."

Misunderstandings are part of every relationship, and certainly, if you wish to nurse a grievance, mixing equal doses of alcohol and paranoia will stand you in good stead. Creel Sump, husband of Vi, is an unhappy man: he thinks he's jealous and he also feels neglected, plus he's afraid he's being made a fool of. But in truth, the real problem is that he's just plain baffled—by life, by women, by his wife—and that makes him lash out. (Of course, a steady infusion of straight tequila will impart a fair dose of Dutch courage, too.)

Meanwhile, Stephen R. Donaldson, orchestrating the proceedings, recognizes that it's just that one little extra touch—the personal note, as it were—that's needed to lift this everyday vignette of free-floating marital rancor into the realm of the unforgettable. His choice for the extra element is an audacious one (hint: it's not human and it wiggles, and it likes dark places) and, ultimately, as you'll see, it proves incisive.

And much of Madness, and more of Sin,
And Horror the soul of the plot.

—EDGAR ALLAN POE

Before he realized what he was doing, he swung the knife.

(The home of Creel and Vi Sump. The living room.

(Her real name is Violet, but everyone calls her Vi. They've been married for two years now, and she isn't blooming.

(Their home is modest but comfortable: Creel has a good job with his company, but he isn't moving up. In the living room, some of the furnishings are better than the space they occupy. A good stereo contrasts with the state of the wallpaper. The arrangement of the furniture shows a certain amount of frustration: there's no way to set the armchairs and sofa so that people who sit on them can't see the water spots in the ceiling. The flowers in the vase on the end table are real, but they look plastic. At night, the lights leave shadows at odd places around the room.)

They were out late at a large party where acquaintances, business associates, and strangers drank a lot. As Creel unlocked the front door and came into the living room ahead of Vi, he looked more than ever like a rumpled bear. Whiskey made the usual dullness of his eyes seem baleful. Behind him, Vi resembled a flower in the process of becoming a wasp.

"I don't care," he said, moving directly to the sideboard to get himself another drink. "I wish you wouldn't do it."

She sat down on the sofa, took off her shoes. "God, I'm tired."

"If you aren't interested in anything else," he said, "think about me. I have to work with most of those people. Half of them can fire me if they want to. You're affecting my job."

"We've had this conversation before," she said. "We've had it eight times this month." A vague movement in one of the shadows across the room turned her head toward the corner. "What was *that*?"

"What was what?"

"I saw something move. Over there in the corner. Don't tell me we've got mice."

"I didn't see anything. We haven't got mice. And I don't care how many times we've had this conversation. I want you to stop."

She stared into the corner for a moment. Then she leaned back on the sofa. "I can't stop. I'm not *doing* anything."

"The hell you're not doing anything." He took a drink and refilled his glass. "If you were after him any harder, you'd have your hand in his pants."

"That's not true."

"You think nobody sees what you're doing. You act like you're alone. But you're not. Everybody at that whole damn party was watching you. The way you flirt—"

"I wasn't flirting. I was just talking to him."

"The way you *flirt*, you ought to have the decency to be embarrassed."

"Oh, go to bed. I'm too tired for this."

"Is it because he's a vice president? Do you think that's going to make him better in bed? Or do you just like the status of playing around with a vice president?"

"I wasn't *flirting* with him. I swear to God, there's something the matter with you. We were just talking. You know—moving our mouths so that words could come out. He was a literature major in college. We have something in common. We've read the same books. Remember *books*? Those things with ideas and stories printed in them? All you ever talk about is football—and how somebody at the company has it in for you—and how the latest secretary doesn't wear a bra. Sometimes I think I'm the last literate person left alive."

She raised her head to look at him. Then she sighed, "Why do I even bother? You're not listening to me."

"You're right," he said. "There *is* something in the corner. I saw it move."

They both stared at the corner. After a moment, a centipede scuttled out into the light.

It looked slimy and malicious, and it waved its antennae hungrily. It was nearly ten inches long. Its thick legs seemed to ripple as it shot across the rug. Then it stopped to scan its surroundings. Creel and Vi could see its mandibles chewing expectantly as it flexed its poison claws. It had entered the house to escape the cold, dry night outside—and to hunt for food.

She wasn't the kind of woman who screamed easily; but she hopped up onto the sofa to get her bare feet away from the floor. "Good God," she whispered. "Creel, look at that. Don't let it come any closer."

He leaped at the centipede and tried to stamp one of his heavy shoes on it. But it moved so fast that he didn't come close to it. Neither of them saw where it went.

"It's under the sofa," he said. "Get off of there."

She obeyed without question. Wincing, she jumped out into the middle of the rug.

As soon as she was out of the way, he heaved the sofa onto its back.

The centipede wasn't there.

"The poison isn't fatal," Vi said. "One of the kids in the neighborhood got stung last week. Her mother told me all about it. It's like getting a bad bee sting."

Creel didn't listen to her. He lifted the entire sofa into the air so that he could see more of the floor. But the centipede was gone.

He dropped the sofa back onto its legs, knocking over the end table, spilling the flowers. "Where did that bastard go?"

They hunted around the room for several minutes without leaving the protection of the light. Then he went and got himself another drink. His hands were shaking.

She said, "I wasn't flirting."

He looked at her. "Then it's something worse. You're already sleeping with him. You must've been making plans for the next time you get together."

"I'm going to bed," she said. "I don't have to put up with this. You're disgusting."

He finished his drink and refilled his glass from the nearer bottle.

(The Sumps' game room.

(This room is the real reason why Creel bought this house over Vi's objections: he wanted a house with a game room. The money that could have replaced the wallpaper and fixed the ceiling of the living room has been spent here. The room contains a full-size pool table with all the trimmings, a long, imitation leather couch along one wall, and a wet bar. But the light here isn't any better than in the living room because the fixtures are focused on the pool table. Even the wet bar is so ill lit that its users have to guess what they're doing.

(When he isn't working, traveling for his company, or watching football with his buddies, Creel spends a lot of time here.)

After Vi went to bed, Creel came into the game room. First he went to the wet bar and repaired the emptiness of his glass. Then he racked up the balls and broke so violently that the cueball sailed off the table. It made a dull, thudding noise as it bounced on the spongy linoleum.

"Fuck," he said, lumbering after the ball. The liquor he had consumed showed in the way he moved but not in his speech. He sounded sober.

Bracing himself with his custom-made cuestick, he bent to pick up the ball. Before he put it back on the table, Vi entered the room. She hadn't changed her clothes for bed. She had put her shoes back on, however. She scrutinized the shadows around the floor and under the table before she looked at Creel.

He said, "I thought you were going to bed."

"I can't leave it like this," she said tiredly. "It hurts too much."

"What do you want from me?" he said. "Approval?"

She glared at him.

He didn't stop. "That would be terrific for you. If I approved, you wouldn't have anything else to worry about. The only problem would be, most of the bastards I introduce you to are married. Their wives might be a little more normal. They might give you some trouble."

She bit her lip and went on glaring at him.

"But I don't see why you should worry about that. If those women aren't as understanding as I am, that's their tough luck. As long as I approve, right? There's no reason why you shouldn't screw anybody you want."

"Are you finished?"

"Hell, there's no reason why you shouldn't screw *all* of them. I mean, as long as I approve. Why waste it?"

"Damn it, are you *finished*?"

"There's only one thing I don't understand. If you're so hot for sex, how come you don't want to screw me?"

"That's not true."

He blinked at her through a haze of alcohol. "What's not true? You're not hot for sex? Or you do want to screw me? Don't make me laugh."

"Creel, what's the matter with you? I don't understand any of this. You didn't used to be like this. You weren't like this when we were dating. You weren't like this when we got married. What's happened to you?"

For a minute, he didn't say anything. He went back to the edge of the pool table, where he'd left his drink. But with his cue in one hand and the ball in the other, he didn't have a hand free. Carefully, he set his stick down on the table.

After he finished his drink, he said, "You changed."

"*I* changed? *You're* the one who's acting crazy. All I did was talk to some company vice president about *books*."

"No, I'm not," he said. His knuckles were white around the cueball. "You think I'm stupid. Because I wasn't a literature major in college. Maybe that's what changed. When we got married, you didn't think I was stupid. But now you do. You think I'm too stupid to notice the difference."

"What difference is that?"

"You never want to have sex with me anymore."

"Oh, for God's sake," she said. "We had sex the day before yesterday."

He looked straight at her. "But you didn't want to. I can tell. You never *want* to."

"What do you mean, you can tell?"

"You make a lot of excuses."

"I do not."

"And when we do have sex, you don't pay any attention to me. You're always somewhere else. Thinking about something else. You're always thinking about somebody else."

"But that's *normal*," she said. "Everybody does it. Everybody fantasizes during sex. *You* fantasize during sex. That's what makes it fun."

At first, she didn't see the centipede as it wriggled out from under the pool table, its antennae searching for her legs. But then she happened to glance downward.

"Creel!"

The centipede started toward her. She jumped back, out of the way.

Creel threw the cueball with all his strength. It made a dent in the linoleum beside the centipede, then crashed into the side of the wet bar.

The centipede went for Vi. It was so fast that she couldn't get away from it. As its segments caught the light, they gleamed poisonously.

Creel snatched his cuestick off the table and hammered at the centipede. Again, he missed. But flying splinters of wood made the centipede turn and shoot in the other direction. It disappeared under the couch.

"Get it," she panted.

He shook the pieces of his cue at her. "I'll tell you what I fantasize. I fantasize that you *like* having sex with me. You fantasize that I'm somebody else." Then he wrenched the couch away from the wall, brandishing his weapons.

"So would you," she retorted, "if you had to sleep with a sensitive, considerate, imaginative *animal* like you."

As she left the room, she slammed the door behind her.

Shoving the furniture bodily from side to side, he continued hunting for the centipede.

(The bedroom.

(This room expresses Vi as much as the limitations of the house permit. The bed is really too big for the space available, but at least it has an elaborate brass headstead and footboard. The sheets and pillowcases match the bedspread, which is decorated with white flowers on a blue background. Unfortunately, Creel's weight makes the bed sag. The closet doors are warped and can't be closed.

(There's an overhead light, but Vi never uses it. She relies on a pair of goosenecked Tiffany reading lamps. As a result, the bed seems to be surrounded by gloom in all directions.)

Creel sat on the bed and watched the bathroom door. His back was bowed. His right fist gripped the neck of a bottle of tequila, but he wasn't drinking.

The bathroom door was closed. He appeared to be staring at himself in the full-length mirror attached to it. But a strip of fluorescent light showed past the bottom of the door. He could see Vi's shadow as she moved around in the bathroom.

He stared at the door for several minutes, but she was taking her time. Finally, he shifted the bottle to his left hand.

"I never understand what you *do* in there."

Through the door, she said, "I'm waiting for you to pass out so I can go to sleep in peace."

He looked offended. "Well, I'm not going to pass out. I never pass out. You might as well give up."

Abruptly, the door opened. She snapped off the bathroom light and stood in the darkened doorway, facing him. She was dressed for bed in a nightie that would have made her look desirable if she had wished to look desirable.

"What do you want now?" she said. "Are you finished wrecking the game room already?"

"I was trying to kill that centipede. The one that scared you so badly."

"I wasn't scared—just startled. It's only a centipede. Did you get it?"

"No."

"You're too slow. You'll have to call an exterminator."

"Damn the exterminator," he said slowly. "*Fuck* the exterminator. Fuck the centipede. I can take care of my own problems. Why did you call me that?"

"Call you what?"

He didn't look at her. "An animal." Then he did. "I've never lifted a finger to hurt you."

She moved past him to the bed and propped the pillows up against the brass bedstead. Sitting on the bed, she curled her legs under her and leaned back against the pillows.

"I know," she said. "I didn't mean it the way it sounded. I was just mad."

He frowned. "You didn't mean it the way it sounded. How nice. That makes me feel a whole lot better. What in hell *did* you mean?"

"I hope you realize you're not making this any easier."

"It isn't easy for *me*. Do you think I like sitting here begging my own wife to tell me why I'm not good enough for her?"

"Actually," she said, "I think you do like it. This way, you get to feel like a victim."

He raised his bottle until the tequila caught the light. He peered into the golden liquid for a moment, then transferred the bottle back to his right hand. But he didn't say anything.

"All right," she said after a while. "You treat me like you don't care what I think or how I feel."

"I do it the way I know how," he protested. "If it feels good for me, it's supposed to feel good for you."

"I'm not just talking about sex. I'm talking about the way you treat me. The way you talk to me. The way you assume I have to like everything you like and can't like anything you don't like. The way you think my whole life is supposed to revolve around you."

"Then why did you marry me? Did it take you two years to find out you really don't want to be my wife?"

She stretched her legs out in front of her. Her nightie covered them to the knees. "I married you because I loved you. Not because I want to be treated like an object for the rest of my natural life. I need friends. People I can share things with. People who care what I'm thinking. I almost went to grad school because I wanted to study Baudelaire. We've been married for two years, and you still don't know who Baudelaire is. The only people I ever meet are your drinking buddies. Or the people who work for your company."

He started to say something, but she kept going. "And I need freedom. I need to make my own decisions—my own choices. I need to have my own life."

Again, he tried to say something.

"And I need to be cherished. You use me like I'm less interesting than your precious pool cue."

"It's broken," he said flatly.

"I know it's broken," she said. "I don't care. This is more important. I'm more important."

In the same tone, he said, "You said you loved me. You don't love me anymore."

"God, you're dense. *Think* about it. What on earth do you ever do to make me feel like *you* love *me*?"

He shifted the bottle to his left hand again. "You've been sleeping around. You probably screw every sonofabitch you can get into the sack. That's why you don't love me anymore. They probably do all kinds of dirty things to you I don't do. And you're hooked on it. You're bored with me because I'm just not exciting enough."

She dropped her arms onto the pillows beside her. "Creel, that's *sick*. You're *sick*."

Disturbed by her movement, the centipede crawled out between the pillows onto her left arm. It waved its poison claws while it tasted her skin with its antennae, looking for the best place to bite in.

This time, she did scream. Wildly, she flung up her arm. The centipede was thrown into the air.

It hit the ceiling and came down on her bare leg.

It was angry now. Its thick legs swarmed to take hold of her and attack.

With his free hand, he struck a backhand blow down the length of her leg that slapped the centipede off her.

As the centipede hit the wall, he pitched his bottle at it, trying to smash it. But it had already vanished into the gloom around the bed. A shower of glass and tequila covered the bedspread.

She bounced off the bed, hid behind him. "I can't take any more of this. I'm leaving."

"It's only a centipede," he panted as he wrenched the brass frame off the foot of the bed. Holding the frame in one hand for a club, he braced his other arm under the bed and heaved it off its legs. He looked strong enough to crush one centipede. "What're you afraid of?"

"I'm afraid of you. I'm afraid of the way your mind works."

As he turned the bed over, he knocked down one of the Tiffany lamps. The room became even darker. When he flipped on the overhead light, he couldn't see the centipede anywhere.

The whole room stank of tequila.

(The living room.

(The sofa sits where Creel left it. The end table lies on its side, surrounded by wilting flowers. The water from the vase has left a stain that looks like another shadow on the rug. But in other ways the room is unchanged. The lights are on. Their brightness emphasizes all the places they don't reach.

(Creel and Vi are there. He sits in one of the armchairs and watches her while she rummages around in a large closet that opens into the room. She is hunting for things to take with her and a suitcase to carry them in. She is wearing a shapeless dress with no belt. For some reason, it makes her look younger. He seems more awkward than usual without a drink in his hands.)

"I get the impression you're enjoying this," he said.

"Of course," she said. "You've been right about everything else. Why shouldn't you be right now? I haven't had so much fun since I dislocated my knee in high school."

"How about our wedding night? That was one of the highlights of your life."

She stopped what she was doing to glare at him. "If you keep this up, I'm going to puke right here in front of you."

"You made me feel like a complete shit."

"Right again. You're absolutely brilliant tonight."

"Well, you look like you're enjoying yourself. I haven't seen you this excited for years. You've probably been hunting for a chance to do this ever since you first started sleeping around."

She threw a vanity case across the room and went on rummaging through the closet.

"I'm curious about that first time," he said. "Did he seduce you? I bet you're the one who seduced him. I bet you begged him into bed so he could teach you all the dirty tricks he knew."

"Shut up," she muttered from inside the closet. "Just shut up. I'm not listening."

"Then you found out he was too normal for you. All he wanted was a straight screw. So you dropped the poor bastard and went looking for something fancier. By now, you must be pretty good at talking men into your panties."

She came out of the closet holding one of his old baseball bats. "Damn you, Creel. If you don't stop this, so help me God, I'm going to beat your putrid brains out."

He laughed humorlessly. "You can't do that. They don't punish infidelity. But they'll put you in jail for killing your husband."

Slamming the bat back into the closet, she returned to her search.

He couldn't take his eyes off her. Every time she came out of the closet, he studied everything she did. After a while, he said, "You shouldn't let a centipede upset you like this."

She ignored him.

"I can take care of it," he went on. "I've never let anything hurt you. I know I keep missing it. I've let you down. But I'll take care of it. I'll call an exterminator in the morning. Hell, I'll call ten exterminators. You don't have to go."

She continued ignoring him.

For a minute, he covered his face with his hands. Then he dropped them into his lap. His expression changed.

"Or we can keep it for a pet. We can train it to wake us up in the morning. Bring in the paper. Make coffee. We won't need an alarm clock anymore."

She lugged a large suitcase out of the closet. Swinging it onto the sofa, she opened it and began stuffing things into it.

He said, "We can call him Baudelaire."

She looked nauseated.

"Baudelaire the Butler. He can meet people at the door for us. Answer the phone. Make the beds. As long as we don't let him get the wrong idea, he can probably help you choose what you're going to wear.

"No, I've got a better idea. You can wear *him*. Put him around your neck and use him for a ruff. He'll be the latest thing in sexy clothes. Then you'll be able to get fucked as much as you want."

Biting her lip to keep from crying, Vi went back into the closet to get a sweater off one of the upper shelves.

When she pulled the sweater down from the shelf, the centipede landed on top of her head.

Her instinctive flinch carried her out into the room. Creel had a perfect view of what was happening as the centipede dropped to her shoulder and squirmed inside the collar of her dress.

She froze. All the blood drained out of her face. Her eyes stared wildly.

"Creel," she breathed. "Oh my God. Help me."

The shape of the centipede showed through her dress as it crawled over her breasts.

"*Creel.*"

At the sight, he heaved himself out of his armchair and sprang toward her. Then he jerked to a stop.

"I can't hit it," he said. "It'll hurt you. It'll sting you. If I try to lift your dress to get at it, it might sting you."

She couldn't speak. The sensation of the centipede creeping across her skin paralyzed her.

For a moment, he looked completely helpless. "I don't know what to do." His hands were empty.

Suddenly, his face lit up.

"I'll get a knife."

Turning, he ran out of the room toward the kitchen.

Vi squeezed her eyes shut and clenched her fists. Whimpering sounds came between her lips, but she didn't move.

Slowly, the centipede crossed her belly. Its antennae explored her navel. All the rest of her body flinched, but she kept the muscles of her stomach rigid.

Then the centipede found the warm place between her legs.

For some reason, it didn't stop. It crawled onto her left thigh and continued downward.

She opened her eyes and watched as the centipede showed itself below the hem of her dress.

Searching her skin every inch of the way, the centipede crept down her shin to her ankle. There it stopped until she looked like she wasn't going to be able to keep herself from screaming. Then it moved again.

As soon as it reached the floor, she jumped away from it. She let herself scream, but she didn't let that slow her down. As fast as she could go, she dashed to the front door, threw it open, and left the house.

The centipede was in no hurry. It looked ready and confident as its thick legs carried it under the sofa.

A second later, Creel came back from the kitchen. He carried a carving knife with a long, wicked blade.

"Vi?" he shouted. "Vi?"

Then he saw the open door.

At once, a snarl twisted his face. "You bastard," he whispered. "Oh you *bastard*. Now you've done it to me."

He dropped into a crouch and searched the rug. He held the knife poised in front of him.

"I'm going to get you for this. I'm going to find you. You can bet I'm going to find you. And when I do, I'm going to cut you to pieces. I'm going to cut you into little, tiny pieces. I'm going to cut all your legs off, one at a time. Then I'm going to flush you down the disposal."

Stalking around behind the sofa, he reached the place where the end table lay on its side, surrounded by dead flowers.

"You utter bastard. She was my wife."

But he didn't see the centipede. It was hiding in the dark water-stain beside the vase. He nearly stepped on it.

In a flash, it shot onto his shoe and disappeared up the leg of his pants.

He didn't know the centipede had him until he felt it climb over his knee.

Looking down, he saw the long bulge in his pants work its way toward his groin.

Before he realized what he was doing—

JACQUELINE ESS: HER WILL AND TESTAMENT

"She almost forgot for a while. But as the months passed it came back to her by degrees, like a memory of a secret adultery. It teased her with its forbidden delights."

In the dark miracle of Jacqueline Ess, Clive Barker has given us what may be the most daring and unnerving story many of you will ever encounter. For in exploring those deepest mythic recesses of female power which exist beyond any known responses, he moves instinctively into the realm of Circe, of Medusa, of Kali, of shape-changing goddesses and demons. Yet, despite its awesomely frightening special effects, for me this story is ultimately an allegory of the nature of desire, which is in itself an endless mystery.

But because there are what can only be termed harrowing perversions of desire on exhibit here, I must also stress the tenderness that unexpectedly breaks through. I could be mistaken, but I do think that Barker provides in "Jacqueline Ess" an utterly original expression of admiration for and homage to the smoldering primal force that is women's sexuality.

My God, she thought, this can't be living. Day in, day out: the boredom, the drudgery, the frustration.

My Christ, she prayed, let me out, set me free, crucify me if you must, but put me out of my misery.

In lieu of his euthanasian benediction, she took a blade from Ben's razor, one dull day in late March, locked herself in the bathroom, and slit her wrists.

Through the throbbing in her ears, she faintly heard Ben outside the bathroom door.

"Are you in there, darling?"

"Go away," she thought she said.

"I'm back early, sweetheart. The traffic was light."

"Please go away."

The effort of trying to speak slid her off the toilet seat and on to the white-tiled floor, where pools of her blood were already cooling.

"Darling?"

"Go."

"Darling."

"Away."

"Are you all right?"

Now he was rattling at the door, the rat. Didn't he realize she couldn't open it, wouldn't open it?

"Answer me, Jackie."

She groaned. She couldn't stop herself. The pain wasn't as terrible as she'd expected, but there was an ugly feeling, as though she'd been kicked in the head. Still, he couldn't catch her in time, not now. Not even if he broke the door down.

He broke the door down.

She looked up at him through an air grown so thick with death you could have sliced it.

"Too late," she thought she said.

But it wasn't.

My God, she thought, this can't be suicide. I haven't died.

The doctor Ben had hired for her was too perfectly benign. Only the best, he'd promised, only the very best for my Jackie.

"It's nothing," the doctor reassured her, "that we can't put right with a little tinkering."

Why doesn't he just come out with it? she thought. He doesn't give a damn. He doesn't know what it's like.

"I deal with a lot of these women's problems," he confided, fairly oozing a practiced compassion. "It's got to epidemic proportions among a certain age bracket."

She was barely thirty. What was he telling her? That she was prematurely menopausal?

"Depression, partial or total withdrawal, neuroses of every shape and size. You're not alone, believe me."

Oh yes I am, she thought. I'm here in my head, on my own, and you can't know what it's like.

"We'll have you right in two shakes of a lamb's tail."

I'm a lamb, am I? Does he think I'm a lamb?

Musing, he glanced up at his framed qualifications, then at his manicured nails, then at the pens on his desk and notepad. But he didn't look at Jacqueline. Anywhere but at Jacqueline.

"I know," he was saying now, "what you've been through, and it's been traumatic. Women have certain needs. If they go unanswered—"

What would he know about women's needs?

You're not a woman, she thought she thought.

"What?" he said.

Had she spoken? She shook her head: denying speech. He went on: finding his rhythm once more: "I'm not going to put you through interminable therapy sessions. You don't want that, do you? You want a little reassurance, and you want something to help you sleep at nights."

He was irritating her badly now. His condescension was so profound it had no bottom. All-knowing, all-seeing Father; that was his performance. As if he were blessed with some miraculous insight into the nature of a woman's soul.

"Of course, I've tried therapy courses with patients in the past. But between you and me—"

He lightly patted her hand. Father's palm on the back of her hand. She was supposed to be flattered, reassured, maybe even seduced.

"—between you and me it's so much talk. Endless talk.

Frankly, what good does it do? We've all got problems. You can't talk them away, can you?"

You're not a woman. You don't look like a woman, you don't feel like a woman—

"Did you say something?"

She shook her head.

"I thought you said something. Please feel free to be honest with me."

She didn't reply, and he seemed to tire of pretending intimacy. He stood up and went to the window.

"I think the best thing for you—"

He stood against the light: darkening the room, obscuring the view of the cherry trees on the lawn through the window. She stared at his wide shoulders, at his narrow hips. A fine figure of a man, as Ben would have called him. No child-bearer he. Made to remake the world, a body like that. If not the world, remaking minds would have to do.

"I think the best thing for you—"

What did he know, with his hips, with his shoulders? He was too much a man to understand anything of her.

"I think the best thing for you would be a course of sedatives—"

Now her eyes were on his waist.

"—and a holiday."

Her mind had focused now on the body beneath the veneer of his clothes. The muscle, bone, and blood beneath the elastic skin. She pictured it from all sides, sizing it up, judging its powers of resistance, then closing on it. She thought:

Be a woman.

Simply, as she thought that preposterous idea, it began to take shape. Not a fairy-tale transformation, unfortunately, his flesh resisted such magic. She willed his manly chest into making breasts of itself and it began to swell most fetchingly, until the skin burst and his sternum flew apart. His pelvis, teased to breaking point, fractured at its center; unbalanced, he toppled over onto his desk and from there stared up at her, his face yellow with shock. He licked his lips, over and over again, to find some wetness to talk with. His mouth was dry: his words were still-born. It was from between his legs that all the noise was coming; the splashing of his blood; the thud of his bowel on the carpet.

She screamed at the absurd monstrosity she had made, and withdrew to the far corner of the room, where she was sick in the pot of the rubber plant.

My God, she thought, this can't be murder. I didn't so much as touch him.

What Jacqueline had done that afternoon, she kept to herself. No sense in giving people sleepless nights, thinking about such peculiar talent.

The police were very kind. They produced any number of explanations for the sudden departure of Dr. Blandish, though none quite described how his chest had erupted in that extraordinary fashion, making two handsome (if hairy) domes of his pectorals.

It was assumed that some unknown psychotic, strong in his insanity, had broken in, done the deed with hands, hammers, and saws, and exited, locking the innocent Jacqueline Ess in an appalled silence no interrogation could hope to penetrate.

Person or persons unknown had clearly dispatched the doctor to where neither sedatives nor therapy could help him.

She almost forgot for a while. But as the months passed it came back to her by degrees, like a memory of a secret adultery. It teased her with its forbidden delights. She forgot the nausea, and remembered the power. She forgot sordidity, and remembered strength. She forgot the guilt that had seized her afterward and longed, longed to do it again.

Only better.

"Jacqueline."

Is this my husband, she thought, actually calling me by my name? Usually it was Jackie, or Jack, or nothing at all.

"Jacqueline."

He was looking at her with those big baby blues of his, like the college boy she'd loved at first sight. But his mouth was harder now, and his kisses tasted like stale bread.

"Jacqueline."

"Yes."

"I've got something I want to speak to you about."

A conversation? she thought, it must be a public holiday.

"I don't know how to tell you this."

"Try me," she suggested.

She knew that she could think his tongue into speaking if it pleased her. Make him tell her what she wanted to hear. Words of love, maybe, if she could remember what they sounded like. But what was the use of that? Better the truth.

"Darling, I've gone off the rails a bit."

"What do you mean?" she said.

Have you, you bastard, she thought.

"It was while you weren't quite yourself. You know, when things had more or less stopped between us. Separate rooms . . . you wanted separate rooms . . . and I just went bananas with frustration. I didn't want to upset you, so I didn't say anything. But it's no use me trying to live two lives."

"You can have an affair if you want to, Ben."

"It's not an affair, Jackie. I love her—"

He was preparing one of his speeches, she could see it gathering momentum behind his teeth. The justifications that became accusations, those excuses that always turned into assaults on her character. Once he got into full flow there'd be no stopping him. She didn't want to hear.

"—she's not like you at all, Jackie. She's frivolous in her way. I suppose you'd call her shallow."

It might be worth interrupting here, she thought, before he ties himself in his usual knots.

"She's not moody like you. You know, she's just a normal woman. I don't mean to say you're not normal: you can't help having depressions. But she's not so sensitive."

"There's no need, Ben—"

"No, damn it, I want it all off my chest."

On to me, she thought.

"You've never let me explain," he was saying. "You've always given me one of those damn looks of yours, as if you wished I'd—"

Die.

"—wished I'd shut up."

Shut up.

"You don't care how I feel!" He was shouting now. "Always in your own little world."

Shut up, she thought.

His mouth was open. She seemed to wish it closed, and with the thought his jaws snapped together, severing the very tip of his pink tongue. It fell from between his lips and lodged in a fold of his shirt.

Shut up, she thought again.

The two perfect regiments of his teeth ground down into each other, cracking and splitting, nerve, calcium, and spit making a pinkish foam on his chin as his mouth collapsed inward.

Shut up, she was still thinking as his startled baby blues sank back into his skull and his nose wormed its way into his brain.

He was not Ben any longer, he was a man with a red lizard's head, flattening, battening down upon itself, and, thank God, he was past speech-making once and for all.

Now she had the knack of it, she began to take pleasure in the changes she was willing upon him.

She flipped him head over heels on to the floor and began to compress his arms and legs, telescoping flesh and resistant bone into a smaller and yet smaller space. His clothes were folded inward, and the tissue of his stomach was plucked from his neatly packaged entrails and stretched around his body to wrap him up. His fingers were poking from his shoulder blades now, and his feet, still thrashing with fury, were tipped up in his gut. She turned him over one final time to pressure his spine into a foot-long column of muck, and that was about the end of it.

As she came out of her ecstasy she saw Ben sitting on the floor, shut up into a space about the size of one of his fine leather suitcases, while blood, bile, and lymphatic fluid pulsed weakly from his hushed body.

My God, she thought, this can't be my husband. He's never been as tidy as that.

This time she didn't wait for help. This time she knew what she'd done (guessed, even, how she'd done it) and she accepted her crime for the too-rough justice it was. She packed her bags and left home.

I'm alive, she thought. For the first time in my whole, wretched life, I'm alive.

VASSI'S TESTIMONY (PART ONE)

To you who dream of sweet, strong women I leave this story. It is a promise, as surely as it is a confession, as surely as it's the last words of a lost man who wanted nothing but to love and be loved. I sit here trembling, waiting for the night, waiting for that whining pimp Koos to come to my door again, and take everything I own from me in exchange for the key to her room.

I am not a courageous man, and I never have been: so I'm afraid of what may happen to me tonight. But I cannot go through life dreaming all the time, existing through the darkness on only a glimpse of heaven. Sooner or later, one has to gird one's loins (that's appropriate) and get up and find it. Even if it means giving away the world in exchange.

I probably make no sense. You're thinking, you who chanced on this testimony, you're thinking: Who was he, this imbecile?

My name is Oliver Vassi. I am now thirty-eight years old. I was a lawyer, until a year or more ago, when I began the search that ends tonight with that pimp and that key and that holy of holies.

But the story begins more than a year ago. It is many years since Jacqueline Ess first came to me.

She arrived out of the blue at my offices, claiming to be the widow of a friend of mine from law school, one Benjamin Ess, and when I thought back, I remembered the face. A mutual friend who'd been at the wedding had shown me a photograph of Ben and his blushing bride. And here she was, every bit as elusive a beauty as her photograph promised.

I remember being acutely embarrassed at that first interview. She'd arrived at a busy time, and I was up to my neck in work. But I was so enthralled by her, I let all the day's interviews fall by the wayside, and when my secretary came in she gave me one of her steely glances as if to throw a bucket of cold water over me. I suppose I was enamored from the start, and she sensed the electric atmosphere in my office. Me, I pretended I was merely being polite to the widow of an old friend. I didn't like to think about passion: it wasn't a part of my nature, or so I thought. How little we know—I mean *really* know—about our capabilities.

Jacqueline told me lies at that first meeting. About how Ben had died of cancer, of how often he had spoken of me, and how fondly. I suppose she could have told me the truth then and there, and I would have lapped it up—I believe I was utterly devoted from the beginning.

But it's difficult to remember quite how and when interest in another human being flares into something more committed, more passionate. It may be that I am inventing the impact she had on me at that first meeting, simply reinventing history to justify my later excesses. I'm not sure. Anyway, wherever and whenever it happened, however quickly or slowly, I succumbed to her, and the affair began.

I'm not a particularly inquisitive man where my friends, or my bed-partners, are concerned. As a lawyer one spends one's time going through the dirt of other people's lives, and frankly, eight hours a day of that is quite enough for me. When I'm out of the office my pleasure is in letting people be. I don't pry. I don't dig, I just take them on face value.

Jacqueline was no exception to this rule. She was a woman I was glad to have in my life whatever the truth of her past. She possessed a marvelous *sang-froid*, she was witty, bawdy, oblique. I had never met a more enchanting woman. It was none of my business how she'd lived with Ben, what the marriage had been like, etc., etc. That was her history. I was happy to live in the present, and let the past die its own death. I think I even flattered myself that whatever pain she had experienced, I could help her forget it.

Certainly her stories had holes in them. As a lawyer, I was trained to be eagle-eyed where fabrications were concerned, and however much I tried to put my perceptions aside I sensed that she wasn't quite coming clean with me. But everyone has secrets: I knew that. Let her have hers, I thought.

Only once did I challenge her on a detail of her pretended life story. In talking about Ben's death, she let slip that he had got what he deserved. I asked her what she meant. She smiled, that Gioconda smile of hers, and told me that she felt there was a balance to be redressed between men and women. I let the observation pass. After all, I was obsessed by that time, past all hope of salvation; whatever argument she was putting, I was happy to concede it.

She was so beautiful, you see. Not in any two-dimensional sense: she wasn't young, she wasn't innocent, she didn't have that pristine symmetry so favored by ad-men and photographers. Her face was plainly that of a woman in her early forties: it had been used to laugh and cry, and usage leaves its marks. But she had a power to transform herself, in the subtlest way, making that face as mysterious as the sky. Early on, I thought it was a make-up trick. But as we got together more and more, and I watched her in the mornings, sleep in her eyes, and in the evenings, heavy with fatigue, I soon realized she wore nothing in her skull but flesh and blood. What transformed her was internal: it was a trick of the will.

And, you know, that made me love her all the more.

Then one night I woke with her sleeping beside me. We slept often on the floor, which she preferred to the bed. Beds, she said, reminded her of marriage. Anyway, that night she was lying under a quilt on the carpet of my room, and I, simply out of adoration, was watching her face in sleep.

If one has given oneself utterly, watching the beloved sleep can be a vile experience. Perhaps some of you have known that paralysis, staring down at features closed to your inquiry, locked away from you where you can never, ever go, into the other's mind. As I say, for us who have given ourselves, that is a horror. One knows, in those moments, that one does not exist, except in relation to that face, that personality. Therefore, when that face is closed down, that personality is lost in its own unknowable world, one feels completely without purpose. A planet without a sun, revolving in darkness.

That's how I felt that night, looking down at her extraordinary features, and as I chewed on my soullessness, her face began to alter. She was clearly dreaming; but what dreams must she have been having. Her very fabric was on the move, her muscle, her hair, the down on her cheek moving to the dictates of some internal tide. Her lips bloomed from her bone, boiling up into a slavering tower of skin; her hair swirled around her head as though she were lying in water; the substance of her cheeks formed furrows and ridges like the ritual scars on a warrior; inflamed and throbbing patterns of tissue, swelling up and changing again even as a pattern formed. This fluxion was a terror to me, and I must have made some noise. She didn't wake, but came a little closer to the surface of sleep, leaving the deeper waters where these powers were sourced. The patterns sank away in an instant, and her face was again that of a gently sleeping woman.

That was, you can understand, a pivotal experience, even though I spent the next few days trying to convince myself that I hadn't seen it.

The effort was useless. I knew there was something wrong with her; and at that time I was certain she knew nothing about it. I was convinced that something in her system was awry, and that I was best to investigate her history before I told her what I had seen.

On reflection, of course, that seems laughably naive. To think she wouldn't have known that she contained such a power. But it was easier for me to picture her as prey to such skill, than mistress of it. That's a man speaking of a woman, not just me, Oliver Vassi, of her, Jacqueline Ess. We cannot believe, we men, that power will ever reside happily in the body of a woman, unless that power is a male child. Not true power. The power must be in male hands, God-given. That's what our fathers tell us, idiots that they are.

Anyway, I investigated Jacqueline, as surreptitiously as I could. I had a contact in York where the couple had lived, and it wasn't difficult to get some inquiries moving. It took a week for my contact to get back to me, because he'd had to cut through a good deal of shit from the police to get a hint of the truth, but the news came, and it was bad.

Ben was dead, that much was true. But there was no way he had died of cancer. My contact had only got the vaguest clues as to the condition of Ben's corpse, but he gathered it had been spectacularly mutilated. And the prime suspect? My beloved Jacqueline Ess. The same innocent woman who was occupying my flat, sleeping by my side every night.

So I put it to her that she was hiding something from me. I don't know what I was expecting in return. What I got was a demonstration of her power. She gave it freely, without malice, but I would have been a fool not to have read a warning into it.

She told me first how she had discovered her unique control over the sum and substance of human beings. In her despair, she said, when she was on the verge of killing herself, she had found in the very deep-water trenches of her nature, faculties she had never known existed. Powers which came up out of those regions as she recovered, like fish to the light.

Then she showed me the smallest measure of these powers, plucking hairs from my head, one by one. Only a dozen; just to demonstrate her formidable skills. I felt them going. She just said: one from behind your ear, and I'd feel my skin creep and then jump as fingers of her volition snatched a hair out. Then another, and another. It was an incredible display; she had this power down to a fine art, locating and withdrawing single hairs from my scalp with the precision of tweezers.

Frankly, I was sitting there rigid with fear, knowing that she was just toying with me. Sooner or later, I was certain the time would be right for her to silence me permanently.

But she had doubts about herself. She told me how the skill, though she had honed it, scared her. She needed, she said, someone to teach her how to use it best. And I was not that somebody. I was just a man who loved her, who had loved her before this revelation, and would love her still, in spite of it.

In fact, after that display I quickly came to accommodate a new vision of Jacqueline. Instead of fearing her, I became more devoted to this woman who tolerated my possession of her body.

My work became an irritation, a distraction that came between me and thinking of my beloved. What reputation I had began to deteriorate; I lost briefs, I lost credibility. In the space of two or three months my professional life dwindled away to almost nothing. Friends despaired of me, colleagues avoided me.

It wasn't that she was feeding on me. I want to be clear about that. She was no lamia, no succubus. What happened to me, my fall from grace with ordinary life if you like, was of my own making. She didn't bewitch me; that's a romantic lie to excuse rape. She was a sea: and I had to swim in her. Does that make any sense? I'd lived my life on the shore, in the solid world of law, and I was tired of it. She was liquid; a boundless sea in a single body, a deluge in a small room, and I will gladly drown in her, if she grants me the chance. But that was my decision. Understand that. This has always been my decision. I have decided to go to the room tonight, and be with her one final time. That is of my own free will.

And what man would not? She was (is) sublime.

For a month after that demonstration of power I lived in a permanent ecstasy of her. When I was with her she showed me ways to love beyond the limits of any other creature on God's earth. I say beyond the limits: with her there were no limits. And when I was away from her the reverie continued: because she seemed to have changed my world.

Then she left me.

I knew why: she'd gone to find someone to teach her how to use strength. But understanding her reasons made it no easier.

I broke down: lost my job, lost my identity, lost the few friends I had left in the world. I scarcely noticed. They were minor losses, beside the loss of Jacqueline . . .

"Jacqueline."

My God, she thought, can this really be the most influential man in the country? He looked so unprepossessing, so very unspectacular. His chin wasn't even strong.

But Titus Pettifer was power.

He ran more monopolies than he could count; his word in the financial world could break companies like sticks, destroying the ambitions of hundreds, the careers of thousands. Fortunes were made overnight in his shadow, entire corporations fell when he blew on them, casualties of his whim. This man knew power if any man knew it. He had to be learned from.

"You wouldn't mind if I called you J., would you?"

"No."

"Have you been waiting long?"

"Long enough."

"I don't normally leave beautiful women waiting."

"Yes you do."

She knew him already: two minutes in his presence was enough to find his measure. He would come quickest to her if she was quietly insolent.

"Do you always call women you've never met before by their initials?"

"It's convenient for filing; do you mind?"

"It depends."

"On what?"

"What I get in return for giving you the privilege."

"It's a privilege, is it, to know your name?"

"Yes."

"Well ... I'm flattered. Unless of course you grant that privilege widely?"

She shook her head. No, he could see she wasn't profligate with her affections.

"Why have you waited so long to see me?" he said. "Why have I had reports of your wearing my secretaries down with your constant demands to meet with me? Do you want money? Because if you do you'll go away empty-handed. I became rich by being mean, and the richer I get, the meaner I become."

The remark was truth; he spoke it plainly.

"I don't want money," she said, equally plainly.

"That's refreshing."

"There's richer than you."

He raised his eyebrows in surprise. She could bite, this beauty.

"True," he said. There were at least half a dozen richer men in the hemisphere.

"I'm not an adoring little nobody. I haven't come here to screw a name. I've come here because we can be together. We have a great deal to offer each other."

"Such as?" he said.

"I have my body."

He smiled. It was the straightest offer he'd heard in years.

"And what do I offer you in return for such largesse?"

"I want to learn—"

"Learn?"

"—how to use power."

She was stranger and stranger, this one.

"What do you mean?" he replied, playing for time. He hadn't got the measure of her; she vexed him, confounded him.

"Shall I recite it for you again, in bourgeois?" she said, playing insolence with such a smile he almost felt attractive again.

"No need. You want to learn to use power. I suppose I could teach you—"

"I know you can."

"You realize I'm a married man. Virginia and I have been together eighteen years."

"You have three sons, four houses, a maid-servant called Mirabelle. You loathe New York, and you love Bangkok; your shirt collar is 16½, your favorite color green."

"Turquoise."

"You're getting subtler in your old age."

"I'm not old."

"Eighteen years a married man. It ages you prematurely."

"Not me."

"Prove it."

"How?"

"Take me."

"What?"

"Take me."

"Here?"

"Draw the blinds, lock the door, turn off the computer terminus, and take me. I dare you."

"Dare?"

How long was it since anyone had *dared* him to do anything?

"Dare?"

He was excited. He hadn't been so excited in a dozen years. He drew the blinds, locked the door, turned off the video display of his fortunes.

My God, she thought, I've got him.

It wasn't an easy passion, not like that with Vassi. For one thing, Pettifer was a clumsy, uncultured lover. For another, he was too nervous of his wife to be a wholly successful adulterer. He thought he saw Virginia everywhere: in the lobbies of the hotels they took a room in for the afternoon, in cabs cruising the street outside their rendezvous, once even (he swore the likeness was exact) dressed as a waitress, and swabbing down a table in a restaurant. All fictional fears, but they dampened the spontaneity of the romance somewhat.

Still, she was learning from him. He was as brilliant a potentate as he was inept a lover. She learned how to be powerful without exercising power, how to keep one's self uncontaminated by the foulness all charisma stirs up in the uncharismatic; how to make the plain decisions plainly; how to be merciless. Not that she needed much education in that particular quarter. Perhaps it was more truthful to say he taught her never to regret her absence of instinctive compassion, but to judge with her intellect alone who deserved extinction and who might be numbered amongst the righteous.

Not once did she show herself to him, though she used her skills in the most secret of ways to tease pleasure out of his stale nerves.

In the fourth week of their affair they were lying side by side in a lilac room, while the mid-afternoon traffic growled in the street below. It had been a bad bout of sex; he was nervous, and no tricks would coax him out of himself. It was over quickly, almost without heat.

He was going to tell her something. She knew it: it was waiting, this revelation, somewhere at the back of his throat. Turning to him she massaged his temples with her mind, and soothed him into speech.

He was about to spoil the day.

He was about to spoil his career.

He was about, God help him, to spoil his life.

"I have to stop seeing you," he said.

He wouldn't dare, she thought.

"I'm not sure what I know about you, or rather, what I *think* I know about you, but it makes me . . . cautious of you, J. Do you understand?"

"No."

"I'm afraid I suspect you of . . . crimes."

"Crimes?"

"You have a history."

"Who's been rooting?" she asked. "Surely not Virginia?"

"No, not Virginia, she's beyond curiosity."

"Who then?"

"It's not your business."

"Who?"

She pressed lightly on his temples. It hurt him and he winced.

"What's wrong?" she asked.

"My head's aching."

"Tension, that's all, just tension. I can take it away, Titus." She touched her finger to his forehead, relaxing her hold on him. He sighed as relief came.

"Is that better?"

"Yes."

"Who's been snooping, Titus?"

"I have a personal secretary. Lyndon. You've heard me speak of him. He knew about our relationship from the beginning. Indeed, he books the hotels, arranges my cover stories for Virginia."

There was a sort of boyishness in this speech that was rather touching. As though he was embarrassed to leave her, rather than heartbroken. "Lyndon's quite a miracle worker. He's maneuvered a lot of things to make it easier between us. So he's got nothing against you. It's just that he happened to see one of the photographs I took of you. I gave them to him to shred."

"Why?"

"I shouldn't have taken them; it was a mistake. Virginia might have . . ." He paused, began again. "Anyhow, he recognized you, although he couldn't remember where he'd seen you before."

"But he remembered eventually."

"He used to work for one of my newspapers, as a gossip columnist. That's how he came to be my personal assistant. He remembered you from your previous incarnation, as it were. Jacqueline Ess, the wife of Benjamin Ess, deceased."

"Deceased."

"He brought me some other photographs, not as pretty as the ones of you."

"Photographs of what?"

"Your home. And the body of your husband. They said it was a body, though in God's name there was precious little human being left in it."

"There was precious little to start with," she said simply, thinking of Ben's cold eyes, and colder hands. Fit only to be shut up, and forgotten.

"What happened?"

"To Ben? He was killed."

"How?" Did his voice waver a little?

"Very easily." She had risen from the bed, and was standing by the window. Strong summer light carved its way through the slats of the blind, ridges of shadow and sunlight charting the contours of her face.

"You did it."

"Yes." He had taught her to be plain. "Yes, I did it."

He had taught her an economy of threat too. "Leave me, and I'll do the same again."

He shook his head. "Never. You wouldn't dare."

He was standing in front of her now.

"We must understand each other, J. I am powerful and I am pure. Do you see? My public face isn't even touched by a glimmer of scandal. I could afford a mistress, a dozen mistresses, to be revealed. But a murderess? No, that would spoil my life."

"Is he blackmailing you? This Lyndon?"

He stared at the day through the blinds, with a crippled look on his face. There was a twitch in the nerves of his cheek, under his left eye.

"Yes, if you must know," he said in a dead voice. "The bastard has me for all I'm worth."

"I see."

"And if he can guess, so can others. You understand?"

"I'm strong: you're strong. We can twist them around our little fingers."

"No."

"Yes! I have skills, Titus."

"I don't want to know."

"You *will* know," she said.

She looked at him, taking hold of his hands without touching him. He watched, all astonished eyes, as his unwilling hands were raised to touch her face, to stroke her hair with the fondest of gestures. She made him run his trembling fingers across her breasts, taking them with more ardor than he could summon on his own initiative.

"You are always too tentative, Titus," she said, making him paw her almost to the point of bruising. "This is how I like it." Now his hands were lower, fetching out a different look from her face. Tides were moving over it, she was all alive—

"Deeper—"

His finger intruded, his thumb stroked.

"I like that, Titus. Why can't you do that to me without me demanding?"

He blushed. He didn't like to talk about what they did to-gether. She coaxed him deeper, whispering.

"I won't break, you know. Virginia may be Dresden china, I'm not. I want feeling; I want something that I can remember you by when I'm not with you. Nothing is everlasting, is it? But I want something to keep me warm through the night."

He was sinking to his knees, his hands kept, by her design, on her and in her, still roving like two lustful crabs. His body was awash with sweat. It was, she thought, the first time she'd ever seen him sweat.

"Don't kill me," he whimpered.

"I could wipe you out." Wipe, she thought, then put the image out of her mind before she did him some harm.

"I know. I know," he said. "You can kill me easily."

He was crying. My God, she thought, the great man is at my feet, sobbing like a baby. What can I learn of power from this puerile performance? She plucked the tears off his cheeks, us-ing rather more strength than the task required. His skin red-dened under her gaze.

"Let me be, J. I can't help you. I'm useless to you."

It was true. He was absolutely useless. Contemptuously, she let his hands go. They fell limply by his sides.

"Don't ever try and find me, Titus. You understand? Don't ever send your minions after me to preserve your reputation, because I will be more merciless than you've ever been."

He said nothing; just knelt there, facing the window, while she washed her face, drank the coffee they'd ordered, and left.

Lyndon was surprised to find the door of his office ajar. It was only seven-thirty-six. None of the secretaries would be in for another hour. Clearly one of the cleaners had been remiss, leaving the door unlocked. He'd find out who: sack her.

He pushed the door open.

Jacqueline was sitting with her back to the door. He recog-nized the back of her head, that fall of auburn hair. A sluttish display; too teased, too wild. His office, an annex to Mr. Pettifer's, was kept meticulously ordered. He glanced over it: everything seemed to be in place.

"What are you doing here?"

She took a little breath, preparing herself.

This was the first time she had planned to do it. Before it had been a spur-of-the-moment decision.

He was approaching the desk, and putting down his briefcase and his neatly folded copy of the *Financial Times*.

"You have no right to come in here without my permission," he said.

She turned on the lazy swivel of his chair; the way he did when he had people in to discipline.

"Lyndon," she said.

"Nothing you can say or do will change the facts, Mrs. Ess," he said, saving her the trouble of introducing the subject, "you are a cold-blooded killer. It was my bounden duty to inform Mr. Pettifer of the situation."

"You did it for the good of Titus?"

"Of course."

"And the blackmail, that was also for the good of Titus, was it?"

"Get out of my office—"

"Was it, Lyndon?"

"You're a whore! Whores know nothing: they are ignorant, diseased animals," he spat. "Oh, you're cunning, I grant you that—but then so's any slut with a living to make."

She stood up. He expected a riposte. He got none; at least not verbally. But he felt a tautness across his face: as though someone was pressing on it.

"What ... are ... you ... doing?" he asked.

"Doing?"

His eyes were being forced into slits like a child imitating a monstrous Oriental, his mouth was hauled wide and tight, his smile brilliant. The words were difficult to say—

"Stop ... it ..."

She shook her head.

"Whore ..." he said again, still defying her.

She just stared at him. His face was beginning to jerk and twitch under the pressure, the muscles going into spasm.

"The police ..." he tried to say, "if you lay a finger on me ..."

"I won't," she said, and pressed home her advantage.

Beneath his clothes he felt the same tension all over his body, pulling his skin, drawing him tighter and tighter. Something was going to give; he knew it. Some part of him would be weak, and tear under this relentless assault. And if he once began to break open, nothing would prevent her ripping him apart. He worked all this out quite coolly, while his body twitched and he swore at her through his enforced grin.

"Cunt," he said. "Syphilitic cunt."

He didn't seem to be afraid, she thought.

In extremis he just unleashed so much hatred of her, the fear was entirely eclipsed. Now he was calling her a whore again; though his face was distorted almost beyond recognition.

And then he began to split.

The tear began at the bridge of his nose and ran up, across his brow, and down, bisecting his lips and his chin, then his neck and chest. In a matter of seconds his shirt was dyed red, his dark suit darkening further, his cuffs and trouser-legs pouring blood. The skin flew off his hands like gloves off a surgeon, and two rings of scarlet tissue lolled down to either side of his flayed face like the ears of an elephant.

His name-calling had stopped.

He had been dead of shock now for ten seconds, though she was still working him over vengefully, tugging his skin off his body and flinging the scraps around the room, until at last he stood, steaming, in his red suit, and his red shirt, and his shiny red shoes, and looked, to her eyes, a little more like a sensitive man. Content with the effect, she released him. He lay down quietly in a blood puddle and slept.

My God, she thought, as she calmly took the stairs out the back way, that was murder in the first degree.

She saw no reports of the death in any of the papers, and nothing on the news bulletins. Lyndon had apparently died as he had lived, hidden from public view.

But she knew wheels, so big their hubs could not be seen by insignificant individuals like herself, would be moving. What they would do, how they would change her life, she could only guess at. But the murder of Lyndon had not simply been spite, though that had been a part of it. No, she'd also wanted to stir them up, her enemies in the world, and bring them after her. Let them show their hands: let them show their contempt, their terror. She'd gone through her life, it seemed, looking for a sign of herself, only able to define her nature by the look in others' eyes. Now she wanted an end to that. It was time to deal with her pursuers.

Surely now everyone who had seen her, Pettifer first, then Vassi, would come after her, and she would close their eyes permanently: make them forgetful of her. Only then, the witnesses destroyed, would she be free.

Pettifer didn't come, of course, not in person. It was easy for him to find agents, men without scruple or compassion, but with a nose for pursuit that would shame a bloodhound.

A trap was being laid for her, though she couldn't yet see its jaws. There were signs of it everywhere. An eruption of birds from behind a wall, a peculiar light from a distant window, footsteps, whistles, dark-suited men reading the news at the limit of her vision. As the weeks passed they didn't come any closer to her, but then neither did they go away. They waited, like cats in a tree, their tails twitching, their eyes lazy.

But the pursuit had Pettifer's mark. She'd learned enough from him to recognize his circumspection and his guile. They would come for her eventually, not in her time, but in theirs. Perhaps not even in theirs: in his. And though she never saw his face, it was as though Titus was on her heels personally.

My God, she thought, I'm in danger of my life and I don't care.

It was useless, this power over flesh, if it had no direction behind it. She had used it for her own petty reasons, for the gratification of nervous pleasure and sheer anger. But these displays hadn't brought her any closer to other people: they just made her a freak in their eyes.

Sometimes she thought of Vassi, and wondered where he was, what he was doing. He hadn't been a strong man, but he'd had a little passion in his soul. More than Ben, more than Pettifer, certainly more than Lyndon. And, she remembered, fondly, he was the only man she'd ever known who called her Jacqueline. All the rest had manufactured unendearing corruptions of her name: Jackie, or J., or, in Ben's more irritating moods, Ju-ju. Only Vassi had called her Jacqueline, plain and simple, accepting, in his formal way, the completeness of her, the totality of her. And when she thought of him, tried to picture how he might return to her, she feared for him.

VASSI'S TESTIMONY (PART TWO)

Of course I searched for her. It's only when you've lost someone, you realize the nonsense of that phrase "it's a small world."
It isn't. It's a vast, devouring world, especially if you're alone.

When I was a lawyer, locked in that incestuous coterie, I
used to see the same faces day after day. Some I'd exchange
words with, some smiles, some nods. We belonged, even if we
were enemies at the Bar, to the same complacent circle. We ate
at the same tables, we drank elbow to elbow. We even shared
mistresses, though we didn't always know it at the time. In
such circumstances, it's easy to believe the world means you
no harm. Certainly you grow older, but then so does everyone
else. You even believe, in your self-satisfied way, that the
passage of years makes you a little wiser. Life is bearable; even
the 3:00 A.M. sweats come more infrequently as the bank balance swells.

But to think that the world is harmless is to lie to yourself,
to believe in so-called certainties that are, in fact, simply shared
delusions.

When she left, all the delusions fell away, and all the lies I
had assiduously lived by became strikingly apparent.

It's not a small world, when there's only one face in it you
can bear to look upon, and that face is lost somewhere in a
maelstrom. It's not a small world when the few, vital memories of your object of affection are in danger of being trampled
out by the thousands of moments that assail you every day,
like children tugging at you, demanding your sole attention.

I was a broken man.

I would find myself (there's an apt phrase) sleeping in tiny
bedrooms in forlorn hotels, drinking more often than eating,
and writing her name, like a classic obsessive, over and over
again. On the walls, on the pillow, on the palm of my hand. I
broke the skin of my palm with my pen, and the ink infected
it. The mark's still there, I'm looking at it now. Jacqueline it
says. Jacqueline.

Then one day, entirely by chance, I saw her. It sounds melodramatic, but I thought I was going to die at that moment. I'd
imagined her for so long, keyed myself up for seeing her again,

that when it happened I felt my limbs weaken, and I was sick in the middle of the street. Not a classic reunion. The lover, on seeing his beloved, throws up down his shirt. But then, nothing that happened between Jacqueline and myself was ever quite normal. Or natural.

I followed her, which was difficult. There were crowds, and she was walking fast. I didn't know whether to call out her name or not. I decided not. What would she have done anyway, seeing this unshaven lunatic shambling toward her, calling her name? She would have run probably. Or worse, she would have reached into my chest, seizing my heart in her will, and put me out of my misery before I could reveal her to the world.

So I was silent, and simply followed her, doggedly, to what I assumed was her apartment. And I stayed there, or in the vicinity, for the next two and a half days, not quite knowing what to do. It was a ridiculous dilemma. After all this time of watching for her, now that she was within speaking distance, touching distance, I didn't dare approach.

Maybe I feared death. But then, here I am, in this stinking room in Amsterdam, setting my testimony down and waiting for Koos to bring me her key, and I don't fear death now. Probably it was my vanity that prevented me from approaching her. I didn't want her to see me cracked and desolate; I wanted to come to her clean, her dream lover.

While I waited, they came for her.

I don't know who they were. Two men, plainly dressed. I don't think policemen: too smooth. Cultured even. And she didn't resist. She went smilingly, as if to the opera.

At the first opportunity I returned to the building a little better dressed, located her apartment from the porter, and broke in. She had been living plainly. In one corner of the room she had set up a table, and had been writing her memoirs. I sat down and read, and eventually took the pages away with me. She had got no further than the first seven years of her life. I wondered, again in my vanity, if I would have been chronicled in the book. Probably not.

I took some of her clothes too; only items she had worn when I had known her. And nothing intimate: I'm not a fetishist. I wasn't going to go home and bury my face in the smell of her underwear. But I wanted something to remember her by; to picture her in. Though on reflection I never met a human being more fitted to dress purely in her skin.

So I lost her a second time, more the fault of my own cowardice than circumstance.

Pettifer didn't come near the house they were keeping Mrs. Ess in for four weeks. She was given more or less everything she asked for, except her freedom, and she only asked for that in the most abstracted fashion. She wasn't interested in escape: though it would have been easy to achieve. Once or twice she wondered if Titus had told the two men and the woman who were keeping her a prisoner in the house exactly what she was capable of: she guessed not. They treated her as though she were simply a woman Titus had set eyes on and desired. They had procured her for his bed, simple as that.

With a room to herself, and an endless supply of paper, she began to write her memoirs again, from the beginning.

It was late summer, and the nights were getting chilly. Sometimes, to warm herself, she would lie on the floor (she'd asked them to remove the bed) and will her body to ripple like the surface of a lake. Her body, without sex, became a mystery to her again; and she realized for the first time that physical love had been an exploration of that most intimate, and yet most unknown region of her being: her flesh. She had understood herself best embracing someone else: seen her own substance clearly only when another's lips were laid on it, adoring and gentle. She thought of Vassi again; and the lake, at the thought of him, was roused as if by a tempest. Her breasts shook into curling mountains, her belly ran with extraordinary tides, currents crossed and recrossed her flickering face, lapping at her mouth and leaving their mark like waves on sand. As she was fluid in his memory, so as she remembered him, she liquefied.

She thought of the few times she had been at peace in her life; and physical love, discharging ambition and vanity, had always preceded those fragile moments. There were other ways presumably; but her experience had been limited. Her mother had always said that women, being more at peace with themselves than men, needed fewer distractions from their hurts. But she'd not found it like that at all. She'd found her life full of hurts, but almost empty of ways to salve them.

She left off writing her memoirs when she reached her ninth year. She despaired of telling her story from that point on, with the first realization of oncoming puberty. She burned the papers on a bonfire she lit in the middle of her room the day that Pettifer arrived.

My God, she thought, this can't be power.

Pettifer looked sick; as physically changed as a friend she'd lost to cancer. One month seemingly healthy, the next sucked up from the inside, self-devoured. He looked like a husk of a man: his skin gray and mottled. Only his eyes glittered, and those like the eyes of a mad dog.

He was dressed immaculately, as though for a wedding.

"J."

"Titus."

He looked her up and down.

"Are you well?"

"Thank you, yes."

"They give you everything you ask for?"

"Perfect hosts."

"You haven't resisted."

"Resisted?"

"Being here. Locked up. I was prepared, after Lyndon, for another slaughter of the innocents."

"Lyndon was not innocent, Titus. These people are. You didn't tell them."

"I didn't deem it necessary. May I close the door?"

He was her captor: but he came like an emissary to the camp of a greater power. She liked the way he was with her, cowed but elated. He closed the door, and locked it.

"I love you, J. And I fear you. In fact, I think I love you because I fear you. Is that a sickness?"

"I would have thought so."

"Yes, so would I."

"Why did you take such a time to come?"

"I had to put my affairs in order. Otherwise there would have been chaos. When I was gone."

"You're leaving?"

He looked into her, the muscles of his face ruffled by anticipation.

"I hope so."

"Where to?"

Still she didn't guess what had brought him to the house, his affairs neatened, his wife unknowingly asked forgiveness of as she slept, all channels of escape closed, all contradictions laid to rest.

Still she didn't guess he'd come to die.

"I'm reduced by you, J. Reduced to nothing. And there is nowhere for me to go. Do you follow?"

"No."

"I cannot live without you," he said. The cliché was unpardonable. Could he not have found a better way to say it? She almost laughed, it was so trite.

But he hadn't finished.

"—and I certainly can't live *with* you." Abruptly, the tone changed. "Because you revolt me, woman, your whole being disgusts me."

"So?" she asked, softly.

"So . . ." He was tender again and she began to understand. ". . . kill me."

It was grotesque. The glittering eyes were steady on her.

"It's what I want," he said. "Believe me, it's all I want in the world. Kill me, however you please. I'll go without resistance, without complaint."

She remembered the old joke. Masochist to Sadist: Hurt me! For God's sake, hurt me! Sadist to Masochist: No.

"And if I refuse?" she said.

"You can't refuse. I'm loathsome."

"But I don't hate you, Titus."

"You should. I'm weak. I'm useless to you. I taught you nothing."

"You taught me a great deal. I can control myself now."

"Lyndon's death was controlled, was it?"

"Certainly."

"It looked a little excessive to me."

"He got everything he deserved."

"Give me what I deserve, then, in my turn. I've locked you up. I've rejected you when you needed me. Punish me for it."

"I survived."

"J.!"

Even in this extremity he couldn't call her by her full name.

"Please to God. Please to God. I need only this one thing from you. Do it out of whatever motive you have in you. Compassion, or contempt, or love. But do it, please do it."

"No," she said.

He crossed the room suddenly, and slapped her, very hard.

"Lyndon said you were a whore. He was right; you are. Gutterslut, nothing better."

He walked away, turned, walked back, hit her again, faster, harder, and again, six or seven times, backward and forward.

Then he stopped, panting.

"You want money?" Bargains now. Blows, then bargains.

She was seeing him twisted through tears of shock, which she was unable to prevent.

"Do you want money?" he said again.

"What do you think?"

He didn't hear her sarcasm, and began to scatter notes around her feet, dozens and dozens of them, like offerings around the Statue of the Virgin.

"Anything you want," he said, *"Jacqueline."*

In her belly she felt something close to pain as the urge to kill him found birth, but she resisted it. It was playing into his hands, becoming the instrument of his will: powerless. Usage again; that's all she ever got. She had been bred like a cow, to give a certain supply. Of care to husbands, of milk to babies, of death to old men. And, like a cow, she was expected to be compliant with every demand made of her, whenever the call came. Well, not this time.

She went to the door.

"Where are you going?"

She reached for the key.

"Your death is your own business, not mine," she said.

He ran at her before she could unlock the door, and the blow—in its force, in its malice—was totally unexpected.

"Bitch!" he shrieked, a hail of blows coming fast upon the first.

In her stomach, the thing that wanted to kill grew a little larger.

He had his fingers tangled in her hair, and pulled her back into the room, shouting obscenities at her, an endless stream of them, as though he'd opened a dam full of sewer-water on her.

This was just another way for him to get what he wanted, she told herself, if you succumb to this you've lost: he's just manipulating you. Still the words came: the same dirty words that had been thrown at generations of unsubmissive women. Whore; heretic; cunt; bitch; monster.

Yes, she was that.

Yes, she thought: monster I am.

The thought made it easy. She turned. He knew what she intended even before she looked at him. He dropped his hands from her head. Her anger was already in her throat coming out of her—crossing the air between them.

Monster he calls me: monster I am.

I do this for myself, not for him. Never for him. For myself!

He gasped as her will touched him, and the glittering eyes stopped glittering for a moment, the will to die became the will to survive, all too late of course, and he roared. She heard answering shouts, steps, threats on the stairs. They would be in the room in a matter of moments.

"You are an animal," she said.

"No," he said, certain even now that his place was in command.

"You don't exist," she said, advancing on him. "They'll never find the part that was Titus. Titus is gone. The rest is just—"

The pain was terrible. It stopped even a voice coming out from him. Or was that her again, changing his throat, his palate, his very head? She was unlocking the plates of his skull, and reorganizing him.

No, he wanted to say, this isn't the subtle ritual I had planned. I wanted to die folded into you, I wanted to go with my mouth clamped to yours, cooling in you as I died. This is not the way I want it.

No. No. No.

They were at the door, the men who'd kept her here, beating on it. She had no fear of them, of course, except that they might spoil her handiwork before the final touches were added to it.

Someone was hurling himself at the door now. Wood splintered; the door was flung open. The two men were both armed. They pointed their weapons at her, steady-handed.

"Mr. Pettifer?" said the younger man. In the corner of the room, under the table, Pettifer's eyes shone.

"Mr. Pettifer?" he said again, forgetting the woman.

Pettifer shook his snouted head. Don't come any closer, please, he thought.

The man crouched down and stared under the table at the disgusting beast that was squatting there; bloody from its transformation, but alive. She had killed his nerves; he felt no pain. He just survived, his hands knotted into paws, his legs scooped up around his back, knees broken so he had the look of a four-legged crab, his brain exposed, his eyes lidless, lower jaw broken and swept up over his top jaw like a bulldog, ears torn off, spine snapped, humanity bewitched into another state.

"You are an animal," she'd said. It wasn't a bad facsimile of beasthood.

The man with the gun gagged as he recognized fragments of his master. He stood up, greasy-chinned, and glanced around at the woman.

Jacqueline shrugged.

"You did this?" Awe mingled with the revulsion.

She nodded.

"Come, Titus," she said, clicking her fingers.

The beast shook its head, sobbing.

"Come, Titus," she said more forcefully, and Titus Pettifer waddled out of his hiding place, leaving a trail like a punctured meat-sack.

The man fired at Pettifer's remains out of sheer instinct. Anything, anything at all to prevent this disgusting creature from approaching him.

Titus stumbled two steps back on his bloody paws, shook himself as if to dislodge the death in him, and failing, died.

"Content?" she asked.

The gunman looked up from the execution. Was the power talking to him? No; Jacqueline was staring at Pettifer's corpse, asking the question of him.

Content?

The gunman dropped his weapon. The other man did the same.

"How did this happen?" asked the man at the door. A simple question: a child's question.

"He asked," said Jacqueline. "It was all I could give him."

The gunman nodded, and fell to his knees.

VASSI'S TESTIMONY (FINAL PART)

Chance has played a worryingly large part in my romance with Jacqueline Ess. Sometimes it's seemed I've been subject to every tide that passes through the world, spun around by the merest flick of accident's wrist. Other times I've had the suspicion that she was masterminding my life, as she was the lives of a hundred others, a thousand others, arranging every fluke meeting, choreographing my victories and my defeats, escorting me, blindly, toward this last encounter.

I found her without knowing I'd found her, that was the irony of it. I'd traced her first to a house in Surrey, a house that had a year previous seen the murder of one Titus Pettifer, a billionaire shot by one of his own bodyguards. In the upstairs room, where the murder had taken place, all was serenity. If she had been there, they had removed any sign. But the house, now in virtual ruin, was prey to all manner of graffiti; and on the stained plaster wall of that room someone had scrawled a woman. She was obscenely over-endowed, her gaping sex blazing with what looked like lightning. And at her feet there was a creature of indeterminate species. Perhaps a crab, perhaps a dog. Perhaps even a man. Whatever it was it had no power over itself. It sat in the light of her agonizing presence and counted itself amongst the fortunate. Looking at that wizened creature, with its eyes turned up to gaze on the burning Madonna, I knew the picture was a portrait of Jacqueline.

I don't know how long I stood looking at the graffiti, but I was interrupted by a man who looked to be in a worse condition than me. A beard that had never been trimmed or washed, a frame so wasted I wondered how he managed to stand upright, and a smell that would not have shamed a skunk.

I never knew his name: but he was, he told me, the maker of the picture on the wall. It was easy to believe that. His desperation, his hunger, his confusion were all marks of a man who had seen Jacqueline.

If I was rough in my interrogation of him I'm sure he forgave me. It was an unburdening for him, to tell everything he'd seen the day that Pettifer had been killed, and know that I believed it all. He told me his fellow bodyguard, the man who had fired the shots that had killed Pettifer, had committed suicide in prison.

His life, he said, was meaningless. She had destroyed it. I gave him what reassurances I could; that she meant no harm, and that he needn't fear that she would come for him. When I told him that, he cried, more, I think, out of loss than relief.

Finally I asked him if he knew where Jacqueline was now. I'd left that question to the end, though it had been the most pressing inquiry, because I suppose I didn't dare hope he'd know. But my God, he did. She had not left the house immediately after the shooting of Pettifer. She had sat down with this man, and talked to him quietly about his children, his tailor, his car. She'd asked him what his mother had been like, and he'd told her his mother had been a prostitute. Had she been happy? Jacqueline had asked. He'd said he didn't know. Did she ever cry, she'd asked. He'd said he never saw her laugh or cry in his life. And she'd nodded, and thanked him.

Later, before his suicide, the other gunman had told him Jacqueline had gone to Amsterdam. This he knew for a fact, from a man called Koos. And so the circle begins to close, yes?

I was in Amsterdam seven weeks, without finding a single clue to her whereabouts, until yesterday evening. Seven weeks of celibacy, which is unusual for me. Listless with frustration I went down to the red-light district, to find a woman. They sit there you know, in the windows, like mannequins, beside pink-fringed lamps. Some have miniature dogs on their laps; some read. Most just stare out at the street, as if mesmerized.

There were no faces there that interested me. They all seemed joyless, lightless, too much unlike her. Yet I couldn't leave. I was like a fat boy in a sweet shop, too nauseated to buy, too gluttonous to go.

Toward the middle of the night, I was spoken to out of the crowd by a young man who, on closer inspection, was not young at all, but heavily made up. He had no eyebrows, just pencil marks drawn on to his shiny skin. A cluster of gold earrings in his left ear, a half-eaten peach in his white-gloved hand, open sandals, lacquered toenails. He took hold of my sleeve, proprietorially.

I must have sneered at his sickening appearance, but he didn't seem at all upset by my contempt. You look like a man of discernment, he said. I looked nothing of the kind: you must be mistaken, I said. No, he replied, I am not mistaken. You are Oliver Vassi.

My first thought, absurdly, was that he intended to kill me. I tried to pull away; his grip on my cuff was relentless.

You want a woman, he said. Did I hesitate enough for him to know I meant yes, though I said no? I have a woman like no other, he went on, she's a miracle. I know you'll want to meet her in the flesh.

What made me know it was Jacqueline he was talking about? Perhaps the fact that he had known me from out of the crowd, as though she was up at a window somewhere, ordering her admirers to be brought to her like a diner ordering lobster from a tank. Perhaps too the way his eyes shone at me, meeting mine without fear because fear, like rapture, he felt only in the presence of one creature on God's cruel earth. Could I not also see myself reflected in his perilous look? He knew Jacqueline, I had no doubt of it.

He knew I was hooked, because once I hesitated he turned away from me with a mincing shrug, as if to say: you missed your chance. Where is she? I said, seizing his twig-thin arm. He cocked his head down the street and I followed him, suddenly as witless as an idiot, out of the throng. The road emptied as we walked; the red lights gave way to gloom, and then to darkness. If I asked him where we were going once I asked him a dozen times; he chose not to answer, until we reached a narrow door in a narrow house down some razor-thin street. We're here, he announced, as though the hovel were the Palace of Versailles.

Up two flights in the otherwise empty house there was a room with a black door. He pressed me to it. It was locked.

"See," he invited, "she's inside."

"It's locked," I replied. My heart was fit to burst: she was near, for certain, I knew she was near.

"See," he said again, and pointed to a tiny hole in the panel of the door. I devoured the light through it, pushing my eye toward her through the tiny hole.

The squalid interior was empty, except for a mattress and Jacqueline. She lay spreadeagled, her wrists and ankles bound to rough posts set in the bare floor at the four corners of the mattress.

"Who did this?" I demanded, not taking my eye from her nakedness.

"She asks," he replied. "It is her desire. She asks."

She had heard my voice; she cranked up her head with some difficulty and stared directly at the door. When she looked at me all the hairs rose on my head, I swear it, in welcome, and swayed at her command.

"Oliver," she said.

"Jacqueline." I pressed the word to the wood with a kiss.

Her body was seething, her shaved sex opening and closing like some exquisite plant, purple and lilac and rose.

"Let me in," I said to Koos.

"You will not survive one night with her."

"Let me in."

"She is expensive," he warned.

"How much do you want?"

"Everything you have. The shirt off your back, your money, your jewelry; then she is yours."

I wanted to beat the door down, or break his nicotine-stained fingers one by one until he gave me the key. He knew what I was thinking.

"The key is hidden," he said, "and the door is strong. You must pay, Mr. Vassi. You want to pay."

It was true. I wanted to pay.

"You want to give me all you have ever owned, all you have ever been. You want to go to her with nothing to claim you back. I know this. It's how they all go to her."

"All? Are there many?"

"She is insatiable," he said, without relish. It wasn't a pimp's boast: it was his pain, I saw that clearly. "I am always finding more for her, and burying them."

Burying them.

That, I suppose, is Koos's function; he disposes of the dead. And he will get his lacquered hands on me after tonight; he will fetch me off her when I am dry and useless to her, and find some pit, some canal, some furnace to lose me in. The thought isn't particularly attractive.

Yet here I am with all the money I could raise from selling my few remaining possessions on the table in front of me, my dignity gone, my life hanging on a thread, waiting for a pimp and a key.

It's well dark now, and he's late. But I think he is obliged to come. Not for the money; he probably has few requirements beyond his heroin and his mascara. He will come to do business with me because she demands it and he is in thrall to her, every bit as much as I am. Oh, he will come. Of course he will come.

Well, I think that is sufficient.

This is my testimony. I have no time to reread it now. His footsteps are on the stairs (he limps) and I must go with him. This I leave to whoever finds it, to use as they think fit. By morning I shall be dead, and happy. Believe it.

My God, she thought, Koos has cheated me.

Vassi had been outside the door, she'd felt his flesh with her mind and she'd embraced it. But Koos hadn't let him in, despite her explicit orders. Of all men, Vassi was to be allowed free access, Koos knew that. But he'd cheated her, the way they'd all cheated her except Vassi. With him (perhaps) it had been love.

She lay on the bed through the night, never sleeping. She seldom slept now for more than a few minutes: and only then with Koos watching her. She'd done herself harm in her sleep, mutilating herself without knowing it, waking up bleeding and screaming with every limb sprouting needles she'd made out of her own skin and muscle, like a flesh cactus.

It was dark again, she guessed, but it was difficult to be sure. In this heavily curtained, bare-bulb-lit room, it was a perpetual day to the senses, perpetual night to the soul. She would lie, bed-sores on her back, on her buttocks, listening to the far sounds of the street, sometimes dozing for a while, sometimes eating from Koos's hand, being washed, being toileted, being used.

A key turned in the lock. She strained from the mattress to see who it was. The door was opening . . . opening . . . opened.

Vassi. Oh God, it was Vassi at last, she could see him crossing the room toward her.

Let this not be another memory, she prayed, pleased let it be him this time: true and real.

"Jacqueline."

He said the name of her flesh, the whole name.

"Jacqueline." It *was* him.

Behind him, Koos stared between her legs, fascinated by the dance of her labia.

"Koo . . ." she said, trying to smile.

"I brought him." He grinned at her, not looking away from her sex.

"A day," she whispered. "I waited a day, Koos. You made me wait—"

"What's a day to you?" he said, still grinning.

She didn't need the pimp any longer, not that he knew that. In his innocence he thought Vassi was just another man she'd seduced along the way; to be drained and discarded like the others. Koos believed he would be needed tomorrow; that's why he played this fatal game so artlessly.

"Lock the door," she suggested to him. "Stay if you like."

"Stay?" he said, leering. "You mean, and watch?"

He watched anyway. She knew he watched through that hole he had bored in the door; she could hear him pant sometimes. But this time, let him stay forever.

Carefully, he took the key from the outside of the door, closed it, slipped the key into the inside and locked it. Even as the lock clicked she killed him, before he could even turn round and look at her again. Nothing spectacular in the execution; she just reached into his pigeon chest and crushed his lungs. He slumped against the door and slid down, smearing his face across the wood.

Vassi didn't even turn round to see him die; she was all he ever wanted to look at again.

He approached the mattress, crouched, and began to untie her ankles. The skin was chafed, the rope scabby with old blood. He worked at the knots systematically, finding a calm he thought he'd lost, a simple contentment in being here at the end, unable to go back, and knowing that the path ahead was deep in her.

When her ankles were free, he began on her wrists, interrupting her view of the ceiling as he bent over her. His voice was soft.

"Why did you let him do this to you?"

"I was afraid."

"Of what?"

"To move; even to live. Every day, agony."

"Yes."

He understood so well that total incapacity to exist.

She felt him at her side, undressing, then laying a kiss on the sallow skin of the stomach of the body she occupied. It was marked with her workings; the skin had been stretched beyond its tolerance and was permanently criss-crossed.

He lay down beside her, and the feel of his body against hers was not unpleasant.

She touched his head. Her joints were stiff, the movements painful, but she wanted to draw his face up to hers. He came, smiling, into her sight, and they exchanged kisses.

My God, she thought, we are together.

And thinking they were together, her will was made flesh. Under his lips her features dissolved, becoming the red sea he'd dreamed of, and washing up over his face, that was itself dissolving: common waters made of thought and bone.

Her keen breasts pricked him like arrows; his erection, sharpened by her thought, killed her in return with his only thrust. Tangled in a wash of love they thought themselves extinguished, and were.

Outside, the hard world mourned on, the chatter of buyers and sellers continuing through the night. Eventually indifference and fatigue claimed even the eagerest merchant. Inside and out there was a healing silence: an end to losses and to gains.

NOTES
ON THE
AUTHORS

Stephen King (American, 1947–   ) is, without question, aptly named, for he has reigned, quite deservedly, over the world of horror fiction during what is now an unbroken span of nearly two decades. Moreover, his enthusiastic affection for every aspect of the genre, along with his great generosity to newer writers, has helped revivify it. Whether imagining the effect on ordinary people and their communities of telekinetic children (in *Carrie*, 1974, or *Firestarter*, 1980), or menacing animals (*Cujo*, 1981, or *Pet Sematary*, 1983), or global pestilence (*The Stand*, 1977 and 1990), he has proved himself an empathic storyteller whose acute perceptions about the sources of human anxiety actually extend far beyond frights and freaks and things that go bump in the night. And although less frequently acclaimed as such, King is also a sly satirist of contemporary American culture.

Valerie Martin (American, 1948–   ) is the author, most recently, of *Mary Reilly* (1990), a tour-de-force reworking of the Victorian horror classic, Robert Louis Stevenson's *The Strange Case of Dr. Jekyll and Mr. Hyde*. In Martin's hands the narrator becomes a young chambermaid keeping a private journal, who records her mounting confusion and anguish as she watches her revered employer struggle against mastery by the evil he has unleashed. In *The Consolation of Nature* (1988), a short story collection, and in the strongly perverse novel *A Recent Martyr* (1987), Martin also showed herself to be influenced by another nineteenth-century master, Edgar Allan Poe, despite the austere (and decidedly un-Poe-like) restraint of her own prose.

Haydn Middleton (British, 1955–   ) is a writer and scholar whose long-standing fascination with British mythology led him to retell, for his first book, the ancient Welsh heroic cycle known in its written form as *Mabinogion*. *Son of Two Worlds* (1987), as it was called, was followed by two novels, *The People in the Picture* (1988) and *The Lie of the Land* (1989). Both, though set in contemporary England, make use of elements rising up from a shadowy, timeless Celtic past; in each, Middleton creates an atmosphere of high erotic tension entwined with incompletely understood situations. In 1991 his novel, *The Collapsing Castle*, will be published.

Ruth Rendell (British, 1930–   ) commands our attention whether she is setting down solidly perceptive detective fiction (*From Doon with Death*, 1965, or *Put On by Cunning*, 1981, to name two) or disturbing tales of explosively vulnerable characters (*To Fear a Painted Devil*, 1965; *Master of the Moor*, 1982; *The Bridesmaid*, 1990; others). In recent years, as "Barbara Vine," she has been justly praised for novels (such as *A Dark, Adapted Eye*, 1988) which skillfully employ flashbacks to illuminate tragic secrets. In Rendell's work, usually both her victims and villains are dogged by cruelly capricious fates, with escape being only an illusion that she has perfected.

T. L. Parkinson's (American, 1949–   ) short stories have appeared in several volumes of *Shadows*, as well as in *Fantasy & Science Fiction*, *Semiotext (e)*, and *Full Spectrum*. His first novel, *The Man Upstairs*, which focuses on "narcissism, unlearning from experience, and sexual violence" will be released in 1991. Like most of the writers in this collection, Parkinson isn't easily categorized, but his wry sympathy for his characters' plights only increases the subtle impact of his carefully escalating shocks and surprises.

Ronald Duncan (British, 1914–82) frequently took death as a theme in his poetry, trying through his art to explore the many human responses to this final mystery. A cofounder, with Benjamin Britten, of the English Opera Company, he also penned three librettos for the composer. His autobiography, *All Men Are Islands*, was published in 1963; he was a translator of Cocteau and of Euripides, and helped to edit an edition of Gandhi's writings.

Michael Blumlein (American, 1948–   ) is a writer and physician whose first novel was *The Movement of Mountains* (1987), an unexpectedly moving tale of interplanetary medical morality. His short fiction has been published in *Omni*, *Fantasy & Science Fiction*, and *Twilight Zone*, among other magazines, and his story "The Thing Itself" was chosen to be included in *Year's Best Fantasy, 1989*. Located stylistically somewhere out on a cutting edge all his own, Blumlein also wrote the text for an independent film, *Decodings*, that won the Special Jury Award of the San Francisco Film Festival in 1988.

May Sinclair (British, 1865–1946), according to the distinguished authority on supernatural fiction E. F. Bleiler, is an underrated writer in the field. The fiction for which she is best known, however, is mainstream, and such novels as *Mary Olivier* (1919), its heroine a young woman growing up in a repressive Victorian household, are still being read today. A feminist, a follower of Freud, and an admirer of Shaw, Wells, and Joyce, Sinclair often experimented with subjective prose technique. Two of her collections, *Uncanny Stories* (1923) and *The Intercessor, and Other Stories* (1931), contain numerous startling and quietly grim tales of love's failures and the damnations of the flesh.

Patrick McGrath (British, 1950–   ) gained immediate recognition with his debut, *Blood and Water and Other Tales* (1988). Employing a dryly ironic tone, he relishes loathsome situations: a Victorian gentlewoman succumbs to caresses bestowed by a hand attached to her dead lover's skull; a coven of merciless blood-drinkers slays a mother and child; an elderly, undying creature survives in a putrescent state. The result: E. C. Comics as they might be presented by "Masterpiece Theatre."

His first novel, *The Grotesque*, appeared in 1989; his second, *The Spider*, in 1990.

Robert Aickman (British, 1914–81) once likened ghost stories to poetry; certainly, if his fiction is an exemplar, the comparison holds. The grandson of Richard Marsh (author of the still-readable, if campily entertaining, *fin de siècle* horror classic *The Beetle*), Aickman actually preferred the term "strange stories" to describe his output. And it is apt, for haunting ambiguity lies at the heart of the effects he creates. His collections, all of them absolutely worth seeking out, are *Dark Entries* (1964), *Powers of Darkness* (1966), *Sub Rosa* (1968), *Cold Hand in Mine* (1975), *Tales of Love and Death* (1977), and *Painted Devils* (1979).

Carolyn Banks (American, 1941–   ) is a novelist and short-story writer whose first book, *Mr. Right*, was published in 1979, followed by *The Darkroom* (1980), *The Girls on the Row* (1983), and *Patchwork* (1986). Fascinated by the darker, violent impulses, she is willing to push her characters to the brink; at the same time, her confidence holds such volatile situations firmly in balance. A frequent reviewer of horror and suspense fiction, she has also taught creative writing.

Robert Hitchens (British, 1864–1950) was a prolific journalist, poet, and novelist whose most successful book, *The Garden of Allah* (1904), was a best seller on both sides of the Atlantic. His weird fiction, written mostly in the earlier part of his long career, ranged from psychological horror to historical fantasy. His occult novels include *Flames* (1897) and *The Dweller on the Threshold* (1911); among his collections are *Tongues of Conscience* (1900) and *Snake-Bite and Other Stories* (1919).

Harriet Zinnes (American) is a poet, translator, and art critic. Her most recent works include a bilingual edition of Jacques Prévert's *Blood and Feathers* (1988) and a short-story collection, *Lover* (1989). One commentator has spoken of the "mysterious transformations" found in her fiction, and another of the "Dadaist games" her poetry (*I Wanted to See Something*

Flying, 1966; *Entropisms*, 1978; others) makes of "the jumble of life."

Jonathan Carroll (American, 1949–   ) has, since the publication of his first novel, *The Land of Laughs* (1980), been admired by a wide assortment of his peers, ranging from Ramsey Campbell to Stanislaw Lem. With each successive book, he has staked out more and more distinctly his imaginative territory, intermingling visionary whimsy with menacing dread. For many years expatriated to Vienna, he has retained, nonetheless, a very American voice: friendly, eccentric, alert to marvels, simultaneously sophisticated and cozy. The most recent of his works are *Sleeping in Flame* (1989) and *A Child Across the Sky* (1990).

Robert Murray Gilchrist's (British, 1868–1917) reputation, if he is remembered at all, is that of a regional writer of dialect novels set around Derbyshire and the Peak district. However, his 1894 collection, *The Stone Dragon and Other Tragic Romances*, emphasized supernatural elements, including *doppelgangers*, ghosts, witches, and lovers returned from the grave. Also active as a journalist, three years before his death he published the novel *Weird Wedlock*.

Christopher Fowler (British, 1953–   ) has written two collections of stories about "urban paranoia" *City Jitters* (1988) and *More City Jitters* (1989). In this loosely related group of misadventures, moments of bad luck and bad timing prevail. His 1988 novel, *Roofworld*, was called by its author "a horror thriller with fantasy aspects"; set in modern London, this depiction of warring sects in an alternative society that survives high above the streets is both convincing and mesmerizing. *Rune*, his newest novel, is being published in 1991.

Eric McCormack (Scottish, 1938–   ) has lived and taught in Canada since 1966. His first assemblage of uniquely uncanny stories, *Inspecting the Vaults* (1987), brought comparisons to Borges, Saki, Michael Ende, and Kobo Abe, and it caused him to be a finalist for the 1988 Commonwealth Writers Prize. *The Paradise Motel*, marking his debut as a novelist, appeared in 1989.

Hugh B. Cave (British, 1910–   ) was born in the west of England but moved with his family to the Boston area as a young boy. He has published in his long career over twelve hundred stories. *Murgunstrumm and Others* (1977), an illustrated collection containing twenty-six of his best, won a 1978 World Fantasy Award. Lengthy sojourns in Haiti and Jamaica produced *The Witching Lands* (1962), and his earlier book, *Haiti: Highroad to Adventure* (1952), is considered an important source work on voodoo. Among his recent titles are *The Lower Deep* and *Disciples of Dread* (both 1990), and in 1988 he was the subject of a biographical study, *Pulp Man's Odyssey: The Hugh B. Cave Story.*

Thomas M. Disch (American, 1940–   ) ranges widely in both style and interest; his output includes poetry, plays, speculative fiction, critical essays, movie reviews, historical pastiches, and children's books. *The Brave Little Toaster* (1986), considered a classic for readers of all ages, has been made into a successful animated film. Among his novels are the splendid black comedy *The Businessman: A Tale of Terror* (1984) and the high-spirited, utterly affectionate gothic re-creation *Clara Reeve* (1975, under the pseudonym "Leonie Hargrave"). His acclaimed short-story collections include *Fun with Your New Head* (1968) and *Getting into Death and Other Stories* (1976).

Angela Carter (British, 1940–   ) was once quoted as saying, "Only horror fiction is a true reflection of the times we live in; only fantasy is true to life." Among her novels are *The Magic Toyshop* (1976), an erotically haunted tale of innocence and obsession, and the exuberantly magical *Nights at the Circus* (1984). Her radio play, *Vampirella*, was broadcast in 1976, and she cowrote the screenplay for a visually memorable reworking of "Red Riding Hood," *The Company of Wolves* (1985). *The Sadeian Woman and the Ideology of Pornography*, a provocative philosophical critique, was published in 1978.

Stephen R. Donaldson (American, 1947–   ) is best known for his pair of heroic trilogies, *The Chronicles of Thomas Covenant* (1978) and *The Second Chronicles of Thomas Covenant* (1981, 1982, 1983), which follow the adventures of "one of the most unusual protagonists in modern fantasy." For Thomas Covenant is a mutilated leper who finds himself transported to a mythical world, the Land, where he must continually do battle with the evil villain Lord Foul. Donaldson's other writings include *Daughters of Regal and Other Tales* (1984) and the two volumes of *Mordant's Need* (1986, 1987).

Clive Barker (British, 1952–   ), at the outset of his career, was dubbed "the future of horror fiction" by Stephen King. Since the publication of his stunningly crafted group of stories *The Books of Blood* in 1984, Barker has continued to dazzle readers with his imaginative nerve. His novels, to date, are *Weaveworld* (1987), *The Damnation Game* (1987), *Cabal* (1988), and *The Great and Secret Show* (1990). He has also scripted and directed the films *Hellraiser* (1987, based on his novella "The Hellbound Heart") and *Nightbreed* (1990, based on *Cabal*).

ABOUT THE EDITOR

Michele Slung's works include *Crime on Her Mind* (1975), a historical anthology of fictional women detectives; *The Absent-Minded Professor's Memory Book* (1985); *The Only Child Book* (1989); and the best-selling *Momilies®* books, *Momilies: As My Mother Used to Say* (1985) and *More Momilies* (1986), which have now been adapted into French, German, Japanese, and Italian editions.

In addition, she served as editor for the Plume American Women Writers series, presenting long-out-of-print fiction in a uniform format, and she was first an editor, then a columnist for *The Washington Post Book World*. Her critical pieces on genre writing have appeared in *The New York Times Book Review* and *The New Republic*, among other periodicals, and in such volumes as *Twentieth-Century Crime and Mystery Writers*, *Whodunit?*, *The Sleuth and the Scholar*, and *The Penguin Encyclopedia of Horror and the Supernatural*.